Joseph Hatton

By Order of the Czar

A novel

Joseph Hatton

By Order of the Czar
A novel

ISBN/EAN: 9783337029180

Printed in Europe, USA, Canada, Australia, Japan

Cover: Foto ©Andreas Hilbeck / pixelio.de

More available books at **www.hansebooks.com**

BY ORDER OF THE CZAR.

A NOVEL.

BY

JOSEPH HATTON,

Author of "Clytie," "Cruel London," "The Great World," etc., etc.

NEW YORK

JOHN W. LOVELL COMPANY

150 WORTH STREET, CORNER MISSION PLACE

INTRODUCTION.

In the summer of 1887 I came upon a pamphlet published by *The Times* five years previously, giving an account of the persecution of the Jews in Russia in 1881. At about the same time I found in the *Brooklyn Times* (U.S.) a tragic incident in the alleged career of a Jewess, which recalled to my mind a grim passage of Russian history. These three records inspired the story I have just concluded. It occurred to me to find in the one village of Russia where the Jews had for a time lived unmolested, a heroine who, falling under the lash of Russian persecution, should survive the keenest of human afflictions, to become, under very dramatic and romantic circumstances, the in strument of Divine vengeance upon her enemy, and probably a type of the fierce injustice which characterizes the civil and military government of Russia. My inspiration for this tragic figure sprung from the following narrative, related as absolutely true by Charles J. Rosebault, in the *Brooklyn Times* during the month of June, 1887 :—

" Not far from the police station on Elizabeth-street is a large three-storey brick building. Years ago it was a handsome dwelling, but time and the small boy have played havoc with its façade, doors, windows, and railing. It is occupied by a well-to-do Russian, who years ago fled his native land for alleged complicity in some plot against the

Czar. It has long been the rendezvous of political refugees of both sexes, Russians, Nihilists, Polish Liberators, French Communards, German Socialists,-and Cosmopolitan Anarchists. The circle met there is composed of educated and clever people. Nearly all are excellent linguists, and more or less successful in trade, literature, or professional life. Owing probably to the terrible scenes in which they have been actors, all are more or less eccentric in behavior, speech, or ideas. Not long since a party of a dozen men and women were spending the evening in the large old-fashioned parlor. All smoked, a few sipped the vitriolic Vodka between the whiffs of their cigarettes, while all the rest assuaged thirst with the cheap wines of the Rhine and Moselle. The conversation had been political and literary rather than anecdotal in character, and had flagged until the room was almost silent. The only person speaking was a handsome Jewess of 24 or 25, whose name or *nom de guerre* was Theodora Ornavitsch. She was of a rare type of that race, being a superb blonde with bright golden hair, large lustrous blue eyes, and exhibiting the powerful figure and splendid health which characterize the Hebrew women to so remarkable a degree. As she paused at the end of an argument and drained a glass of Josephshoefer, some one asked, ' What made you a Nihilist, Dora ? '

" ' Nothing very remarkable to us Russians,' she replied. ' I belong to a good family in a small town in the Warsaw Province. I married the Rabbi of our Synagogue, and we were very happy for a few months. The Czar then made a change, and sent down a new governor from St. Petersburg to replace our old one, who was a good and just man, although a Russian general. The new comer had every vice, and no virtue of any kind. He was so bad and cruel that our friends and relatives wrote us when he came warning us against him. My husband the next Sabbath, in the Synagogue, told our people about him, and advised them to be over cautious in not violating any one of the thousand tyrannical laws with which we were cursed. Though he spoke in Hebrew, for fear of spies, someone betrayed him to the governor. He was arrested, tried, flogged on the public square into insensibility, and sent to Siberia for life. I was present when he underwent his agony, and stood it until I became crazed. I broke through the crowd toward the wretch of an official, and cursed him and his master, the Czar, and swore vengeance against both. I, too, was arrested, tried at court-martial, and sentenced to receive a hundred blows with the rod in the public square. I, a woman, was taken by drunken Moujiks and heathen Cossacks to the place, tied by my hands to the whipping post, my clothing torn from my body to the waist, and beaten before all the soldiery and the people of the town. At the twentieth blow I fainted, but the ropes held me up, and the full hundred were counted on my body. They cut me down, rubbed rock salt and water and some iron that eats like fire into my back to stop the bleeding, and carried me to the hospital. I lay there two months, and was discharged. I had but one idea then, and that was vengeance. By patience I managed to get employment in the governor's palace as a seamstress. One after-noon he was in his bath, and he sent for towels. The attendant was tired, and I volunteered to take them. I threw them over my arm, and under them I held a long stiletto, sharp as a needle. I entered the room, and he was reading and smoking in the bath. I laid the towels by his side with my left hand, and at the next moment with my right I drove the knife through his heart. It was splendidly done. He never made a sound, and I escaped to this land. That is why I am a Nihilist : Do any of you doubt ? ' She sprang excitedly from her chair, and in half a minute had bared herself to the waist. The front of her form from neck to belt might have passed as the model of the Venus di Milo. But the back ! Ridges, welts, and furrows that crossed and interlaced as if cut out with a red-hot iron, patches of white, grey, pink, blue, and angry red, holes and hollows with hard, hideous edges, half visible ribs and the edges of ruined muscles, and all of which moved, contracted, and lengthened with the swaying of her body. There was a gasp from everyone present. The aged host rose, silently kissed her on the forehead, and helped her to put back her garments. Then again the wine passed round, and what secret toasts were made as the party drank will never be known."

The historic chapter which this newspaper paragraph brought to my mind was the story of Madame Lapoukin ; the briefest account of which is probably the following, from *The Knout*, by Germain de Lagny :—

In 1760, under the reign of the indolent and luxurious Elizabeth, who had abolished capital punishment, Madame Lapoukin, a woman of rare beauty, of which the Czarina was envious, was condemned to the knout and transportation, in spite of the privilege of the nobility never to suffer the former punishment. She had been fêted, caressed, and run after at court, and had, it was said, betrayed the secret of the Empress' *liaison* with Prince Razoumowsky. She was conducted by the executioners to the public square, where she was exposed by one of them, who rolled up her chemise as far as her waist; he then placed her upon his shoulders, when another arranged her with his coarse dirty hands in the required position, obliging her to hold her head down, while a man of the lower classes, squatting at her feet, kept her legs still. The executioner cut her flesh into shreds by one hundred strokes of the knout, from the shoulders to the lower portion of the loins. After the infliction of the punishment, her tongue was torn out, and a short time subsequently she was sent to Siberia, whence she was recalled in 1762 by Peter III.

For the successful development of these journalistic literary and historical facts and suggestions into a full three volume novel, with truthful as well as characteristic accessories, it was necessary that I should make a study of Russian village life, and refresh my memory with such chapters of Russian history as should enable me to hold my imaginary characters and their actions within the reasonable control of probability. I was already fairly well acquainted with some of the best works of Russian fiction, which are full of strong local color and fine characterization, Gogol's stories more particularly, but in order that I might not stray from the path of truth any further than is reasonably permissible, I followed up the narrative of *The Times*, in the files of the *Daily Telegraph* and the *Jewish Chronicle;* traced the anti-Jewish riots throughout their lurid march of fire and bloodshed ; talked to several traveled authorities as to their experiences of Jewish life in Southern Russia ; and settled down to a careful study of the literary, topographical, political and historical literature of the subject, in the course of which, for the purposes of this story, I have consulted and read : " The Jews and their Persecutors," by Eugenie Lawrence ; " Scenes from the Ghetto," by Leopold Kompert ; " The Knout and the Russians," by Germain de Lagny ; " Elizabeth, or the Exiles of Siberia," by Madame Cottin ; " Russia under the Czars," by Stepniak ; " Prison Life in Siberia " and " Crime and Punishment," by Fedor Dostoiffsky ; " The Russian

Revolt," by Edmund Noble ; "The Jews of Barnow," by
Karl Emil Franzos ; "Russia, Political and Social," by L.
Tikhanirov ; "Called Back," by Hugh Conway ; "Dead
Souls," by Nikolai V. Gogol ; "War and Peace," and
"Anna Karenina," by Count Tolstoi ; "A Hero of our
Time," by M. V. Lermontoff ; "Russia before and after
the War," by the Author of "Society as it is in St. Peters-
burg," "The Encyclopædia Britannica," "Russians of To-
day," by the Author of "The Member for Paris ;" "The
Russian Peasantry," by Stepniak ; "Stories from Russia,
Siberia, Poland and Circassia," edited by Russell Lee ;
"Chambers' Encyclopædia ;" George Kennan's *Century*
papers on ":Plains and Prisons of Western Siberia," and
"Across the Russian Frontier ;" Theodore Child's "Fair
of Nijnii-Novogorod " in *Harper's Magazine;* The *Times*
pamphlet (before mentioned), "Persecutions of the Jews in
Russia, 1881 ;" "Venice," by Yriarte ; "Venetian Life," by
Howells ; "Sketches from Venetian History ;" "New Italian Sketches," by J. A. Symonds, and other miscellanous
literature. It will be seen that I name these works without
any view to classification or order. A foreign criticism
upon the Venetian chapter of the story makes it desirable
for me to state that the introduction of a Russian interest
in the Royal Fêtes on the Grand Canal is pure invention.
The pageantry is true enough ; the presence of the King
and Queen of Italy ; the illumination and the rest ; but
the red gondola and the ghost of the lagoons belong to the
region of fancy ; though they might easily have formed
part of the events of the time. I saw a dead swimmer
towed into an English fishing port under very similar circumstances to those which I have described as occurring
in the waters of the Adriatic.

With all due apologies for this personal note, I venture
to express a hope that my readers may feel an interest in
the Milbankes, the Forsyths, the Chetwynds, and the

Klosstocks. If I shall make these people half as real to them as they are to me, they will keep them in their remembrance as acquaintances, if not as friends; and in reflective moments their hearts will go out to an old man and his daughter who in the spirit of chastened content are fulfilling their voluntary exile, their happiness a dream of the past, their chief hope in a future "where the wicked cease from troubling and the weary are at rest."

J. H.

BY ORDER OF THE CZAR.

CHAPTER I.

THE KLOSSTOCKS.

SHE might have sat to Titian, as the lovely daughter of a Doge of Venice in the romantic days of Christian chivalry ; and yet she was only the daughter of a Polish Jew, and lived on sufferance in the Russian village of Czarovna.

The God of Jew and Gentile alike is kind in hiding from all His creatures the book of Fate, otherwise Anna Klosstock might have cursed the hour in which she was born. Nevertheless at the opening of this history we find her rejoicing in her life, and grateful to her Creator for the exceptional blessings with which her girlhood was endowed. She had—above all things desired of woman—the gift of beauty ; and as there is no beauty without health, Providence had blessed her with a physical capacity for enjoyment, and an intellectuality beyond that which as a rule accompanies the comely attraction of good looks.

Indeed, at the beginning of this story of persecution, love and vengeance, it might have seemed to the optimistic philosopher that Fate had gone down into the lowliest walks of life to prove the equality of the general distribution of happiness, and that Anna Klosstock had been selected as an example of the divine impartiality. For although Anna lived only in the shadow of liberty, she had never known what its sunshine is, and in her captivity was a queen—the elect of every man, woman and child of

the community in which she was born.   It is true her subjects were a despised race, but the Ghetto or Pale of
Settlement in the populous village of Czarovna was the
most contented, the happiest, the most flourishing of the
Jewish towns of Southern Russia ; so much so, indeed,
that instead of encouraging the Imperial Government to
persevere in a policy of liberality towards both Jew and
Gentile, it had more than once excited the suspicion, fear,
and duplicity of the reigning powers.   At Czarovna both
Jew and Christian lived on fairly amicable terms.   The
Governor, General Ivan Poltava, credited the peace of it
to the exceptional liberality of the merchant, Nathan
Klosstock, Anna's father ; but General Poltava was as
great a rarity of honesty in the administration of his office
as Nathan Klosstock was of generosity in a Jew merchant.
Were there more of such there would be fewer troubles in
the land ; though neither Russian Imperial policy nor the
local Hebrew education tend to develop just and upright
governors, or fair-dealing and high-minded Jewish subjects.

Czarovna was an example of how possible it is, even
under the grinding laws of Russia, for a community of
mixed nationalities and alien races to live, if not in harmony, at least without the miseries of a perpetual feud ;
but there was an unusual principle of give and take on
both sides between the Jews and Christians of this exceptional village in the province of Vilnavitch.

If the Jews in Russia are tainted with the worst characteristics of the race, their grasping and dogmatic idiosyn-
crasies are the result of a systematic and cruel persecution.
The conditions under which they exist are miserable beyond
all imagination.   They suffer again the persecutions of
Egypt, without the hope or prospect of deliverance.   The
Imperial legislation of St. Petersburg seems to aim at
nothing short of their annihilation. . They are legislated

for as if they were a criminal class—condemned to pass
their lives in circumscribed districts. The ancient Ghetto
of the Middle Ages exists for them in some districts of
Russia with all its penal severities. They may not own
an inch of Russian land ; they may only occupy themselves
in certain limited licensed businesses ; they are compelled
at intervals to present themselves at certain official stations
for the purpose of reporting themselves and renewing their
passports ; they are open to insult and derision at the
hands of any Christian who chooses morally and physically
to wipe his feet upon them. Nevertheless, as a class, they
succeed in ekeing out an existence and maintaining a religious independence with an obstinacy that is little less than
miraculous. The intensity of their application to the art
of money-making also develops, even under the severest
conditions, a moneyed class. In every village there is at
least one rich Jew—a local Shylock—who lends money at
usury, buys up or mortgages the crops of his urban neighbor, rents some noble's distillery, controls the taverns, and
commands from his co-religionists the respect which is
denied him by his Christian fellow-subjects. The child of
a thousand years of ill-treatment, it is not to be expected
that he will deal any more charitably with the Christian
than the Christian deals with him. If the Christian despises
him, be sure he hates the Christian with a deadly hatred.
Should his child, under the milder influence of Christian
precepts, give way to a proselytizing influence, she or he
is considered dead to all intents and purposes, the bitter
feeling going so far as to comprehend a funeral service,
with an empty coffin and a cemetery record. There is no
forgiveness for the deserter among the Russian Jews.

Nathan Klosstock would probably have resented as
fiercely as Shylock himself the defection of his only daughter Anna, although in his financial reign at Czarovna he
had won the title among the better class of Christians of a

liberal Jew. Under the unusually mild governorship of General Poltava the strict limits of the Ghetto had been practically wiped out. The mayor of the little town, being particularly anxious to stand well with the General, who lived in an old palace on the uplands overlooking the straggling village, acted with an outward show of sympathy for the Governor's mild and beneficent edicts.

Czarovna chiefly consisted of one long broad street, with houses and shops in a strange picturesque jumble, a fine church, and in this case a more or less dilapidated palace on the outskirts, in which the Governor (who in this instance also exercised authority over much of the surrounding district, with the approval of the Governor-General of the vast province of Vilnavitch) resided, and the barracks where there were generally quartered a troop of Hussars. At the northern end of the town, creeping up from the rocky bed of the river, that wound its way into the distant forest, was the Jewish quarter, which even in this exceptional district considered it necessary to put on an outward appearance of poverty in keeping with tradition, but which had many contrary examples to show to those who excited in them no dread of plunder.

The house of Moses Grunstein, for instance, externally looked what it professed to be, the abode and warehouse · of a struggling trader and merchant, who found it difficult to make both ends meet; but in reality it was in its way a palace, with a subterranean annex, that was one of the mysteries of Czarovna, and its owner's particular and special secret. Nathan Klosstock, however, made but little disguise of his prosperity, for he believed no one grudged him his wealth, because he made good use of it, and was as generous as any Christian could possibly be, and far more so than many really were. But the native who lives in the track of the tornado grows accustomed to danger. People live without fear beneath the shadow of

Vesuvius. Every man is mortal but oneself. There might be troubles in other villages of Southern Russia, but to Nathan Klosstock Czarovna was safe. Life is a matter of habit; one may become used to anything. Happiness is a question of comparison. A prisoner having been sub-ject to a severe discipline is awakened one morning with the companionship of his dog; in future he is to have books, there is a jar of flowers in his cell, he may take exercise, and he is to suffer no more hard labor : he thinks himself the happiest man in the world. Nathan Klosstock, though recognized in a friendly way by the Governor, had to cringe and grovel before the great landlords, and he dared not resent the bold looks and insolent compliments which were now and then paid to Anna by some of his noble patrons. But oh, my brethren, to what a gulf of misery and death he was walking all this time, he and his ! —the way strewn with flowers, as if to enhance the horrors of the impending gulf—walking hand in hand to the music of their own grateful hearts, at which every fiend in hell might have laughed, so grim, so awful was the pit that Fate had cast in their way.

During some years past a few of the later generations of Jews had ventured, with proper authorization, to live in the town proper and its outskirts, where they could see the sky and have the privilege here and there of something like rural occupation. There were troubles now and then with such of these as the Governor permitted to hold taverns or public-houses, and it was no doubt a legitimate complaint on the part of the poorer class of farmers that these miserable Jews, having lent money to the even more miserable mujiks, encouraged them to drink and spend the money they had borrowed. But whenever anything like a serious situation was developed in this direction Nathan Klosstock came forward and settled it. He had also propitiated the few nobles and better class of land cultivators in the province, by fair and honorable advances of money, at fair and honorable rates. He was the general merchant of the district, dealing in everything ; was a shipping agent, importing goods from almost every part of the world ; was a pleasant, hearty, genial, fairly educated man, and had induced the young rabbi Marcus Losinski, of St. Petersburg, to take up his residence as the Chief Rabbi at Czarovna. Klosstock's house was the Mecca of many traveling pedlars, students, and beggars. He was known throughout all the lands where Jews are known. His wife during her short lifetime had been worthy of his fame, and his daughter Anna was a lovely type of Semitic beauty, with a grace of manner that was eminently in keeping with the name she bore.

The Klosstocks lived at the very entrance to the Ghetto, where in olden days the gates that had shut in the narrow streets of the despised community had swung night and morning upon their grating hinges, to the order of the hostile guardian whom the Jews themselves had to pay for exercising his barbaric authority over them. It was an unpretentious house, though somewhat glaringly painted ; and it served as shop, counting-house, office, museum, and living apartments, where Klosstock's forefathers had founded the little fortune which had prospered in the hands of their now aged son.

It was after a visit to the province of Vilnavitch, and a pleasant call, *en route*, at the house of Klosstock, that Nathan had induced the young and distinguished rabbi to accept the vacancy at Czarovna. Not that the rich Jew had given his daughter to Losinski, as he might have done, but he had promised him that if he should find favor in Anna's eyes the betrothal should take place as soon as possible. Anna had already received much more than the customary tuition which the Jews of her father's class permit to their daughters. She could speak German, had a fair knowledge of French, was almost learned in Biblical lore, and had the natural taste of her race for music. Her voice and her lute were heard at the Jewish festivals, and her charities might have won the commendation of the strictest worshippers of that Messiah for whom her race suffer still under the ban of having crucified.

Marcus Losinski, coming to take charge of the morals and religion of the Jews of Czarovna, was to Anna a pilgrim of light from the outer world. He was wiser than his years; had traveled through the East, even to Jerusalem. He could tell her of the wonders of the great capitals. He had fulfilled missions to Paris and London, although he was only some ten or fifteen years her senior.

No queen could have held Losinski in a firmer allegiance of love and worship than Anna the Queen of the Ghetto.

" It is accounted a sin among the Christians," he had one day said to her, " to love even maid or wife beyond the man they have made their God; and I am glad to have been born a Jew, Anna, if it were only to be untrammeled by law, human or divine, in my love for you."

" Do you not think," Anna replied, " that God's laws are as easy as man's are difficult.

" Yes, Anna, truly I do. Religion lies not in law nor in knowledge, but in a pure and holy life."

" And yet, dear love," said Anna, " I sometimes think you chafe here in Czarovna, and long for a wider sphere of usefulness."

" It is not so, Anna. My ambition is satisfied to be with you, whatever my sphere of work; but sometimes I wonder if it were not wise to leave this land of doubt and fear, and travel further afield where our people are not everlastingly within the clutch of tyranny and abuse, where indeed they are safe from public persecution and private contumely."

" Ah, you envy Andrea Ferrari," Anna replied. " You

would like to go up and down the world as he does, seeing fresh peoples, noting the wonders of strange lands."

"Nay; I have seen much of the great world, Anna. My only desire is to be sure that your future shall be as happy as your past; that neither you nor your father may ever be the victims of some sudden change of policy on the part of the Government. For myself, my life is nothing to me if it brings no special good to you. Martyrdom in such a cause would be happiness."

"You are sad!" Anna said quickly. "Do not talk of martyrdom; you make my heart stand still. What martyrdom, dear love, could there possibly be for you in my behalf?"

"None that would be martyrdom," said Losinski. "But how do we come to be talking in such a doleful strain? Forgive me, Anna, Ferrari comes to your father's house presently. I met him an hour ago at the barber's. He is particular about his toilette when he comes to see the Queen of the Ghetto.'

"He is very welcome," said Anna. "Is he not something like the dove returning to the ark with news of the outer world? There are no books of travel so interesting as the travelers themselves."

"For which sentiment," said a voice in the doorway, "I return you my best thanks; and I believe, if I am not considered too egotistical, that I am of your opinion.

"Ah, Signor Ferrari," exclaimed Anna, rising, "welcome; it is true we were talking of you."

"Again good-day to you," said Losinski. "Anna finding me in a doleful mood began to talk of you; I hope you will make us merry."

"That must be our duty to Andrea," remarked Nathan, the master of the house, who had entered the room with the traveler; "our guest has journeyed far and wants rest and refreshment. He reserves for after dinner his news and gossip—and he has news that is not altogether good, he says; so let us eat, drink and be merry, for the present is ours, and who knows aught of the morrow? Come, Anna, be of good cheer."

"Nay, I am, dear father; and our good friend Signor Ferrari shall tell us of his city in the sea. That will make him happy, and we will share his joy. You have only good news from Venice?"

"None other, dear mistress," the Italian replied; "Venice is paradise."

"Venice is your home, signor; and home is paradise wherever it is. Come, let us go to dinner."

Nathan smiled at Ferrari and laid his hand lovingly on Anna's shoulder as they left the small entrance hall or porchway into the general room of the old house, where dinner was ready.

"It is a sentiment that does you honor as well as your daughter," said the Italian in reply; but turning to Losinski he added, "Is it good after all, a Providence that gives the children of the desert a proverb instead of a home?"

"God be thanked," said the rabbi, "for the comfort of Anna's loving sentiment."

"Amen," said Ferrari: "long live the grateful heart;" and then to himself, "Shall we, the so-called chosen, always have to fawn on the hand that smites us?"

CHAPTER II.

HAPPY CZAROVNA.

IT was an interesting and characteristic group, the Klosstock household, with Ferrari and Losinski as guests, a few days before the year of Anna's bethrothal to the young and learned rabbi was ended.   They sat round about the great stove, after dinner, Klosstock in his brown gabardine, looking venerable and picturesque; the young rabbi similarly attired but in black, a heavy signet ring upon the forefinger of his right hand, his face singularly handsome, with soft, dreamy, hazel eyes, a brown beard, not unlike the beard which painters give to their imaginary portraits of Christ; Andrea Ferrari, the Italian Jew traveler, a shrewd, keen-looking man of middle height, with a watchful manner, a dark olive complexion, a straggling black beard and moustache, a low compact forehead, as much of his mouth as you could see denoting firmness of character, his hand strong and nervous, boney, almost clawlike, his dress of a far more artistic cut than the others, with a girdle of tanned leather and of ample proportions, large enough and strong enough to carry treasures even more valuable than their weight in gold; and hidden in his breast both knife and pistol—for while Andrea could play the humble Jew, he knew also how to protect himself on occasion.   There had been times when he had found it useful—and his conscience took no affront at it—to pass himself off as a Christian citizen of Venice.   He hated Russia with the intensity of an unforgiving nature; his father, an inoffensive pedlar in the land, having lost his life in a street brawl at the hands of a drunken crew of

Moscow revelers, his mother falling a victim to grief at her husband's death.

Apart from these inducements to revenge, Andrea Ferrari had imbibed the doctrines and some of the hopes of the latest propaganda of the Nihilists of Russia ; but this he kept a strict secret in his own breast, he well knowing that in Russia even a secret so well guarded as his sometimes gets out, not by open or private confession, but through a keenly interpreted look, a sudden interrogation, or an ill-considered remark.

The somewhat sinister expression of Andrea's face, a habit he had of dropping his eyes, an introspective manner, was very much in contrast with the frank, open countenances of the host, the rabbi, and the young girl who was not only known within the Pale of the Settlement as the Queen of the Ghetto, but outside the Jews' quarter as the good daughter of the Liberal Jew.

Anna loved to hear Andrea Ferrari talk of his travels, and the rabbi, by whose side she sat, an attentive listener to the general conversation, was also much interested in him.

" Tell Anna," said the rabbi, " of Venice ; of those olden days of our people, and how our brethren have progressed in wealth, in power, and in freedom ; moreover, such advancement is an encouragement for hope, even here in Russia."

" Would to God that all our neighbors, far and near," said Klosstock, lighting his big German pipe, " were as well considered and as justly protected in their rights as we of Czarovna ! "

" Rights ! " exclaimed Andrea, in a fierce but suppressed tone, " what rights, my father ? "

" The right to live without being beaten—the right to pray to the God of our Fathers—the right to buy and sell."

" Yes, we are well off at Czarovna," remarked the

rabbi; "but that should not make us content when our brethren in the east and west are ground under the heel, beaten in the streets, cast into prison, crucified; and even here in the south, Czarovna is one of the few exceptions, where we may do more than herd together like animals content to feed on the husks their masters fling to them. But it was so in Venice, where to-day our brethren hold up their heads in the blessed sun, and walk with the Christian merchants, their equals in respect and in power.

"Not quite that," said Andrea, "but of a sufficient freedom of action and life; it is only in London where it may be said the Jew is equal to the Christian. And if it were not that some of our brethren, steeped in the prejudices and vices that have been engendered of a thousand years of persecution, did not trespass upon the English liberal and human sentiment by ill acts that we as a community would be the first ourselves to punish, London would come to forget entirely that a man were Jew or Gentile, except, if he were a Jew, to glorify him all the more for his good works. It is thus that we are cursed from generation to generation; the offspring of the dead, bitter past, the child of persecution; the seed of misery and dependence, waxes strong, and in his strength develops the cunning of a past in which it was his only weapon, and brings down upon individuals the curses of even the great liberal-minded people of London."

"If thou wert not a Jew, and true as the ring of thine own gold, Andrea Ferrari, thy words would be thine own condemnation; but, friend of many countries, do thou tell our daughter Anna of that city of the sea, which is like the dream of a poet rather than a sober incident, from the book of real experience; and whither our dear son, the rabbi, doth propose to travel with our loving daughter Anna—mayhap accompanied by their father—what sayest thou, Anna?"

"It is too much happiness to think upon," she replied.

"You may go to bed, Amos Negrusz," said Klosstock, addressing a serving-man, whom both the rabbi and Ferrari had eyed with something like suspicion. The man bowed, but said nothing, not even "Good-night." He was a sinister-looking person, and had probably noticed a certain watchfulness on the part of the guests that was peculiar to their manner on this occasion, for though he had only been in the Jew Klosstock's service a few weeks, he had come with such excellent credentials, and was so willing and so anxious to all appearance to please, that both the rabbi and the master were inclined to trust him, and to regard him as an acquisition to the household.

"Forgive me," said the rabbi, lifting the heavy curtain over the door whence Amos Negrusz had disappeared, and standing for a moment in a listening attitude, "and I will explain later."

Klosstock looked inquiringly at his daughter, whose hand seeking his, he raised it to his lips, and she laid her head upon his shoulder.

"I do not like the man Amos," said the rabbi, in a low voice.

"Nor do I," added Ferrari.

"Nay, what has the poor fellow done?" asked Klosstock. "You thought him a good man and useful, my son, until now."

"I did," said the rabbi. "It is only to-day that I doubt him; only to-night that I fear him."

"Fear him?" said Klosstock. "Do I hear aright?"

"Where did he come from?" asked the Italian.

"From Elizabethgrad," said Klosstock.

"Recommended by one worthy of trust?"

"Yes, truly," replied Klosstock, "the merchant Chane."

"I thought so," said Ferrari significantly. "Do you know the merchant Chane?"

"Not to speak with him," said Klosstock, "but I know him by repute as one whose word is his bond, and who has large possessions."

"Ha!" ejaculated the Italian, rising and pacing the room for a moment, and at the same time pausing near the door, as if he listened for footsteps.

"Do you know him?" asked the rabbi.

"I do," said Ferrari.

"I fear a cloud is gathering about us," said the rabbi, "but one which may break far away if we are careful. I have kept watch over my words this evening that your servant might not hear of the warnings which have reached me within the last few hours from a trusted friend in St. Petersburg."

"Is it touching the new Governor?" said Ferrari interrupting him.

"It is," said the rabbi.

"Alas, I can indorse it; and I, too, have observed a reticent demeanor, for the reason that this Amos is not what he represents himself to be."

"Forewarned is forearmed," said the rabbi. "The new Governor is on his way to Czarovna; it may be possible to propitiate him; I know that it is possible for him to reduce our lives to the miserable level of those of our brethren at Kiew. That we are an exception is due to exceptional causes. The hand of persecution lies heavy on our brethren all round about us."

"Our brethren are themselves much to blame," said Klosstock. "They make hard bargains; they thrive on the Christian need; they do no acts of charity outside the Pale of Settlement; they forget that God made us all."

"They remember," said Ferrari, "that the Christian has ground them beneath his heel; they remember that from age to age in all countries they have been harried by Christian fire and sword; and that even in these days of .

so-called charity and education, and especially in this land of the Czar, they are the victims of harsh laws, aliens alike from freedom and justice, and compelled to kiss the rod that stripes them. No, my father, blame them not that they take their revenge."

" But I do blame them, my son," said Klosstock, " and I present to them and to you the example of Czarovna as proof of the good that comes out of toleration."

" Toleration !" exclaimed the Italian, but in a hoarse whisper. " The merchant Chane is a tolerant man. Hush ! But we alarm our good young hostess."

" I have spoken something of this to Anna already," said the rabbi, "and we are accustomed to discuss many things outside the ordinary lines of education."

Anna crept closer to her father's side, and looked up wistfully at the handsome young *savant* who was to be her husband within the next few days, and whom she loved with the devotion of her fervent and affectionate nature.

CHAPTER III.

" A BOLT FROM THE BLUE."

A WARM ruddy glow from the great stove fell lovingly upon the group, which had an Oriental picturesqueness of detail that might to an artist have recalled the lights and shadows of the master painters of old, with the exception that there was something modern in the beauty of Anna, with her violet eyes, her rich red-gold hair, and her fresh complexion : a beauty more akin to pure Venetian than to that of the Semitic race.

" Anna, it were well thou went to rest," said Klosstock ; " our guest and friend Andrea is over anxious about this new governor. He will alarm thee ; and even our dear Losinski is inclined to exaggerate the possibilities of the

2

change in the governorship. It is true we are parting
with a kind and benevolent man, and we should rejoice in
his promotion."

" If it is promotion," said Ferrari.

"Yes, my son, it is—the Governor has told me so himself ; and as a good wife makes a good husband, so do
good subjects make good governments, and there is some
truth in the credit which General Poltava gives to me for
the peace and happiness we enjoy in Czarovna. I have
conciliated our masters, propitiated our neighbors, our
people have placed their interests in my keeping. I have
in my dealings followed the example of my father ; and
the result of this policy is seen in the gates of the Ghetto
having for years rusted on their hinges, unused and forgotten, and in the neighborly relationship of Christian and
Jew, such as exists at this day, Ferrari—as you were telling
me when last you favored us with your welcome presence
—in that city of the sea, which once was the seat of persecutions and butcheries of our race beyond the power of
pen or tongue to describe."

‘ It is so, my father ; and it would be to Southern
Russia as if the Messiah were with them, could our people
enjoy the blessings their brethren enjoy in Venice and in
London."

"And in regard to which Czarovna stands only second,
eh, Ferrari ? "

" Czarovna has many blessings," said the Italian.

"Thou art my blessing, Anna," said Klosstock, "and
it grows late."

The Jewish maiden rose, embraced her father, took her
leave of the rabbi and their guest, and taking up a quaint
old lamp retired, her heart full of the hope that if she and
he whom she loved did bend their steps to other lands
where the original yoke of the Egyptians had indeed fallen
clean away from the Jewish shoulders, her father might be

induced to accompany them; though she knew how he would cling at last to the spot where her mother, the beloved wife of his youth, lay in her everlasting bed. But she hoped all would be as she wished, and she was glad that the journey had been talked of before the rabbi's friendly messenger had brought the bad bad news, which might otherwise have made the departure of her father seem like an act of desertion.

"Listen, both of you—Nathan Klosstock and you, my dear friend Losinski," said Ferrari. "The butchers are abroad. The red fury of barbarism is once more marching through the land. The prediction that the anti-Semitic trouble of Germany would spread to Russia has been pushed on by Panslavist emissaries from Moscow. The flame has broken out at Elizabethgrad. The Jews, being forewarned of trouble, applied to the authorities for protection. They were treated with scorn. While I speak to you the Jews' quarter is a wreck. Placards were issued, informing the orthodox Russians that the property of the Jews had been given over to them, and that they might take it. The Government did not deny the outrageous notification. The orthodox rose. The military being called out presented themselves at the scene of the massacre, but only to look on, their criminal sympathy with the mob only tending to encourage the cruel excesses."

"Didst thou say massacre?" asked Klosstock, looking aghast at the Italian.

"I said massacre. But it was worse than massacre, my father; twenty-five good women, our dear sisters, were violated, ten dying in consequence."

"Holy Father!" exclaimed the rabbi.

"At the house of one Mordecai Wienarski, the mob, disappointed of plunder, caught up his child and hurled it through the window. The infant fell dead at the feet of a company of Cossacks, but they moved neither to take it

up nor to arrest the murderers. Two thousand of our
brethren are houseless : six have gone to their long rest ;
many are grievously wounded, and the community has
been plundered of property of the value of forty thousand
English pounds."

"Thou strikest me dumb, Ferrari!" said the host.
"What dost thou advise?

"Nay, calm yourself," said Losinski ; "this is not the
first rising against our brethren ; and while all Russia has
suffered much in this way, do not forget that Czarovna
has been free from trouble. We must not seem to know
of this terrible news ; we must show no fear ; we must not
let it change our manner towards our neighbors ; General
Poltava is still with us, and his officers are kind and
considerate."

"Do not be deceived," said Ferrari ; "to-morrow, perhaps to-night, your new governor will arrive at the palace ;
I passed him on the way ; he was traveling incognito. By
this time General Poltava is under arrest."

Klosstock leaned back in his chair and groaned.

"I almost hate myself for being the bearer of such ill-
tidings," said Ferrari ; "it is the bolt from the blue.
I found you steeped in the happiness of virtue, good-feel-
ing, and sweet content ; I am a moral earthquake to your
household bliss. But it is in one's happiest hours that
Fate strikes us down."

"Let us pray!" said the rabbi.

Nathan Klosstock fell upon his knees in a paroxysm of
grief. Ferrari bowed his head, mumbling to himself that
he would rather cut the throat of the servant Negrusz,
before he had time to do him, at least, a mischief.

The rabbi offered up an eloquent appeal to the God of
their Fathers, recalling the many favors He had accorded
to His chosen people, and especially the blessings He had
vouchsafed to Czarovna, bewailing the persecutions which

His people suffered round about them, and more especially asking for the protection of this house of Klosstock, and of His servant Anna, light of her father's old age, and soon with His favor to be a wife unto the humble petitioner, and so on—a prayer of faith and hope and humility, to which Klosstock said " Amen," and Ferrari " So mote it be ! "

Then there was a dead pause, and the three men stood up and listened, as if they expected an answer to the rabbi's prayer in the shape of some good omen or token of peace. But all was still as death, except for the howl of some restless dog in a distant street.

The moon had risen and was pouring its beams into her chamber as Anna set down her lamp upon a quaint old chest by the window. She sat right in the midst of the lunar radiance and thought how beautiful it was, how lovely was life—her life—what rich blessings God had lavished upon her. There was not a single tremor of fear in her heart. If trouble was coming to Czarovna, she and those she most loved would be able to leave it. It would have been too much to have expected her to think of any others at that moment besides her father and her lover. Nor could she realize the bitterness of a persecution which she had not felt, and which Czarovna had not known in her time ; and while the rabbi had spoken of these things, he had been jealous not to overshadow Anna's happiness with tales of horrors, the recitation of which, while they might cast a shadow upon her thoughts, could serve no useful purpose. For she was born with sensibilities and a sympathetic nature, and would find in life itself, as she grew older, quite enough that was sad, without lavishing her sympathies upon sorrows and troubles she could neither influence, amend, nor control.

Anna did not dream of the shadowy form that crept out of the moonlight, crouching beneath her window, as

she closed the shutters and betook herself to her prayers.
Neither did the rabbi, nor the guest, nor good old Father
Klosstock.   For the three men now lighted fresh pipes,
and gathered about the stove to be free and confidential
in their conversation, Anna having retired.

"This new governor," said Ferrari, "is General Petronovitch, a man of a cruel disposition, who hates our
chosen people, and aids and abets their persecution.
Nay, dear host, my good friend, be not impatient with me.
I know what I say ; know more than I dare to communi-
cate to you; know more than some might say I ought ;
more I hope than is good for such as Petronovitch."

"I have never asked thee, Ferrari, whence thou comest,
or whither thou goest ; but I trust to thy love and discretion not to compromise this household with anything
that can be called political."

"Your trust is well placed ; I am here for the last time.
Czarovna will see me no more, nor, indeed, will Russia,
after I leave her accursed soil on this last journey.
Indeed, but for the love I bear you and your daughter I
should have not been here to say farewell ; for I passed a
long distance out of the way I was going to bring you the
warning which the rabbi Losinski has haply received
before me.   It is well ; you might otherwise have thought
less of what I had to tell you."

"If you are compromised in the eyes of the Government, Andrea Ferrari, it is hardly kind to have made this
your chief house of call in Southern Russia," said the
rabbi.

"I have had no reason to believe that I was suspected
until I left St. Petersburg this time, intending to go to
Paris ; but some sudden knowledge of the change of
government here and the departure of a certain man from
the capital for Elizabethgrad and Czarovna, forced me, as
I said before, out of the love I bear this household, to
make my way hither."

While he was speaking, the man who had crept out of the moonlight entered the old house by a side door in the courtyard, which was opened to him by an inmate ; and at the same time there emerged from an archway in the street at the entrance to the Ghetto a file of soldiers, and a wagon came rumbling along the thoroughfare, awakening the otherwise quiet echoes of the night. •

"What is the noise outside ? " asked Ferrari, feeling the knife, which he always carried handy in a belt on his hip.

" Some late carrier from the country," said Klosstock.

" You seem much disturbed," remarked the rabbi.

" I had a bad dream last night ; I thought I was sitting here among you, and that suddenly there started up behind the stove a man, who said, ' Andrea Ferrari, thou art my prisoner.' The noise outside struck me curiously as if it were the prologue to my captivity."

" Hast thou been drinking, Andrea ? " the old man asked.

" Nay, I am in my soberest senses ; a little over-anxious for thy welfare perhaps ; for know this—Governor General Petronovitch is a sensualist, and a tyrant ; he is believed to have instigated the rising against our chosen people at Elizabethgrad, and your friend Poltava's withdrawal from the province is not promotion, it is disgrace ; he is even suspected of sympathy with the Nihilistic propaganda."

" God forbid ! " exclaimed Klosstock.

" Moreover thy new servant, Amos Negrusz, is a Government spy—— "

" And he arrests thee, Andrea Ferrari, as a traitor ! " said a voice, which seemed to come from the earth, as the three men started to their feet and the servant emerged from a dark corner of the room, covering Ferrari with the shining barrel of a revolver, while at the same time another person appeared from the doorway whence Anna had retired, and a loud knocking was heard at the front door of the house.

" Do thou open thy door to the police," said Negrusz.

Ferrari had stood perfectly still, his heart beating wildly, but hand and head ready for the slightest chance of escape. The arrogant act of the servant in ordering the master to open his own door gave Ferrari the opportunity. It was only for a second that Negrusz was off his guard, but in that second Ferrari, with the agility of a cat, was upon him, his knife in his throat, the pistol wrested from him, and the next moment the lithe Italian had disappeared through the open doorway in the rear.

A scene of confusion followed : hurried orders of military men, the screams of women, and presently the report of firearms in the principal street of the Ghetto.

CHAPTER IV.

AN ESCAPE.

His teeth set, his red knife firmly grasped, Ferrari sped through the narrow streets, down strange passages, now crouching out of the moonlight, now dashing through its beams, until he found himself on the bank of the river that skirted the settlement. Here, in the shadow of a bridge, he rested, and hoped Losinski's prayer had indeed been heard, and half believed it had, his escape so far having been nothing less than miraculous ; and breathless as he was, panting for very life, he rejoiced that the spy Negrusz had been delivered into his hands.

Presently he looked back towards the village. Lights were appearing in the previously darkened windows. He thought he heard the hum of voices. No doubt the whole place was up in arms. He feared for the safety of Anna, and for the lives of his dear friends. What would happen? Could he be of use to the Klosstocks, upon whom it seemed to him he had brought disaster and ruin? How could he hope to escape? He was now known to the police, denounced by Negrusz—a sleuth hound of the St. Petersburg Detective Force, who had found reason to suspect Ferrari about the time of the murder of the Czar. While, however, he was making up his mind to act, Ferrari, in the very house where Negrusz thought he had him safe, had managed to disappear, which was sufficient evidence to satisfy Negrusz if ever he again encountered him. From that moment Ferrari had assumed one of his various disguises, which he had only laid aside on his way to Czarovna, and this was the last visit he had intended to pay to his friends in Southern Russia.

Ferrari had, for several years, been associated with the propagandists ; but until this night his hand had shed no blood in the Nihilistic cause, and now that he had whetted his knife he felt a thirst for more.

What should he do ? Take advantage of the disturbance and sensation of the affair at the Klosstocks to sneak back into the Ghetto and find shelter there? Or make his way to some distant village ? Or seek refuge for a time in the adjacent woods?

There was a certain Count Stravensky, a landowner near Czarovna, of whom Ferrari had in secret conclave heard as " one of us." If he only knew whether he might trust the count ! If he only knew where to find his place ! This Count Stravensky was one of the old nobility, who had been grossly insulted by the Pristav of the district during a search for secret printing presses, and piqued at the treatment his complaint had received, and nettled at his exclusion from Court, he had indeed joined the forces of that vast agitation which was shaking the social order of Russia to its foundations. As the count is destined to figure in these columns, it may be well to refer to the peculiar kind of persecution to which even the highest as well as the lowliest of the land are subjected—Jew and

Gentile, noble and peasant, men and women, gentle and simple.

During the periods of what Stepniak calls "the White Terror," which generally follows on great attempts or detected plots, when searches are made by the hundred, there is hardly a family belonging to the educated classes who, on retiring to rest, do not tremble at the thought that before morning they may be roused from their sleep by the emissaries of the Czar. The Count Stravensky, during one of these general raids, felt thoroughly entitled to sleep in peace. But as it turned out, he had offended the Procurator of the district, who had some personal scores to settle with the local nobility. The count was not one of the most amiable of human beings, it is true; but he was faithful to the dynasty, and had inherited from his progenitors a love of home and country. He was a widower, and his only son had died fighting for the Czar in Central Asia. One day, with drums beating and banners flying, the Procurator marched into the woodland country beyond Czarovna, and infested the house and grounds of the count. No one was permitted to leave and none to enter, until the officer and his men had ransacked the place for a secret printing press or for incriminating papers. They found neither; but a few *versts* away they discovered, in the library of the count's nearest neighbor, a newspaper calling upon the Czar to give the country a Constitution. The editor and proprietor of the journal had already been imprisoned for this offence. The count's neighbor could not say how the paper came into his room; he vowed he had not only not read it, but had never seen it until it was taken from his desk; and it afterwards was clearly shown that he spoke the truth—a discharged servant confessed that he had placed it where it was found, and afterwards given information to the police. Nevertheless, the count's neighbor, who had been carried off to prison, was not released upon this evidence, but died on his way to Siberia. The count was forcibly confined to his house for several days, and, though he escaped the fate of his neighbor, he was subjected to much annoyance, until the Procurator was dismissed from his office for a glaring offence against a more favored individual. When the local noble's name occurred to Ferrari, he had just previously received an official token of the Imperial favor and at the same time a large acquisition of wealth. But all this was too late so far as his allegiance to the Czar was concerned ; he had long since lent his secret aid to the general agitation, but with a secrecy which defied the keenest eye.

Ferrari, unfortunately, had no knowledge of these details, and so keenly did the count protect himself that it is possible, had the Italian sought refuge on his estate, he would have given him up to the police. That would have entirely depended on circumstances ; for Stravensky was a man of moods, and of late he had given the new Procurator every reason to believe that he was active in the interests of the Czar and his officers.

While Ferrari was holding within himself a council of war, there issued from the village a dozen troopers, no doubt from the local barracks, who came sweeping across the plain in the direction of the spot where he lay concealed in the shadow of the bridge.

At first blush, he gave himself up for lost, but determined to die hard. Sheathing his knife, he drew his revolver, and crouched behind the timbers of the bridge, that he might, at least, empty every barrel before he was taken. But the horsemen dashed across the bridge and disappeared over the plain and away into the woods beyond, on their way, no doubt, to the residence of Petronovitch, the old palace of the Provincial Government.

The Italian, with an involuntary prayer of thankfulness, now crept from his retreat and made his way back to the

Ghetto. If he could only find shelter he knew that he could rely upon his fellow Jews to conceal him. He had such words of brotherly responsibility for them, such tokens of strength and power in the rings he wore upon his fingers, that he had only to find a corner to put his head into to be sure that he might keep it there so long as it pleased God not to guide the hunters to his hiding-place.

Changing his appearance in various little ways, in the hope of being able to pass the scrutinizing eyes of the policeman who had seen him, and taking out his knife with a determined resolution of using it if necessary, he managed to reach the back streets of the Pale of Settlement without being observed. He could hear the sound of many voices in the distance, and there were lights in some of the humblest of the half mud and wholly thatched homes of his fellow religionists.

Beneath a heavy archway he noticed at a corner of one of the streets a more than usually spacious house, the door open, a lamp burning in the outer hall, and he entered. It was evidently the home of poverty, large as was the house, unless it was one of those instances of opulence which often in Jewish quarters hides itself in back rooms behind squalid exteriors.

Passing through the outer room, ill-furnished and of evil smell, Ferrari heard someone speaking in the next apartment. Laying his head to the ground, he came to the conclusion that two persons were in the room, a man and a woman. Going back to the entrance to the house, he closed the door, drew the bolt behind him, passed through the outer hall, then boldly lifted the latch of the further room and entered.

Raising his right hand with an eloquent benediction, he invited, nay commanded, aid and sympathy, both of which he received, and at once.

The home he had entered was the house of Moses Grunstein, who lived with his young wife and one servant in the utmost seclusion that was possible in the Ghetto. He had married a second time, had no children, was rich in this world's goods, and was honored and respected. He carried on a large general business, and had made money by dint of saving his profits and lending them at fair usance to his Russian neighbors, and to the landowners of the district. Few persons—never a Christian if he could help it—ever saw the inner glories of his house, where he lived in good style, surrounded with valuable articles of furniture and decoration, which rejoiced the heart of his young wife, Deborah, who was content to wear her jewels on high days and holidays, and in the intervals for her own pleasure in the private rooms of her husband's house.

" A fugitive," said Moses, repeating Ferrari's explanation, "the friend of Joel Strackosch, of St. Petersburg, with a mission to the Rothschilds, in London, and the victim of a conspiracy of the Russian police. It were enough that thou art the esteemed guest of our brother Klosstock. For I have seen thee there."

" Do you not know, then, what has happened ? " asked the Italian.

" Where ? When ? "

" Now—in the village—almost in the next street ! "

" No," answered the old man, his young wife clinging to him in an attitude of alarm.

" Have you not heard the report of firearms ? "

" No ; we spend our nights in prayer and contemplation."

" Where are your servants ? "

" We have only one. Where is Esther ? " He turned and addressed his wife, who at once went forth to find the servant. Returning, she said Esther was not in the house, and yet the doors were barred.

Ferrari explained how he had found the place open and how he had himself bolted the doors after him. "No doubt," he said, "your servant heard the noise, and has gone out to see what is the matter." Then he related what had happened, whereupon the host said, "My son, this is of serious moment; surely it is the breaking up of the peace of Czarovna; every house will be searched, but thou couldst not have entered one where thy secret is so safe. The Ghetto has not always been the abode of security. Deborah, do thou undo the doors and await thy handmaid's coming. Our brother Ferrari's secret is our secret, and we pledge ourselves to that before God."

Deborah bowed her head, and as she lifted up her face the old man kissed her upon the forehead.

"Follow me," he said, taking up a lamp and addressing Ferrari, who followed him straight, the old man leading the way through various passages and lavishly furnished rooms, into what appeared to be a cloth warehouse, and thence into a narrow courtyard, shut in by the tall front of the warehouse and overhanging rock. In a corner of the dark and gruesome *cul de sac* was what appeared to be a well, by the dark side of which the old man paused as if they had arrived at their destination.

"Be not afraid, my son, I mean thee well," said the old man : " a wary correspondent of mine, two days ago, gave me a note of warning that trouble was falling upon Elizabethgrad, and that the blast of persecution might even blow in this direction, but although I showed my wife this refuge yesterday for the first time I did not think I might have to use it, and I take thy coming as a sign from God."

"But where is the retreat, my father?" asked Ferrari, the damp mouldy odor of the place promising anything but a comfortable sanctuary.

"It is at hand. Wouldst thou have it easy of access?

They who made this refuge were thoughtful of their fugitives and of their lives ; follow me."

The old man, handing Ferrari the lamp, proceeded to descend the well, not with the aid of rope or bucket, but by steps which he sought with his feet while clinging to the side. He knelt down, then feet foremost literally went into the well. His head resting upon the coping stone, he said : " Thou wilt feel niches on the right and left for thy feet ; the water would not drown thee if thou wert to fall, which is impossible ; Deborah descended yesterday ; lower thyself by means of the niches for thy feet, and I will conduct thee further : give me the lamp."

Ferrari, following these instructions, presently entered a small subterranean passage, now lighted by the lamp of his host, who stood upright at the further end, whence a door swung open at his touch, and closed upon them with a spring that seemed to clutch the rock through which the place had been excavated. They were within the outer halls of an immense natural cave, their way marked by stalactite and stalagmite, their footsteps awakening echoes that were accompanied by the distant sound of falling waters.

Suddenly coming to a standstill, Ferrari's guide lifted his lamp high above his head and pointed onward, where streaks of daylight seemed to penetrate the gloom afar off. They paused here to make a turning to the right, through a narrow way, where the darkness was so intense that the lamp fairly blinked at it. Then suddenly they were obstructed by what appeared to be solid rock. The aged Jew stooped and apparently turned a key, and the next moment a heavy door swung upon its hinges and disclosed a lighted chamber, fairly well furnished, with comfortable rugs and skins, cupboards and cabinets, the latter roughly made but strong and evidently filled with treasures.

" I have made these," said Moses Grunstein, " with my

own hands," pointing to the furniture; "it has been a labor of love for twenty years, and here you may rest and be secure.   My wife has been here, but without my aid no person could discover this sanctuary, nor finding the passage could suspect the door, nor finding the door could open it except by siege, and besieging it could not prevent the inmate's escape, as I will show thee when thou hast refreshed thyself and surveyed thy new abiding place."

Ferrari found his curiosity as well as his gratitude excited to the utmost, and was as anxious to know the story of the cavern as Moses Grunstein was to know the details of what had passed at the house of his dear friend Klosstock.

"First be seated," said Grunstein, "and I will disclose to thee thy store of wine and food."

Ferrari's kindly host lighted another lamp and produced candles from a spacious cupboard, where there were stores of biscuits in tins, unleavened bread, dried fish, jars of honey and fruits; beneath this cupboard was a lower one containing wines and medicines; while close by were various cooking utensils, and wood and charcoal.

"It is rarely cold here," said Grunstein, "and I am disposed to believe there is a natural warmth in this part of the cave arising from a hot spring; for there is a warm mist always rising beyond the further compartment, and I hear a bubbling of waters; but I have made a cheerful fire, and with perfect security.   At first I feared that the smoke thereof might betray me; but it has not; it seems to me that this cavern is almost endless; five and twenty years ago I discovered it, and I have spent days within its hills and valleys but have never found any ending of it.   Did the Russian law enable a Jew to buy land I would have purchased this estate and made money by exhibiting this wonder of Czarovna, as money is made in other parts of the world by similar exhibitions.   I know the history of every known cavern in the world, so far as their histories are related in books. And while I tremble lest thou shouldst deceive me, I feel a glow of pleasure in showing thee my treasures."

" I have sworn to thee, Moses Grunstein, and that binds me ; but a very devil might be trusted out of his gratitude to be true to thy secret, if thou hadst saved him from a Christian saint as thou hast saved me from Christian devils. And I say saved, with a kind of revelation that it is so ; for know, dear friend, that I am master of so many disguises that with thy aid I need not remain here longer than is necessary for thee to provide me with the means to make myself someone else, and happily I have more than one passport which I can fit with more than one disguise.

CHAPTER V.

AN ARREST.

WHILE host and guest were thus entertaining each other in Grunstein's remarkable retreat, the police were seeking Ferrari in every house of the Ghetto, and troops were scouring the country in all directions. Poor Anna was aroused from her dreams of bliss to be declared a prisoner in her father's house. The officer placed in charge had every room ransacked for seditious papers. Her own virgin chamber was not sacred from their prying eyes. Before it was well day the new governor, General Petronovitch, made his appearance. He sat in Nathan Klosstock's great room, and had the owner and his daughter brought before him as if they were criminals.

" So," he said, " you are the vile reptiles that have found so much favor with my predecessor?—like governor, like subject."

"We are no reptiles, may it please your Excellency," Nathan Klosstock replied.

"Dog of a Jew!" exclaimed Petronovitch, "how comes it then that my Imperial master's mandate is treated with contempt, and his trusted officer murdered in thy house, and by the hands of thy guests, traitors to His Imperial Majesty?"

"If I may be permitted to answer I would say we are no traitors to His Imperial Majesty, but humble, loving subjects."

"Loving subjects? I spit upon thee, thou cursed Jew!" and he spat accordingly.

"Nay, sir, have mercy upon my daughter; she has been trained to pray for His Imperial Majesty, and to honor her father."

"Has she so?" said Petronovitch, turning his cruel eyes upon her; she does not honor thee in her handsome face, nor in her graceful figure. Stand up, girl, thou needs not fear; where is the man to whom thou art betrothed, as they tell me thou art?"

"The rabbi Losinski, your Excellency," said Anna, in a voice trembling with agony and distress, "was driven forth."

"The Jew Losinski," said the officer, "we thought it well your Excellency, to keep apart from the other prisoners. He is without."

"Bring him before us," said Petronovitch.

Two soldiers appeared with Losinski.

"The rabbi Losinski?" said Petronovitch with a note of interrogation.

The rabbi bowed his head.

"The famous student of St. Petersburg?"

"Your humble servant," said the rabbi, "and your Imperial Master's faithful subject."

"For the present, to show that we are the merciful

officers of a merciful Emperor and Father of his people, be they Jew or Gentile, Turk or Persian, thou art released. Betake thee to thy home."

The rabbi lingered for a moment and then advanced towards Anna.

" Begone, I say."

Anna raised her eyes full of appeal and tears.

" This woman is my betrothed," said Losinski ; " permit me to remain."

' Ill-mannered cur ! " said Petronovitch, " out of my sight ! '

Then turning to the officer, he said, " Thrust him forth."

And forthwith the rabbi was hustled into the street, where the sun was finding its way into the dark corners of the Ghetto, and a wild song-bird, straying from the meadows by the river, was singing somewhere in the blue sky.

With what a heavy heart did Losinski turn towards his home ! As he appeared in the midst of the Jewish dwellings, men and women came out of their houses, and many were trooping in from their pleasant homes outside the Ghetto. They were making their way to the Synagogue in response to the triple knock upon their doors—the usual call to prayer—at this time both a surprise and a warning.

" We need thy counsel," said one of the foremost of his flock ; " we need mutual advice."

" And prayer," said the rabbi.

They pressed on their way, encompassing the burial ground of their race, and more than one of the aged people remembered the martyred dead who lay there. Czarovna had a history of cruel rule and bitter persecution ; and in more than one breast of those who followed the rabbi arose the fear that the peace and happiness of the past ten years was but a passing ray of light in the gloom of their ancient records, and that once more they were about to enter upon a period of misery and tribulation,

The news of the previous night had spread like wildfire ; reports of the massacre of Elizabethgrad had come in, and during the day strange men had taken up their quarters at the inns, without any apparent object of business or kinship, or for any purpose of pleasure. Occasionally a traveler would appear in the village, to inspect the old cathedral church and palace, or to wander over a strange group of rocks that rose in curious shape beyond the Ghetto and down to the river—as if they had been thrown up by some sudden revulsion of nature—and beneath which Grunstein had made his interesting and useful discovery ; but the newly-arrived strangers seemed to have no business of any kind, and it was said by a traveler from the West that it was thus the troubles began at Elizabethgrad.

Arrived at the Synagogue, after an earnest prayer for guidance and help, the rabbi related to the people what had taken place at the house of Nathan Klosstock, and he advised his brethren to have a care how they conducted themselves and their affairs in presence of the affliction that had befallen them. He spoke with emotion of the arrest of the late Governor, Poltava, and of the helpless prospect that was before them under his successor. Passing over his own great trouble with much self-denial, he warned his hearers with impressive eloquence to take care they gave the new Governor, His Excellency General Petronovitch, no excuse for afflicting them, no reason for professing to suspect their allegiance to the Czar, no opportunity for affording him a hasty conviction ; for they knew how great was his power, the more so in times of political excitement, and in presence of an active hostility of the Orthodox Christian against the Orthodox Jew. The reports which had preceded the new Governor provided him with a character exactly the opposite from that of General Poltava ; and the rabbi gave point to its truth by telling his flock that he himself had already had bitter proof that neither in charity, religion, nor justice had they anything to hope from General Petronovitch. He did not say this in any bitterness of spirit; he was content to leave himself to the hands of God; but he said it that they might understand how they stood; that the reign of security was at an end, but that the day of tribulation might be at least mitigated by circumspect conduct, patience, humility and prayer.

CHAPTER VI.

A SENTENCE.

DURING the remainder of the day, Czarovna was like a place torn with some internal calamity, and full of a dread of worse to come. To typify the community as one man, it was as if he was stricken with the first symptoms of the plague, and knew that his hours were numbered, and that he would die in dreadful agony. Police and soldiers ostentatiously paraded the little town. The Governor and his staff took up their quarters at the old house of the Ghetto. "It is on the scene of hostilities," said Petronovitch, "and will serve as a convenient court of justice; for we must needs have prisoners. Unless these cursed Jews give up the murderer, Ferrari, they shall smart for it; he cannot have left Czarovna; he is in hiding. I will whip every cursed man and woman of them, but I will have the ruffian they are concealing."

Anna was permitted her liberty on condition that she held no communication with her father or with Losinski. Petronovitch had her watched in the hope that she might unconsciously lead them to their quarry. How could she obey the Governor's inhuman order! The sentinels who guarded her father in an upper room of his house prevented her from seeing him ; but there was no officer to bar her way to the humble lodging of Losinski, whither she flew for counsel and advice.

"Oh, if we could but leave this place !" she said. "If my father gave them all he possesses, would they release him and give us our liberty to go forth and starve?"

"Be comforted, my dearest," said Losinski, "we have only one resource, our Heavenly Father."

"But will He hear us? Oh, will He hearken to our prayers ?"

She was distraught, the poor child—mad with fear, and with a dread she dared not speak of. Petronovitch had addressed her in soft, if not kindly words. She would rather he had spat upon her.

"God will surely help us," said the rabbi ; "it cannot be that so much true religion, such a good and honorable life as your father's, shall not find approval in His sight and therefore protection ; and it cannot be that such love as He has permitted me to be blessed withal shall be blighted."

"Oh, my dear love," exclaimed Anna, "I sometimes fear we are not His chosen: that after all we did crucify Him whom we should have accepted !"

"Nay, Anna, thou art beside thyself !"

"Surely I am," she replied, wringing her hands ; "passing the great crucifix by the church, it seemed to me as if the eyes of Him in His agony sought mine, and that He pitied me."

"For God's sake, Anna, no more of this, lest the judgment of Heaven fall straight upon us."

"Say not 'lest it fall,' dear love," said Anna ; "surely it has fallen. I am homeless, my father a prisoner, and I am going mad, for I know they will take thee from me. Hark ! they are coming !"

She fell fainting into his arms, and as he laid her upon a seat and called the woman of the house, the police knocked at the door and entered.

" You are my prisoner—come ! " said the first officer.

" What is my offence ? " asked Losinski.

" No words," said the officer, laying a rough hand upon him, " come ! "

Losinski was hurried before the Governor, who attacked him with brutal effrontery as " a conspirator, a traitor, a cursed Jew ; " and repeating the very words of caution Losinski had used in addressing his flock : " I am cruel, am I ? I am not the weak fool your previous Governor was, eh ? No justice or charity is to be expected from me ? You denounce the faithful servant of His Imperial Majesty to your people, do you ? You would foment a rebellion, would you ? Speak, Jew, what have you to say ? "

" Arraign me before the judges in open court and let me know the charge you bring against me, and I shall know how to defend myself."

" I do arraign you now, before this Court Martial, this Council of War," said the General, waving his hand so as to indicate his staff, who bowed their hands with the submissiveness of slaves. " Do you deny the truth of what I allege ? You shall see that I am just if I am severe, as it behoves justice to be in these days of conspiracy and rebellion. Stand forth, you Judas, there ! "

He named him well—the witness—for he was a member of Losinski's flock—a half imbecile, God-forsaken wretch, whom the police had suborned by threats and money to betray the rabbi.

" You heard the Losinski warn his flock against me, the Governor, appointed by our holy father, the Czar ? "

" I did," said the witness.

" He said they might neither expect justice nor charity from me ? "

" Yes," replied the poor creature.

"You hear, Jew? You shall see how just I am, how generous are my brother councillors. What have you to say?"

" May I ask your witness, my unhappy brother, a question?"

" You may."

" Did I advise anything but gentle submission to the new Governor—a careful observance of the law?"

" No," said the wretch. " Oh, God forgive me!"

"Stand up, Judas," said the Governor. " That meant, 'Be careful how you rebel, but rebel; don't do it in the open day light; but the Governor Petronovitch is unworthy of his position; he is a tyrant. His Imperial Majesty has sent amongst you an unjust and cruel officer; rebel against him, but have a care, do it secretly.' You, Losinski, are a cut-throat Jew—a rebel, a traitor to the State—and for this I will make an example of you. You are condemned to receive fifty blows of the knout in the public place of execution! Officers, remove him and let his punishment take place with all convenient speed; direct the Commander of the District Prison to attend us at the Palace of the Government within the hour."

Losinski staggered under the sentence and turned pale to the very lips.

" Mercy! mercy!" he cried; "do not condemn me on the evidence of a miserable wretch such as this."

He pointed to the suborned witness as he spoke, and the poor creature turned away his head and sobbed.

" Why ask me for mercy," said the Governor with a cruel sneer, " since I am a tyrant, without pity, without remorse?"

" I did not say so," the rabbi replied, "and whatever I said was in the cause of peace."

" It is in the same cause that thou art condemned."

" Great God ! " exclaimed the rabbi, casting his eyes upwards, " help me, for Thy name's sake—for her sake, for the sake of Thy poor servant, Anna ! "

" Away with him ! " exclaimed the Governor, and the next moment the rabbi, beside himself with grief and terror, was dragged into the street.

CHAPTER VII.

THE KNOUT.

CAPITAL punishment is abolished in Russia, but there are tortures worse than death, and there are deaths from star-vation and cruelty in Russian prisons far more numerous than the decapitations in France and the hangings in En-gland. What English punishments were two hundred years ago Russian tortures are now and worse, and they are conducted with an hypocrisy that is wholly Russian. The truth is, according to more than one historian and commentator, strangulation, crucifixion, the gallows and decapitation were considered too mild for salutary influenc on criminals and political offenders. The Russian legis⁄ho tors, therefore, invented other deterrent instrumenther's keep the people straight ; the rod, the whip, the kno·money the mutilation of the face were introduced, but fre⁄aste no only as supplementary to the deadly mines of Sibeɪ

In the entire language of civilization it is maiɪ that there is no word which conveys an idea of ꝗh the cruelty, more superhuman suffering, than is conveyeɑpro-the Russian word, knout. To hear it in Russia is ere shudder ; and it is all the more terrible that the puniʂed ment of the knout does not necessarily mean death. ɜr ; the friends of the victim have influence enough or suꝰds. cient money to bribe the executioner to kill the condemɪl no then it means death, but this is not a mercy always obtainable.

Anna met the minions of the Council dragging her lover to the prison of the District Court, for Losinski was more dead than alive. He was no coward, but he knew what the knout meant. His very blood had frozen at the sentence. For the moment he even forgot Anna, only thinking of the horror of his situation. He had seen the administration of the knout more than once in St. Petersburg; he had seen the half-naked victims strapped upon the machine so tightly that it seemed impossible that the body could move so much as a hair's breadth, and yet with the skin as tight as racking screws could make it, to the very dislocation of the bones, the wretch would bound under the very first blow. Losinski seemed to see himself undergoing the torture, and he had fought his captors with the vigor of a wild despair. When Anna came upon the grim procession he had simply collapsed; they were dragging along a man half-dead with fright and wholly insensible.

It had been some little time before the rabbi's people had made Anna understand why at parting Losinski had solemnly commended her to God. When she realized had happened, when she knew that he was a pri- she rushed out with no other intention at the than to find him.

" calm," said an old man, standing in her way, "be

"Who are you?" she asked.

"A friend," said the stranger.

"I have never seen you before."

"Yes, you have. Let me whisper a word to you."

She bent her head.

"Thank God," she exclaimed, in answer to the whis-

d word.

Almost immediately a little group of anxious people had gathered round them, mostly Jews, though there were several mujiks in their sheepskin jackets standing in the roadway.

" What shall I do ? " Anna exclaimed, pressing her hand upon her heart, and trying to prevent herself from uttering a cry of anguish.

" Go to the Governor," said a neighbor, " ana fling yourself at his feet; the rabbi is condemned to the knout ! "

" Oh, great God ! " gasped the wretched girl. " Oh, Father in heaven, thou wilt not desert him, Thy servant ! Oh, merciful God."

She staggered, and would have fallen, but for the old man who had been the first to accost her.

Almost as suddenly as she had given way she seemed to recover herself.

" This is no time for tears," she said, wiping her face with her handkerchief, " what shall I do ? Advise me, friend."

She addressed the old man, who, leaning upon his staff, surveyed the scene with much apparent composure.

" There is only one way," exclaimed the neighbor who had previously spoken ; " the Governor is in your father's house, go to him, plead for the rabbi, offer all the money you have for his release, make any bargain, but waste no time ! "

" You are right," said the girl ; " I will go."

Without another word she pushed her way through the throng, and hurried homewards, to meet the terrible procession. The old man was at her elbow, so also were several of her neighbors. Seeing Losinski, Anna rushed in among the soldiers and flung herself upon their prisoner ; only, however, to be thrust back again among her friends.

" Oh, my love ! " she cried. " Merciful God ! will no one protect us ? "

"Go to the Governor," said the neighbors, "pray to him; kneel to him."

"Yes, yes," she said, all her efforts to be calm availing her but little, the danger having been so suddenly revealed, the catastrophe so overwhelming.

"Where is my father?" she asked, addressing the old man.

"Nay, I know not; a prisoner, I believe."

"In his own house," said the neighbor, "or was; where he may be now who shall say?"

"I shall go mad," exclaimed Anna.

"Daughter, be calm, everything depends on that!"

"Yes, I know," she replied; "I will."

"You are going to the Governor?"

"Yes."

"Take this," he said in a whisper; "you may need it; hide it in your bosom."

She took it; it was a knife.

"There is a dishonor worse than death," he said, "and it is lawful to kill in self-defence; daughter of a despised but noble race, be worthy of your father, be worthy of your lover!"

"I will," said Anna, her form no longer trembling, her hand firm, her teeth set, a great resolve in her heart.

"Tell him that you and yours are willing to go forth penniless, that he is welcome to all you possess, that you will show him your father's store, and that Joel Rubenstein, the rich banker of Moscow, shall indemnify his future in a hoard of wealth he little dreams of. You are strong now?"

"Yes."

"Go, my child!"

When she arrived at her father's house, the Governor had gone to the palace of the Government, his new home, and had left instructions that the commander of the prison

should attend him there. The officer on duty informed
her that she was to have full permission to remain in her
father's house or leave it; that no restraint was to be
placed on her liberty, except that she could have no interview with her father.

" I must see the Governor," she said.

" You know the way to the palace," said the attendant.
She did ; and she at once directed her steps thither.

Down the long street of the Ghetto, over the bridge
where Ferrari had prepared to sell his life dearly, across
the plain, over the uplands and through the piece of forest
where she had walked with her father in happy days to join
him in paying his respects to General Poltava and Her
Excellency his amiable wife, the distance from Czarovna
was about a couple of English miles.

It was now nearly an hour after noon. Winter and
summer are sudden incidents in Russia ; one day the land
is snowbound, the next there is a great thaw, the next is
the beginning of summer : on this sad day the last of the
snow had disappeared, the swollen river ran merrily along
its sedgy course, and the sun was shining brightly in a
blue sky.

A mile beyond the bridge a horseman accosted her ; he
was attended by several servants.

" You are the daughter of the merchant Klosstock ? "

" Yes."

" We have met before ; I know your father ; I have
heard what has happened ; I desire to assist you, but I fear
it is impossible. I am the Count Stravensky."

" Oh, thank your highness; my father is a prisoner in
his own house, my betrothed, the learned and beloved
rabbi, is condemned to the knout. I am going to the
Governor to throw myself at his feet and beg for mercy."

The noble boyar looked upon the girl with a world of
compassion in his brown eyes ; her hair was falling all

about her pale handsome face, her eyes were red with weeping.

"I have just now ventured to say to His Excellency the Governor all I know that is good of all of you," said the count, "and hope you may be successful; but I fear, my poor girl, I fear—and there is no lady at the old house so recently adorned by Her Excellency the Lady Poltava to soften the discipline of the place. Are you not afraid to trust yourself alone there?"

"I am alone in the world; I have no one belonging to me now; two days ago I was the happiest of God's creatures."

"And they called you Queen of the Ghetto. Heaven help you! Would that I could! You are not afraid to go alone, you say? I have the Governor's permission to speak with your father; that is why I am now riding into Czarovna. But I will return and go to the Governor with you if you think——"

"No, no, go to my father, dear sir, thank your highness; my loneliness may be the best appeal to the Governor than even your kind aid; and my father needs comfort. Tell him I am well; that I am free; and oh, conjure him to buy his own and the rabbi's liberty if money will buy it; and if not "—lifting her head high for the first time—" tell him we will die together!"

"I will say so," the count replied, not without emotion, "and if I can be of any service to you—I fear my influence is not great—command me."

And they went on their several ways, Anna running to make up for this short delay, the count turning upon his horse to look back after her.

"What a lovely creature!" he said to himself, "brave as she is lovely and good as she is brave! Is it wise to permit her to see Petronovitch unattended?"

"God be with you!" said the old man who had spoken

with Anna in the street, and who had followed her through
the Ghetto, over the bridge and out upon the plain much
more briskly than his age and staff would have seemed
possible.

" And with you, friend," said the count. " I had not
observed you; where did you spring from? "

" Your attendants are out of hearing? "

" They are."

The old man uttered a password and gave a sign. The
count, beckoning to an attendant, requested his retinue
to ride into Czarovna, and await him at the house of
Klosstock, the Jew:

" You were pitying Anna."

" The Queen of the Ghetto? " said the count. " Is it
not so she is called? "

" By those who desire to compliment her and her fatner s
position," said the old man, "yes; but to-day she is de-
throned, and her kingdom is like to be in ruins. There is
no time to stand on ceremony, Sir Count. I gave you a
sign and a word."

" Well? "

· " Is it well? " said the old man.

" I am sorry for these Jewish people," said the count.

" You encourage me. You are sorry for your country
also ? "

" Say on, but do not forget that the very trees and stones
have ears and tongues in these days."

" And I will trust you," said the old man. " I am Andrea Ferrari. I bring messages for you if I think it wise
to deliver them. The brethren did not quite know how
to regard you."

" Since you have placed yourself in my hands, were I
otherwise than their friend I respond to your trust—confidence for confidence. You have had a narrow escape;
your peril is by no means over."

" I am not thinking of myself, but of these poor people ; more particularly this girl, her father, and the rabbi. Can anything be done for them ? "

" I fear me not. Petronovitch is cruel by nature and by policy; Poltava is in disgrace for his leniency; and your arrest, the death of one of the Emperor's officers at your hands, and in the Jew's house, so entirely justifies the change of Governors and policy that Petronovitch is master of the situation, and will be encouraged to take a big revenge. We are under martial law, and he hates the Jews ; indeed, it is hard to say whom he loves."

" I will follow the girl Anna," said the old man ; " good day, Sir Count."

" *Au revoir !*" responded the count. " Let us meet soon."

It was wonderful with what rapidity the old man, our unfortunate friend Ferrari, got over the ground. He soon disappeared in the wood ; and meanwhile Count Stravensky cantered into the town of Czarovna, which he found under the influence of strange and disturbing incidents.

CHAPTER VIII.

THE AWFUL NEWS THAT CAME TO CZAROVNA.

WITHIN the few months previous to the change of Governors in the province of Vilnavitch, the chief towns and villages of Southern Russia were ablaze with riot, violence, and bloodshed. In the provinces of Cherson, Ekaterinsolav, Poltawa, Taurida Kiew, Czeringow, and Podolia there had spread like wildfire the idea that the Jews and their property had been handed over to the tender mercies of the populace, an idea that seemed almost justified by the inertness of the Governor-General in his treatment of the riots at Elizabethgrad and Kiew.

The Times in London made a statement to this effect,
and gave particulars of some of the outrages ; and London
knew more about what was going on in the unhappy towns
of Southern Russia than was known even a few miles from
them. And no wonder that the news traveled tardily to
Czarovna, for here neither Jews nor Christians interested
themselves in political or other affairs outside their own
town, which was a model of good government and exceptional in its general contentment. Several towns had been
wrecked, many a Jewish woman outraged, many a poor
Jew slaughtered, before the full importance of the awful
tidings reached Czarovna, the first agents of trouble arriving
in the prosperous town on the very night of the attempted
arrest of Ferrari.

In each instance of the risings, agents had arrived in
the towns with copies of an alleged ukase empowering His
Imperial Majesty's orthodox subjects to seize all the property of the Jews and put down all resistance of the
transfer. The mayor of one town actually read this pro-
clamation in public, and the place was only saved by the
wisdom and courage of the chief priest, who denounced
the ukase as a forgery and forbade the townspeople to act
upon it ; but at many other towns and villages near by it
was literally interpreted, and the property of the Jews was
taken over, in some cases partly destroyed, and the transfer
accompanied with barbarities and ruffianisms unknown in
this age outside Russia. Children were roasted alive.
Women were outraged in the presence of their offspring.
Men were murdered ruthlessly and without giving the
victims a chance of defence. At one place women appeared
among the assailants and assisted the men in their devilish
orgies and crimes. But it is not within the province of
this narrative to enter into the details of these barbarisms,
which are duly recorded in the newspapers of the time.

The statistics of the terror are appalling, and the worst

feature of the whole affair was the barbarities committed
against the Jewish women ; even the Czar's commanding
officers seeming to think the honor and lives of the poor
creatures of no account, so small were the efforts which they
made to temper the brutalities of the rioters, who were frequently supported and aided by the soldiers and police. The
latest phase of the blind passions of the Christian Russians
was that of arson. So common did the vengeance of fire
become that the mujiks gave it the name of the red cock.
This is the technical term of the peasants for the deliberate
firing of towns. The red cock crowed over many a Jewish
place of settlement ; and within the short time of the riots,
which came to an end only at Czarovna, a hundred thousand Jewish families were homeless, and their property, to
the extent of sixteen million pounds, either taken from
them or destroyed. And the date of these events was not
later than 1881.

There was one beautiful exception to the generality of the
success of the ukase. It was a small unsophisticated town,
something like Czarovna ; the Christians called upon their
Jewish neighbors and warned them of what was going on,
telling them that the agents and rioters from an adjacent
village which had been sacked were coming on to them,
and saying, " Now if it is true that the Emperor has given
your property over to his orthodox subjects it will be
better for you to let your neighbors take it than have it
wrested from you by strangers, and if the ukase is not true
we can hand you your property back again." So when
the band of thieves and rioters came to that town they
found the Christian inhabitants already in possession of
their neighbors' houses, shops, and goods. In this instance
the demon of blood and fire and plunder was outwitted ; he
had to pass on, and in due course the Jews got their property back again.

The Government took no action in denying the forged

ukase, but after the outbreaks issued a Commission of Inquiry in such form and with such instructions as made the persecution of the Jews seem justifiable ; and such added restrictions have followed the commission that the Russo-Jewish question is summed up by a great publicist of the day in these words : " Are three and a half millions of human beings to perish because they are Jews ? " The answer, judged by the present active policy in Russia, is " Yes."

All of which the present narrator hopes will not discount the reader's interest in the house of Klosstock and the doomed community of Czarovna, whence by-and-bye we shall travel to London, there to pick up other human interests and human fates, that are strangely linked with such of the actors in these opening scenes as may not fall victims to the lust and greed of their assailants, and the tyrannical and cruel despotism of the Government.

CHAPTER IX.

THE CRY OF A BROKEN HEART.

GENERAL PETRONOVITCH had finished a hasty meal, and was smoking a cigar over some heavy red wine, when Anna was announced.

" The Jew merchant's daughter," said his military servant. " I told her you could not give audience to anyone."

" You are a fool ! "

" Yes, your Highness," said the man ; " I said I would inquire if you had leisure."

" Admit her ; see that we are not disturbed."

The man withdrew. The General smiled and drained a tumbler to the dregs.

" By the mass, a pleasant encounter ; I would not have

wished for a more agreeable visit. She comes to beg for her lover."

" Pauloff," he cried, ringing a bell which had been placed by the side of his cigar box, " Pauloff."

The attendant returned.

" Listen."

" Yes, your Excellency."

" If I call you and give you an order to postpone the punishment of the man Losinski, in presence of this Jew girl, you will not deliver it. Do you understand? written or verbal, do you understand? "

" Yes, your Excellency. She is here."

" Let her come in. Guard the door without ; admit no one."

The attendant bowed, and Anna entered the room.

" No, no ; you may not kneel to me," said Petronovitch, advancing towards her.

" Mercy for the rabbi ! Save my father," said Anna. " It can be no gladness to you to bring such terrible suffering upon us, it can do no good to our great Emperor; better it would be to take our money, our jewels, our property ; that will buy soldiers clothes, feed your poor, make your ladies happy ; take it, give us our lives and liberty—we ask no more."

She was almost out of breath with the utterance of her little speech, that she had formulated in her despair as she entered the old palace of the local government.

" My dear young lady," said Petronovitch, and the courteous words chilled her, " do not distress yourself; I am not the tyrant your Losinski would make out ; but I owe a duty to my Imperial master. I do not want your money, nor does my Government; we only want peace and order. We are pained to find such reputable persons as your father harboring a conspirator who, on being arrested, cut the throat of our Imperial master's officer and escaped by the connivance of your father, the master of the house; and when we are in our most generous mood of narrowing justice down to the criminal only, and considering the previous good conduct of his associates, the rabbi, a learned and scholarly man, incites his flock against us the Governor, and denounces us as the corrupt and cruel agent of a corrupt and unjust Government."

He knew not what he said, your Excellency !" Anna exclaimed. "Oh, forgive him—His Greatness the Czar has no truer subject ; mercy ! oh, be merciful ! "

"Be seated, child, and let us talk the matter over."

Remaining standing until now, he offered her a chair and sat down himself.

"Do not ask me to sit ; when I flew here for succor they were dragging the rabbi through the streets I know not where, and they said he was condemned to a punishment worse than death. Great God ! while I stand here he may be suffering."

She turned upon Petronovitch her pale, frightened face, her eyes ablaze with excitement and terror.

"Oh, sir, spare him ! Hark ! I hear his voice ; he calls me—he is dying ! "

"This is madness ; listen, my poor girl, I *will* spare him. There ! he is saved ! "

"Heaven bless you," she cried and seized his hand and kissed it. "God will bless you. But how is he to know you will spare him ? How will they know he is to be saved ? "

"If you will promise to be quiet and remain here, and let me know your wishes and not distress yourself, you shall hear the order given for the postponement of his punishment, and you shall yourself bear away with you the order for his release."

" Bless you," said the girl, her eyes now filling with tears as she staggered to a seat.

"Pauloff," called the General, ringing his bell. The attendant entered, Anna looked up.

"Pauloff, bring me pen and ink."

Pauloff went to a cabinet and brought the writing materials. Petronovitch wrote upon a sheet of paper, folded it and handed it to Pauloff with these words—"An order for the postponement of the punishment of the rabbi Losinski ; send a messenger to the commander of the prison forthwith."

Anna covered her face with her hands and wept tears of joy.

"Will you read the order, madame ? " said Petronovitch, showing it to her.

"No, no, I trust you."

"And the messenger will inform the commander that the order for Losinski's release shall follow, you understand ? "

"Yes, your Excellency," the man replied, leaving the room, Petronovitch following and quietly raising the *portière* to bolt the door.

"There, we are not so black as we are painted, are we ? " he said, approaching Anna, and laying his hand upon her shoulder.

"You are very merciful," she said.

Petronovitch took a seat by her side.

"And what is to be my reward for all this, and the much more I am to do for you ? "

"Eternal thanks and prayers, and the blessed consciousness of a great act of charity ! "

"Just so," he said, his sensual face paling with the emotion of an unholy passion. "And so you are to marry the rabbi ? "

"Yes," said Anna, permitting his near approach without a movement one way or the other, willing, poor creature, to submit to some amount of insult for those she loved.

" He is to be envied," said Petronovitch, stealing his arm round her.

" Your Excellency is pleased to be merry after your act of goodness," Anna replied.

" I am pleased with you, too, and I hope you are not displeased with me ? "

" You are very good ; I owe you a deep debt of gratitude."

" It is easily paid," he said, taking her hand in his hot grasp.

" It can never be sufficiently acknowledged," she said, now moving a little way from him ; " my father and my future husband will never cease to bless you."

" I prefer to be in your thoughts," he said, his hot lips close to her own, " and in your arms," and he kissed her roughly, brutally.

She struggled free from his grasp, but did not lose her self-control nor upbraid him, as he expected she would.

" You propose too much honor for a poor Jewess ; pray now, sir, permit me to withdraw," was all she said.

" You are worthy of an emperor," he said : " no Christian is more beautiful."

" But your Excellency knows I am to be married to one of my own people."

She would not allow him to think for a moment that she believed he intended anything more than to make love to her with a view to marriage. " You may not marry a Jewess, be she ever so wealthy."

" Oh yes, I may," he said, " we are not so particular when beauty is in the case—such beauty as yours."

She retreated before him ; he followed her.

" I frighten you. Nay, let us talk about that release ; I have only to write it."

She stood still and allowed him to approach her ; she permitted him to take her hand ; he led her to a couch of skins.

"Now let me go, dear sir," she said, in her gentlest voice, "and I will come again to morrow."

"You make me jealous of the very man I am about to release," he said, his arm about her waist once more.

"Let me see him free," she said, her heart beating, every nerve strained with fear and apprehension, "and I will come to you the next moment."

"Nay, my darling, I cannot spare you," he said roughly, taking her into his arms and half stifling her, his hot breath upon her cheek, but the next moment she was free, and the knife Ferrari had given her flashing above her head, the fire of a tigress in her eyes.

"Let me go, or call in your servant to carry out my corpse."

For a second Petronovitch was checked. But he was not daunted, either by the knife or by Anna's threats. though he pretended to be.

"Forgive me," he said. "I had an idea that you Jewish girls were kind and generous. I had no idea you carried such formidable greetings for lovers as that. We are to know more of each other before we are friends ? Well, so be it. Forgive me, and I forgive you. Put up your knife, and keep your promise, for I am now going to put your word to the test—the moment you see him free, you will come to me ?"

"I said so," Anna replied, off her guard and replacing her knife in her bosom, as Petronovitch took up his pen to write the order for Losinski's release.

But Anna had not gauged the fiendish deceit of the man she had hoped to content with such complaisance as she had struggled to permit herself in her desperate case.

"I give you my word," he said, "I will not molest you. Be seated. I only now desire to have your rabbi released that I may see how you ladies of the chosen people keep your word."

Entirely accepting this view of the case as the denouement of her visit, Anna sat down and calmly awaited the
order for her lover's release.

Petronovitch, having written, read it to her, and as
she held out her hand for it he flung his arms round her,
snatched the knife from her bosom, and at the moment
that angry voices were heard in altercation at the door
(one of them the voice of Ferrari), he dragged her into an
adjoining room, where the crash of a heavy door closing
behind her silenced—except, let us hope, for heaven—the
cry of a broken heart.

CHAPTER X.

THE DEATH-BLOW OF THE KNOUT.

It seemed as if the curse of the Lord had fallen upon the
house of Klosstock and upon all the chosen of Czarovna.
The light was suddenly gone out. That good Providence
which for years had watched over the ghetto now turned
from it, and there fell upon it the winter of misery, persecution and death. They bowed them to the east and
prayed for succor, and there came fire and sword from the
west.

In the middle of the night when Anna was held in a
terrible bondage Nathan Klosstock was fettered and removed. Morning saw him on his way to the House of
Preventive Detention at St. Petersburg, *en route* for what
is called administrative exile   This kind of captivity has
for the authorities none of the inconveniences of public or
even private trial. The prisoner disappears from the
world. Neither friend nor foe may know him again. It is
possible for his identity to be as thoroughly wiped out in
this way as if he were secretly murdered and buried in an
unknown grave. He has been changed from a man into a

number, from a human being into a caged animal. If
Heaven is merciful, he will, in a little time, be attacked with
some fatal disease, and so be released from the benevolent
judicature of the only country which has abolished capital
punishment—abolished it as a fiend might, with his forked
tongue in his cheek.

And when that same morning broke upon Czarovna, in
the Province of Vilnavitch, Heaven appeared to be more
than angry with its servant, Klosstock, and its minister,
the learned Losinski, for it made its sun to shine gloriously
throughout the land. The radiant ruler of the day lighted
up the gruesome procession that formed and marched from
the district prison to the place of punishment.

The platform of the executioner was set up opposite the
barracks of the hussars, and was supported by a company
of the Imperial troops. In the police cart Losinski, half
naked and bound, was supported by two gaolers, and at
the barracks he was literally handed to the executioner, for
he was still in a condition of mental and physical collapse.
To this extent God had been kind to his poor servant,
who, despite his nobility of nature and his intellectual
strength, did not possess the qualifications for martyrdom.

Among the crowd was Ferrari, in the disguise of the
Moscow banker, and with the Moscow banker's passport
in his pocket. It was he whose voice was heard at the
doors of the Governor on the previous day, and he had
had a narrow escape of detention; but the judgment to
know when to speak and when to be silent, and the discretion to know how to use money and when, had kept
Ferrari free from the hard hand of the enemy, though
neither his judgment, his discretion, nor his power had
enabled him to help Anna.

It was with a heavy heart that he had returned to
Czarovna and communed with his friend Moses Grunstein
who had counselled him to bribe the executioner not to

spare Losinski, but with merciful consideration to kill him outright.

Such as German de Lagny described the punishment of the knout twenty years ago, so is it to-day, for Russia is singularly conservative in its Imperial despotism. A man is condemned to receive, say fifty or a hundred lashes. He is dressed in a pair of linen drawers, his hands tied together, the palms flat against each other, and he is laid upon his face, on a frame inclined diagonally, at the extremities of which are fixed iron rings. His hands are fastened to one end of the frame, his feet to another. He is then stretched in such a way that he cannot move, "just as an eel's skin is stretched in order to dry." His bones crack and are dislocated under this operation. Five and twenty paces away stands the public executioner, attired in a colored cotton shirt, velvet trousers (stuffed into a pair of jackboots), his sleeves tucked up over bare brawny arms. He grasps his dreadful instrument in both hands. It is a thong of thick leather cut in a triangular form, four or five yards long and an inch wide, tapering off at one end and broad at the other. The small end is fastened to a wooden handle or whipstock about two feet in length. It is akin to the buffalo whip of the Western States of America, the crack of which is like the discharge of small artillery. The signal given, the executioner advances a few steps, bends his athletic body, grasping the knout in his two strong hands, the long lash dragging like a snake along the ground, and between his legs. Within three paces of the victim he flings the creeping lash above his head, then with a curious cruel knack lets it twirl for a moment before bringing it down upon the naked object, around which it twines with malignant force—"in spite of its state of tension, the body bounds as if it were submitted to the powerful grasp of galvanism." Retracing his steps, the executioner repeats the stroke with clock-like regularity, until the prescribed number of blows is counted. It is a ghastly sight; the present narrator will spare the reader a detailed description of its horrors. But in Russia where so much may be purchased for gold, and indeed where so much must be purchased—the venality of every official class being notorious all over the world—the family of the wretch condemned to the knout may buy from the executioner what he calls the death-blow; in that case, the operator slays the victim at the very first stroke "as surely as if it were an axe that he held in his hand."

The drums had beaten, the Governor and his officers had taken their places around the scaffold—for the knout is administered with much ceremony, more especially when the punishment is intended for a salutary warning during some political crisis—the crowd, awe-stricken, yet anxious to see the awful exhibition, were holding their breath with fear, the lash was writhing through the air, when a mad woman tore her way through the crowd, her hair all disheveled, her face white as her bare arms, her eyes bloodshot. But the sensation she created did not stay the flying lash. It came down with the thud of death upon the body of Losinski. The very life was beaten out of him. Ferrari knew it. Grunstein knew it. The executioner knew it. But Anna only saw the lash swing and fall, stroke after stroke, while she fought with the crowd, and at last was seized upon by Ferrari and Grunstein in the hope of saving her from the police.

"Are ye men?" she cried, when for a moment she was at rest. "Oh, my brothers, will you stand by and see your master murdered? Great God, curse this cruel host of the fiendish Czar?"

"Peace, daughter, for Heaven's sake!" urged Grunstein.

"Anna!" whispered Ferrari.

"Yonder!" she cried. "Look at him—the false governor, the traitor, the liar, the Christian Tarquin!

A few men of the ghetto gathered about her threaten-
ingly, for the Jews of Czarovna, through many years of
something approaching to freedom, were not altogether
devoid of courage, and at once, half crazy as she was,
Anna seemed to see her advantage.

" Men of the ghetto ! " she cried, " look to your wives
and daughters. You knew me a pure, good woman;
your vile governor Petronovitch has put upon me an everlasting curse ; avenge me, for the love of your women and
babes ! "

" Down with the Governor Petronovitch ! " shouted the
imbecile who had betrayed Losinski.

And the knout continued to fall upon the dead rabbi.
When the last blow was struck there was a movement
towards the crowd where Anna was haranguing them, and
this was encountered by a hostile rush of the multitude
that had now gathered about the outraged woman. The
Governor could be seen giving orders. Several officers
left his side and made for the spot where Anna was conspicuous, her arms tossing to and fro above the crowd,
her tall figure a rallying point for the riot, that now began
with a quick ferocity, in defence of the wretched queen of
the ghetto, to capture whom it was at once seen was the
object of the Governor's officers.

All at once there was fighting, from one end of the
street to the other. The foremost band was led by the
imbecile, who fairly leaped upon the police as they charged
the crowd, only, however, to be transfixed by a bayonet
thrust. Anna seemed to be the very centre and object
of the riot. The men of the ghetto defended her with a
devotion that was as noble as it was ill-advised and futile.
It is true that several of the Imperial troops and police
bit the dust, but the Jews fell by the score, and before
Losinski's body was removed from the scaffold and carried
as a matter of form to the hospital, a fresh company of

troops came marching out from the barracks. The Jews retreated to their homes, and the populace, influenced by the agents who had arrived at Czarovna the night before from the east with the false ukase, began to rise against their Semitic neighbors.

CHAPTER XI.

PANDEMONIUM.

BEATEN back and retreating, the Jews left their forlorn sister as needs must to the mercy of the Governor. Unsatiated with the blood of Losinski, in a passion of brutal rage he condemned Anna to the lash, and to instant punishment.

In the midst of the red excitement of the moment, men's passions alive with fear, terror and vengeance, with the sound of musketry following the retiring Jews, and with the murmur of a gang of prisoners whom the hussars were dragging towards the Governor, Petronovitch's inhuman order was given, and Anna was stripped to receive fifty strokes of the knout.

There were Russian women on the scene, the wives of some of the officials; they are supposed to attend such terrible functions as the knout on special occasions, for the purpose of assisting to emphasize a public deterrent example offered on such occasions for the benefit of the people. They had borne the sight of the rabbi's death with the nerve of official dignity. But a palpable murmur of horror and protest was heard among them as they realized what was about to happen to Anna. The Count Stravensky, venturing on the spur of the moment to make an appeal to the Governor on behalf of the woman, received a prompt and significant snub: "Are we to maintain the authority of the Government or not? Is open defiance, and in presence of the officers of the law itself, making riot under the very banner of his Imperial Majesty nothing, Sir Count? Begone, sir, to your home!"

As the count, biting his lips, moved away, Anna Klosstock, stripped to the waist, was laid upon the reeking frame to receive her punishment.

From such of the crowd as were left, Jew and Gentile, a cry of horror went up to heaven, but the sun shone brightly and the measured beat of the executioner upon the peeling flesh fell stroke by stroke fifty times.

The quivering body was then carried with a strong escort of soldiers to the hospital, and the riots of Czarovna began in downright earnest. "Better we take their goods than the strangers from Elizabethgrad," said some of the Christian townsfolk. Others remembered wrongs or imaginary wrongs which they had suffered at the hands of their neighbors. The mujiks thought of the money they owed the Jews. Others were fired with a sort of patriotic zeal, preferring to believe that the Emperor wished them to take over their property. "They are delivered into our hands by the Government," said the agents of the other risings against the Hebrews.

Outside the ghetto, the Jews' houses were sacked without much defence; they were mixed up with the wooden and mud houses of their Christian neighbors. The beerhouses and taverns were occupied with ignorant throngs, who, having drunk themselves into a frenzy, presently sallied out into the ghetto, mad, wild, irresponsible savages.

The Jews fortified themselves in their houses and fought for their lives—fought with knives and staves, and here and there with firearms; but as a rule they had little or no knowledge of guns and pistols, and while they had the instinct of self-preservation to push them on, their assailants were fired with drink and greed, and stimulated with a natural barbarity. The more their cruel passions were fed, the more they desired; and Pandemonium was let loose.

A woman with her babe, because she stood before her son, a youth who had fought against the entrance of the mob into her room, had the child dragged from her arms and its brains dashed out before her face, herself being subjected to the last insults that men-fiends can offer to helpless women.

At the lodging of Losinski, on the other hand, the woman of the house received the leader of the attack with a coal hammer, and laid him dead at her feet, at which the mob passed on and left her.

The keeper of the synagogue, whither many timid Jews had sought sanctuary, fought the mob single-handed upon the stairway, until he fell covered with wounds.

Klosstock's house was ransacked without even a show of protest. "Thine ox shall be slain before thine eyes, and thou shalt not eat thereof; thine ass shall be violently taken away from before thy face, and shall not be restored to thee ; thy sheep shall be given unto thine enemies, and thou shalt have none to rescue them. Thy sons and thy daughters shall be given unto another people, and thine eyes shall look and fail with longing for them all the day long ; and there shall be no might in thy hand.

It did not enter into the divine invention of mischief to curse his rebellious people with the knout and the dungeon, the husband torn from the wife, the daughter stripped and flogged in the market place, the babe dashed to pieces in sight of the mother, brutal might everywhere triumphant, virtue, modesty and right trodden in the gutter, spat upon, massacred. But such has it been of late with the Jews in Russia ; such it is feared will be again.

Is it, then, a matter for wonder that so many of the Nihilistic authors of anti-Russian books have been Jews ? Is it surprising that the Jews have aided the propaganda

against the Russian Government? Under such disabilities
is there anything astonishing in the fact that there is a
good deal of wretchedness, knavery, dirt, squalor, and
deceit among the commoner class of Jews in Russia? What
kind of a miracle would it be that, in spite of persecution,
stripes, murder, enforced penury and hunger, with debarred
constitutional, social, or any other rights, except now and
then to see the light of heaven, should raise a people to
the level of the masses of free countries, such as England
and America?

CHAPTER XII.

VOWS OF VENGEANCE.

THE Count Stravensky rode homewards with a conflict of
many harassing feelings stirring his heart. He would have
done much to save Anna Klosstock. Ever since he had
met her on the road to the old palace of the Government,
her face had been continually before him. Had he been a
man of a stronger will, he would probably have prevented
her from going to that fatal house. But he knew his own
weakness; it was not so much want of courage as the
knowledge that he was not a true subject of the Czar;
true to Russia, yes—but untrue to his oath of allegiance,
untrue to his order, and would have been openly hostile if
any good could have come of it.

Meanwhile, however, he was one of the powers behind
the popular movement of the time, and with the hope that
the day would come when he might strike a blow for
liberty in open daylight and lay down his life, if need be,
to some purpose, to sacrifice himself now either to suspicion or to personal malice would be a useless waste of
power and possibility.

Count Stravensky had already been able to help on the

chances of the coming of that glorious future of which many patriots were dreaming, and he knew better than to forfeit his place and position voluntarily and to no good. But for the knowledge that he was already deeply compromised and might be charged at any moment, though he had every reason to believe his secret was well kept, he would have resisted the Governor's arrogant order. It would have been an inopportune moment to have defied the administrative authority—the town on the eve of open revolt, the Governor anxious to signalize the opening of his government.

The count ground his teeth and vowed to himself as speedy a vengeance as a calm discretion would permit him to take in the interest of the great cause to which he was secretly pledged. He had been publicly insulted; but that was as nothing compared with the outrage which had been committed upon the beautiful girl with whom he had spoken on the previous day upon the road he was now traversing. While he bit his lips and clenched his right hand with rage and indignation, the tears streamed down his rugged cheeks, as the two pictures of human misery rose up before him—the pale, lovely face of the Jew's daughter as he had seen her on the previous day, her great violet eyes full of mute appeal, her bronzed locks in picturesque masses about her face, her red lips and white teeth, her fine noble figure, and the mad, bloodshot eyes that had met his gaze near the scaffold, to which she had been brutally and ruthlessly condemned.

" Are we men or fiends that we can do such deeds? What sort of miserable cowards are we to stand by and see them done ? "

His hand upon his sword, he turned his horse in the direction of the once happy but now wretched town of Czarovna, but only to wheel round again and continue his ride home. He resolved, however, if the poor creature lived through her terrible punishment, and escaped Siberia, or were vouchsafed years enough to pass the ordeal of both knout and Siberia, he would do something towards making the remainder of her life bearable. And he recalled to mind the case of Madame Lapukin, who, some hundred years before, was flogged almost to death, her tongue torn out, and then skillfully saved from death to be sent to Siberia, whence she was released by Peter the Third when she was an old woman.

This awful example gave the count a passing hope that if Anna did not die, as he prayed she might, he would, in some way, be able to help her, if it were only to make her a witness of the downfall and punishment of Petronovitch ; for of the Governor's ultimate ruin and death he felt a moral certainty, and he humbly asked God to save him a red hand in this.

They all prayed, you will observe, on whichever side they were. Even Petronovitch knelt publicly and helped the priest to give thanks for the discovery of plots against the Czar and the punishment of the instigators thereof. If the Divine Power were one that could be influenced by these miscellaneous petitions, what a complication of investigation would be involved in the answering of their conflicting requests ? But God's laws against tyranny, persecution, murder, are irrevocable ; they are often slow of operation, but in the end the wrongdoers are punished. The end may seem to us long in coming ; it is not so when we remember what atoms we are, and that our lives are only as a moment in the longevity of God and the great world

Stravensky, among other things, came to the conclusion that his life and work would be of more value to the cause of Liberty, and his chance of success against Petronovitch greater, if he lived in St. Petersburg ; and when he reached his estate and sat down to converse with his steward he

informed him that he had resolved to let his property in
the province of Vilnavitch, the governorship of which was
no longer to his liking, and take up his abode in St. Petersburg.   He did not give his faithful servant any further
information, but he had in his heart a big scheme of
intrigue against Petronovitch, and in favor not only of the
Jews but of Holy Russia.   Possessed of great wealth, he
would devote it now in earnest to the great cause; he
would lay himself out for popularity; he would seem to be
a Royalist of the Royalists; he would win his way to the
Czar's confidence; he would be a social and political
power, in order that he might the easier swoop to his
revenge, and be all the more able at the right time to turn
and rend the personages with whom he would make a pre-
tence of friendship.   How far the part which the count
proposed to himself was a noble one the reader must judge
for himself; how far he succeeded in his plans of patriotism and vengeance the narrator will inform the reader in
due course.

If Andrea Ferrari had been the arch-fiend of evil himself, he felt that he could not have brought more calamities
upon his friends than had befallen them, as he conceived,
through his unconscious agency.   While he upbraided himself, he nevertheless could not but be conscious of the fact
that after all he had only hastened the troubles that were
about to fall upon Czarovna.   Given Petronovitch for
Governor, and the agents of the false ukase in the town,
something terrible must have happened sooner or later; at
the same time, but for him there might have been time to
save Anna and the rabbi and Nathan Klosstock.

These thoughts raced through his mind even at the height
of the rioting about the scaffold.   His usual grip left him.
He hesitated and was lost—or rather saved; for had he
not hesitated he would have rushed into action, and to
what purpose?   The knout, imprisonment, or death!

When Anna was captured he was borne away with the retreating crowd to the ghetto, pressed upon by the soldiers, and presently hustled and struck by the gathering rioters and agents of the false ukase, who were already assembling in the streets of the Jewish quarter.

With a deep vow of vengeance against Petronovitch, he hurried on to the assistance of Grunstein, and with a view to reach the good old Jew's hiding-place.

Pushing open the front door, leading through the porch into the house, he found Grunstein, torn, tattered and bleeding, his wife bathing his temples.

The threatening cry of the mob could be heard from far away. It was like the first booming of the coming storm. It would come nearer and nearer every minute, until it fell with a crash, and with lightning and sudden death in it.

Ferrari locked and bolted every door behind him. "Bloodhounds," he growled between his teeth, "wait awhile!"

"I am not hurt; it is nothing," said Moses Grunstein, rising as he spoke. "Deborah was alarmed, but it is nothing; would that I might have died to save that poor victim of our neighbor Klosstock!"

"We are indeed a cursed race," exclaimed Ferrari.

"To-day, it is true, our Father Abraham is on the side of the Philistines," said Moses Grunstein. "'And thy life shall hang in doubt before thee; and thou shalt fear day and night, and shalt have none assurance of thy life.' The curse is upon us."

"But He shall yet bring us to the land which our fathers possessed," said Deborah, "and do us good, and we shall be blessed."

Deborah not only comforted her husband with plaster for his body, but with plaster for his perturbed mind.

"That will do," said Ferrari. "I expect, the truth being known, the Lord has nothing whatever to do with it, the trouble is somehow in ourselves; but, mistress, where is your servant?"

"She is in my chamber, packing my jewels."

"Call her down."

Deborah called the maid, who came with a small box in her hand and a bundle of rich silk shawls on her arm.

"Listen," said Ferrari; "listen, all of you! The wolves are without, there is no time to lose. Is all prepared for our retreat?"

"All," said Grunstein.

"Then let us waste no time."

For the moment there was a lull outside; it seemed as if the mob had passed on.

"As if," said the old man, divining Ferrari's thoughts, "they had seen the ancient sign and we are saved."

"Did any one see you enter?"

"When?" asked the old man.

"When we were separated, and you made for home."

"I think not."

"A stranger followed me," said Ferrari: "one of the agents of the rising—an Eastern man, I'll swear. I had nearly stabbed him on the doorstep; but he can wait. Come, dear friends."

"I heard thee bar the doors; we are safe, my son, at present; let us refresh ourselves; thou art pale, thy lips are dry."

At a nod, Deborah, his wife, brought wine and cakes from a little cabinet.

"I like your courage, old friend," said Ferrari, "it rebukes me; my nerves are shaken."

"I know how easy it is to retire to those chambers within," said Grunstein, "and there is no need to run now."

"Would to Heaven we might have stood yonder by that scaffold," said Ferrari; "surely, after all, it would have been best to die like the idiot, who atoned nobly for his betrayal of Losinski."

" That did he," said the old man.

" It is hard for me to persuade myself that I am not as guilty of Losinski's death as the suborned witness was," said Ferrari. " It was I who brought the police spy upon the house of Klosstock ; my intention was to warn and save —instead of that I was the trail the bloodhounds followed ; the face of Anna Klosstock will haunt me to my dying day ; I only consent to live that I may stab Petronovitch to death with the same ghastly memory uppermost in his black heart. Hush ! did you not hear a noise in the outer hall ? "

As he spoke there was a hurrying of feet in the street outside, then the crash of a window, followed by the report of firearms.

" They are coming," said Deborah, creeping to the side of the old man.

" Yes," he said, " have no fear ; all will be well."

" Pray God it may," Deborah answered.

" Go forward with the shawls and jewels," said the old man, addressing the girl ; " and be not afraid."

" I am not afraid." said the maid, " now that our guest has come."

Ferrari smiled and bowed. " Madame," he said, turning to the mistress, " I hope my sojourn under your roof will bring you better fortune than my presence at the Klosstocks has brought to them and theirs."

" You blame yourself without a cause, my generous Moses says, and I can well believe it."

" You may trust to my good intentions," Ferrari replied ; " you shall also find me grateful."

" We are in the hands of God ! " she answered.

" Amen ! " said the old man.

A thundering at the outer door was the defiant reply of the mob to these pious ejaculations.

"Come," said Ferrari, and they followed him at once.

"Now, my friend," continued the guest, "we will escort the women to safety."

The old man rose and led the way. Ferrari locked and bolted each door as they went along ; intending, nevertheless, to return and unbolt some of them, for it was not in human nature to slink away and not strike one blow for his friends and the bleeding cause of Freedom.

Arrived at the well, the women were soon placed beyond danger.

"And now, good friend," said Ferrari, "do thou await me here ; descend, keep watch at the entrance below, and I will join you anon."

Grunstein begged him to run no further risk, but rather make good his retreat and safety.

Ferrari made no answer, but laying aside his Jewish gabardine and the wig and beard of the Moscow-banker, turned up his sleeves to the elbow.

CHAPTER XIII.

A GREAT FIGHT ; BUT THE RED COCK CROWS OVER THE GHETTO.

THE entrance to the well, which was the narrow way to the underground palace of the wise old Jew, was a small open square or yard leading into the back of the Grunstein warehouse or store room, a not very safe place if the mob made their way through the strong iron-bound door that gave upon it. But Ferrari was master of the situation, seeing that, go as far as he might through the premises, he had strong doors between him and the rioters, unless through any indiscretion arising out of his excitement they should score an advantage against him. The yard in question was unapproachable from without, seeing that on one side it was shut in by the warehouse before-mentioned, and on the other by the beginning of the overhanging rocks which were the commencement of that curious geological formation the secret of which Moses Grunstein had discovered long ago, to his great satisfaction if not to his financial profit.

Ferrari, with the master key of the place in his hand, being also on the right side of all the bolts and bars, stood in the little courtyard of the underground retreat, and listened. He had given the knife which had served him so well on the night of his escape from Klosstock's house to Anna—alas! to so little purpose—but he had replaced it from Grunstein's store with a superb example of the cutler's art. It was not a dagger in the general acceptation of the term; it was something between a butcher's knife and the stiletto of the Spaniard; it had the fine temper of the latter with the strength of the former, and it rested in a heavy leathern sheath; it had not the handle of the dagger, but was attached by a strap to the wrist. In a pocket upon Ferrari's hip was a revolver, and in his resolute eyes there was a whole armory of weapons; for whatever one may have previously seen of the ugly side of Ferrari was as nothing compared with the murderous look there was now in his face as he stood listening for the mob, conscious of his power and full of a determination to avenge on somebody the death of the rabbi and the almost worse than assassination of Anna Klosstock.

Let us glance at him in the streak of sunny daylight that falls into the narrow gorge we have called the courtyard, between the well and the Grunstein warehouse. Wearing a coarse grey shirt of woolen texture, a pair of breeches with high boots, he is stripped for battle. He is of medium height, bony, lithe, some would say thin, and his muscles are of iron. His shirt is open at the throat,

showing a shapely neck ; no Adam's apple in it, but strong
muscular bands right and left; his head well fixed upon
the neck ; and one notes that, in repose and not under the
tension of strong passion, head and shoulders would be
singularly graceful, but now the head was stiffly borne up
as if all the muscles of the body were strung for some big
athletic action. His face at first blush would have struck
you as more or less ascetic ; but there was something both
sensual and sensuous in the mouth, and just now there
was a drawing up and a twitching of the right corner of the
upper lip that suggested the snarl of a dog that is going
to bite. His eyes, black as night, only showed the whites,
except that there was a touch of the sun by way of reflection in the pupils, that made a lustrous suggestion of their
depths. The forehead was square, and had two strong
wrinkles above the nose and a decided scowl right across
the frontal bone. He had torn off the disguise of beard
and moustache, leaving only a short, downy moustache as
black as his long hair that hung about his forehead and
was in artistic harmony with his sun-tanned skin.

It was the face of an enthusiast, with the cunning of the
Jew and the hot passion in suppression of the Italian
bravo. But when he stretched his two arms above his
head, as if he were giving himself a pull together for a
great leap, you could see that with all the fire of physical
passion there was also present a capacity for restraining it
until the time was ripe for action. He suggested the tiger
getting ready for a spring.

Behold him creep to the great door and fling it back
upon its hinges. Behold him leave it wide open for easy
egress. Behold him pass along to the next door and
listen. He hears no sound. He draws the bolts, releases
the bar. He is now in the midst of bales and boxes of
skins and rich textiles. Still no sound? Yes. A murmur that is not far away. He opens the next door ; he is

in the Jew's living room, the apartment where he and
Grunstein had drunk confusion to the foe. The mob is
at the door ; they have broken down the two other doors,
and are thundering at this. Ferrari draws his knife,
kisses the blade and snarls. The mob have broken in
one of the panels. There are two bolts on the upper
half of the door. Ferrari undoes one of these, whereupon
half the panel gives way, and there is a yell of triumph
without, followed by a yell of pain. Two arms that were
thrust into the opening have been instantly seized by Ferrari in one bony hand, to be literally scored from wrist to
elbow with red gashes that leave the flesh hanging like
loose bandages.

And now Ferrari's lips are red, for he has kissed his
knife again, and he laughs like a maniac. "Come on,
scum of the earth ! Don't be bashful. Come on ; there's
room for all of you, and to spare ! " But they did not
hear a word, although they had paused for a moment to
let the wounded assailants fall to the rear.

Bang, bang, crash came the blows upon the door, as if
a very battering-ram of old had got to work. They were
determined men, these ; not the sort who passed on
because they met a strange resistance ; besides, they knew
the value of Grunstein's store. Down came the top half
of the door, and crash into the faces that looked in went
Ferrari's knife amidst howls of pain and execration.

And they saw Ferrari, those who were not blinded
with his knife, and he laughed aloud, and yelled, and
leaped, and flourished his weapon, and had nearly lost his
life, as a consequence, the sharp crack of a pistol and the
whiz of a bullet causing him at once to dodge his head
and rush for the second room. He had only just time to
swing the door upon the jambs and bolt and bar it when
the mob were inside the next room and had flung themselves upon the door ; but it was made of stronger and

sterner stuff than the other, and it had the additional protection of an iron bar.

"Don't be a fool, Andrea," Ferrari said to himself, almost hissing the words, as if he were addressing some second person. "Don't be a fool; would you let them catch you and skin you alive? Don't be a fool, I tell you!"

His hand sought his hip pocket and then withdrew.

"No, not yet," he said; "you will empty your pistol at the last stand."

The door was thick, but he thought, between the blows upon it, he could hear the ruffians dragging away the Grunstein bales; he saw them indeed as much as heard them, in his imagination, gloating and yelling over their spoil, and maddened with the drink they must have found in the first room of the strange old house. The door cracked. He tightened his belt, examined his knife, gave his shirt sleeves another roll above the elbow, that snarling curl of the upper lip showed one of his teeth, the one called the canine tooth, and his delicate nostrils dilated. How curiously the daintily-modelled nose seemed to contradict the sensuous and somewhat cruel mouth.

A piece of the door flew past him in splinters followed by a shout of triumph, but no venturesome arm was thrust through the ragged aperture. Ferrari thought he recognized the voice of the man who had been a ringleader in the first rush upon the Jews near the scaffold—one of the strangers who had come into the town from Elizabethgrad. It was different from the voices and accent of the Czarovna men.

Another aperture in the door was made, and it was as if the assailants had kept silence as a signal for their leader to speak. "Now, you rat, we've got you; say your prayers, you filthy Jew."

Yes, it was the voice of the ruffian who had come into Czarovna with the false ukase and the pistol and dagger.

"Come and take me, then," said Ferrari, his face as near the hole as he dared to place it, and his voice as calm as if he were speaking to some one in the open street, and without fear. "Make a hole big enough to let in one at a time, and I'll fight you all, you wretched *canaille* of the earth—cowards, thieves, cut-throats, and assassins of women !"

The challenge seemed to be accepted with a howl of anger and derision, and the blows at the door were renewed. They were now literally battering on the bar, and they made no way. Another pause ; but no arm came through the broken panel.

"I'll open to you if you will thrust in your filthy leader," shouted Ferrari.

"Open then," responded the stranger ; and the mob gave a yell that was something in the nature of a cheer.

At that moment some kind of reinforcement arrived, and it was as if a dozen men at one swing flung themselves upon the door armed with blacksmiths' hammers. The iron bar bent before the assault, the door shook upon its hinges.

Ferrari glanced at his base of retreat, and held his breath. The blows were repeated again and again, and presently the timber began to give, and in an incautious moment a hand was thrust through to seize the bar with a view to lift it. In a moment the venturesome hand was almost severed from the wrist, and a cry rang out fierce enough to chill even the hot Italian blood of Ferrari—a cry not alone of one man, but of a score, a rasping howl of vengeance, followed the next moment with a renewed attack.

That which struck the only note of fear in Ferrari's breast was the sudden firing of several muskets into the broken door. But he was as cunning as he was brave ; he only had one desire at the moment, and that was to have his hand on the leader of the gang. Silence followed the firing, and the Italian guessed its object and humored the hope of the foe.

"You have done for me, you cowards," he screamed, and then gasped and fell heavily; but he was on his feet in a second, his knife clutched firmly in his right hand.

"Ha, ha, ha!" laughed the leader at the top of his voice, and the rest joined him in chorus—such a cruel, brutal laugh! Then there was a scuffle and a rush, and the next moment the leader squeezed his body through the half-open door, and in an instant was seized and dragged through the room, and beyond the next door and into the little courtyard of the Aladdin's Palace underground, the great door swinging back, with a closing and shutting of automatic bolts like the ring of doom. Before he could hardly breathe the man from Elizabethgrad was disarmed and stamped upon.

"Wait, my friend, wait," said Ferrari, fastening the remaining bolts of the great door. The mob pouring into the breach of the previous door had evidently paused to look for the dead Ferrari and their live leader; not finding them were puzzled, and before attacking the next barrier had spent some of their energies in ransacking the warehouse, which gave them a very satisfactory plunder.

Meanwhile Ferrari, taking his opponent by the throat, raised him to his feet. He was a powerful, low-browed, shaggy-haired Russian, in a sheepskin jacket, worn, no doubt, more particularly to please the mujiks, for whose interests he professed to be fighting. He was dazed and stunned, but shook himself free of Ferrari, and looked at him with a threatening eye.

"Well, Christian," said Ferrari. "Well thief, murderer, beast! How will you die? Will you be crucified? That is a death you talk about a deal, you gentle religious folk. Ha, you brute, I have a great mind to rip you into a thousand pieces!"

Ferrari flashed his knife in the man's face. The Russian did not flinch. He fixed a dull gaze upon Ferrari's bony face and sparkling eyes.

" Give· me a chance," at last said the leader from Elizabethgrad.

" A chance to kill me ? "

" A chance of my life."

" Ho, ho ! " laughed Ferrari, " do you ask a Jew to do that ?   Do you ask a Jew who crucifies babies and makes sacrifices of Christians at his bloody feasts ?   Do you ask me to save you ? "

" To save yourself," said the man, sullenly.

" You will kill me, then ? "

" They will," said the man, pointing to the closed door.

" Have you not read in what you call your Scriptures what the God of Abraham, Isaac and Jacob did for His people in the old days ?

No reply.

" Answer me, you thief, or I will stab you."

" I have answered," the man replied.   And now there began a fresh assault upon Ferrari's last barrier, and the long ears of the man from Elizabethgrad moved as a horse's might, and a tremor of hope ran through every muscle.

" Your friends are coming ; are you not sorry you left them ? " said Ferrari with a sneer.

Just as the spy in the opening chapter of these records lost his life to Ferrari's knife by a glance aside in a moment of victorious pride and cynicism, so for the twinkling of an eye was Ferrari off his guard with his unbound prisoner, who sprang at him and held him with the hug of a bear. Neither of them spoke.   They fell to the ground with a thud ; they writhed ; Ferrari's knife fell from his grip, but it was still fastened to his wrist.   He could not recover it within his hand ; his opponent was feeling for it, and also trying to seize Ferrari by his right wrist ; the fight on both

sides concentrated in this. The man from Elizabethgrad
held Ferrari in so strong a hug that the Italian could not
move his hand sufficiently to clasp the handle of his knife.
The Russian's knife and revolver were on the ground only
a few yards away; the man from Elizabethgrad was trying
to drag Ferrari in their direction, but Ferrari had twined
his strong muscular right leg round the two heavy limbs of
the other wrestler, and worked it as a rudder; and moreover his left hand was on the throat of his assailant, and he
fairly gripped the wretch's windpipe as in a vice. At the
same time the man from Elizabethgrad held Ferrari with a
close persistence that only had to last long enough to be
fatal, for it would in time have squeezed the very life out
of him.

And the thunder of the attacking party without fell upon
the great door, fell upon it in measured strokes; a veritable
ringing file fire of blows, with now and then an added rush
in force, that shook the timbers and drew forth grunts and
screams from bolts and bars.

These sounds were like bells of hopeful song to the man
from Elizabethgrad, who under their inspiration made a
sudden and almost superhuman effort, as also at the same
moment did Ferrari, who with the breath nearly battered
out of his body recovered his knife. Feeling the handle of
it within his grasp was the one touch of magic needed for
his salvation. With a sense of fainting coming over him,
he made a last attempt to free his right arm. He had held on
to his opponent's throat, who was also getting weak from
approaching suffocation. It was the supreme moment for
both of them. Ferrari wrenched his arm free, clutched his
knife, drew it steadily upwards, thrust it into his opponent's
side, and fainted.

At the entrance to the retreat, just within the well, had
stood awaiting the return of Ferrari his friend and host.
Between his sighs and prayers he had heard all that had

transpired in the little courtyard ; heard it and prayed and listened, looked up to the sky, and had seen nothing. Once he was on the point of ascending to the daylight, but hearing that Ferrari had a prisoner, who of course would be bound, did not consider his assistance necessary ; then he had gone back into the cavern to reassure Deborah and to bring some weapon away—he knew not why, so bewildered was he. When he returned all was still ; he heard, as he thought, hard breathing, and thought perhaps Ferrari had executed his prisoner, and was waiting to learn the outcome of the attack on the old house.

" Andrea Ferrari ! " he called in a soft voice. No reply. "Andrea ! " he exclaimed. No answer. Now louder, " Andrea Ferrari, my dear friend ! Art thou there ? "

Then the old man crept from his hiding-place and peered out above the coping stone of the well. There lay the two combatants. He issued forth and hurried to Ferrari. At the same time he glanced cautiously at the enemy, taking also the precaution to unsheathe the knife he had brought from his retreat. The Russian was dead. Ferrari moved and sighed. Moses Grunstein knelt down beside him and poured down his throat a measure of brandy from a flask at his girdle. The Italian sighed more deeply and opened his eyes. For a moment there was a look of agony in them ; it gradually changed into a smile, and then he struggled painfully to his feet.

At the same time the mob thundered upon the great oaken door with a din of terrible resolution.

" Come, my son, come ! " said the old man, " or we are lost."

" Yes," said Ferrari ; " thank God in the meantime that we are saved."

As he looked up and uttered this brief prayer he turned the Russian over with his foot and spat upon the bleeding body.   ·

" Come—come," said Grunstein.

Ferrari with a look of hatred in the direction of the mob stood aside while Grunstein descended the well.   Then shaking his fist at the mob he could not see he followed his leader.   Standing at the entrance to the approaches of the cave the old man said, " Now, my son, to perform a miracle.   It has pleased God to afflict us sorely ; it has pleased Him at least to let His hand fall upon one of our persecutors ; it may please Him to save us for a happy future.   For the present we are safe, and we shall emerge again free ; these storms of persecution and death come and go ; the fury past, there will be peace, and Moses Grunstein has some treasures left.   Listen ; it is a powerful barrier, the last one, is it not? "

" It laughs at them," said Ferrari.

" But it will give way anon," said the old man, "and then it cannot be that they will not examine the well ; possibly suspect its secret.   So now for the miracle I told thee of."

The old man took Ferrari by the hand.   " A few steps to the left, my son."

Passing to the left they went a few steps forward, and then the old man stopped.

" What do you hear? " asked Ferrari's host.

" A rush of water."

" It is the stream that passes through the cavern at the further end ; a small stream, but confined to a narrow gully it makes a great noise.   I turn it aside, and it enters the well until the water rises above the entrance."

He stooped as he spoke, and with considerable effort turned a heavy screw that creaked and creaked with a painful sound, and presently the old man rose to his feet. There was a change in the noise of the water ; it was now heard as if falling from a height, and with a splashing sound.

" We retrace our steps," said the old man.

They returned to the entrance of the cave. A stream of water was falling into the well.

" Now, my son," said the old man, " turn thine eyes to the right."

" Yes," said Ferrari.

" Raise the lamp."

Ferrari held the lamp above his head.

" You see a ring of iron ? "

" Yes."

" Grasp it."

Ferrari laid hold upon it.

" Stand back and pull it. Keep free from the entrance."

Ferrari pulled the ring. There fell down a slab of metal or hard wood, entirely closing communication with the well and the exit above.

" The water will rise up in front of it," said the old man, " and no skill in Russia will find out its secret. When it is time for us to go forth, we open our door and admit our watery guard, which will scatter itself in these passages in ten minutes and our egress remains as before. Without this sentinel some prying devil more clever than his fellows might find our hall of entrance ; but now if he has a mind to drop into the well he finds no rest for the sole of his foot ; only the water. And didst thou notice a rope hanging from the rock over the yard ? "

" No."

" They will notice it when they beat down the door, and close by pieces of rock and soil as if someone had clambered up to the daylight ; and that will be regarded as thy means of escape, and so peradventure the well may claim no attention whatever. Come then, my friend, let us go within and praise the Lord, for His mercy endureth for ever ! "

Ferrari shrugged his shoulders at the invitation, thinking of the dead rabbi, and the worse than dead Queen of the Ghetto.

And while they prayed and feasted, and slept and ate and drank in security—Moses and his wife and servant, and the stranger within his gates—the storm of civil and unholy strife, the red waves of persecution passed over Czarovna like a blight from hell.   Helpless women and children fell before the lust and savagery of ignorance, fanaticism, blood-guiltiness, and revenge. Once more the cruel fate of their predecessors of Egypt had sought out the Israelites in this remote corner of the world, and they were beaten with many stripes, tortured with rod and fire, their household goods taken fiom them, their altars and shrines desolated, their numbers decimated with fire and sword. Czarovna was almost wiped from the face of the earth. In the daytime the ghetto resounded with cries of death and yells of drunken vengeance. At night the red cock crowed over the long street, and flamed high above the eaves and chimneys of the home of the Klosstocks.   And when the work of desolation came to an end, the country round about was filled with houseless Jews seeking the shelter of wood and forest, making their way to the river that held its course through hostile town and village to the distant sea.

The historian's duty in regard to this part of his narrative is complete with the simple record of the sack and burning of Czarovna, and the intimation that out of this flame and smoke of desolation came forth at last safe through the furnace Andrea Ferrari, Moses Grunstein, his wife and servant. How Ferrari eventually made his way through the spies and police of Russia is not a matter of so much account as what he did with his liberty, which it will be the business of the narrator to set forth in future chapters ; but it is important to relate that he left Anna Klosstock a miserable wreck in the Christian hospital at Czarovna, subject to the treatment of local medical science, which prided itself on the roughest and readiest means of curing those victims of the knout whose friends had not been able to purchase the death-blow—curing them that they should be enabled to undergo such further punishment as their crimes involved by order of the Czar.

There were in particular two men in the world—Count Stravensky and Andrea Ferrari—whose hearts bled for Anna Klosstock, and who had sworn to avenge both herself and her father upon Ivan Petronovitch, if not upon the Czar himself, under whose government such deeds were possible as those which blasted the house of Klosstock, giving over its virtuous inmates to the pangs of exile, torture, infamy, and untimely death.

CHAPTER XIV.

" TRAGEDY."

A group of prisoners on the march, attended by Cossacks of the Dun and Tartar Guards. The wiry steeds and tall lances of the former break up the monotonous line of the travelers afoot, emphasizing the crouching despondency of some and the defiant carriage of others, among the forlorn crowd of human misery.

In the foreground a man has fallen by the way. He is young, and has apparently collapsed through sheer bodily fatigue. The one woman of the group, in the act of stooping to assist him, is thrust back, with the butt end of a trooper's rifle. She turns towards the soldier with a mingled look of appeal and hatred. It is a beautiful face, stamped with a suffering that has no resignation in it. The eyes are sunken, but full of fire. The low well-knit forehead is wrinkled with pain. The mouth is pursed into an expression of angry revolt. If ever the time for vengeance came, you feel that this woman would not abhor the

assassin's knife or the dynamiter's shell; and in regard to
the captive whose physical strength is not equal to the
spirit of the martyr, you find yourself hoping that he may
now once for all be released from the living death to which
his companions are journeying.

It was only a picture, and hardly that.. It was the
rough hurried sketch of a first idea; yet there were lines of
suggestion in it that might have belonged to the finished
intentions of a great work. The woman was more than a
sketch; or, if not, the brush was an inspired one; for there
was a world of suffering and agony in it, mental and physical. You would say to yourself as you gazed at it,
"that woman was once a lovely girl; she has endured
wrongs the most terrible; she has fought against a cruel
destiny and been worsted at every turn; but she has one
hope left—the desire for revenge; and the artist who has
told us this must know her history; and her history is a
tragedy."

When you look close into the picture you saw what
appeared to be confused and random strokes, wild splashes
of color, faces and forms hinted at; but standing apart a
little way you found that the work took form and shape
and became a living story of human persecution, with a
background of dreary waste and clouds full of wintry
anger. The woman's face of all others stood out an almost
finished study.

" And last night," said the young artist, " I dreamt I
was that poor wretch falling by the way, and that an angel
interposed between that woman and the victim of a tyran-
nous rule, and I was borne to heaven; and when we reached the sunshine, the angel was the woman—and she was
beautiful."

" Yes, it is given to genius to have dreams and to see
visions," said Dick Chetwynd, laying a friendly hand upon
the young man's shoulder, and at the same time standing

in a critical attitude before the picture, "and it is given to genius when it paints to realize its visions. Something of a nightmare this one, eh, Phil? Tell me all about it. For a bit of rapid work it is marvelous."

"You think it is good? Well, I am glad, because I rather fancied it myself," said the artist, putting in a fresh touch or two in order to heighten the effect of the figures standing out against the sky. It was a long almost un-broken sweep of lurid cloud, suggesting the hopelessness of the prisoners, as much as the weakness of a setting sun that had beneath it the cold dreary waste of a Siberian landscape in winter.

"You are a genius, Phil; that woman's face is a stroke of inspiration."

"How particularly amiable you are to-day," was the young artist's reply.

"Just, Philip, not amiable; just. If I have hitherto been more critical than complimentary, I have been influ-enced by a desire to keep you from taking the bit into your mouth and bolting with some wild idea; but when one has evidence of power in a friend's work, why not admit it? I don't hesitate in your case, because I feel sure you will appreciate the responsibility of what is called genius."

How little Dick Chetwynd imagined that his previous efforts to guard Philip Forsyth from letting his genius run away with him would all be discounted in the history of this picture, though in a direction of danger utterly dif-ferent from anything that could possibly have occurred to him! We are all more or less engaged in protecting our-selves from dangers and troubles that never occur, to fall into pits and snares and toils the least looked for among all our forecasts of possible misfortunes.

"Don't think for a moment that I accept your kindly verdict about genius," said the artist; "it gives me plea-sure when you like my work, but what, in your estimation, is genius?"

Philip laid down his palette and brushes, and offering Chetwynd a cigarette, began to smoke one himself.

" The very question the editor of *The Evening Critic* has been asking in his very interrogatory journal ; and not a bad vacation subject either."

" And what is the conclusion? " asked the artist.

" That talent does easily what others do with difficulty, while genius does what talent cannot do ; in other words, or rather in Lord Lytton's, 'genius does what it must and talent does what it can.'"

" And what is your own opinion ? "

" When I consider my own particular work," said Chetwynd, " I come to the conclusion that Carlyle was right when he said that genius is the infinite capacity of taking pains ; and when I look at your sketch, Philip, I believe genius to be the capacity to do with a snap of the fingers or a wave of the hand that which talent with all its infinite pains can never quite succeed in accomplishing."

" You are so much cleverer than I can ever hope to be at logical definitions of things, and in every other way, that it would be absurd on my part to debate so difficult a matter, but I believe *industry* is genius. Look at the fable of the tortoise and the snail ! I have sketched this thing in quickly, but only under the influence of a sudden feeling for it. Perhaps it will end here ; whereas Smith, who took the medal for design, would, given such a subject, settle down to it, plot away at its details, finish it elaborately and a hundred chances to one win the prize."

" It is a quality of genius to underrate its power, to hate drudgery, to rest on its oars ; but you have the higher quality of talent as well as genius, Philip ; you work, and you will paint that subject—' Prisoners on their way to Siberia.' "

" How did you know the subject ? " asked the artist.

" It does not need that angel of yours to come down

from heaven to tell one the subject. Besides you have been talking Siberia, the Ravelin, Russian tyranny, and the hopelessness of Nihilism for weeks past."

" I have been reading Stepniak, Dostoieffsky, Gogol, Lermontoff, Tolstoi, Tourgeneff, Kompert, Noble, Tikhomirov and the rest ; and I seem to have realized in their revelations some of the vague dreams and suspicions of my youth. You forget that I was born in St. Petersburg."

" No, I forget nothing as a rule that is worth remembering ; and besides your mother, Lady Forsyth, does not permit one to forget your life in Russia, especially when she is entertaining some of the distinguished—and otherwise—exiles of the North—I say ' and otherwise ' advisedly."

" My mother is too magnanimous," said the artist ; " she takes everybody at their own estimate."

" Our *Evening Critic* friend is engaged just now in summing up his latest question upon the forces of character, with illustrations of suppressed force and so on. But what two forces are there that are equal to industry and earnestness ? "

" You are my forces, Dick ; without your encouragement I should do nothing."

" Oh, yes, you would."

" If any other fellow said half the kind things you say to me I should turn from him as I would from a flatterer who had some purpose to serve in sweetening his words to please me. But if you say ever so much more than I deserve, I know it comes out of your kind interest in me, and when you criticize me—and you have not done that to-day —I know you are right."

" You are a disagreeable and an ungrateful young vagabond if you doubt that I do not know that every word I say to you is the truth, so far as I am capable of speaking it ; and in spite of my journalistic career I have not forgotten the difference between truth and its opposite, between flattery and criticism, and between sincerity and humbug ; and, moreover, I believe I am still capable of an honest friendship."

"I would like to hear any man say to the contrary," exclaimed Philip, shaking his fist at an imaginary foe.

" Would you ?   Talk to some of my friends on the subject then.   They will give you satisfaction."

" If we lived in another country or age, and they libelled you, Dick, they would have to give me satisfaction."

"Ah, we live in a far better age, Philip, and the pen is not only mightier than the sword, but it is keener than its sharpest edge.   And think of the stabs it can give in the dark ; think of the quiet secret revenges it has in its power. When a man insults you or your friend it is not necessary to call him out ; besides, that is a troublesome business and dangerous to oneself also.   No, you simply go down to your newspaper—your *Evening Critic* say—and you pink him there ; and next day you can rub in a bit of salt, and later still you can reopen the wound and make the man's life a misery to him."

" You are a woful cynic, Dick ; and when I note that side of your character how can you blame me if I am apt to wonder whether you are only amusing yourself at my expense when you tell me I am a genius and all that kind of thing ? "

" What you are saying now is the cynicism of the heart ; my cynicism is the cynicism of the head. And so you doubt me, do you ? "

" No, Dick, I only doubt myself.   When I doubt myself most I ask you questions.   You have not told me what you think of my Siberian sketch for the medal."

When the Royal Academicians gave " Tragedy " as the subject for the gold medal and traveling studentship, the road to Siberia leaped into the mind of Philip Forsyth, a flash of inspiration, full of vague memories of his childhood and of definite stories heard from suffering lips in his later years, and he straightway sketched the picture which is briefly described in the opening words of this chapter. It was the work of a few hours, directed by the feeling of his entire life, and inspired by an enthusiastic and lofty nature.

Dick Chetwynd knew how rapidly the sketch had grown under the young fellow's hand; hence his remark about genius. He had also guessed the intention of the sketch, but hesitating as to the wisdom of the choice of subject for the Academy competition, had left it for his young friend to mention the special object of it. Friendship is never officious in the direction of advice or sympathy; it is anxious to give pleasure, even in its good advice; and where Art is concerned it takes into account the sensitiveness of its disciples, knowing how small a word of opposition randomly spoken may shrivel up a great idea, or make a wound most difficult of healing. Dick Chetwynd had given Philip advice without hesitation in its frankness, but it was given at the right time. Had he objected ever so much to this remarkable sketch, he would not have chosen the moment when the imagination was hot with it, and the hand fresh from its ideal interpretation, to express his hostile opinion; but truth to tell, in regard to this somewhat modern view of " Tragedy," as suggested on the wet canvas before him, he saw far greater evidence of power than Philip had hitherto exhibited, and he was perfectly sincere in his compliments.

The two men were in remarkable contrast, both in appearance and character. Philip Forsyth—in a brown, more or less threadbare, velvet jacket, with a loose black silk handkerchief round his neck—was three and twenty, of medium stature, lithe of limb, with black hair that fell about a forehead with strongly marked eyebrows, eyes that were of a deep blue, singularly out of harmony, you would think on first meeting their pathetic gaze, with the rich olive complexion of the young fellow's face. His lips indicated both refinement and passion. According to those who read character in the fingers, his hands were the hands of both the artist and of the executant, but there were not wanting seeming contradictions of his moral character in his physical anatomy. He gave you the idea of an interesting enthusiastic lad ; for young as he was he did not look his years. When he talked, however, his conversation was far beyond them, and you soon discovered that he was more a creature of impulse than a youth of anything like settled ideas ; but at the same time you could not fail to be convinced of his tremendous capacity for the art he had chosen to follow. If in his conversation with Chetwynd he was inclined to depreciate himself, it was not from any want of confidence in his powers, but from a certain feeling of modesty and in protest against the extravagancies of his friend, who saw further ahead than Philip's most ambitious dreams, but who, had he looked into the future with the true eye of prophecy, with the vision of second sight, would have been sorely and sadly troubled at the prospects of his *protégé* and friend.

Philip Forsyth was an art student, his father English, his mother Irish ; his father a railway contractor, who had made and lost a fortune in Russia, and who had been knighted for some special services rendered in connection with an English Industrial Exhibition. Philip was born in St. Petersburg, which city he left with his widowed mother, ten years prior to the opening of this romance, for London.

His mother, Lady Forsyth, had a secured income of a thousand a year, and she added to it a not inconsiderable sum by her contributions to the rebel press of her native city of Dublin. She received at her pleasant rooms at

Bedford-square the shining lights of the Irish party, as well
as the distressed refugees of foreign nationalities. Dick
Chetwynd doubted the lady's sincerity and her hatred of
" the brutal Saxon," and used all his influence with Philip
to keep him clear of the Irish conspiracy. He might perhaps have best served Philip's interests by attaching the
young fellow to the Irish cause in preference to that of the
despairing organization which seems to lead its chief directors to untold miseries of torture and death.

Whatever Lady Forsyth's opinions might be, they did
not prevent her from mixing in the best Saxon society that
would open its doors to her. If she sang " The Wearing
of the Green " at her own exclusive parliamentary parties,
she would all the same modestly join in the anthem of
" God Save the Queen," when she found herself in the
more representative circles of London life. She was of a
poetic temperament, had the gift of eloquence, and was
looked up to by a section of young art students, who
chafed against the stiff rules of the Royal Academy, and believed in the more rapid and generous curriculum of the
French schools. She wrote tolerable and fiery verse on
heroic subjects, talked clever criticism, was a humorous
satirist of political parties, dressed more or less æstheti-
cally, gave her afternoon receptions in rooms of a semi-
religious darkness, was a pleasant, cultured, odd, out-of-
the-common hostess ; and while some people laughed at
her, others admired her, many thought her exceedingly
clever, and most people liked to go to her receptions.

Philip was devotedly attached to his mother, but he
doubted the sincerity of certain men and women who,
while they upheld the rebel sentiments of the Green, managed to make themselves very happy with the Red among
the fleshpots of London. But for himself he had no very
strong convictions either one way or the other, nor in fact
had his mother. He was deeply moved at all times by a

tale of sorrow, and the more so if he could suggest it with his brush. He was like a musician who dramatizes events and emotions in musical rhapsodies, only that he tried to put them on canvas, and he confessed to Chetwynd that the incidents of so-called Irish rebellion did not inspire him with a single subject worth painting. On the other hand, the struggle of Liberty with Tyranny in Russia ennobled the cause of Freedom; it made men heroes, it made women divine.

How far these feelings and opinions were the outcome of serious reflection or the evanescence of an artistic habit of thought, influenced by a poetic temperament and fostered by the conversations of Dick Chetwynd, must be left to the judgment of the reader and the elucidation of events. Not only had Philip heard his father speak of the shameless dishonesty of Russian officials, the barbarism of the Russian law in the matter of political offences, in regard to which the English law is so especially lenient, but he imbibed from some of his mother's foreign visitors a desperate hatred of Russia. He knew by heart the story of Poland, the disabilities of Russian serfdom freed only to have to endure worse hardships than slavery; he had heard from their own lips some of the horrors endured by political prisoners, though it was a perpetual wonder to him how any of the refugees he had met could ever have escaped Russian vigilance, without the talismanic assistance of gold.

When he thought of the struggles of brave men for constitutional rights in Russia, of their desperate plots, and their fiendish punishments, he found no word of defence against Chetwynd's impeachment of more than one of his mother's Irish friends, who were enjoying all the freedom of the crowned Republic of England, living luxuriously in her great metropolis, and still prating of her tyranny and oppression, and who, the time being opportune, would be

ready to play the part of traitors to their friends and country.
All this seemed to him to heighten the despotism and
cruelty of the Russian system, and to confirm the right-
eousness of the Nihilistic fight against the Czar. But
Philip's was not a logical mind ; it was moved by impulse,
by instinct, it was emotional, artistic, sensitive, and it had
a fateful habit of thought and feeling, which qualities possibly may belong to the attributes of genius. At all events
Art has nothing to do with political principles, with the
philosophies of government, or with constitutional rights ;
it has to do with sentiment, love, nature, the affections, and
with the portrayal of noble actions and fine emotions,
with the reproduction of landscape on canvas, the illustra-
tion of great events, the glorification of virtue, heroism,
patriotism, but it has nothing to do with political debates,
with revolutionary action, with real fighting, with the for-
mulation of administrative principles ; it is the handmaiden,
not the soldier ; the rewarder of noble deeds and the en-
courager thereto. Such at all events was the idea of Art
which Chetwynd tried to convey to Philip Forsyth, whom
he loved with a sincere friendship.

As a political journalist Dick Chetwynd was not a
success ; as a politician he was too honest to be anything
more or less than a failure. He believed that if the Par-
nellite faction were sincere in their desire to promote the
material interests of Ireland, the question at issue between
the two great parties in the State would have been settled
long ago. Not that he defended the Tory party in the
past any more than he approved of the Gladstonian Administration. It was his firm belief that on many an occasion
the Irish question was simply used on both sides as a
political shuttlecock, without the slightest reference to
what was best for Ireland, England, or the Empire. .At
the same time he despised the rank and file of the Irish
party ; believed Parnell to be more or less the victim of

the thing he had created; thought America had shamefully abused the privileges of blood and friendship in permitting a gigantic conspiracy to be hatched and kept alive
on her free soil, to the detriment and danger of the mother
country; thought Gladstone had only one desire in life,
and that to be in office; regarded Hartington and Cham-
berlain as patriots of the noble type; looked upon the
principle of hereditary legislatorship as a grand old traditional farce; would to-morrow give Ireland such a measure
of local self-government, or Home Rule, or whatever it
might be called, as would enable her to conduct her own
internal business without reference to local committees at
Westminster; was fully of opinion that the margin of personal and constitutional liberty in England was so wide
and deep that any person who stepped beyond its barrier
should be shot; was at heart a Republican, but above all
things an Imperial Unionist, and would defend to the
death the merest scrap of soil over which the flag had ever
floated; in this he was a Cowenite, as he said; loyal to
the Crown as long as that remained our legitimate form of
government. He would go to war to-morrow for India
against Russia or all the world; would fight France for
Egypt rather than revive the dual control; would make
every possible sacrifice for the honor, prestige, and glory
of his native land; and any Government, Radical or Conservative, that would continue to give us the security of
personal liberty and maintain the integrity of the Empire
would have his vote and interest. It need not be pointed
out to any practical politician that Dick could not be
successful on these lines, any more than Joseph Cowen, the
patriotic member for Newcastle, could.

Dick was a Yorkshireman, five-and-thirty, married, and
the father of a young family. He was of a medium height,
broad of shoulder, strong of limb, inclined to make adi-
pose tissue (as his doctor told him), the only antidote to

which was exercise, and Dick's exercise consisted chiefly
in walking up to Philip Forsyth's studio from his house in
Dorset-square.   Dick was of fair complexion, wore his
beard broad and curly, had a massive forehead, grey eyes,
a rich unctious manner of speech, and was known rather
for his pluck and cleverness than for the solidity of his
character or the perspicuity of his political views, though
he was an established and independent journalist and
something more.   As a descriptive writer and a war correspondent he was a decided success.   In other enterprises of later days he had not failed.   His literary work
and his criticisms in the world of art were clearer, sharper,
and better defined than his political opinions, though in
his somewhat complicated politics he had before him the
encouragement of many melancholy examples.   As a journalist on the warpath he had told the story of the Zulu
War, and had marched with Roberts through Afghanistan.
He had exploited the Irish revolt in the American cities,
had cabled the earliest declarations of the American-Irish
plotters from Mill-street, had written the first interview
with Rossa, and had reported one of the secret meetings of
the Dynamiters in New York.   He had traveled through
Russia on a journalistic mission, and had seen the world
under many and varying circumstances, having begun his
newspaper career at eighteen.

When we make Dick Chetwynd's acquaintance he had
settled down to the pleasant work of independent journalism
and the secretaryship of an Art Club, which had under his
excellent management become a monopoly of art-trading
in a quiet but profitable groove of what seemed dilettante-
ism, but which in reality was solid business.   " The
Rossetti " was a club and gallery controlled by half a dozen
wealthy noblemen, who were guided by the discreet and
clever hand of Dick Chetwynd.   It gave parties, held
exhibitions, published an Art Magazine, dealt in art

7

treasures in a high and exclusive manner, and made a big annual income, fifteen hundred pounds of which Chetwynd enjoyed as a salary ; and he had perquisites, besides an unique position in artist society.   His wife was a bright, buxom, clever woman of the world, a Londoner with all a Londoner's prejudices, and they had a family of half a dozen children, and lived in good style in Dorset-square, where they had a music room and an art gallery at the rent of two hundred a year, which in the more fashionable regions of Kensington would have been worth five or six.

CHAPTER XV.

"THAT WOMAN'S FACE."

" AND you think you interpret the subject in this sketch of a company of prisoners on the way to Siberia?" asked Chetwynd, once more forcing the conversation in the direction of Philip's work.

"Yes, I cannot imagine anything more tragic, can you?"

" I could think of many subjects more poetically tragic," said Chetwynd, " but none which in your hands will make a more remarkable picture."

" An Irish eviction?" said Philip, smiling, not sarcastically, but recalling a discussion in which Chetwynd had considered it necessary to dwell upon certain cruelties of eviction in order to keep Philip up to what he considered the right pitch of democratic sentiment—for Dick was more Radical than Rebel, more Reformer than Republican; and in all this he was one of the anomalies of English political life in these days of political evolution and change.

" No, not an eviction, Mr. Cynic," said Dick ; "don't think I am blind to the due proportions of things, and I love art beyond politics. If I did not I should be engaged at this moment in projecting an English Republic."

" I wonder your Rossetti nobility put up with you."

" They have to put up with me, old man ; besides we don't talk politics, and (with a self-deprecatory smile) even noblemen like to be associated with intellect, especially when it pays."

" Yes, that is a great matter," Philip replied ; "it is the rock upon which I shall split."

" Not at all," said Chetwynd ; "it is the artist's business to think of his art, and to leave the question of paying to Fate."

" And yet I fancy you were thinking just now that I should have a much better chance of the medal with a conventional treatment of tragedy than with a realistic study of the tragedy side of Russian tyranny and Russian heroism. Sometimes in one's hatred of Russia one is apt to forget that the tyranny and heroism go hand in hand ; that they come from the same people."

" It is generous to think so ; you do not regard Ireland as the Poland of our day, and I don't ask you to think of it in that light, though it is an oppressed nationality, and I have faith in my fellow countrymen when I find so many of us acknowledging our misdeeds."

" But if we are to go back to the past for misdeeds it seems to me that the English themselves have had a hard time of it, not to mention the Scotch and the Welsh. But of course all this is nonsense, the Irish troubles are to be mended as the disabilities of the masses have been amended ; but if there is the tyranny in Ireland, the abuse of Irishmen, some of my fellow bogtrotters aver, let them rise and be free ! That is what other nationalities have done ; and if they have the cause let them fight ! "

" We were talking of Art, and the interpretation of Tragedy," said Dick ; "you are no politician, and you are so pleased with your life in London that your gratitude to us brutal Saxons overcomes your judgment. I think you would have a better chance of the medal if you took a classic subject from Roman History. Moreover, it would give you an opportunity of showing your skill as a student of the figure. Siberia gives you no chance of a careful study of the nude or the semi-nude."

" No, but it gives me composition, color, sentiment, feeling, intensity of expression."

" If it engages your enthusiasm," said Dick, "do it, Philip ! Never mind whether you get the medal or not. Success at the Academy is a good deal of a lottery, and a medal won by pandering to Academic methods of faddism is not worth having."

" Thank you, old fellow," said Philip ; "you are to me as great a stimulus as success itself. Have a drink, and I will tell you about that woman you see in the foreground looking defiance at the brutal Cossack."

It was one of the first days of the early spring. A few flakes of snow were flying about in the sunshine, looking like scattered cherry blossoms. Philip called Dick's attention to them as he drew down a blind to keep out the sudden sunshine that sent a white beam right across his picture.

" Let us welcome the Spring," said Philip, going to a cabinet and producing a bottle of champagne. " You have had luncheon ? "

" Yes. You are a luxurious dog, Philip."

" No. I sometimes don't drink a glass of wine for days together, not even at dinner. This is a brand you will approve of ; it is like the English Spring, a flash of liquid sunshine."

" Here's success to ' Tragedy ! ' " said Dick, taking up the glass his host had filled.

" And here's to Spring !" said Philip. " The loveliest

season of all the English year, whatever cynics may say about it ! "

" As champagne is the finest of all wines," said Dick, " and this is more than superb ; Philip Forsyth, I repeat you are an extravagant dog ! "

" And I reply I am none, as the prisoner said to Dog-berry. But if I were, I am spending my own money, and I have no false pride. I make it a rule never to let a week pass without its pot-boiler."

This was quite true, and it was another contradiction of the ordinary interpretation of genius, if Philip really was a genius. The young fellow did not believe in draw-ing all his supplies from his mother; if he dreamed he worked. There was none of the careless, indifferent impecuniosity that people associate with genius in this young artist's disposition. He not only made a sufficient income to supply his modest or luxurious desires, but also to enable him to contribute occasionally an article of *vertu* to his mother's rooms in Adelphi Terrace, the most picturesque and inspiriting situation, he contended, in all London. But his pot-boilers were not mere convention-alities. They were bits of color, impressions, fancies, replicas of studies, musings in tone, and trifles of various kinds—which cost him neither trouble nor labor, and of which he thought nothing—for his ambition, if he had an ambition, was heroic—it soared, but it was emotional, and required an object.

" About that woman : last week at the opera I saw a face that I shall never forget. It was partially hidden by the box curtains which draped it, the neck being in shadow, the remainder of the figure hidden. It was a woman of thirty, I should say, with the suffering of a century in her eyes ; suffering and a consuming passion ; the pallid face one sees in prisoners who have been long in confinement, but without the sad resignation that mostly accompanies it.

The features were Grecian in their regularity, but with the capacity for passion thrown in as an artistic contradiction; a straight nose, but a low, square forehead; a perfect mouth in form, but the curves tending to cruelty; the face long, the expression suggesting the lofty scorn, the high sense of duty of a Marie Antoinette, with the determination and murderous fire of a Charlotte Corday. Clytemnestra and Diana in one; a something lovable and lovely with homicidal tendencies; an indescribable creature, whose face I have tried to suggest in that sketch, and whose story might well be the history I want to convey in my competition for the medal! Do you know the story of Madame Lapukin, in the days of Elizabeth of Russia?"

"No," said Chetwynd, watching the play of Philip's mobile features, as the enthusiast endeavored to convey to him an idea of the woman whom he hoped to make live again on canvas, wondering at the same time where he would get his model if he could not find the woman of the opera and induce her to sit for him.

"One Germain de Lagny tells the story, in his account of Russia, translated by John Bridgman and published by Bogue. In 1760, Madame Lapukin, a rare beauty, the envy of the Czarina, said to have betrayed the secret of the Empress' liaison with Prince Razoumowsky, was condemned, in spite of the privilege of the nobility never to suffer the punishment of the knout, to be publicly whipped and her tongue torn from the roots! Think of it. This lovely woman, who had been fêted and caressed by society, the beauty of a luxurious court! She was stripped, submitted to other indignities, and her flesh cut into strips from her shoulders to her hips. Her tongue was torn out, and then with a refinement of cruelty which is carried out to this day she was sent into hospital, and cured of her wounds sufficiently to enable her to be marched to Siberia. She did not die by the way, but lived to be recalled by Peter the Third, in 1762. When I saw that face at the opera I said to myself, it might have been the face of Madame Lapukin, waiting for an opportunity of vengeance, and when the Academy announced their subject I thought of that terrible tragedy, and I saw the woman ministering to the dying on the road to Siberia, praying for death as she must have done, and seeing more fortunate ones stumble and fall, to be left in the wind and the snow, that was not so cold and bleak as man's inhumanity. I saw her moved by the tender impulse of her sex in the midst of her own suffering to lay a gentle hand upon the shrinking arm of her fellow prisoner, and followed by the Cossack's rough interposition, and then I saw that look of hate, of unavenged grief, of tiger-like defiance that fascinated me in the face draped by the opera curtains. Around this incident grew at once all the rest, and I have written right across it in my mind's eye, ' Tragedy.' "

" You are a brave, wonderful fellow," said Dick, rising and taking him by the hand; " if you were not a painter to have this outcome for your feelings, or a poet to put them into print, you would be a Nihilist, and possibly a victim to some mad plot to overtake the future by blowing up the Winter Palace and shouting ' victory' as you fell under the crashing timbers."

" Do you think so?" he said, with a sad smile, the color returning to his face, which had become as pale as the imaginary Lapukin's, while he was telling the woman's story.

" I do; but this saves you," pointing to the sketch; " and it is a greater power than dynamite, a bigger reformer than the knife or the revolver. Put your heroism into your pictures, Philip, and I will forgive you for not being a politician."

" That's all right," said Philip ; " anyhow we shall always be friends, and if I can satisfy your critical opinion I shall be content to lose the medal."

"In the meantime," said Dick, smiling, "we must find that woman who combines the beauties and terrors of the tiger and the gazelle."

"Ah, if we only could!" exclaimed Philip.

"If we only could," said Dick; "is she then only a dream?"

"In my sketch, yes; but at the opera she was flesh and blood."

"And did you not try to find out who she is?"

"Yes."

"On the night?"

"Yes."

"And since?"

"Yes: she has vanished without leaving a trace."

"How do you know that she has disappeared so completely?"

"I will tell you."

CHAPTER XVI.

TWO MERRY SISTERS.

"It was the opera of Carmen, said Philip: "a favorite opera of mine, because it seems to me to be a consistent and possible story, the music and words deftly wedded, the chorus people coming in naturally, as part of the story and not merely to sing. Indeed, it is the only opera in which one's imagination does not seem to be especially or remarkably handicapped, when at a tragic moment the hero begins to sing, and when the heroine, being stabbed to the heart, or dying of poison, does not also burst out into a wonderful effort of vocalization."

"Oh, you demand realism in opera, do you? And yet I hear you prefer a light melodramatic work, such as Carmen, to the great Wagnerian dramas."

"But I don't make any sweeping criticism for or against any opera or any composer," Philip replied. "Carmen always appealed to me somehow for its utter naturalness : I may be wrong, I dare say I am. Well, it was at the scene where Michavel tries to persuade the soldier lover to go home—the scene with the banditti in the mountains, you know—when I was suddenly conscious of a new pres- ence in the house, not upon the stage, but in the theatre. I had glanced aside for a moment, and in the box imme- diately opposite—Lady Marchmount's box, in fact—I saw a face partially hidden among the curtains, pale, earnest, with great bright eyes, and a halo of dark red hair ; the lips were parted, the face all eager and wonderfully beautiful, and it seemed to me as if the eloquent eyes fell upon mine. I was fascinated ; as I gazed the face gradually withdrew into the shadow of the box. When the act was at an end I visited Lady Marchmount. While I shook hands with her ladyship, I looked round her box. 'You expected Lord Marchmount?' she said. 'He is obliged to be at the House ; but I think he will come before the end of the last act. My girls are with their aunt ; I am quite alone. Will you 'not sit ?' I thought she seemed to be talking and explaining why she was alone for the sake of putting me off my inquiry as to the lady who was in the box during the bandit scene ; I don't know what made me think so. 'But the lady,' I said, 'who was here a few minutes since ?' 'What lady?' she asked. 'She was at the back of the box,' I said. 'I have had no visitor that I am aware of, except yourself.' 'I beg your pardon, perhaps it was in the next box ; I am sure you will forgive my curiosity, Lady Marchmount, but it was a very remarkable and beautiful face, and it went straight home to my imagination as the very face I want for a picture I am going to paint.' 'That is a convenient excuse you artists make for introductions to pretty women, but I have had no lady in my box to-night. If, however, you are in search of beauty, what say you to Madame Petronovitch?' She indicated the royal box with her fan, and handed me her glass.

"I looked over the way and saw a handsome foreign-looking woman, chatting with a distinctly Russian officer; both animated, the lady evidently happy, the officer somewhat constrained in his manner, and with, as I thought, a cruel mouth, and a cold resolute eye. 'General Petronovitch,' said Lady Marchmount, 'the famous Russian diplomat and soldier making a tour of Europe by way of honeymoon, coupled with official business; is to honor the Italian Court during the coming festivities at Venice; a compliment to Italy which troubles France and does not delight Germany. Lord Marchmount was to have come to bring the General to my box, and no doubt will. Won't you stay?' 'Thank you, Lady Marchmount,' I said, 'I have a friend who is a stranger to the town,' which was true; a young fellow to whom my mother was anxious I should pay attention. So I left the box, and made a survey of the house from various points, but my mysterious and beautiful vision was nowhere to be seen."

"It was not a vision after all, eh? not a dream face, incident and all?"

"No, it was a reality, and I cannot help thinking Lady Marchmount had some reason for saying she had no other visitor except myself."

"But surely she would not have told a deliberate lie about it?"

"She might have done so with a reservation."

"But why?"

"Ah, there you bring me to a dead stop."

"Would it have been possible for the lady to have gone into the box and Lady Marchmount not have seen her?"

"Yes, if the door had been left open, and Lady March-

mount had been deeply interested in the play; but she
was not. Her interest was in the Russian party in the
Royal box."

" Was the stranger long in the box?"

" About as long as it took me to tell you of her."

" She was very much in earnest, you say; was she deeply
interested in the opera?"

" On reflection it seems to me she must have been
directing her gaze upon the Russian box; and yet also I
fancied she looked at me as well. But the incident was
brief, and what struck me was the wonderful, sad, tragic
beauty of the face."

" Madame Lapukin's ghost, Phil!"

" No ghost," said the artist, his eyes upon the face he
had drawn.

" Then we will find her. You have all one requires,"
pointing to the picture, " to assist an independent search.
'Wanted, a mysterious lady, last seen at the opera of
Carmen in Lady Marchmount's box, half hidden in the
curtains, reminded an enthusiastic artist of——'"

" Don't scoff, Dick," said Philip; "you have no idea
how serious I feel about that face."

" Of course you do. One only wants the assurance of
your canvas to know that. But what other steps, if any,
have you taken to find madame?"

" I have been to the opera every night since, in and out,
making calls; I went into Milbanke's box. Then another
night took my mother; another went into the stalls. I
strolled into the Row, cold as it is, and I have called upon
Lady Marchmount."

" And no clue?"

" Not the slightest."

" What does Dolly—Miss Norcott—say to it?"

" To what?"

" To your search for the mysterious beauty?"

" I have not mentioned the subject to her."

"But I thought a young fellow mentioned pretty well everything to his *fiancée.*"

"Dolly is not my *fiancée,*" said the artist.

"Is it all off, then?"

"It was never all on."

"Oh, indeed; excuse me, I thought from what your mother said the other night it was settled, and that you were going with the Milbankes to Venice."

"I am thinking of going to Venice."

"And taking a studio there for a month or two?"

"Yes."

"Convenient to have Dolly and her very amiable sister there at the same time; save you from *ennui,* and enable you to forget that woman's face."

"I shall never forget it."

"Nor will the public," said Dick, "if you finish your picture as you have begun it. I don't want to surprise your secret, but Miss Norcott is a very bright, charming, and desirable young woman."

Philip's reply was interrupted by a triple knock at the door, followed by a merry, musical voice which asked, "Is anything dreadful going on? May we come in?"

"That is Dolly," said Philip.

"Sounded to me like Mrs. Milbanke," said Dick.

"She said 'we,'" observed Philip, going to the door, "and that 'we' means Dolly and her sister, Jenny."

"Of course you may," said the artist, leading in a pretty fashionable girl of a little over twenty.

"Jenny is with me—she stayed to speak to the porter's wife. Here she is; come in, Jenny, there is nothing dreadful going on, only Mr. Chetwynd," said the young lady, in a pleasant voice. "Oh yes, there is," she continued, all in the same breath, and looking straight at Philip's sketch. "What a miserable lot! But how clever! Is this yours, Mr. Forsyth?"

"Yes, I think so," said Philip, his manner somewhat constrained as compared with his frank conversation with Dick Chetwynd.

"One of Forsyth's dreams," said Chetwynd, at the same time greeting Dolly's sister, Mrs. Milbanke.

"What a queer dream," went on Dolly, "but Mr. Forsyth has ugly dreams."

"Not always," said Dick, smiling in his bland, calm way. "*You* are looking charming this morning."

"Oh, I am not one of Mr. Forsyth's dreams; I am a very sober reality. Am I not, Mr. Philip Forsyth?"

Here she turned her merry eyes upon Philip, and was the very antithesis of the woman in the picture. Dolly was beaming with good health, a pretty blonde, with a dainty figure; very modern, an artist would say, and so she was in dress, style and manner; a tennis player, a flirt, and yet at heart a good-natured pleasant London girl. And she was London, every inch of her, with all the London *chic* and audacity; fearless in her pleasant ignorance of art and all its branches, except the art of dress and the art of small talk; she would talk on anything, art or what not —the musical glasses or the music of the spheres; she laughed at her own ignorance when it became too apparent, but she could waltz divinely, sing snatches of all the modern operas, comic and otherwise, play bits of Wagner, Chopin, Mendelssohn, Sullivan; never finished anything, however, and was altogether a pretty, dainty, amusing, light-hearted London girl. And her sister, Jenny, was a great deal like her, only a little more staid in manner and conversation, she being married and Dolly only on the eve of being engaged. They were of medium height, both of them, the one a little prettier than the other, both merry, both touched with the Society mania of knowing the "smartest people, don't you know?" both flirts, both genial, pleasant and good women. Once in a way some

conceited person of the opposite sex would mistake their
free and unconstrained manners, and trespass by suggestion or remark upon what they considered their good
nature, and then it would be revealed to him and sundry
that Dolly and her sister "stood no nonsense," to use a
favorite phrase of Mr. Samuel Swynford, an admirer of both
the sisters and especially of Dolly, for whom it was generally known he cherished a more or less secret passion.
"They both like a bit of fun," said Sam to a friend, who
had heard of a snub Mrs. Milbanke had administered to a
certain noble lord, "but they know just how far to go, and
any fool who is not equally well informed comes a cropper,
I can tell you, if he presumes upon their good nature. It's
like a bear transaction against a strong syndicate. I knew
a fellow who did a big bear on Nitrates just as the rise
began ; he did not know how the north wind was blowing
any more than did your noble lord when he ventured to
discount the high, unblemished and beautifully moral characters of Dolly Norcott and her sister Jenny."

They were daintily dressed, the two merry sisters. Dolly
might have been called a harmony in pink ; for if her cloak
was of dark plush, the lining was of soft pink silk, and her
hat was of some indescribably pinky salmon color, in tone
and sympathy therewith. Jenny, her sister, was dark, not
a brunette, but her hair was a very deep brown, her eyes
hazel, her complexion what Disraeli would have called
rich, and while there was a strong family likeness to her
sister, she was not as pretty as Dolly ; nor had she the
freshness of youth, that was Dolly's precious possession
both in fact and in appearance. Dolly was twenty-three,
Jenny was thirty. Jenny wore a plush cloak of a dead
gold color, and, unbuttoning it, disclosed a lovely dress of
ruby silk. She wore a plush hat to match her cloak, tall and
stately with nodding decorations, such as gentlemen find
very awkward at theatrical matinees, and against which

one of the free and independent States of America is about
to pass a law. Before it comes into force it is to be hoped
the fashion of exaggerated hats will have changed, though
it must be admitted that the prevailing fashions are not
unpicturesque. Dolly Norcott and Mrs. Milbanke might
have been presented to the most querulous American critic
of tall hats as very pleasant arguments in their favor, and
one would not object to have had the two ladies put into
competition with any two American beauties of their age,
or indeed in competition with any two sisters of any other
country, though of late years America has claimed the
palm, and many Englishmen seem to have conceded to
them the claim for feminine beauty over the old country
and every other.

But no woman in all the world grows old as gracefully
or beautifully as an Englishwoman! There is Lady
Marchmount, for instance. She is nearly sixty; she looks
forty, has the voice of thirty, the manners of a matron, the
heart of a girl; there is not a wrinkle in her face, nor a
white hair in her head. And yet she does not, as do many
American ladies of her age, dress as if she were twenty;
she accepts the fact of her age, assumes the *role* of a matron
who is a grandmother, and preserves, as she will to her
last days, a charm of manner and a womanly grace, which
is exceptionally the inheritance of Englishwomen.

" Don't go on our account, Mr. Chetwynd," said Mrs.
Milbanke ; " we only called because we were passing, and
Dolly wondered what Mr. Forsyth was doing. We have
been calling on Lady Marchmount."

" Many people there ? " asked Philip.

" No, twenty or thirty," said Dolly. " The usual set:
members of Parliament's wives, a prima donna engaged to
sing, a thought reader, and several persons from the Italian
Embassy."

" Many ladies ? " asked Philip, his mind running on the
woman of the opera.

"Why, I told you," said Dolly, "the same old set; are you still dreaming? There was a very pleasant man who knows Venice well; he says we ought to stay there at least two months—that for his part he could live there for ever, and Jenny told him you are going to have a studio there and paint, at which he was deeply interested."

"Oh, here you are," said Mrs. Milbanke, as the porter's wife entered with tea. "I ventured to ask for some tea, Mr. Forsyth," said Mrs. Milbanke. "I always think it is so delightful, tea in a studio; and especially when there is no fuss and the men can go on smoking. 'Liberty Hall,' as Mr. Samuel Swynford says."

"Just so," said Chetwynd. "Has Mr. Swynford made a fortune yet?"

"I am sure I don't know. He was very mysterious the other night with Walter about some Transvaal mines that are a certainty. I don't quite know whether he is a bull or a bear, but he says they will go up to ten premium, and that when they do he is going to have a holiday. He has let Walter have a few shares."

"Which I fear will settle poor Sam's prospects," chimed in Dolly, "as Walter told him; for if there is an unlucky fellow in the world, it is Walter."

"He does not think so," said Chetwynd; "at all events he does not look it when he is out with his wife and sister."

"Ah, he is a dear fellow—Walter," remarked Dolly, sipping her tea, and suddenly remarking to Philip, "Won't you make me a cigarette? I might take one whiff, eh? There was a Russian woman at Lady Marchmount's who smoked a cigarette, much to everybody's surprise; it is true she only smoked it in the hall when she was leaving. They say cigarette smoking grows on one like dram-drinking; your mother, Lady Forsyth, allows it at her Sunday evenings, Mr. Philip?"

" Yes," Philip replied, " she allows many things which I don't think I should permit."

" Walter won't let us smoke," said Mrs. Milbanke ; " not that we want to, but he won't have it at all, although he himself smokes from morning till night."

'' Walter is very funny about his smoking," said Dolly ; " he says it is a good thing for the house, and a good thing for him, but a bad thing for women—taints their breath, makes them mannish, which he hates.   But you have got a rather mannish woman in your picture, Mr. Forsyth."

" Do you think so ? "

" Yes, but I suppose she is intended to be tragic, eh ? "

" Yes."

" I thought so ; the young man is dying of cold and weariness, and she wants to help him, and that Cossack soldier won't let her.   What a look she gives him !   It will be a fine picture."

" Do you think so ? " exclaimed Philip, with a smile of satisfaction.   " Dick is pleased with it."

" Then it must be good," remarked Jenny, " if Mr. Chetwynd thinks so, and is not afraid to put his thoughts into words."

" Indeed, you seem to know me, Mrs. Milbanke.   What a pleasant thing it is to have a character that every one can read like a book—to wear one's heart upon one's sleeve, as Shakspere has it."

" For daws to peck at, eh ?   Then I'm a daw, Mr. Chetwynd, thank you.   You didn't think I knew my Shakspere, I suppose.   Come, Dolly, now we must go.   I have scored off Mr. Chetwynd, and I will not stay a minute longer."

" That is so like Jenny," Dolly remarks to Philip ; " whenever she wins anything she leaves off.   Some people lay down their cards or their bat or leave the tables when they lose, Jenny always leaves when she wins."

" Except that once, Dolly, at Monte Carlo ; do you

remember? Don't think I gamble, Mr. Chetwynd, but at Rome do as the Romans do. We were at Monte Carlo last winter with Walter, and, of course, we went to the tables. I know nothing about Faro and that kind of thing, I simply backed the red—it was the day before we left—it came up five times, five times ten pounds, and then I put all the fifty on; it came up again, and then I would leave. Don't you think I was wise?"

"You are always wise, and always delightful," said Dick.

"Come along, Dolly. Good-bye, Mr. Forsyth. I know Mr. Chetwynd is going to say something sharp and cutting; I won't hear it. Come along, Dolly; I can hear the carriage on the gravel. I told him to come for us in a quarter of an hour. Au revoir, Mr. Forsyth; you are coming to dinner."

"To talk over Italy, and especially Venice," said Dolly, turning the battery of her eyes upon Philip. And what lovely eyes they were, blue as an Italian sky, her lips as red as its coral, and her whole figure, appearance, manner, voice, the warm pressure of her hand, radiating health and sensuous good nature.

CHAPTER XVII.

THE MILBANKES AT HOME.

"By Jove, you are to be envied," exclaimed Dick when the two women had left; "as fine a woman as the most fastidious Sybarite with a love of life and domestic happiness could desire. Just the kind of girl for you; not too learned, no dreams, enough appreciation of art to give you a frank and useful opinion—the outside opinion, the opinion of the public; no sulks, no mad passion, plenty of common sense, good spirits, a nice little fortune, would entertain

your guests right merrily. I think your mother is very
wise to encourage the match. And the right sort of family
to go into. Walter Milbanke is as good a fellow as there
is going; got a snug conveyancing practice left by his
father. His mother is rich. Dolly's people are in good
society and well off, and Mrs. Milbanke is one of the most
charming and agreeable of hosts. Why don't you settle it
all, Phil? You are the sort of young fellow who should
get married. You want sympathy, and you want a comfortable and well-managed home."

" She is a delightful girl, Dolly—as you say, Dick, very
pretty. I am sure she is generous, in spite of that suggestion of worldliness that comes out in her conversation. But
she is not like that with me. I think it is part of the current coin of Society ; but I hate Society."

" No, you don't, old chap ; you hate what people call
Society, but you like what we call Society, what your mother
calls Society, what my wife calls Society ; you enjoy that,
and you can make your own set. When you marry Dolly,
you can interpret your own idea of Society, and translate
it as you please. Come, old fellow, don't brood over the
gold medal ; don't think too much of the model you want
for the forlorn woman in the foreground. We will find
her, or another as good. Come up into the East End one
day (your tragic heroine has a Jewish cast of countenance),
I will take you to a Jewish quarter where you will find
several Polish faces that might sit for your Siberian picture."

" The despair would be there, perhaps," said Philip,
" but not the beauty, not the dignity, not the strength, not
the threat of vengeance in the eyes, not the deep strange
reminiscence of suffering I saw in the mouth, and in the
clenched, bony, but refined fingers ; no, that is a face I
should say one is likely to see once in a lifetime."

Let us follow Mrs. Milbanke and her sister home.

Dolly Norcott lives with her parents at Norwood, but spends most of her time at Westbury Lodge, St. John's Wood Road. They call it Westbury Lodge because Walter Milbanke has an estate at Westbury, near Bristol, and there is a little territorial vanity in this association of name. It is a picturesque, two-storey house, fenced in, and looking the daintier for the fencing when the front gate is open and you get a glimpse of a long grass-covered path, at the end of which there is a tesselated hall, and beyond a back garden, with tennis nets and flowers.

Westbury Lodge is by no means palatial, but it is sufficient for the wants of the Milbankes, Walter often declaring that if he were worth twenty thousand a year he would not want a larger house, nor would he desire to live one jot more ostentatiously than at present; though his wife ventures to remark that she hopes if ever he has twenty thousand a year he will go into Parliament, and work his way into the Cabinet as So-and-So has done, and as So-and-so means to do.

Walter meets his wife and sister in the hall, kisses them both, asks where they have been, what the news is, and tells them he has only just come from the office; hopes dinner will not be late—he has asked Sam Swynford to join them. Jenny says she thinks that unfortunate, and asks if he has forgotten that Philip Forsyth is coming, and that the occasion is the talking over the Venice trip. No, Walter says he has not forgotten; and the fact is, he says, he does not choose to have this fast and loose business of Mr. Philip Forsyth, and he is not sure that Sam Swynford would not be a much better match. Anyhow he regards it as a good idea to bring the two young fellows together as much as possible, that Dolly may make up her mind, or that the two young fellows may kill each other or do something. For his part he does not intend this affair to go on; if Philip accompanies them to Italy, why, of course, that may be said to settle the question.

" But he would go, Wally dear, whether we go or not. He has taken a studio there, or intends to do so."

" He expressed no intention of the kind until he knew we were going there."

" That is true," the wife replied.

" And his mother has twice spoken to me about Dolly, and expressed a hope that she and Forsyth would make a match of it at once. ' How happy could I be with either,' eh ? " continued Walter, putting one arm round Dolly and another round his wife, and leading them into the drawing room. " That's your sentiment, eh, Dolly ? "

" Oh, I don't know, Wally. I think I like Philip best. He is romantic and interesting ; far more distinguished in appearance than Sam ; and is likely to make a name and a great position."

" When you will have to do all the worshipping," said Walter. " These artistic geniuses, these men of distinction —authors, painters, artists, actors—they don't make good husbands as a rule ; they have whims and humors—moods, I believe they call them ; the more successful they are the more dreamy and exacting. Society spoils them."

" But I am bound to say Philip puts on no airs," Dolly replied ; " he is very modest, considering how clever he is."

" Oh, yes, no doubt ; but when success comes then comes hero-worship and all that sort of thing. For show, I daresay Forsyth would make the best husband ; a fine, handsome, young man to sit by your side at the opera, to drive in the park with, if he had ever time to drive in the park, and for other women to envy and try to get him away from you. But for a good, honest, devoted, useful, and wealthy husband—and I say wealthy advisedly, he knows what he is about—I would back Sam Swynford. You could have your own way with him, just as Jenny has with me." This Walter said with an audible chuckle, adding, " Sam is by no means the fool some people affect to think him ;

I know that he made ten thousand pounds last week in Primitivas—bought them at seventy and held on like grim death till they went up to two hundred and twenty. Think of the courage of a stroke like that, and the knowledge ; there is not a cooler head nor a softer heart on the whole Exchange. And now, my dears, as you are in full possession of my views, I vote you go and dress for dinner and act accordingly."

They dressed together, the two sisters. Never were two young women more devoted to each other. Dolly was as proud of Jenny's clever domestic abilities as Jenny was of Dolly's beauty. Jenny admired Dolly's singing beyond even the vocalization of Patti. Dolly thought Jenny the most charming of conversationalists. There were two couches in the room to which Walter had dismissed them for the mysterious ceremony of dressing. The lounges were speedily occupied by the two ladies, in dressing gowns and slippers, attended by a clever French maid, who brought them tea in two tiny pots and then left them to decide what they would wear on this momentous occasion, for on this night Dolly was expected to bring Philip Forsyth to book, or make up her mind to accept Sam Swynford ; not that Sam had proposed, but it was believed that he would do so on the slightest provocation.

"You ought to be a very happy girl," said Jenny. " How happy could *you* be with either."

"How did you ever make up your mind to marry Walter?" Dolly asked in a half drowsy kind of way.

"Easily enough ; he was a good fellow, not a bit jealous, had a good, sound, settled income, and loved me to distraction, as he does now."

"Yes," said Dolly, "but you had lots of offers, mother says."

"Well, I don't know ; I might have had, but the fact is I hadn't any more than you have, Dolly, dear."

" But could have, Jenny, could have, only that spoils
the fun. Best to lead them on a little and stop short of
that, eh? You said so, you know, when I came out."

" And was not the advice good ? "

" Yes, I think so."

" Well, I declare, Dolly, you are going to sleep."

" I am very tired; only forty winks. Is there time?"

" Plenty, my darling," and as Jenny said so Dolly buried
her face in the great sofa cushions, and composed herself
·to enjoy her siesta. "Don't trouble about thinking of
waking, I will call you in time," added Jenny, taking up
one of the latest French novels, which she had smuggled
into Westbury Lodge without Walter's knowledge, for
Walter had vowed many a time that he would no more
think of having an objectionable, fast, immoral book in his
house, than he would think of inviting a bad lot to dinner.
But what was the good of being able to read French with
facility, coupled with possessing a taste for racy fiction,
without going to the fountain head for it ? Not that Jenny
understood half that was insinuated or set forth in the
direction Walter denounced, and she hated to have anything like a scene with the dear fellow; so she deceived
him a little, "not in any serious way, don't you know?"
as she explained to Dolly, but just to protect both Walter
and herself from scenes. In the same way she occasionally
permitted what Society butterflies termed tributes to her
beauty, in the way of a little flirtation, which she did not
mention to Walter because she did not want him to be
" punching men's heads or calling them out, don't you
know?" She had with these little shortcomings of Eve
all the other good qualities, and the historian is not disposed
to quarrel with her, the more so that she always strove to
make herself attractive and interesting in the eyes of her
husband, for whom she had a real sentiment of love and
respect, except once in a way when he had a preaching fit

on, and talked a little louder than necessary about what he would have in his own house and what he would not have.

It was Jenny's dressing-room, adjoining Walter's chamber, to which the sisters had retired, but Dolly and Jenny literally lived together when Dolly was on a visit at Westbury Lodge, and the room had been fitted up with this understanding ; so that there were two almost facsimile toilette tables, flashing with cut glass bottles, radiant with silver-backed brushes, sparkling with gems, and furnished with the various luxurious appointments of a fashionable woman's room. The walls of the apartment were decorated in what Jenny called complexion colors ; the curtains white lace and pink silk, the mirrors Louise Quinze, the atmosphere pleasantly perfumed, the floor of sandal wood, covered with Persian rugs. It is fitting that we retire while the doves of this pretty nest plume themselves for their guests, to return presently, after pinning and scheming of maid and mistress, the last touch of rouge or powder, and the last critical glance into the glass.

The result must be pronounced satisfactory. Jenny poses before her mirror in a pale yellow tea gown of soft silk, trimmed at the throat and wrists with Mecklenburgh lace, a trail of daffodils on the right shoulder *a la* Bernhardt, a chain of old Dutch silver round her neck, and on her yellow silk shoes buckles to match, ornaments that had once belonged to a rich burgomaster's wife. Her black hair had in its folds old silver pins, one of which might have been used to stab a rival queen in some sensational novel. She was pleased with herself, as well she might be. Having adjusted the last pin and arranged the last flower, Jenny turned with merry eyes to Dolly, who was a perfect picture of health, happiness, and mischief, in the simplest of white crape Empire dresses, a pair of tiny diamond earrings, her hair dressed high in loops and curls, a bunch of lilies of the valley at her white throat, devoid of orna·

ment, a simple diamond ring on one finger, and a flush of pride and ambition upon her fair cheeks. Dolly looked conscious of her beauty; she already in imagination had Philip at her feet, and saw herself sitting by his side in a Venetian gondola, listening to the love songs and choruses of minstrels, floating with the tide past Desdemona's window.

"Now, girls, are you ready?" asks Walter, putting his head just inside the doorway. "I see you are. That's right. Nothing like punctuality; and, by Jove, how well you look. I don't know which to admire most. But you have both your own individual styles of beauty. Dolly, you look like a picture I once saw in a book of beauty— one of the mezzotint school, called the Dove of Amsterdam; just as fair, just as soft, just as full of health and fun. Come along, Jenny; you need no compliments to maintain your courage. You have not to meet the momentous question of your life to-night; that was settled long ago, and you have never regretted it, have you, dear?"

"Never, Walter," she replied, "and I hope Dolly will be able to say the same with as clear a conscience as I can, ten years from now."

"Then, it is to be settled to-night, Walter, is it?" Dolly asks.

"I suppose so, my love. Jenny says so, Lady Forsyth says so—I called there on my way home this afternoon, and she was full of it—and I conclude that I am expected to say the same."

"And do you mean to say that before the door closes upon our two friends for the night, that I shall be engaged to marry one of them?"

"Well, I don't know that I go so far as that," said Walter; "I thought it was to be understood that if Forsyth accepted my invitation to accompany us to Italy, that would be considered as tantamount to a declaration."

"Yes, that is the nonsense Lady Forsyth would talk," said Jenny, "but that is not what I mean, and it is not what Dolly means. If ever Mr. Philip Forsyth is to pro. pose, he will do so this very night ; and if he does not, Sam Swynford shall to-morrow."

"Oh, that's the programme, is it? " said Walter.

"That's the programme," Jenny replied, in her pretty but emphatic way ; and so the trio went down into the drawing-room, almost at the same moment that Mr. Philip Forsyth was announced.

————

CHAPTER XVIII.

MAN PROPOSES.

WALTER MILBANKE was under the impression that he was master in his own house, and his wife was clever enough to keep this belief alive. She had her own way without appearing to oppose Walter in the smallest thing. His father had made it a rule to govern, his household auto- cratically. "Have a wife, and rule a wife," was his motto, and he instilled it into Walter, but Walter's was a far more gentle nature than that of his deceased father, and Jenny Norcott had had sense enough to discover this the very first day she was introduced to him, and on which very first day she had made up her mind to have him to pro- pose to her, and to promptly accept him. Within twelve months of that very first day they were married.

This was ten years ago, and they had lived a happy life ever since—Jenny, a clever housekeeper, fond of society and dress, Walter decrying "that sort of thing," but enjoying it all the same, and Westbury Lodge being known among a certain set of pleasant people as a Paradise of good management and merry receptions.

The children—there were three of them—were not
allowed to interfere with the social pleasures of the house;
they had good nurses and well-arranged apartments, and
only now and then were permitted to be in evidence in
drawing or dining room. Their mother visited them once
a day, and romped with them or read them stories, or
heard their lessons, and at night, when she was at home,
they said their little prayers at her knee. They came to
dinner at birthdays or at Christmas, they went out in
the carriage for a daily airing, and sometimes into the
park, wonderfully dressed, and with French servants picturesquely attired. Walter, while he said Jenny was fond
of showing off the children when they went out, liked to
see the display, and was a happy well-to-do fellow, with a
good word for most people, rarely a bad word for anybody,
except once in a way, when the attentions to his wife of
some snob or other, who did not understand her free and
frank manner, aroused his marital dignity, and on one
occasion he actually slapped a fellow's face, and then
called him out. This was in the first year of his marriage.
He had since learned what a man must put up with,
having a pretty and charmingly-dressed wife, who, assured
of her position, is somewhat too fearless in what she says
and does before strangers.

Under these conditions of domestic administration it is
hardly necessary to say that the dinner to which Walter
had invited Swynford, and Mrs. Milbanke Philip Forsyth,
was an adequate, pleasant and cheery repast; no fuss,
no formality—as Walter said, *en famille*—eight o'clock,
bright fires (it was the last week in March, and the English Spring was setting in with its accustomed severity),
two good dishes among the kickshaws, a bottle of dry
champagne, no nonsense about whitewash after dinner, but
a drop of Margeaux and as quickly as might be afterwards
a good cigar and a thimbleful of black coffee, and join the
ladies in half an hour.

Walter had a glib and happy vocabulary, a touch of the Charles Mathews manner, and which his wife in moments of badinage said had come to him ever since he played, at some private theatricals, the leading part of "Patter *versus* Clatter."

During that one good cigar after dinner, Walter had tried to talk of the Venetian trip, which had often been discussed by the Westbury Lodge household, to be at last finally settled upon. Philip had of his own accord expressed a wish to accompany the party, and his mother had secretly confided to Mrs. Milbanke that this proposal was preliminary to a second one of a more important nature.

The Milbankes were well satisfied with this arrangement. Dolly, while she flirted with Sam Swynford, and indeed with any other eligible gentleman who came in her way, was far more serious with Phil Forsyth than with anyone else, had indeed gone so far as to dance with him at Lady Marchmount's ball five times, to Phil's entire satisfaction and to the envy of several of his acquaintances.

Philip Forsyth, being of a more or less reflective turn of mind, and a student in name and in reality, enjoyed the light-hearted chat and merry ways of Dolly, and it must be confessed she was a very bright and pretty girl. She had dark brown eyes, a fair complexion, light brown hair with a suggestion of sunshine in the tone of it, a straight little nose, that had in early youth made up its mind to be *retroussé*, and had become more demure later on, to develop into a coquettish something between humorous snub and serious straight, the effect of which was, to quote Sam Swynford, "awfully taking, my boy." She had a dainty, willowy figure, not too willowy, but with sufficient roundness to suggest generosity of living and generosity of nature. Coupled with all this she had a musical little laugh, which in an ugly girl would have been called a giggle, but in the case of Dolly was a pretty trill of gaiety and good humor. In her own heart she did not quite know which of her two lovers she liked best. In her merriest moods she fancied Sam, who was always " on for fun," as he said ; who brought none of his business worries to dinner—a contrast to Philip, who when he had difficulties with his painting managed to cast the reflection of them on the party.

Once in a way, when Dolly had a headache or had been disappointed in the fitting of a dress, or when her sister had not got the box at the opera which Walter had promised for a Patti night, she preferred the society of Phil, who was always more or less ready to be doleful ; but she liked him best when she met him out at a " swagger literary party," to quote Sam again, and the conversation turned upon a big subject, political or artistic, and Philip Forsyth came out with some of his strong and well-expressed opinions, and the table became silent to listen, and she heard men say he was a very clever fellow, and how eloquent he was, and how sincere, and how refreshing it was to hear a young man talk well and not be afraid to be honest and even sentimental.

But this was no doubt a matter of pride on Dolly's part, and on these occasions her sister would take the opportunity, just in a delicate way, to let it be known to the biggest gossip in the room that Mr. Forsyth was in love with Dolly, and Dolly would sing like an angel the moment she was asked, and the gossip in question would make an opportunity to remark to his friends what a lucky fellow Forsyth was, and so on. Both Phil and Dolly would be pleased with all this, and so that possible engagement was fostered up to the days of the proposed Venetian trip, the making of which was to settle the one great question of two households, the Milbankes' and Forsyths' ; for Lady Forsyth had come to the conclusion that a cheerful wife like Dolly, with an equally cheerful fortune, would be of all things the best for Phil, whom she loved as ardently as her somewhat frivolous and too impulsive nature would permit. She loved him intensely, while the fit was on, just as she loved her friends while they were there, with this additional weight in Philip's favor, that he was her son, that she was proud of him, and that all of her impassioned affection that was not absorbed in politics, society, and in those memories of the past about which she wrote so much in the magazines, was absorbed in her darling—the apple of her eye, the joy of her widow-hood, "the genius of a line of brilliant men and women," to borrow her own words, as we have borrowed some of Sam Swynford's vocabulary.

"The fact is," said Walter, as he handed his choicest brand of cigars to Swynford and Forsyth, and he was ad-dressing the former, "Philip is going with us to Venice I believe."

"Lucky dog," said Sam, "I wish I could."

Walter didn't dream of saying, "nobody asked you, my boy," but in a sidewink at Phil he allowed the artist to understand that such was the case, and that for his own part, even setting aside the question of Dolly, he would prefer the cultured society of Phil to the more vulgar if more genial companionship of Sam.

"Too busy making money just now," said Sam, "to get away even for a day." He said this as cheerily as if he had not absolutely lost half the ten thousand we have already heard about.

A true speculator, Sam, no whining, no despondency over losses, just the same keen firm grip of things whether he lost or won, just the same looking forward to the big fortune he meant to win, with the exception that losses were a sort of tonic to him.

"The city is very lively just now?" said Walter inter-rogatively, addressing Sam.

" Yes, and will be livelier yet," said Sam.

" A tremendous company boom on—the Americans call everything a boom. Everybody with a fine flourishing business making thousands a month wants to share their profits with the public," said Walter.

" Quite so," said Sam. " Traders, manufacturers, brewers, miners, have suddenly become philanthropists."

" No other desire than to endow the general public with twenty-five per cent. for capital for which a niggardly Government will only give two and a half."

" *Punch* couldn't put the situation better," said Swynford, laughing, " unless, perhaps, it added that the Peerage, the Army and Navy, and the House of Commons had joined in the benevolent scheme as directors, with a unanimity of belief in joint stock enterprises that made guinea-pigging a positive virtue."

Philip drank his wine, stretched his legs, and looked into the fire, feeling himself entirely out of the conversation.

" You don't speculate, Forsyth ? " said Walter, turning to Philip.

" I do indeed, very much," replied Philip.

" Do you, though ? " said Sam.

" Not in the city," the artist replied ; " but in many ways and about many things."

" Ah, yes," said Walter ; " but you have not to pay for your fancies."

" It don't matter, for example," remarked Sam, " whether *your* futures come off or not ; but in the city, whether you bull or bear futures, the results are matters of the highest banking importance, eh, Walter ? "

" Yes," said Walter, examining his cigar as if he loved it. Walter was a luxurious smoker ; he literally fondled his cigars.

" It is a good thing we are not all in the same line of

business," remarked Philip. "But I am not so sure that speculations which do not involve the passing of money are not perhaps in some respects nearly as important as dealings in stocks."

"More so," said Sam. "It's a vulgar business, dealing in stocks, but it has its fun, and if you are lucky it enables a fellow to help the other chaps who speculate about art, and the future, and all that sort of thing. We are rare hands in the city at buying pictures and books, and doing the right thing by art and intellect, don't you know? There ain't an atom of pride in the city, and we are always deuced glad for one of you intellectual swells to come up and see us."

"Yes, that's true," said Walter. "They even treat me well; but I confess I generally drop in upon city friends at lunch time—and don't they lunch! And what snug taverns! Busy clubs! And there are gangs now—North gangs, Rothschild gangs, Nitrate gangs, South-African mining gangs; seems to me men operate in syndicates now, is it not so, Swynford?"

Walter was warming again to his city subject, and Swynford beamed on him gratefully.

"Yes, don't know that they might almost be called conspiracies. I can tell you, a fellow who has to fight for his own hand as I do is lucky if he comes out with his hair on. But the public is so confiding. The rigging of companies' shares, before and after allotment, would give thimblerigging odds, and win easy."

"You don't seem to approve of the city, Mr. Swynford," said Philip.

"Oh, yes I do, bless you! it's a game. I don't know that it is much worse than the law, with all respect to our host; it is honester than politics, and you can get a deuce of a lot of fun for your money."

"It beats the law there," Walter rejoined, fondling his

cigar. " But Art I fancy has its mirthful side, eh, Forsyth? well let us say its rosy side, if mirthful is too flip-
pant."

" Art is a cap and bells under a cassock," said Phil,
addressing himself to the fire.

" And the city's a pleasant fellow, with a flower in his
buttonhole and a swindling prospectus in his pocket," said
Swynford with a hearty laugh.

" Swynford wouldn't like to hear anyone else attack
the old lady of Threadneedle Street in that fashion," said
Walter, addressing Philip ; " but let us drop that venerable nonentity—she must be deaf with the recent financial
booms—Venice is more in our way, is it not, Forsyth ? "

" I daresay Mr. Swynford gets quite as much pleasure
out of the city as we do this side Temple Bar, and I am
quite sure he would find as much real enjoyment in Venice
as we shall. Don't think, my dear Mr. Swynford, that I
imagine my profession is a more noble one than yours.
On reflection, and notwithstanding what I said a little
while since, I am inclined to think trade, business, finance,
have the best of it. I sometimes wonder if painting and
acting and writing novels and plays, and indeed if all the
other fields of art are not the mere play grounds of men
who think they are tilling a splendid soil, and after all do
not succeed in providing mankind with either food* or
raiment ; they are not producers who keep the world
going, they grow no corn, dig up no coal, make no iron,
weave no cloth ; they are after all nothing but——"

" Producers of the salt of life," said Walter. " It is the
artists and craftsmen who make life worth living. What
is the moneyed man's highest ambition ? To surround
himself first with their work and then with the artists
themselves ; which brings us back to the Venetian question.
Those old fellows of the great Republic : they knew how
to combine trade with art, how to glorify money, how to

make it and how to spend it. Is it settled, Forsyth, that you are to be one of our little party? We go next month. Our plan at present is not to stop until we get to Milan; then on to Verona; next to Venice; stay there six or eight weeks, and after a run through the Lakes, return *via* Switzerland and Paris. Is it true that you have taken a studio in Venice?"

"I have had one offered to me. I should like to go; indeed, it is one of the dreams of my life that I would like to realize."

"You have a good many dreams, you fellows who paint," replied Swynford.

"Yes," said Phil, his mind running on the face in his sketch, "any fellow might be excused for dreaming over such cigars as Milbanke's, not to mention his claret. What a capital dinner you have given us. But your cook is a treasure."

Philip felt he must make an effort to get away from his picture. His work always took strong hold of his imagination, but "Tragedy" seemed to be taking full and entire possession of him; he began to wish he had never seen the woman at the opera. "Shall we join the ladies, Milbanke?"

"By all means. Shall I tell them you will join us in our Italian holiday?"

"Yes, I think so."

"Bull or bear in that stock?" said Sam Swynford to himself as the three left the room. "I suppose he will take the pool; just my luck!"

Mr. Swynford was a stock-broker and he looked it. There was a certain city go and swagger in his manner, which gave confidence to his customers and made Sam welcome both in artistic society and among his city friends. He was breezy and alive with animal spirits, dressed well, wore a flower in his button-hole summer and winter, was

always groomed " up to the nines," as some of the most
slangy of his acquaintances described the polish of his
boots, his waxed moustache, his close-cropped hair, and
his well-brushed coats. He was what would be termed a
young man with a fair complexion, and accordingly on that
account Mrs. Milbanke was inclined to think that Philip
Forsyth had the best chance in the competition for Dolly,
because in love, like does not like like, but its opposite.
Sam was of medium height, inclined to be what is called
stout, was broad of shoulder, his hands of a generous type,
and he had a fat cheery laugh. He wore tight coats, a
showy watch chain, and carried a big silver-mounted
stick.

On the present occasion his dress clothes were in the
height of fashion—silk facings, silk collar and white vest,
with a single small gem in the way of a stud for his imma-
culate shirt front. His somewhat florid cheeks shone with
health, his grey eyes sparkled with his host's wine. He
had no peculiarities of manner, but was a type of a fairly
bred young Englishman, in a big way of business, perfectly
at home with himself except when he was near Dolly Norcott, with whom he was over head and ears in love ; and
without, as he feared, the remotest chance of ever winning
even her esteem, he yet thought of the possibility of making a heap of money for her, whenever he entered upon a
more than ordinary large hazard either as a bull or a bear.
He had never dared to propose to Dolly, because she had
more than once given him to understand that any familiar-
ity of that kind would be fatal to their friendship ; that she
was not for him in any other capacity than one of friendship ; that as a friend she liked him better than any other
of her brother-in-law's guests, and she hoped he would not
compel her to ask Walter not to invite him any more to
Westbury Lodge. Although this had been said more or
less jestingly, Sam knew that for the time being Dolly meant

it; but he had a lurking hope that in the course of the chapter of accidents he might have a chance. Possibly his city experiences encouraged him to think of his prospects in this way, because he had so often seen the unexpected happen on the Stock Exchange, and he did not see why the doctrine of chances which affected his operations there should not also influence his speculations in regard to Dolly, the one line of matrimonial stock which he desired to inscribe in his book of options. Somehow, however, on this night of his latest little dinner at Westbury Lodge he had misgivings as to his prospects in that quarter; but he made it a rule to appear cheerful and happy under all circumstances, so he sailed into the drawing-room after Philip and Walter, with the smile of apparent confidence and unconcern.

There was just enough of the decorative craze of the day in the arrangement of the Milbanke drawing-room to give it an air of modern prettiness, but not so much as to destroy the sense of comfort, which is often sacrificed to artistic show. It was neither a harmony in yellow nor a symphony in pink; it was not an inspiration from Japan, nor a copy of a Chippendale idea adapted to parquette flooring and Queen Anne windows; there had been no paragraphs in the Society papers about it; probably neither Mr. Whistler nor Mr. Menpes had ever seen it, and if they had they would most likely have condemned it. Nevertheless you felt that the decorator had worked at it with artistic feeling, and that the hostess had supplemented his labors with ideas beyond the reach of art. There was a copper kettle singing on an old hob-grate, a cluster of candelabra on the mantel, a sconce or two of gas on the walls, a dozen or so fine examples of Cox, Haleswelle, Herkomer and Carot on the walls, a cabinet of Venetian glass, a many-legged table with a crown Derby coffee service upon it, and a dainty liquor case; the floor was covered with Persian

rugs, there was drawn up before the fire a big much-
cushioned seat; and the general tone of the room was
yellow, but whether it'was the yellow of warm light or the
yellow of curtains and walls one did not think of inquiring,
though one might wonder about all this afterwards, reflect-
ing on the pretty, comfortable, unusual kind of room it
was.

Mrs. Milbanke was seated at a pretty tea table, lighted
with a pretty copper lamp. Dolly was half buried in an
easy chair with the last new book in her lap. Swynford
hoped she was enjoying her literature. She looked up with
a mischievous smile and said she was, though she must
confess it was full of sadness, not to say horrors. Stepniak's " Russia under the Czars," she continued, this time
turning her blue eyes towards Philip, who, of course, became immediately interested. Her sister had suggested
the book as a desirable one to have lying about since they
had seen the sketch on Philip's easel, and they had driven
down to Mudie's for it before going home after they had
left the studio that very afternoon. It had not taken Dolly
half an hour, the half hour after dinner, to get at the tone
of the work, and to know just enough to let Philip see that
she was interested in the subjects which interested him.

" Yes," he replied, sitting down by her side, ": it is a
painful subject, though one might be forgiven for expecting
to find something noble in pages inscribed with such a
title—but there is in the record of its martydoms."

There was something fateful in Philip's appearance and
manner; he was pale, his black hair was dishevelled, it
fell in a great shock over his forehead, his long hands were
particularly white, and there was a poetic melancholy in
the expression of his sallow face that suggested much
thought and work. All this made him interesting in Dolly's
estimation, and she was also taken by the air of distinction
which seemed to belong to those student-like character-

istics which were so opposite to the happy professional air
of her brother-in-law, and to the smug city cheerfulness of
Samuel Swynford, of Lombard-street.

"I have always been deeply concerned in regard to the
fate of political prisoners in Russia," continued Philip,
"and just now I am thinking of little else. I suppose there
is a touch of selfishness in this increased devotion, because
I am putting my feelings and my imagination into commission as it were ; I hope they will assist me to carry off the
Gold Medal."

"Oh, that is the secret of the sketch we saw this afternoon ?" said Mrs. Milbanke. "You forgot to tell us ; or
perhaps it is a secret."

"Forsyth thought he would not spoil a good subject for
conversation this evening," chimed in the host. "Yes,
my dear, I will have a cup of tea ; don't approve of tea as
a rule, 'but to-night we'll merry be,' as the song says, eh,
Swynford ?"

Walter did not quite know what he was saying ; not that
he had had too much wine, but his wife had been making
signs at him, and he tried to hide his non-understanding
of them under a ripple of talk. "A good old song,"
he went on ; "I remember my singing it when I was
a boy at a birthday—yes, my dear, Mr. Swynford will take
a cup of tea, and by the way, Swynford, you are a judge of
water colors. I would like to show you a little portfolio I
bought last week—a collection of landscapes and figures
—two little Turners, half a dozen David Cox's, a Calcott,
and a couple of sketches by Landseer ; here it is, my
boy."

And Walter, having suddenly caught the meaning of his
wife's nod, had led Sam to the furthest end of the room
away from Philip and Dolly, and was soon deep in the
mysteries of the portfolio in question, getting Sam's ideas
of its value, not only artistically but financially, together

with his views of the present inflated state of the money
market and other matters of current interest.

Meanwhile Philip responded to Dolly's sympathetic
inquiries about prison life in Russia, the high-handed
character of what was termed administrative arrest, and
what he intended to convey in that sketch, in which the
woman's face was so remarkable as to have set Jenny talking of nothing else ever since they had seen it. Philip rode
his hobby gracefully, with eloquence and with knowledge,
and paused more than once to note how beautiful Dolly
was, and what a happy contrast were her red lips, her bright
genial eyes and warm healthful flesh, compared with the ·
woman of the opera, " the ghost of Madame Lapukin," as
Dick Chetwynd had styled her.

Presently Jenny had drawn her chair near the two young
people, to hear Philip's story of this woman at the opera,
and his desire to have her as a model for the face in his
medal picture ; and by and by she led the conversation up
to their trip to Italy and the poetic loveliness of Venice,
where she assured him he would find a model in every
woman of the people whom he met. She had only been
to Venice once, and then only for a week, and she thought
she had seen more beautiful women during those seven
days than ever she had seen in her life before.

Philip in reply could not resist the suggestion that it was
not necessary to go to Venice to look for beauty ; and if
he accompanied them he should ask the favor of putting
Dolly into a Venetian picture, for so far as he was any
judge of the peculiarities of the Venetian face he thought
Dolly herself possessed that curl of the lip and that sunshine in the hair which was supposed to be thoroughly
Venetian.

Without seeming to say it, the clever little matchmaker
let Philip also understand that Dolly was also blessed with
a certain golden sunshine in the Three per cents., which

his mother, Lady Forsyth, thought an important item in the charms of marriageable young ladies.

It is difficult to fathom the thoughts of man, and to say whether the best of God's creatures is mercenary or not ; whether the most virtuous may not be influenced now and then by the worst passions. So far as the narrator of this history is concerned, he is inclined to think Philip did not note the worldly hint of Mrs. Milbanke, or, if he did, that it had no influence with him, though the hostess more than once made some passing reference to the responsibilities of marriage being so greatly lessened if there was money on both sides ; or if there was money on one side and genius on the other, quite in a more or less inconsequential way getting in a reference to an artist whom they both knew who was very clever but still could not sell his pictures, and what an important thing it was in art for a man to be more or less independent of dealers, so that he could afford to follow the bent of his genius or his inclination, and do the work he liked best ; and so on—an eloquent rush of worldly wisdom, most useful in regard to young people, about to contract a marriage, and especially to a couple of young people, the bride pretty, with money and social position, and the bridegroom an artist, also with social position, a little money, perhaps, and no end of genius and ability, if he could only paint what he wished and be independent of the Academy and of dealers ; and somehow Philip found himself, before he quite knew where he was, discussing these delicate matters, as if he or Dolly, or both, were personally concerned in them.

And once, Dolly's hand being near Philip's, he laid his upon hers, and she, not withdrawing it, he pressed the fair hand, and was very sensible of its soft pliability. The gentle pressure that responded to his, when he ventured a little further and took Dolly's hand fairly within his own, set his heart beating, and he forgot everything except Dolly and his mother's praises of her. It came into his mind that it would please his mother very much if he married Dolly, and that she was very beautiful, had golden hair, a sweet voice, and cheerful manners, and that sometimes Fate met one half way, as it were, and sometimes clapped one on the shoulder unawares, and that after all it would be a pleasant Fate to be entitled to take Dolly to one's arms, and have her for a lifelong companion.

While Walter Milbanke was fooling Samuel Swynford, it was as good as settled that his hopes were to be utterly crushed. Why, therefore, prolong the description of this evening one moment more than is necessary to aquaint the reader with the main incident of the night? Swynford felt uncomfortable, and said he must go earlier than he had intended ; he spoke of some important business he had in the city the next morning at ten, and took a cheerful leave of Westbury Lodge two hours before Philip ; and long before that favored young gentleman said " Good-night," he had been alone with Dolly for three parts of that time, both Walter and his wife having business in another corner of their pretty house ; Mrs. Milbanke to see the children put to bed (though they had been in bed for hours), and Walter to answer a couple of letters which had come in by the last post.

It was a blissful time for Philip while it lasted ; a dream of a new and unexpected kind of happiness ; a dream in which hands clasped hands, and lips touched lips ; a dream in which a soft, sweet, blushing girl confessed that she loved him ; a dream in which he believed he loved her better than anything or anybody in all the world.

And so it was settled that a fortnight later Philip Forsyth should accompany the Milbankes on a tour through France, Italy and Switzerland, with a long vacation in Venice, and that during their wanderings they should settle the month in which Philip should make Dolly his wife.

" Man proposes "

CHAPTER XIX.

"WHAT FATES IMPOSE, THAT MEN MUST NEEDS ABIDE."

THEY awoke to a new life the next day, several persons in this history. The old order of things had changed in a night. Dolly had a new position in the eyes of herself, her relations and friends; she was "engaged." Mrs. Milbanke entered upon a fresh phase of existence; her sister had "accepted" Mr. Philip Forsyth; Lady Forsyth would be Dolly's mother-in-law. Mr. Samuel Swynford might no longer feel that in his city operations he was working for a future in which Dolly Norcott would have the leading part. Dick Chetwynd believed that the career of his friend Philip Forsyth had now become secure. Hitherto his prospects had needed the ballast of responsible duties. Married to Dolly, his ambition would be fostered by an absence of what the young fellow had considered the absolute necessity of earning his own living : for although Lady Forsyth had a fair income, she spent every penny of it and did not keep out of debt, and the possibility of her death and his inheritance of the property left by his father did not for a moment enter into Philip's calculations.

Lady Forsyth felt something like a sense of triumph in the engagement of Philip and Dorothy, for many reasons ; it secured her son's independence, it relieved her of a kind of responsibility as to his future, she liked Dolly, thought the Milbankes pleasant successful people, and the excitement of the wedding and getting ready for it would be an agreeable break in her life, which, lively as it was in a general way, the tune of it was all on one string.

Philip went to his studio on that memorable next day, unhitched his bell, wrote "Out" on his wicket, locked his door, put the key in his pocket, and entered upon a reflective solitude.

The Regent's Park studios were a pretty, red-brick cluster of buildings north of Primrose Hill, designed and erected for art work, and for personal comfort, by an enterprising architect who recognized the progressive movement of the times, and in the right spirit provided a calm retreat for workers who could afford to pay a fair rent for their accommodation. The studios had a general portal, in which resided the porter and his wife, who kept a small staff of servants for the purpose of attending to the domestic and culinary requirements of the tenants. Passing through this general portal which had its gates and hours on the principle of an old-fashioned college or inn, you came into a courtyard, around which the studios were ranged, each with its individual retiring rooms and offices. Some of the men lived there altogether; one occupant, after some protests and difficulties with the landlord, had been permitted to bring home his wife there; another house was occupied by a lady artist, and thus the humanizing influence of woman had entered through the general portal, and given a pleasant tone to the place. From the moment that Hymen had come in there, æsthetic blinds, red-raddled flower pots, outside mats, birds in cages, and gay flower-beds had appeared; while the harmless, necessary cat had had a ribbon tied round its neck, and the colony had made itself look just as gay and merry as it undoubtedly was. There had been little luncheons and an occasional reception prior to the entrance of Hymen with his torch; but they were as nothing compared with the gatherings which had made the place musical and floral in these latter days, when the Regent's Park studios have become famous not only for the work they turn out, but for their social gaieties. Nobody would ever be able to work and play as well in the same place, it was feared, when Hymen was permitted to light his torch within the sacred precincts ; but " Out " made any studio safe from interruption. " Out," communicated to the Porter's Lodge, was as powerful a talisman of protection from callers as if the painter who had exhibited the legend on his wicket had been leagues away ; and so the opportunity for serious work was secured. It was a tribute to the earnestness and industry of the region, during the weeks immediately preceding the Spring Exhibitions, that, as a rule, the entire colony was " out " from early morn till dewy eve ; and Philip's " Out " was therefore not singular on this bright and breezy April morning.

There was a cheerful fire in his stove. The sun was streaming in at his western window. Having promptly drawn a blind down against the radiant light, Philip took off his black morning coat and waistcoat, and put on his brown velvet working jacket, removed his boots in favor of a pair of white tennis shoes, and took up a position of observation with his back to the stove, which was a handsome terra cotta construction, German in appearance, but with the advantage of an open grate, making it a compromise between England and the foreigner so much as to retain the national prejudice in favor of an open fire, while it secured the German and Russian practicability of a real heating stove.

Philip stood with his back to the fire and surveyed the room ; not that he saw anything in it, but he surveyed it all the same, looked round it, up at the roof, and down at the floor, the couch with its tiger skin, his low easy chairs with their fluffy cushions, his parquette floor with its rugs, his screen full of rough sketches, his throne for sitters, his two great easels, his cabinet crowded with papers of all kinds—drawings, old engravings and new

sketches—and his wardrobe full of costumes, the sketch
on his easel covered with a piece of silk, the door opening
into one of his retiring rooms, with its cartoons in the
little passage way, his small collection of plastic ware
scattered here and there, and his statuettes of a Russian
peasant, and a baked clay model of a Polish patriot.

All these things he looked at but did not see ; his mind
was occupied with other images, with other thoughts ; it
was not altogether absent from the studio, but it was
making curious and strange journeys outside the porter's
lodge, and busy with thoughts that went out far away,
and with strange day-dreams.

Did he love the girl to whom last night he had engaged
himself in a lifelong bond ?

Or in what he had said was he pledged to that serious
compact of marriage ?

If Love was that absorbing passion he had dreamed of,
was he in love with Dolly ?

Was not his last night's engagement a sudden impulse,
in which there was a good deal of passion and very little
love ? Was Dolly the ideal of womanhood he had dreamt
of as an artist, and read of in the poets ? Was she not
rather a pretty, clever, little woman of the world, her heart
in the studio of the milliner rather than in the studio of
the painter ?

Did she really care for Art ?

Was beauty without the refining grace of culture and
sentiment really Beauty ?

Would any man have been happy with the most perfect
goddess of the Grecian sculptors ?

Did Providence for that matter ever combine true
physical beauty with intellectual grace ?

Had not Dolly and her sister, and even Walter, seemed
last night to enter into a charming conspiracy to get him
to ask Dolly to be his wife ? Had not Walter's genial

wine, the sweet incense of admiration, the soft, cozy, healthful charms of Dolly, been sensuous, as opposed to the
spirituelle temptations which should guide the choice of a
lover who looked for a wife superior to the wiles of Society
and to the frivolous attractions of dress?

These questions, not exactly in definite shape, but
shadowy, passed before him, without answers. They
seemed to have the accompaniment of some strains of
music from Carmen, and his thoughts wandered away to
the Opera, and to the beautiful, sad face in the curtains of
Lady Marchmount's box.

He listened, and could hear faintly the strains of a street
band, which was playing a passage from the very scene
which had for him been interrupted by that strangely
fascinating presence which he had endeavored to suggest
in his medal picture.

His eyes wandered to the easel, and as they did so the
remnant of grey silk which had covered his sketch gradually slipped down upon the floor, and there was the face
looking at him through its deep red halo, and its accompanying figures of misery and suffering. There was nothing
supernatural in this, though it exercised an uncanny kind
of influence upon Philip. The truth is, the drapery had
been gradually slipping away for hours, influenced by the
increasing gravitation of the heaviest part to the floor and
the entrance of Philip, the shutting of the door, and his
moving about, so that it fell away just at a critical moment
in Philip's reflections, and his imaginative nature found in
the incident a shadow of a protest against the chief event
of the previous night.

If Dolly's face only gave you the idea that there was
something behind it, he went on mentally saying to himself,
an intellectuality beyond mere worldliness, how much more
beautiful it would be! But he could lead her in the
direction of the studies he liked ; he could give her an

ambition higher than that of shining in Society ; he could
bring her sympathies within his own control. Could he?
There was the rub. And there, still before him, was his
idea of the face which of all others he had ever seen possessed intellectual fire, poetic sentiment, but had withal a
something fearful in its great eyes, and something thril-
lingly mysterious in its sudden appearance and in its no
less startling disappearance.

He walked to the easel, picked up the silk remnant, and
glanced round the room as if he expected to see some one ;
then mechanically wrapping up the piece of silk, placed it
carefully away in his wardrobe, took up his palette, wiped
it, and commenced to squeeze a series of color tubes
upon it.

While he is thus engaged, let us glance at him critically.
It is a promising youth, not quite rugged enough perhaps
for the making of a man of action, but at the same time
betokening firmness, good health, ambition, checked, however, by one physiognomical drawback, a somewhat weak
chin, and with eyebrows that as a rule rarely accompany a
happy disposition. Lavater has some notable views upon
the meeting eyebrows held by the Arabs to be so beautiful,
and by the old physiognomists to be the mark of craft, but
regarded by the master as neither beautiful nor betokening
craft, but rather, while giving the face a somewhat gloomy
appearance, denoting trouble of mind and heart. Similarly
with the pointed chin ; many people believe it to be the
accompaniment of acuteness and craft, but Lavater knew
many honorable persons with such chins, and he noted
that their craft is the craft of the best dramatic poetry.

Philip Forsyth had the melancholy eyebrows and the flaw
of weakness in the chin, not as to the pointed chin, but to
the want of angularity, and the suggestion of retreat, coupled
with a something negative in both its form and size ; but for
these drawbacks Philip's face was the face of an artist, and a

man of nobility of mind and ambition.   The compact forehead, the thick black hair, the perfect nose—suggestive of
the keystone to the Gothic arch, as Lavater regarded it—the
dark, steadfast eyes, the strong hands with the long dexter-
ous fingers, the well-proportioned limbs, moderate breadth
of shoulder with narrow hips and easy graceful movements,
all belonging to masculine beauty, and to a nature of keen
sensibilities.   Meeting Philip for the first time, you would
have regarded him as a young man out of the common ;
but you might have credited him with nursing an ambition he could not realize, or with a melancholy turn of
disposition—qualities which are not without attraction in
the young, who are just beginning to realize the responsibilities of existence.

There was perhaps a further touch of weakness in Philip's
individual characteristics—namely, in his gait and manner.
He did not walk straight and direct to anything : there was
a something akin to feline gracefulness in his movements.
He approached an object with a certain swerve of motion,
as if he, more or less, walked in curves, as graceful actors
do ; and this also was characteristic of his mode of thought.
It was to the line of retreat in the chin, its slight under-
size, that physiognomists would credit this peculiarity,
combined with a strong imagination not under the full
control of the logical or executive faculties.

But these very weaknesses helped in many respects to
add to the attractiveness of Philip's work and conversation.
They made, for instance, Dick Chetwynd feel perfectly
safe in giving him advice, and added to Dick's satisfaction
with the young fellow's matrimonial engagement to a pretty,
sensible girl not likely to be led away by will-o'-the-wisps,
and with sufficient money in the three per cents to give
stability to his social and domestic position.

Philip, having laid his palette and brushes down by the
easel, took from his pocket a cigar case, selected a cigar,

lighted it, dragged a chair in front of his sketch, sat cross-legged upon it and looked at the canvas steadfastly, smoking all the time, and occasionally looking upwards, watching the blue wreaths break upon the cross beam, from which swung specimens of old flint guns, spears, bows and arrows, and a Roman corslet.

With the eye of imagination he saw his picture grow into what it might be, what he hoped it would be, not only a great work of art, but an everlasting rebuke to Russian tyranny—not simply the study to which the Academy had awarded the Gold Medal, but the study which had perhaps brought the awful political disabilities of the Russians home to the sufferers, helping the champions of the people to break the chains that kept Liberty in prison, galled its flesh, and wore its brain to madness.

He had once seen of band a political prisoners and criminals start on their weary way to Siberia, and he had never forgotten it, nor would, though he was not more than nine years old at the time. It was during the years his mother and father had lived in Moscow. Wherever they are condemned to Siberian exile by order of the Czar—everything is by order of the Czar in that vast, despotically-governed empire—they proceed first to Moscow, where, after a brief sojourn in the great convict prison there, they start on their awful journey. The prison is some distance from the city, and Philip remembered that he and his father rose very early to see the exiles leave, his father having some mission of benevolence to one of them, which he was allowed to undertake by order of the Czar. The penal settlement was a series of huts and houses surrounded by a high wall. There were numerous sentinels, and they had many formalities to go through before Philip's father saw the wretched man for whom he had brought the last parting messages from a broken-hearted wife. The prisoners included both men and women, and they were as a rule attired in a uniform kind of dress, which seemed to Philip's memory to be a long, loose great coat of a rough grey cloth. As they left the prison they saw the first gang begin their march, and it was the recollection of this that had enabled Philip to give life and reality to the more terrible narratives of which he had since read and heard—incidents on the road, deaths by the way, tragedies *en route*, during which the Czar had been relieved of many prisoners, the innocent and the guilty, the hardened criminal and the spotless victim of his infernal rule. Philip remembered the heavy rings that were riveted upon the legs of the convicts, one for each ankle, united by a chain, which fetters were linked with others, holding groups or companies together to render the surveillance of their guards easy and complete, as they held their weary way across the vast steppes into the Siberian wilds, where even Nature allied itself with the Czar to torment and kill them.

It did not require much knowledge or imagination to introduce into a group of the poor, wretched creatures that young student falling by the way, nor to bring a suffering woman to his aid, nor to invoke the interposition of the brutal Cossack against both of them. This was the incident upon which Philip concentrated his mind and his brush, and to-day, having promised himself models for these three figures, he still went on painting from memory, a touch here, a correction there.

Unconsciously he found that he was sketching himself as the dying student. Every touch he put into the figure made it more and more like him, but every touch upon the woman he rubbed out again. It was an inspiration, that woman's face. He felt it as such, and now the fear took possession of him afresh that he would never be able to finish it. He therefore came to the wise conclusion not to touch the original sketch again, but to make new studies for any alterations in its development.

The face took fresh possession of him as he worked; and when presently he began to think again of Dolly, and to picture in his mind the scene she had forecast of a floating gondola on the Grand Canal, with only they two and the gondolier in the moonlight, with music rising and falling in the sweet Spring air, that face had gradually as it were eclipsed Dolly's cheerful, love-inviting features, and it was at the feet of the strange woman he was sitting, and the music changed to the appealing and the defiant strains of the mountain scene, with the loving maiden fresh from the innocent village and the dying mother, and Philip again looked round the studio as if someone had come in without opening the door.

Then with a sigh he laid down his brushes, and staggered, rather than walked, into an inner room, that was fitted up as part bedroom, part sitting-room and dressing-room, flung himself down before a crucifix, and prayed with all his heart for guidance, for aid, and for comfort.

When he rose from his knees he returned to the studio and paced to and fro in a steady, steadfast manner, occasionally running his fingers through his hair, but never pausing until after nearly an hour of this physical and mental exercise—for he was thinking and revolving all manner of ideas about himself, the picture, Dolly, and the woman of the opera box—he drew a couch before the stove, lay down, and, tired in mind and body, drifted into that kind of sleep which Dickens speaks of as stealing upon us sometimes, and while it holds the body prisoner does not free the mind from a sense of things about it, but enables it to ramble as it pleases.

Philip, resting with a sense of the happiness that comes with the redressing of every physical want, wandered off into pleasanter dreams than those which had hitherto filled his waking mind. Once more it was Dolly at whose feet he reclined on the waters of that city of the ocean he had longed to visit, and which he was now to see for the first time in loving company, with blue eyes that would return his admiring gaze, with soft hands that would respond to the tender pressure of his own, his love and hers set to glorious music, and basking in Italian sunshine. And so the time passed away. The sun had gone down, and the mists had fallen all over Primrose Hill when he awoke, his fire out, and only a faint glimmer of the gaslight from without showing him where he was, the half waking sleep of his first hour having changed into a dreamless time, out of which he rose, however, cold, and feeling the prosaic sensations of hunger.

At about the same time that he woke up Dick Chetwynd arrived at the Lodge. "Out" was the answer.

"But 'In' and working," said Chetwynd.

"Well, yes, sir," said the porter's wife, "and what we considers a little odd, he have had nothing to eat all day ; not rung his bell for nothing, and come ever so early."

"Sure he has not gone out?"

"Quite sure."

"Then I think I might break the rules and see what he is about, eh?"

"Well, sir, you might, being his most intimate friend, and exonerating me and my husband."

"Quite so," said Dick, passing through the barrier and going straight to Philip's quarters, which had a separate porch or passage-way and were especially private and secluded. It was now too dark to see the legend "Out" upon the wicket, the gas lamp at the entrance only seeming to cast the floor in darker shadow."

"What the mischief can he be at?" Dick said to himself as he performed a stirring fantasia upon Philip's knocker.

The door was almost immediately opened, but the studio was in darkness, every blind down, the only light being a faint gleam from some outside lamp. "Hello!" said Dick. "What's going on here?"

"I don't know, I believe I am," said Philip. "Come in, Chetwynd; have you a match?"

"A match, yes. What's the matter?"

"Nothing's the matter," said Philip, "only that I have been to sleep."

"What, all day long?" asked Dick, lighting a match.

"I don't know; I think I have, or else been dreaming. It is awfully good of you to come, old chap."

·Philip took the match from Dick, lighted a lamp, and shivered. "Is it not very cold? What's the time?"

"It is very cold and the time is seven o'clock. You have not dined?"

"No," said Philip.

"That's right," said Dick, "I have not. Come home with me.'

"My mother expects me to dinner."

"No, she does not. I have seen her ; met her at Martinotti's studio ; an exhibition of his models for the Garibaldi statue. I told her I should call for you and carry you off. But what have you been doing, my dear fellow? You are as white as Martinotti's plaster!"

"I have been trying to work."

"I expected to find you radiant after what happened last night. I suppose the new impulse it has given to your ambition has set you working too hard to-day? You must not do that. I congratulate you, my dear boy ; it is a most desirable match in every way."

"I hope so," said Philip.

"You hope so, you young vagabond?" said Dick—he always called him a young vagabond when he liked him most—"you know it is."

"She is a sweet girl," said Philip ; "I wish I was worthy of her."

"Worthy? Fiddlesticks! Go now and dress and let us be off; you don't mean to say you have been here all

day without luncheon, and not even open your newspapers !
This will not do, Phil, even when a young fellow is in love.
So you have been working on the sketch, have you?
Humph ! I don't think I should touch it any more ; get at
the picture, dear old chap, that's the thing to do now.
And I have tremendous news for you ! "

" Indeed ? "

" Yes, dress, and I'll tell you as we go Dorset-square."

Philip lighted another lamp, and went into the next
room.

" I shall smoke while you dress."

" All right," said Philip, " but come in."

" No, I shall amuse myself with the gold medal ; imagine
you carrying it off, and having a silk rope round the picture at the Burlington house, or at another Gallery we wot
of if you like."

" But what is the news ? " asked Philip, now busy dressing.

" Great news, Phil ; the making of your picture. I shall
not tell you until you are dressed."

Philip, now thoroughly aroused, was fairly back again in
the every-day world ; he put his head into the washing
bowl, and was soon all aglow ; it did not take him ten
minutes to dress, and the porter's wife answered the bell
with unwonted alacrity.

" I have a hansom at the gate," said Dick, when Philip
asked the porter's wife to have one ordered.

The attendant being gone, " now," said Philip, " what
is your news, Dick ? "

" Let me help you on with your overcoat; it's a cold
night, bright starlight, frosty ; you must not get a chill."

" Oh, I'm all right," said Phil.

" But you do not exactly belong to yourself any more,
you know ; you have to take care, for Dolly's sake."

" Very well," replied Phil, just a little impatiently ; " let
me shut the door; all right, mind the step."

Studio lights were burning in the windows, the married quarters of Hymen with the torch looking more cheerful than any other of the homes of Art. There was a faint perfume of wall-flowers from an adjacent window box ; the porter's lodge was radiant with a crackling and cheerful fire ; and in the street was a hansom with two white lamps, which were presently dancing along the Albert-road by Primrose Hill and away down Baker-street towards Dorset-square.

"And now, Phil," said Dick, turning to his friend, "pull yourself together for the news."

"I have been doing that for the last half hour," said Philip.

"I have found her."

"Great heavens, whom?" exclaimed Philip; his heart beating wildly, in spite of himself.

"Your ghost of Madame Lapukin. But more like Cleopatra than Lapukin, I fancy."

"Do you mean the woman I saw at the opera?"

"Who else could I mean?'

"How do you know it is her?"

"From your description and your portrait of her. A superb woman ! But not half so melancholy as you make out ; and her hair is chesnut, not red ; a chesnut that will drive you crazy ; great violet eyes set in a colorless face of æsthetic loveliness ; but her mouth ! well, it is the mouth of Clytemnestra !"

"It is not the same woman, Dick."

"Yes, it is, and to-night you shall see her and talk to her, and ask her to sit to you."

"And who is she then?" Philip asked, "and why did she appear in Lady Marchmount's box like a vision and disappear like a dream?"

"You can ask her yourself. I saw her this morning at the Gallery ; and she is the famous Russian Countess, Olga Stravenski."

"And I thought she might have been a Nihilistic spy, the victim of some vile conspiracy," said Phil, in a tone of been disappointment. "A Russian Countess! To ask her to see my sketch would be to insult her; to sit for that suffering angel she has inspired, an outrage. I don't wish to see her."

"Oh yes, you do! Here we are."

The cab pulled up at one of the best houses in the square, well-known in art circles, a home of taste and social geniality.

"She is coming here after dinner; and I have to thank you for the honor," said Dick, as he turned the latch with his key. "I told her all about you, and she shall sit for the medal."

CHAPTER XX.

HOW CHETWYND MET THE COUNTESS.

MRS. CHETWYND was as buxom as her husband was genial. She was a woman of the right sort to help a man on in life. More particularly was she just the woman for Dick. In his early days of journalistic struggles she had not only enabled him to keep up a good appearance in the world, but she had made his home comfortable, if not luxurious. on two pounds a week; and to-day she made his fifteen hundred a year go as far as most men's five thousand. Often in past days Mrs. Chetwynd had cooked a dinner and left the kitchen to preside over it, and had played the part of both cook and hostess equally well. Nor was she lacking in artistic taste or literary culture. She was a bright, clever woman, not above a woman's duty, not ashamed of her domestic work, and happy because she had made Dick's position a certainty.

" We have always been equal to either fortune," Dick
would say in confidential moments, when discussing the
difficulties of the London battle ; " we could have lived
in a garret at any time, and got as much happiness out of
it as if it had been a palace ; and that is the only way for
a man and woman to fight the battle of London together."

" We are dining in Dick's room to-night," said buxom
Mrs. Chetwynd, " because we have a reception, and I want
the lower rooms of the house free, and, morever, I like to
give the servants every chance to keep their heads, and we
do not have any assistance on these occasions, Mr. Forsyth. Dick does not believe in hired waiters and manufactured food."

She always quoted Dick as if she consulted him on
everything, which she did not. But she was always
anxious to have it understood that Dick was at the head
of affairs as much in Dorset-square as at the Gallery, or at
his editorial office in Fleet Street. She was a rosy, pleasant,
frank hostess, Mrs. Chetwynd. Hawthorne, who spoke
of English women as beefy, would probably have noted in
her an absence of what might be termed the dainty
spirituelle side of the feminine character which is very
attractive to some men, but she was a type of that
English womanhood which has given to the English character, in all ages, its energy, its muscle, its open fearless
features, and its national dignity. She was the picture of
a refined Rubens. She had the rounded limbs, but they
were firm and shapely ; she had the blonde face, but it
was neither fat nor thin ; the fair hair ; but she had the
mouth and eyes of an intellectual as well as a beautiful
English woman ; and Dick's friends noticed that she continually grew more and more like her husband, the result
of perfect unity of sympathy and a sincere and abiding
love.

" The moment she came into the Gallery to-day," said

Dick, telling his wife and Philip how he had met the Countess Stravensky, "I was struck with her appearance ; so
sad yet so beautiful ; and thought of the face in the sketch.
She was attended by an Italian Jew, one Andrea Ferrari,
who is said to be her private secretary; he seems to be
both footman and secretary, man-of-all-work to her ; a
curious, wiry, active, though watchful little chap, just the
sort of person one could imagine as the agent of a revolutionary conspiracy ; a firm, thin mouth, shaggy eyebrows,
a low but compact forehead, black hair with streaks of
white in it, all nerves and muscles, and with two ferret-like
eyes deep set in his head.   And somehow it was not only
the countess' appearance that brought the woman of the
opera to my mind, but Ferrari ; for he seemed to me, at
once, to belong to the situation, and I added him mentally
to the Siberian group.   Very odd all this ; but life is odd,
eh ?   Don't pass that sherry, Philip, it is the purest
Amontillado and it positively helps the soup ; ask Agnes."

Mrs. Chetwynd was Agnes, and she at once endorsed
her husband's recommendation of the sherry.   Philip
allowed his glass to be filled, but made no reply to Dick's
remark, by the way, dropped in really for the purpose of
helping Philip to take the subject of the woman of the
opera as nearly like ordinary conversation as possible.

" But she is a Russian countess ? " said Philip.

" Yes, that's the trouble—I mean that is the difficulty
about getting her to sit.   Her secretary handed me a special note of introduction, from an old friend of mine con-
nected with continental journalism, and I made a point of
talking to her and to him.   She made a romantic marriage,
it seems, in Moscow, to the dying Count Stravensky—one
of the most devoted of the Czar's nobles, whose patriotism
had been greatly tried, who had indeed suffered persecution at the hands of the Czar, and still remained faithful ;
and as if to make up for the dead man, the Czar has since

shown much favor to his widow, who is now travelling for her health."

" And you think her beautiful ? " asked Philip.

" She is your picture, and as sombre in expression, until you rouse her interest ; then her eyes—they are of a rich violet—light up, and her smile is simply divine."

" And you will find the chicken not to be despised," remarked Mrs. Chetwynd, " if you will allow me to suggest anything so mundane ; the Surrey chicken ought to be canonized in the cook's calendar."

" Yes ; don't let the countess take away your appetite ; and here's to the gold medal ! "

Dick nodded to his guest over a glass of champagne, and Mrs. Chetwynd said : " But you did not tell me why I am to have the honor of this paragon of beauty's presence to-night without a formal invitation ? "

" She informed me that she expects to leave London to-morrow or on the next day," said Dick, " and may not return ; which emboldened me to say how much I regretted you had not had the pleasure of meeting her, in order that you might have invited the honor of her company at your ' at home ' to-night, and so on. Then I told her all about Philip and his picture ; how it had been inspired ; intimating with a poetic and mysterious touch that I believed you had dreamed you had seen her at the opera, and how you had tried to suggest such a face as hers in the very last position possible, and that you were searching London for the face you vowed you had seen, in order to ask the owner to sit for your picture. She seemed more interested in what I said than she cared to exhibit. I thought she winced, and that a shade of color spread over her pale, handsome face when I mentioned your having seen her at the opera. She turned and spoke to her secretary, who, while she appeared to talk quite familiarly with him, treated her with the greatest deference, if not with slavish

humility. 'You interest me in your friend,' she said, in
a voice that was soft and musical. 'Since that was my
object,' I said, 'I am very glad to hear you say so. You
are an artist yourself, perhaps?' 'No, I love art,' she
replied, 'I have lived in Italy and France.' 'Then you
would not be offended if I say that if you had been going
to stay in London for any length of time I would have
petitioned you to sit to my young friend.'"

"You are very kind, Dick," exclaimed Philip, "and
you have a lot more courage than I have!"

"You are not a journalist with ten years of experience
as a war correspondent," said Mr. Chetwynd.

"I would not like to ask the countess anything at
which she might take offence," said Dick. "There is
sorrow in her eye, and softness in her voice, but there is
the devil there also. And mark me, Philip, you are right
in thinking there is a remarkable history behind that
face.

"How do you mean, Dick?" Philip asked.

"I mean that it appealed to you as a face that had seen
a world of persecution and trouble. You have more than
hinted at a woman who has suffered and will be revenged.
Your artistic instinct is right, I believe."

"But do you really think she is the woman I saw?"

"I know she is."

"How?"

"By your portrait, and from her anxiety to see you."

"Her anxiety to see me!" exclaimed Philip, the blood
rushing to his temples.

"Don't blush, Philip—I mean do," said Dick, "I like
to see a young fellow blush; I sometimes wish I could.
When I had fired that shot, about you having seen a face
at the opera which you had gone home and put into a picture of a tragic character, she tried to disguise her interest,
I had almost said her alarm; and she smiled sweetly, but

with an effort, when I told her your name and spoke of
your mother; she knew your mother's name, and her
private secretary or guardian, or official executioner or
whatever he may be, said Lady Forsyth was well known
in Russia. 'She is a rebel,' I said smiling, 'as much a
rebel possibly against Queen Victoria as she is against the
Czar, so you must forgive her; and besides we play with
revolution in England, toy with Socialism and so on, just
as we do with æstheticism and private theatricals.' 'Yes,'
she said inquiringly, and inviting me to go on. 'And the
young artist I am speaking of was born in Russia, and of
course he will take the sentimental and romantic side of
Russian politics.' 'Then his picture is political?' she said,
with a strong note of interrogation. 'More or less,' I
said; 'it is a fanciful sketch at present of the road to
Siberia, and—don't smile—and pray do not be angry—its
central figure is very much like your ladyship.' She
started at this, and said as if amused, 'You alarm me, Mr.
Chetwynd; if we were in Russia, and you talked to me in
this way, I should suspect you were an officer in disguise,
and that you had a file of soldiers at the door.' The secretary
stood by and watched me closely. I felt his little ferret
eyes upon me, though every time I looked up he was apparently gazing upon Holman Hunt's 'Scapegoat,' and I
wondered afterwards if it suggested to him anything beyond
its realistic ugliness. She had taken a seat beneath one of
the palms in the Western room of the Gallery, and the
more I talked to her the more she invited me to go on—
that is, she listened with attention and made an encouraging remark now and then. I told her that my wife took a
deep interest in your career. She said she would have
liked to meet my wife; I said my wife had a reception to-
night, and that you would be coming to us, and if she
would deign to accept so late and informal an invitation,
how much honored we all should be. She said at once she

would, and before the day was over, in response to a telegram, Agnes had called and left cards, and this morning we had her ladyship's acceptance ; and here is her letter ; a firm, sharp hand, is it not ? "

Dick handed the letter to Philip, who looked earnestly at it, and returned it.

" Yes, what I should call a fine, cultured hand, rather pointed in style ; but a noble signature."

"You seem to be both worshippers at this Russian shrine," said Mrs. Chetwynd, " I hope I shall not be disappointed. Now you are going to smoke, so I shall leave you ; we will meet again, Mr. Forsyth, in the drawing-room at ten, and later I will tell you what I think of Madame la Russe."

Philip opened the library door for the hostess, who passed out with a bow and a smile, and presently he and Dick over cigars and coffee continued to discuss the Countess Stravensky.

" How old do you think she is ? " asked the artist.

" Thirty or more," said Dick, " and a widow. Not too old to make a certain young lady jealous."

" Do you think she will sit for me ? " Philip asked, disregarding Dick's badinage.

"'Not if she is leaving London to-morrow."

" You think she is going away ? "

" No, I don't."

" Why ? "

" Because she spoke of leaving town as if she were in doubt about it ; and when a woman is in doubt she does not do what she says she thinks she will."

" If she sat for me of course I need not show her my sketch."

" Why not ? "

" Because she would be entirely out of sympathy with it. It would be like asking Lady Salisbury to sit for the heroine of an Irish eviction."

"Who knows. She may be favorable to the young Russian party."

"What, as the widow of a Russian nobleman, devoted to the Czar?"

"The possibility I suggest is, of course, very remote; but her secretary, Signor Andrea Ferrari, who is evidently her right hand, looks anything but the character of a Russian loyalist; moreover he is a Jew, and furthermore he is an Italian Jew."

"Might it be possible that he is in the pay of the Russian Government?"

"It might; anything is possible," Dick replied, "but I thought a passing glimmer of satisfaction passed over his otherwise Sphinx-like face when I said your mother was a rebel. Anyhow they are a strange couple; and the lady is a wonderfully fascinating and lovely woman. Why she should be peering about in Lady Marchmount's box, as you seem to have seen her, is an odd thing, the more so that in the opposite box, or at least the one nearly opposite, was a distinguished Russian party; one would think that the Countess Stravensky would have known her compatriots, and would have visited them or they her!"

"Yes," said Philip in a thoughtful way; "and what is equally strange is that Lady Marchmount says she was not in her box."

"True; you had not got into an unhealthy state of mind over your work and fancied you saw her, eh?"

"No, and I cannot help thinking she had some secret curiosity to satisfy in regard to that Russian General Petronovitch and his bride. When I thought of the incident later I wondered if she were afraid they might see her; whether the bride might have been a rival; or if she wished to recall the appearance of some person in that box whom she had not seen perhaps for a long time. Lady Marchmount was, to my thinking, telling a diplomatic lie when she said no one had been into her box."

" But you did not see her speak to Lady Marchmount ? "

" No."

"Therefore, it would be in keeping with the mystery you have managed to surround what after all is not extraordinary incident, if the countess, walking along the corridor, had mistaken Lady Marchmount's box for her own ; or finding the door open had looked in and availed herself of the opportunity, from behind the curtain, to take a glance at the Russian box."

"I can't say," Philip replied, "but nobody except myself seems to have seen her in the theatre ; that's the puzzle ! "

CHAPTER XXI.

"A KIND OF MONTE CHRISTO IN PETTICOATS."

MRS. CHETWYND'S reception began at half-past nine. At ten o'clock there was a fair sprinkling of arrivals. The people who meant to get away early, or who had other places to go during the night, came with something like punctuality. But the lady's intimate friends and the lions of the night did not begin to arrive until eleven, and some of them came after the opera and the theatres.

Dick and his candidate for the gold medal went into the drawing-room at ten o'clock, and found pleasant opportunities of assisting the hostess to entertain her guests. Among the early arrivals was Phil's mother, Lady Forsyth, who was attired in soft black silk, with handsome jewellery of diamonds and emeralds, among her finest ornaments being her favorite four-leaved shamrock, in gold enamel and emeralds, and an Irish harp for a brooch. She was still a handsome woman, though her hair was almost white, and the roses had long since faded from her cheeks. She

entered the room at about the same time as Lady Marchmount, whose husband was one of the Radical leaders, and
had, under Mr. Gladstone, fulfilled semi-official missions
both to Rome and Russia ; her ladyship posed somewhat
as a political wire-puller on her own account, and delighted
to be considered as in the secrets of foreign Governments.
She found a pleasant occupation in patronizing the Irish
party, and holding out a friendly hand to Lady Forsyth.

" Mrs. Chetwynd tells me that she expects the Countess
Stravensky," said Lady Marchmount to Lady Forsyth,
when, after receiving the homage of some lesser lights,
they found themselves pretending to listen to a brilliant
pianoforte fantasia in one of Mrs. Chetwynd's most comfortable seats.

" Indeed ? " was Lady Forsyth's reply.

" A remarkable woman, who only arrived in town a
week ago. I hope to see her before the night is over at the
Russian Embassy."

" Remarkable in what way ? " asked Philip's mother.

" She made a death-bed marriage, the story of which was
told the other day in the *Gaulois.* A lady of no family in
particular, poor but clever, a widow of a young and learned
Jew ; the Count Stravensky, a very wealthy Russian nobleman, met her in France, old enough to be her grandfather,
fell in love with her and obtained the Czar's permission to
marry her. He had rendered the Government great services both civil and military, was taken ill in Paris and
they were married two hours before he died ; she took his
body to Russia, saw it ceremoniously buried in the church
of Vilnavitch or some such place—I forget the name—entered into possession of his vast estates, sold them, left
Russia, and consoled herself for her double matrimonial
disappointment by traveling from place to place, entertaining herself with acts of charity, especially in the interests of the Jews, actually went and lived in the ghetto at

11

Venice three years ago—think of it!—and, in spite of the
Russian persecution of the chosen people, is said to be
hand and glove with the Russian Government in its fight
with the Nihilists—a curious story, is it not?"

"Very!" said Lady Forsyth; "an eccentric evidently
—some women find delight in compelling the world to talk
about them."

"You have only to be very rich, a widow, handsome,
and affecting a mission, to have all the world that is worth
knowing interested in you," responded Lady Marchmount.
"The Countess Stravensky is a woman to know."

"A kind of Monte Christo in petticoats," suggested
Lady Forsyth; and as she said so Philip came up, and
Lady Marchmount moved away.

"She is coming here to-night, mother," he said.

"And who is 'she' when she comes—Dolly?" asked his
mother, making room for him to sit by her side.

"No; the lady I saw at the opera whose face I suggested in the medal sketch. Chetwynd assures me it is the
very woman."

"Then I believe I can guess who she is," said his mother;
"Lady Marchmount has been telling me about her."

"Yes?" said Philip. "Lady Marchmount knows her
then?"

"If it is the Countess Stravensky, who has been married
twice and widowed with curious promptitude—in the case
of one husband, at all events——"

Before she could finish the sentence, both mother and
son yielded to the same impulse to look towards the door
at the announcement (which then immediately followed
the close of that little-noticed fantasia) of the Countess
Stravensky.

Mrs. Chetwynd went forward and received the lady with
unusual *empressement.* The countess responded with
graceful informality, almost interrupting Mrs. Chetwynd's

society bow by extending her hand to be shaken, and at the same time addressing some pleasant word of thanks for being permitted to accept Mrs. Chetwynd's invitation so unceremoniously. The next moment she was speaking with Dick, all unconscious of the admiration she was calling forth on all hands.

She wore a long, trailing Empire dress of straw-colored silk, covered with crape of the same dainty hue, trimmed with garlands of golden laburnum, that seemed to accentuate the rich gold of her hair, at the same time deadening the paleness of her cheeks and giving death to the violet of her eyes. Her jewellery consisted of the topaz and the diamond exquisitely blended. In harmony with her costume, her hair was dressed in the Empire fashion, giving an added height to her imposing figure; her tresses were held up, as it seemed, by one magnificent pin of topaz, set in a shimmering halo of diamonds. Long gloves draped her arms, she carried a yellow-ostrich-feather fan, and from one arm depended a crape shawl, the fringe of which swept the floor with her train. Upon her left wrist was an ancient Arabian amulet composed of topaz, through which in Arabic was bored in curious stars the word "Vengeance." Mr. Chetwynd's guests only saw the sombre yellow bangle; they little dreamed of the great, solemn, terrible oath that had been sworn upon it.

The countess was no otner than our Queen of the Ghetto, poor Anna Klosstock. The reader will know how to correct some of the information which Lady Marchmount gave to Lady Forsyth. Though it was not quite unexpected, the marriage with the Count Stravensky will be new to them. In regard to the details of that interesting and romantic union, it is possible we may hear the story from the lips of Andrea Ferrari, or from the mouth of the countess herself. Meanwhile the reader's interest especially at the moment will be with Philip Forsyth, who, sitting with his mother within the shadow of the window-seat, had noted the beautiful image that had inspired his tragic picture, though now and then it seemed to him as if there were a world of comedy also in the lady's smile ; but the young artist was not sufficiently experienced in the dramas of real life to be well acquainted with the acting that is often more intense on the real than on the mimic stage. The countess had a part to play, and she played it to perfection when the audience was in evidence. When she was alone with her Fate there were even times when she tried to forget herself, or only to remember those happy early days of Czarovna, the awful eclipse of which the reader has a melancholy knowledge. Phil noted her pale fair face, her soft violet eyes, her wealth of deep-red hair, her grace, her imposing figure, her distinguished manner ; but never once did he find a suggestion of the sad, somewhat weird look in her eyes, until he had talked with her, as he did presently, after Mrs. Chetwynd had brought him where she was sitting beneath a cluster of tall palms, near the great open ingle nook which Mrs. Chetwynd had constructed in her drawing room in defiance of many rules of art, but with singularly picturesque effect.

" Mr. Chetwynd has told me of your picture," she said, in a rich musical voice, and with an accent of a somewhat composite character, neither French nor German, but with a touch of both, and perhaps also a suggestion of Russian. " Your picture interests me."

" You are very kind to say so."

" I say so, not simply to be kind, but for the truth that it is so."

" I fear my friend has exaggerated its merits," said Philip, beginning to feel at his ease after the first flutter of nervousness and admiration.

" It is of the subject that I am also interested ; it has the merit, that of sympathy. You were born in Russia ? "

" Yes," said Philip. " I was partly educated in Moscow."

" Ana perhaps it is that you saw some of the exiles on their long journey; their sufferings touched your heart, you were so young. Is it not so ? "

" It is not necessary to be young, madame, to feel sorry for the wretched."

" Ah, you say well ; you have a good nature, and I would I might be your friend, but I was the friend and more of one of whom your face reminds me. But my friendship does not make good for those I love," and Philip saw that sad look of the theatre come into the expressive eyes and harden the mouth for a moment, to give way to a softer look and a more tender tone of voice ; and he was right in his observation ; for the moment the countess saw Philip Forsyth, she said to herself, " That young man has the eyes and the expression in them of my beloved Losinski, and the same tender heart ; it is strange that I should have been interested in him before I saw him." As she spoke to Philip there seemed to be tones in his voice that reminded her of Losinski, and with the memory there came the shadow of Petronovitch and the knout ; but with a great effort she kept to the softer side of the memory, and she talked with Philip as she had never talked to human being since the tragedy, from which she emerged not only alive but with a strange power and a strange beauty.

Philip felt the magic influence of her sudden awakening to human sympathy. For ten years she had not until now felt one throb of human feeling that had not been accompanied with a pang of hatred, revenge, and revolt at the world and everything in it. Her charities had been as much in the way of protest and revenge as any other action of her life. She had lain next door to death for twelve months in the Czarovna hospital, half the first months of the time in terror of mind and body indescribable. When she was sufficiently recovered for removal, the new Governor, succeeding Petronovitch, who was promoted for his patriotic quelling of the riotous Jews, found means to comply with the wishes of the Count Stravensky, and Anna Klosstock found friends in France, friends and fellow sufferers, friends and agents of the propaganda, friends and work ; disappearing for five years, losing all identity with Anna Klosstock, she made an entry into Parisian life that was more or less distinguished, and soon afterwards married the Count Stravensky—his last act of enmity towards the Government of the Czar.

"And if I am a friend of the great Czar, our Russian Father, I can still feel for those who suffer," said the countess to Philip ; "it is not that we must be of what is called the young Russian party to be sorry for the exile, the prisoner, the miserable, and those who give their liberty and life for a cause, or for a sentiment ; for me, suffering is of no party, misery of no nationality. You interest me ; I will go to your *atelier* and sit for that sad woman in your picture. Mr. Chetwynd shall make a convenient arrangement that shall be agreeable to you, and I will do myself the honor to make a call upon your mother. Till then, adieu ! "

When the countess' carriage was called, it had already an occupant. Andrea Ferrari stepped out, gave his hand to madame, and closed the door upon her. The lookers on saw him address the lady as if for instructions. What he said was rather in the way of giving orders. " Petronovitch and his wife left London for Paris by the mail. We are in good time for the Reception at the Embassy ; we shall drive thither ? "

The countess bowed her acquiescence, the Italian took a seat on the box, the carriage drove rapidly away, and the countess soon afterwards, between the elaborate courses of an elaborate Anglo-Russian supper, listened to an English duke's assurances of sympathy with the Czar and his Government.

CHAPTER XXII.

FACE TO FACE.

A MONTH of strange atmospheric vagaries—the month of April in the English Metropolis—a month of sun and shade, of calm and storm, of east winds and southern breezes, of rain and sleet, of cruel chills and softened tenderness ; and all the while a month of budding blossoms, of waving leaves and scented sweetbriar; a month, so to speak, of ups and downs, like a man's life. It lacked, perhaps, the violent contrasts, nevertheless, of the career of the Countess Stravensky, who, despite the blasting cyclone of ill-fortune, stood when all was over like a poplar that had been able to defy the storm, but stood all alone, with the forest torn and ragged and uprooted around it.

When Philip Forsyth, the morning after Mrs. Chetwynd's reception, walked from Gower Street to his studio beyond Primrose Hill to receive his new and strangely fascinating sitter, London was a summer city, though it was still only April, and there had been a fall of snow and a hailstorm in the preceding week. Regent's Park was radiant with a sunshine that had in it the warmth of June with the freshness of the most genial of Spring days, and there were pleasant shadows in it from the trail of morning clouds, and the air was full of the perfume of flowers. The brown tanned beds in the broad walk were gay with budding hyacinths, and the fountain was making music in its granite basin. The chestnuts were full of white promise of early bloom, and the leaves were as fresh and green as if they were the new-born leaves of some remote wood far away from city smoke and fog. The first swallows of the year twittered as they floated overhead, and blackbirds were making late breakfasts upon the green sward which they investigated with hurried and flashing beaks.

Philip in a dull kind of way was conscious of all this: it came as an accompaniment to his thoughts of other things, more particularly to his meeting with the Countess Stravensky, and to the object of his early and delightful walk to his studio. He went swinging along through the Park and out into Albert Road, quite in the spirit of the time. He recalled in a dreamy fashion, that was, however, somewhat out of harmony with it, every word and every look of the mysterious beautiful woman of Mrs. Chetwynd's reception. He saw her eyes looking into his with tender interest, he heard her say she might be his friend. The soft tone of her voice when she said she was interested in him came back to him. He comprehended in one long reflection the memory of her ˙lovely form, her red-gold hair, her becoming dress, her distinguished manner, the fascinating melancholy of her face when it was in repose, the depth of her eloquent eyes when she turned their violet light upon his. He might have been walking on air every now then, so unconscious was he of his surroundings, and yet he found the influence of the buds and blossoms, the wooing breeze, the perfume of flowers, and the drowsy plash of the first water cart of the season, that laid the dust after the first swallow had skimmed along the road, not in very wantonness of the gaiety and pleasures of life, as the poets think, but as earnestly bent upon the practical sustenance thereof as the blackbirds in the park.

The aspiring artist did not pause to ask himself what sort of absorbed interest this was he was taking in the Countess Stravensky: whether it was the absorption of the painter in a great subject, or the pulsations of the romantic passion of an impulsive young man. It was quite certain that for the time being the beautiful foreign lady had occupied a place in his thoughts which should have been alone occupied by Dolly Norcott, to whom only two days before he had become engaged.

This fact was recalled to him by the Countess Stravensky herself within an hour of the time when he was walking more or less on air, as we have seen, to his studio beyond Primrose Hill, for the condescending model arrived punctually to the time which she had fixed with Philip's mother on the preceding night. He had had the place specially prepared to receive her, and she had come quietly attired, as if in sympathy with his subject.

It was eleven o'clock when she passed through the porter's gate. Her single brougham stood outside with one servant on the box. On the pavement was a gentleman in waiting—a foreigner who strolled about the neighborhood enjoying the fresh spring morning, and a cigar strong enough to have thrown an ordinary smoker into a narcotic fever.

Philip received his visitor with a calm sense of triumph. She wore a grey soft cape, which she laid aside almost as soon as she entered the studio.

" It is very kind of you to come," said Philip, not attempting to disguise his pleasure.

" Kind of you to ask me to do so—and Mr. Chetwynd made such a point of it ! " she said, with her fascinating foreign accent. " What a charming hostess—Mrs. Chetwynd ! Sorry I could not remain as long as I could have wished ; but there was a prior engagement, which duty required I should observe, at the Russian Embassy ; it was a ball, and I had the satisfaction of arrriving for the the little supper, as they so call it, and I was escorted by one of your great ministers ; a friend, so he said, of Russia. Ah, thank you, they are lovely ! "

This in response to a bouquet of lilies of the valley which Philip offered to his visitor, as he invited her to take a seat upon the sitter's platform.

"You are business-like, you do not forget that my time is much occupied; but I am to sit in character, is it not so?"

He thought her voice wonderfully sweet, her foreign accent giving to the tone of it an added charm.

"I wish I had designed for you a subject in which the study should have been one of beauty and happiness instead of beauty in misery and despair. But may I not first sketch you as you are?"

Whether it was that the countess desired to check the exuberance of Philip's frank admiration of her, or that the question arose out of a real interest in his welfare, she suddenly forced him back upon the duty he owed to Dolly Norcott.

"Your mother tells me you are engaged to be married."

"Indeed!" he said.

"And when are you to be married?"

"I do not know," he said.

"The happy day—have you not already marked it with white in your calendar of bliss?"

"No," he said, busy with his brushes and his easel.

"You do not care to talk about the betrothal. Is it so?"

"I care most to hear you talk," he replied, his dark eyes turning towards her.

"That is a trick of the painter, eh? He thus will get the expression of his sitter's face. Well, it depends what the expression is to be. But am I not to see what you have already desired it should be? Mr. Chetwynd was concerned with the thought that I might be displeased at your painted opinion of the miseries inflicted by my country on the exile and the prisoner! Not at all. That I sympathize with you in this, brings me here."

"Mr. Chetwynd," Philip replied, "overrates my sketch, but since your ladyship wishes to see it, it is here."

He wheeled towards her chair an easel upon which he lifted the sketch we have already seen. He did so in a somewhat perfunctory manner, for he had found some of his enthusiasm for the countess evaporate at her mention of his engagement. Not that it had set him thinking more of Dolly, as a lover should, but it had appeared in his mental groping to have projected a shadow between him and the delirious pleasure of having the countess all alone to paint, and at the same time to study—to worship perhaps—for he had encouraged an indefinite kind of anticipation in regard to .this visit in which art was not the only factor, and almost the first words of his sitter appeared to him to have set up a barrier against the romance of it.

The countess rose from her seat, stepped down from the platform, and gazed at the medal sketch. The light fell effectively upon picture and reality. Philip noted the fair, round figure of the woman, simply clad in a pale silk gown draped to her figure, her red-gold hair dressed high as on the night before, her bonnet designed as if to set off rather than hide it, her pale face, with the dark lashes of her eyes shadowed upon her cheeks, her entire appearance singularly graceful and queenlike.

"And you think this woman like me!" she said, after standing before the picture as it seemed to Philip for quite five minutes.

"Chetwynd thought it like you."

"Chetwynd did?" she said, still looking at the sketch.

"Indeed he recognized you from this clumsy description of you."

"Not clumsy but remarkable," she replied. "You painted it after seeing me at the opera?"

"Yes."

"What if I have not been at the opera?"

"Then I have dreamed it," said Philip.

"It reminds me of a girl I once knew years ago," she said.

"I did not wish to show it you : I felt it was a libel on you."

"It is beautiful," she replied, now looking at him, and with a sad expression in her eyes.

"It shall be, if you give me the opportunity to study the original."

"I suppose you have in your mind a story for your picture. It is called Tragedy, your mother tells me."

Philip wished that his mother had not said so much to the countess ; but he only replied that it was the subject for the Academy gold medal.

"And in your mind the tragedy is the situation of that young man who is to die in the arms of the woman—in mine, eh, Mr. Forsyth ? I am to be the poor creature who extends her arms with all her good kind suffering heart in her pale face to the poor dying student—is that so ? "

"And the general group ; the old man is an incident of the tragedy. The spirit of the subject also lies not alone in the fact pourtrayed, but the idea of the road to Siberia."

"Yes, yes—do not be afraid to say all you may think or feel of that, the most enormous of all tragedies it is true ; but there is worse than Siberia—there are perils worse than the road to it and the arrival. Perhaps in your picture the young man is her lover; ah, my friend, to have been his companion in exile would have been bliss to that young girl whom the face recalls to me ; her love was so great Siberia would have been heaven with him. Do you ever think of all the horrors of the Inferno of Dante ? They are as nothing compared with the fate of that young girl whom I knew in a Russian village long ago. But, my dear Philip, why ask me, who am rich and happy and of the *noblesse*, to sit for this poor mad creature ? "

Philip's heart stood still for a moment when she called him her 'dear Philip,' and then began to beat fast and furious.

"That is why I did not wish you to see it," he said, his face aflame, his tongue running on at a rapid rate. "You, who are so beautiful; you who should rather sit for a Queen of Beauty—a goddess for men to worship and women to admire—for Arthur's Queen, or Cleopatra. And in that there would also be tragedy, but the tragedy of the poet, not the vulgar tragedy of a troop of prisoners. Let me blot the libel out."

He advanced towards the sketch, as if he would have carried out his suggested threat. She laid her hand upon his arm, and he thrilled at the touch.

"Not so, dear friend," she said; "it is a compliment to me that you can think of me as pathetically as that," and she pointed to the picture. "Ah! if you only knew! And she was beautiful, that girl I am thinking about; but Siberia was too good for her; she was of the cursed race of the Jew, and they called her Queen of the Ghetto in the place where she lived in innocence, and was engaged as you are, and more, with the day fixed for the wedding, and the year of betrothal at an end; and she, be sure, marked it in the calendar, and he her betrothed. You are in the right—it is tragic, this picture of yours! It has also enough of sorrow in that one incident of the woman or her lover to call it tragedy—and perhaps the old man might be her father, eh? Was that in your thought?"

While she spoke she removed her bonnet, and drew her hair about her head as suggested in the picture, as Philip had seen it at the Opera, and she took her seat, and he followed her, palette in hand.

"There, my friend, go on with your study; it is not the first of the times I have sat for the artist. I can make that expression, perhaps, for you; I try to look back to the poor girl I tell you of. There!"

The mouth fell into an expression of despair, and the eyes looked up with a tearful idea of pain in them ; the hair fell around the pale beautiful features. Philip gazed but did not paint.

"Why do you pause ?—will you not have me for your model ? Do I not act well ? "

Then she arose from the crouching attitude she had assumed and laughed almost hysterically.

" You cannot realize that I who am so gay and rich and so high-born should act such a part as the miserable woman of the prison—the lash perhaps. Well, you are right—do not alter the picture ; it has all the spirit of the misery of persecution—outrage, the rod, the lash ; you have felt it in your heart ; I am glad I have seen what you feel ; but go seek the wretched, not the happy such as I for your model ! "

She was putting on her bonnet.

" But you are not going ? " exclaimed the artist.

" Why not ? " she said ; " you will not paint me.   You do not think I can be of use in your picture ! "

" Forgive me, " he said, " you have perplexed me ; I was not prepared for so wonderful a realization of the woman I saw at the Opera—the face I have tried to paint."

" Some other day, then," she said, " when we are both less embarrassed.   I have other engagements—a luncheon, dinner, a dance—and I must get up my Society spirits, eh ? It is not for me to think of such sorrowful things."

She comprehended in a long sweeping action of her arm Philip's entire sketch.

" You are angry with me," said Philip.

" No, no," she said, " I am never angry ; despair is not anger ; revenge is not anger ; longing is not anger. Ah ! I see I bewilder you ! Thank you."

She had pointed to her cape ; Philip assisted her to put it on.

" You have excited into action some old memories," she said, " and you have a strange resemblance to that poor girl's lover; he had marked the day as I tell you with a white stone, and its sun set in blood ; you are not so engrossed with the betrothal of your love. It is well; I admire your English *sang froid;* it is the reason why you are great ; you can look love and destiny, victory and defeat, heaven and hell in the eye straight, and you do not flinch. Indeed you are a great people ! "

" Ah ! madame, for some reason you mock me," said Philip. " I have offended you ; if I dared say all I think and feel about you—the admiration you have inspired in me, the ambition that lies beyond that mere daub you have been good enough to praise, that boyish fancy, the weakness of which since last night I see with the eyes of a man ! "

" Another day," she said, interrupting. " Please ring for my carriage ; and believe what I say when I tell you I am not angry ; that I feel all you say deep in my heart ; that you have awakened there sensations that have been dead for years ; and if we do not meet again, let me beg of you to finish that picture ; it will bring you fame ; I commission it; paint it for me ; it shall have the first place in my gallery ; it shall have a home in my heart." She turned as if to go ; then with her eyes full upon him, she said, quickly : " In my country there is the kiss of friendship and there is the kiss of peace ; I give to you that salute, and with me it is the kiss of a sweet memory that lasted for a moment, to be lost in the shadow of a tragedy more terrible than that you have dreamed of in your art and in your tender sympathies with the persecuted and distressed. Adieu ! "

She kissed him on both cheeks and was gone out at the open door before he could attend her. While the wheels of her brougham rattled out at the portal of the court-yard he stood in a heat of strange delightful surprise, looking amazed and bewildered at the open doorway where the sun came streaming in like a benediction.

———

CHAPTER XXIII.

DOLLY IS DETERMINED TO BE HAPPY.

PHILIP had not seen Dolly since he had asked her to be his wife : it seemed an age—it was only two days ago. What an eventful two days ! To Dolly they had seemed also a long time, but somewhat uneventful. Mrs. Milbanke had not refrained from remarking that it was odd Philip had not called the next day ; and on this morning of the countess' visit to Philip's studio, she had expressed some wonder as to Philip's health.

" He must be ill, my darling," said Jenny at breakfast, after Walter had started for the city. " It is Lady Forsyth's day, I will call ; you shall not go ; I will go alone ; if he is ill we ought to have had the fact made known to us ; if he is well his conduct must be explained.   When I was engaged to Walter every day that I did not see him I had a letter from him."

" He must be ill," said Dolly, taking up one of the last remaining strawberries that had come up from Walter's place in Gloucestershire.   " Poor Sam would have been here every five minutes if he had been allowed." .

· " You must not think what Sam would have done," said Jenny.   " It is not proper, and it is not wise.   Why, I declare it is twelve o'clock ! Walter is later for the city every morning."

" It is all owing to my engagement," said Dolly ; " before it was settled he talked of nothing else, now it is settled he finds it an equally absorbing topic, and one would think our trip to Venice was my honeymoon, he makes so much of it."

" He is a dear, good fellow," Jenny replied : " lives for
everybody except himself, more particularly for you and
me, Dolly. You must not think to get as good and devoted a husband as Walter, but Philip Forsyth is far
cleverer, and he is famous, or will be, and one day you will
be Mrs. Forsyth, R.A., and perhaps Lady Forsyth—who
knows? There is no end to the possible triumphs of the
wife of a great artist—and Philip will be great, Mr. Chetwynd says so ; and there is no more severe critic and
perhaps none so influential—he is said to have been the
critical godfather of Burne Jones and Watts and Albert
Moore, and several others."

" But, my dear, Watts is old enough to be his father."

" I can't help that," Jenny replied, fastening a sprig of
white lilac in the bosom of her dress—the white lilac from
Walter's place in the country, a bunch of which had
adorned the breakfast table, making a sort of little bower
for the nest of plover's eggs which had formed part of the
menu.

" I suppose I ought to be very unhappy," Dolly remarked as her sister rose to leave the table, " and yet I am
not."

" You don't feel things as I did," said Jenny ; " we live
in a more practical age, I suppose."

" Indeed, since when? " asked Dolly. " You are not
old enough to be my mother, if Watts is old enough to be
Chetwynd's father ; and sometimes I could almost imagine
you to be my younger sister."

" Then you don't love Philip as I loved Walter ? "

" I don't know how much you loved Walter."

" Then you are not a person of much observation," said
Jenny.

" I suppose one loves a man according to how much he
loves us. You seem to think Philip has neglected me
already."

"No, I do not; I think he is ill; and if you had been me, and Philip had been Walter, I should have been so certain of it that I should have made immediate inquiries, in person or by telegram or both. And, what puzzles me, is that you take it all as quietly as if you had been married five years, and one day your husband had not come home to dinner, and had not sent you word that he was detained."

"I suppose it was such a strain upon me to get him to propose that the reaction has left me limp and played out, as that American lady said the other day."

"She said 'wilted,' my dear," Jenny rejoined; "but I am sorry to hear you speak as if you had given Mr. Forsyth positive encouragement to propose."

"Now don't be a hypocrite, Jenny; you know I did, and that it was in its way quite a little conspiracy on all our parts, and that Walter was in it as bad as any of us, the darling."

"Dolly!" said Jenny reprovingly, but at the same time linking her arm within her sister's and leading her into the morning room where they generally amused themselves with needlework and novels, mostly novels. "You are trying to be cynical because you feel annoyed with Philip; I know you are; as if it was necessary for you to try and force his hand!"

"It might not have been necessary," said Dolly, "but we did it."

"Oh, Dolly, you are in a wicked temper."

"Not at all. I know that what you did was out of your great love for me, and that Walter had no other object; and I will not deny that Philip seemed to like it, that he was very devoted and very eloquent, and that he proposed to me with fervent *empressement;* but for all that we had prepared the little trap for him, had we not, dear?"

" Not more than it has to be prepared for all of them, the awkward creatures ; they must have assistance. But one does not prepare the way for unwilling lovers ! Philip loves you, are you not sure of that ? "

" Oh, yes," said Dolly ; " he thinks I have beautiful eyes and a fine complexion and a good temper, and that I dress well and have an independent fortune, and all that ! "

" And all that ? " exclaimed Jenny, "and much more. What silly novel have you been reading lately ? "

" Only the novel we really see about us all the time—the novel that nobody writes—the reality of London society and London life—the truth of every day. I don't mind, Jenny, I take it all as it is ; but when you and I are alone, dear, don't expect me to pretend, as I do when Walter is with us or anybody else."

" Walter ? Dolly ! Do you mean to say I deceive Walter ? "

" Deceive him ? No, my darling, not more than he knows you do ; we all deceive each other; it is necessary to our happiness more or less. But you and me, Jenny, we are generally perfectly frank ; we have no two natures to keep separated for each other. I love Philip and he loves me, but not in that ecstatic devoted Romeo and Juliet fashion that you have been trying to think of for me in a sentimental moment."

" Oh, Dolly, you are growing worldly—I am sure you are. I would not have believed it if you had not told me ! "

" I have not told you anything of the kind. I am not growing anything different from what I have ever been, but I do not try to persuade myself that I am different ; and I am not going to make out that I am breaking my heart because Mr. Forsyth has not called or written or done something that is usual with young men when they ask young women to marry them. I like Philip well enough, I quite appreciate all you say about the possibilities of the future, but, as the song says, if he does not care for me what care I how fair he be."

"In the first place the song does not say anything of the kind," Jenny replied, "and in the next place please to remember that you are engaged to be his wife, and that all London knows it—that is, all that part of London that we care anything about."

"My dearest sis, it is of no good your lecturing me. I was born under a merry star, and nothing is going to make me sad."

"Oh, don't say that, dear; it is like a challenge to Heaven!"

"I was going to say nothing was going to make me sad except old age," went on Dolly, defiantly. "I mean to enjoy my life, and I am sure Heaven does not desire any of us to do otherwise so long as we fulfil our duties, visit the poor, go regularly to church, bear no malice, and covet no man's goods, neither his ox, nor his ass, nor anything that is his."

Jenny had never seen Dolly in so curious a mood, and did not quite know what to make of it.

"I mean to enjoy my life," her sister continued, "and if Philip Forsyth likes to enjoy it with me he is welcome. I have accepted his proposal of partnership, but if he is going to be stiff about it, and formal, neglectful, proud, or grumpy, I can't help it; he will find he is not going to make me unhappy—at all events without a struggle on my part to be happy."

"A struggle, dear!" said Jenny. "Happiness is not obtained by struggling; it comes of itself, free and bright like a summer morning; you don't get it by fighting and wrangling. I do not understand you to-day, unless it is that you are really troubling about Philip; that you care for him a great deal more than you would for some strange reason have me believe."

"Jenny, let us drop the subject."

"I will not, Dolly. I know exactly what you feel, and what distresses me is that you should try to conceal it from me."

"Then, dearest, if you know all you say, why not act upon it, without making all this fuss?"

"Fuss!" exclaimed Jenny. "With all your determination to be happy whatever may occur, Dolly, it will be a sad day for both of us that casts a shadow upon my love for you and your love for me!"

Jenny's voice had tears in it; and Dolly could fight no longer. She flung herself sobbing into her sister's arms; which Jenny afterwards explained to Walter, fully endorsed all she (Jenny) had said about the serious character of the situation between Dolly and Philip—a situation which was more or less modified, soon after this unusual scene between the sisters, by a call from Philip himself.

CHAPTER XXIV.

DOLLY AND DUTY.

THE candidate for the Academy's Gold Medal, and the affianced of Dolly Norcott, was received by Mrs. Milbanke in her afternoon warpaint, just ready to go out, her brougham at the door, in her hand one of those formidably mounted parasols that an American satirist had named "the husband queller." It was a Paris purchase by Walter, the handle of solid gold, with a jewelled rim that suggested some regal symbol of high office, or at least a civic mace; a detail to be noted as one glances back a season or two upon tall hats, dress-improvers, and other inventions of Fashion. Mrs. Milbanke herself must have had in her mind the ostentatious importance of that formidable parasol; for she told Walter that when Philip was announced she felt like a warrior of old in full armor, and with a glove in his casque, ready for anything or anybody, but more particularly Mr. Philip Forsyth.

" My dear Mrs. Milbanke," said Philip, " I called to see if I might have the pleasure of taking you and Dolly " (yes, he called her Dolly) " to my mother's Afternoon."

" You might," said Mrs. Milbanke, her bonnet on, her golden sceptre in her hand, " and you might not : I really cannot say ; we thought you had forgotten that there was such a place as Westbury Lodge ; at breakfast this morning, Walter wondered whether you had been called abroad."

Mrs. Milbanke's brown cheeks glowed with suppressed anger.

" I hoped to have called yesterday," said Philip, looking at his boots.

" It is two days since my sister accepted your proposals, the most momentous occasion of both your lives ; for two days she has neither seen you nor heard from you ; and to-day you call as if nothing had happened ; what is the meaning of it, Mr. Forsyth? What are we to understand by it? My sister is positively ill with vexation or anxiety, I really do not know which."

" I am awfully sorry," said Philip, " the truth is I have been unusually busy ; I went to Mrs. Chetwynd's At Home last night—more on business than for any other purpose ; Chetwynd came and fetched me away from the studio; and I hoped to have seen you at Dorset-square—you and your sister."

" I don't know why you should have expected either of us ; we do not know Mrs. Chetwynd ; we have met her once or twice it is true ; and we know Chetwynd, a very pleasant sort of person ; but we do not visit Mrs. Chetwynd."

Mrs. Milbanke had made up her mind to be calm, if spiteful, the moment Philip was announced ; but she found it impossible to control herself. Her tongue wagged at a tremendous rate. "Moreover," she continued, "if you had any wish or any curiosity about it, you could have asked us if we were going to the Chetwynds. A young man does not get engaged every day; it is an incident, at all events, in a young girl's life which is more than ordinary; but——"

"Really, Mrs. Milbanke, I don't think I have deserved to be so severely lectured; and without a hearing," said Philip, interrupting Dolly's sister in her mad career of rebuke. "I was going to explain that I have been unusually busy; you know of what importance it is to me that I should lay in that medal picture before I go to Venice; and I met the lady at Mrs. Chetwynd's whom I wanted to sit for the central figure; she kindly consented to give me a sitting this morning; she came, and the moment she left I drove here."

"What lady?" said Mrs. Milbanke.

• And then Philip remembered that the entire story of the mysterious lady of the opera was between himself and Chetwynd—and of course Chetwynd's wife. You tell a man something he is not to repeat to anyone, not even to his wife; he gives you his word, and keeps it, no doubt, as a rule, except in regard to the pledge not to tell his wife. Philip did not quite know why he had not told the story to his dear friends the Milbankes. Perhaps he had not had time; perhaps he thought Mrs. Milbanke would talk too much about it. He had it in his mind to tell Dolly on the night when he proposed to her, but for some reason or other he did not.

"The lady whom I thought I saw at the opera," Philip replied, "and whose face gave me the idea for the sketch of 'Tragedy.' Did I not tell you?"

"No," said Mrs. Milbanke, pursing up her little mouth and waiting for further explanation.

"Well, there was not much to tell. I saw a remarkable face at the opera; it gave me an idea for the picture. Chetwynd found the original. She was at his wife's At Home. She consented to give me a sitting."

"Yes?" said Mrs. Milbanke, "and so you could not come and see Dolly; nor send a telegram nor a letter, nor a bouquet, nor anything; and have we the pleasure of knowing the lady?"

"I think not. She is a Russian countess—Lady Stravensky."

"The woman we met at Lady Marchmount's—that was the name; I mentioned her to you the day we met at the studio; the foreign woman who smoked cigarettes, an adventuress I should imagine."

"I don't think so," said Philip, "but whatever she is, her face is a wonderful study."

"No doubt," said Mrs. Milbanke.

"She is received at the Russian Embassy."

"And at Mr. Philip Forsyth's studio," retorted Mrs. Milbanke.

"And why not?" asked Philip, "surely you do not think——"

"Don't ask me what I think or I may tell you and we might both be sorry afterwards; I love my sister Dolly, and know how good and sweet and forgiving and gentle she is; and it grieves me to see her miserable; it is something new, terribly new, to see her cry; this is one of the happiest households in the world, Mr. Forsyth: but yesterday and to-day we have been all of us positively wretched."

Here Mrs. Milbanke began "to give way" as she afterwards told Walter, for Philip did look so mournfully apologetic that she could not find it in her heart to continue the attack.

"And all this on my account," he said, and it must be admitted he was truly sorry. "Believe me I am deeply grieved; I hope you will not think I am trying to make an excuse when I say Dolly was not out of my thoughts; for all the time I have been thinking of my work and doing it, my ambition was engaged as much on her account as my own. And I was anxious to make my arrangements for our trip to Venice."

"I told Dolly," said Mrs. Milbanke, now laying down her sceptre and sinking gracefully into a chair, "that you could not fail to have a proper explanation; but she is a sensitive girl, and of course she very much expected to see you yesterday. I was going to your mother's when you were announced. If you will bring Dolly I will send the carriage back for you."

"I shall be delighted," said Philip.

Whereupon Jennie went upstairs to her sister, who, much engrossed with a popular authoress' last novel, had for the time being forgotten her own troubles in those of a romantic hero, who, despite his Oriental palace and his many conquests amongst princesses and beauties of the purest blood, married and otherwise, was unhappy on account of some village maiden who had unconsciously made a hot and fierce onslaught upon his hitherto un-touched sensibilities.

"You must come down, my darling," said Jennie, "Philip is here, very contrite, awfully unhappy; he has been very busy on a work which he hopes to finish in order to be able to get away with us next week. I talked to him rather severely, but I am sorry now, because he is so sorry. Come down, dear; I will go on to his mother's and he will bring you; he looks very handsome."

Dolly laid aside her novel; got up from her luxurious little couch, which was quite a decoration at the foot of her dainty little bed; looked at herself in a convenient mirror; the investigation was satisfactory, both to herself and to her sister; and might have been to any male connoisseur of female beauty. Soft, rosy cheeks, a wealth of silken hair, a round undulating figure, the lovely lines of which were indicated in the graceful folds of a flowing muslin tea-gown.

" How long will it take you to dress ? "

" Half-an-hour."

" Then Philip shall escort me to Lady Forsyth's and return for you, he need not go in."

" I ventured to ask your mother one day when I was in an inquisitive mood, why she insists upon living in Gower-street," said Mrs. Milbanke, when the brougham was rolling quietly upon its rubber tires by the north side of Regent's Park, and making its way through the north gate and along by the Zoo, " one of the ugliest—not to say the most unfashionable of streets."

" And what did she say ? " Philip asked, anxious to take an interest in any subject which Mrs. Milbanke might consider worthy of discussion.

" Because her house at a hundred and fifty a year was worth six of the Mayfair houses at three or four times the rent, and because she had bought the lease, and further-more because she liked the house, and furthermore still— you know your mother's graphic manner—because a fashionable neighborhood is not necessary to a woman who can bring fashion to her rooms wherever they may be."

" My dear mother has a great opinion of her social position," said Philip, " and the best people so-called and certainly the most interesting do go to see her."

" That's true," said Mrs. Milbanke, " but I have not told you all she said ; she asked me what I meant by liv-ing in St. John's Wood—did I call that a fashionable local-ity ? I said if it was good enough in the past for Landseer, George Eliot, Douglas Jerrold, Charles Dickens, and in the present for an old lady friend of Her Majesty's, half-a-dozen R.A.'s, and no end of literary men of the first mag-

nitude, not to mention bankers and divines, it was good
enough for the wife of a mere city solicitor."

And thus, after sundry discussions of an equally momentous character, Philip and his prospective sister-in-law drifted into the very smallest of small talk, which was happily
brought to an end very quickly, for Walter Milbanke's
horses were as good as his wines and his dinners, Walter
priding himself on having everything of the best.

When Mrs. Milbanke made her way through Lady
Forsyth's crowded hall to the drawing-room, Philip Forsyth in a somewhat perturbed state of mind was driven
back to Westbury Lodge.   He hardly felt master of himself; a strong consciousness of the claims of duty took
possession of him.   He had proposed to Dolly; Dolly
was a beautiful girl, she might easily make a much better
match.   His mother liked her very much.   Mrs. Milbanke
was a kind, genial woman, devoted to Dolly.   Walter Milbanke was a good fellow.   They were well-to-do, and they
paid him much respect.   Chetwynd had said Philip
needed the anchorage of marriage ; and after all the Countess Stravensky was a strange creature, with no doubt a
remarkable career.   She went about in a queer way with a
private secretary, who was a very cut-throat looking person ;
and she was Philip's senior by several years.   He admitted
to himself that she exercised a strange fascination over
him ; but why did he admit this ?   Why did he think about
her at all beyond the realm of art, any more than he would
think of any other good subject ?   He asked himself these
questions in a desultory kind of way, and shuddered with a
pleasant thrill as he thought of her kissing him ; but this
was followed by an unpleasant kind of feeling that there
was something motherly or sisterly, or merely friendly in
her kiss and in her farewell, nothing suggestive of passion
or of love except in the abstract.   She had said " Good-
bye ; " she had treated him as if he were a memory, not a

living entity. As he thought in this wise his mind began
to take a cynical view of what had happened ; " she kissed
me for someone else, kissed me because I reminded her
of someone she had known when a girl, or that some other
girl had known ; " Let me kiss him for his mother " —the
song ran through his brain with a laugh, as if the thought
had been bracketed with the word *Laughter*, as the re-
porters put it in their chronicles of funny speeches.
Indeed Philip felt himself in a very bewildered state of
mind, inclined at one moment to make fun of himself and
his aspirations, then to fall under the influence of the pale
face and the red-gold hair, and finally to stretch out mental and physical arms towards Dolly and Duty. The
alliteration of the words struck him, Dolly and Duty, and
he smiled. He was mentally intoxicated. He hated himself for having behaved inconsiderately to Dolly, who had
been so deliciously kind to him only two nights previously,
and to whom he had pledged a life's devotion. He felt
that he had deserved all that Mrs. Milbanke had said in
his disparagement, and all indeed she had not said, but
had hinted at ; and sitting by her side with her sensuous
perfume still clinging about him, the consciousness of her
pretty dresses and in her soothingly luxurious atmosphere,
and remembering that Dolly was almost ten years younger
and ten times prettier, and with soft round arms and pout-
ing red lips, and hair like the richest yellow silk, he tried
to snap his fingers .at the poetic, intellectual, Oriental
beauty of the strange foreign woman who for a few hours
had threatened to fill his very soul with her violet eyes
and her stately figure and her red-gold hair.

It is quite questionable after all if Dick Chetwynd was
right in advising Philip to get married. And it was equally
questionable whether Dolly Norcott was the woman for
such an erratic and unstable nature as Philip's seemed to
be. Philip's was an emotional nature, liable to fall under

evanescent influences. He was imaginative, had mixed
ideas of duty, a longing ambition, was proud, had thoughts
that were the outcome of momentary influences, good
impulses but a short memory for them. He had one great
redeeming quality—industry ; but for this he might have
been classed among the geniuses who are content to dream,
the geniuses who only lack for success the spur of industry.
If the narrator of these adventures believed in the evil eye
or in interposition of some supernaturally evil factor in a
young man's life, he would declare that the face at the
Opera had for Philip the evil eye under whose influence he
would fall and suffer ; but that is perhaps only because
one has to record what appears to be a strange, sudden
change in the young man's conduct and destiny from the
moment he saw the face of the Countess Stravensky at the
Opera ; anyhow it is certain that when the shadow of the
Countess Stravensky fell upon the life of Philip Forsyth
he became another being, and probably Richard Chetwynd
might say " and all the better for Philip Forsyth," since
the inspiration of. the face at the Opera had given the
young fellow's art just the touch of imagination it needed,
just the idea of purpose and intention which had made it
for the first time in the opinion of Chetwynd a tremendous
reality of promise.

As the brougham glided along that most wearisome and
monotonous of all London thoroughfares, Albany-street,
Philip recalled what Mrs. Milbanke had said about the
foreign lady who smoked cigarettes at Lady Marchmount's,
and then for the twentieth time he wondered what could be
the meaning of Lady Marchmount professing to ignore the
countess' presence in her box on that memorable night
at the Opera. For the twentieth time he went over the
whole of the circumstances ; and for the twentieth time
came to the conclusion that there must be some feud between the countess and the young wife of the Russian

General Petronovitch, whose name he had noticed in the papers that very morning, by the way, as the representative whom Russia in a semi-official way was sending to Venice, to be present at the function, on which occasion Venice was to put on some of her ancient glories, gondolas of past centuries, so far as decoration was concerned, gondoliers in all the glories of the greatest days of the Queen of the Adriatic. Russia was not willing, it appeared, to let England and Germany have it all their own way even with Italy; and in that gorgeous procession of boats was to be a barge belonging to General Petronovitch, and probably a military and civic staff. At least that is what the papers said. Philip hoped he might be there to see; and how could he see the show in better company than that of Dolly and her sister and Walter Milbanke, who knew Venice, and would be sure to do the thing as it should be done?

If Philip had been confronted with this mixture of prosaic, artistic, worldly, and incongruous interpretation of his multifarious reflections and thoughts as he drove from Gower-street to St. John's Wood, he would probably have denied the correctness of the report; but much as it might have surprised and perhaps annoyed him, it would nevertheless have been perfectly true; therefore, in your estimate of the character of Philip Forsyth, do not forget this somewhat inconsequential record of his state of mind on this notable day.

CHAPTER XXV.

THE PATIENCE, HOPE, AND PRACTICAL PHILOSOPHY
OF SAM SELWYN.

EARLY spring sunshine was making pretty lacelike shadows upon the dusty roadway, as the Milbanke brougham
emerged into the picturesque thoroughfare by the Zoo.
Presently it drew aside to permit a royal cavalcade to pass.
Her Majesty was paying her usual visit to her old friend,
mentioned by Mrs. Milbanke in her defence of St. John's
Wood. No sooner was the Queen in town for a day or
two than her carriage with its escort was seen in Regent's
Park and St. John's Wood.

It was a bright, inspiring day. Philip with the remembrance of Dolly and that strong determination of duty in
his mind felt the influence of the Russian shadow slipping
away from him ; though if he had cared to be perfectly
frank with himself he would have had to acknowledge that
his sudden realization of the claims of duty had something
to do with exorcism of the pale face and the red-gold hair.

When he arrived at Westbury Lodge he found Dolly
waiting for him in the little morning room. How lovely
she looked ! You might have asked Philip how she was
dressed and he could not have told you. She seemed to
him like the embodiment of the day, floral, fresh, sunny and
sweet. Whether she wore a bonnet or a hat, what was
the color of her gown, would have been questions as difficult to him as abstruse points in Algebra ; but the general
effect was a dream of English girlhood, sunny hair, soft,
glowing cheeks, red lips, arched like Cupid's bow, and

when she spoke a musical voice that had nothing in it but forgiveness and love, and no other suggestion than a desire to be amiable and happy. He felt the contrast between this and his intercourse with the Lady Stravensky, as a restful, calm delight.

Dolly submitted to be kissed, and accepted Philip's apologies with a pretty smile, saying, " Oh, it did not matter." Of course she had thought when people were engaged that —but she would say nothing, Jennie had said quite enough she was sure, and it was all her fault for taking it to heart. " And I did somehow take it to heart," she went on, " but I am spoiled, Jennie spoils me, Walter spoils me, and I expected you would; perhaps it is as well—besides it is a mistake not to allow each other a little freedom, is it not ? "

" So long as you allow me the freedom to love you with all my heart," said Philip, kissing her again, " that is enough for me," and in saying so he said exactly what he thought at the moment, his ecstasy being enhanced by a responsive embrace that blotted out every thought of the Countess Stravensky, her violet eyes, red-gold hair and all ; for in the matter of beauty, for pleasant companionship, to live with, to go to receptions with, to have at a young man's side, to make other young men envious of, Dolly Norcott could, to quote Sam Selwyn, give any other girl in all the wide world as many points as the severest handicapper could desire and beat her by miles !

Poor Selwyn, he had made it a point to be at Lady Forsyth's At Home ; he had long been on her ladyship's visiting list ; and an off day on the Stock Exchange and other considerations drove him to Gower-street. Moreover he hoped to meet Mrs. Milbanke and her sister. He had heard of the engagement between Philip and Dolly almost as soon as he was awake the next morning, but he had no intention of resenting it. He had not proposed to Dolly, therefore he had no grievance. He liked Walter Milbanke, and occasionally did business with him. He enjoyed Mrs. Milbanke's little parties; and he loved Dolly devotedly; why, therefore, should he give the Milbankes reason to fight shy of him? No, he would continue the friendship if they would let him. He could not help thinking Philip a bit of a snob; but for Dolly's sake he would try and like him. Besides, there is many a slip betwixt the cup and the lip; the safest stock would occasionally collapse. Nothing was certain except settling day; even that had a bright side to it now and then; and he determined to keep alive just for his own smoking, as he called it, his fancy for Dolly Norcott.

The fellows at the City Club where Sam was lunching with these reflections in his mind, while Dolly and Jennie were having their after-breakfast discussion, gave Sam credit for a very different line of thought from that which engaged him. It was known that he had made what they called a haul in nitrate rails and primitivas. A genial, clever, merry fellow, Sam had attracted the friendly notice of the master of those stocks, who over a chop and a bottle of Roederer had confided to Sam certain information upon which the young broker had acted with a lively faith and a firm hand, which had had remarkable results.

"Just bought an estate in Surrey, I hear," said Cordiner. "Well, I congratulate you."

"I've had one in Spain any time this ten years," said Sam. "It won't run to Surrey."

"There is no fellow going whose good luck is less envied than yours, Sam."

"And you?" said Sam, looking up from his simple repast and contemplating his suave, genial, well-fed, clean-shaven, fashionably-dressed friend.

"Oh!" said Cordiner, "if my doctor did not interfere with my champagne, and Providence invented for one's
13

sins a less severe form of punishment than gout, I should be the happiest man alive."

"You are married?"

"Rather," said Cordiner; "happy, though married, as the bookstalls have it."

"I am a bachelor," said Sam, and the information vouchsafed on both sides was not so much out of place in the conversation of City friends as might at first appear; it is common enough in the City of London for men to know each other intimately within the shadow of the Stock Exchange, and even at certain West End clubs, without having the smallest knowledge of each other's domestic relations.

"Then you don't want the estate in Surrey at present," said Cordiner—"no good without a wife."

"I suppose not," said Sam, "unless——"

"No, no, don't do that, old chap; no fun to be got out of that."

"No?" said Sam, his thoughts running in quite a different direction from those of Cordiner.

"None; morality pays, my boy; requires a bit of a struggle; perhaps some experience; but in regard to women it comes within the proverb about honesty being the best policy."

"I dare say," said Sam, who by this time had come to the cheese and to a consideration of which frock-coat he would wear for the Forsyth afternoon, and how long it would take him to get home and dress; and he wondered if Dolly would be there, and what she would say to him, how she would receive him; how Philip would treat him —haughtily, of course. The conquering hero game and all that; well, he did not care—he was not going to allow himself to be shut out of a corner of Paradise because he could not range all over it.

"Are you off?" said Cordiner, who had made some other remark to Sam which had not been answered.

" Yes."

" You are wool-gathering a little, eh ? "

" Am I ? " said Sam.

" Yes, you are," replied Cordiner, ordering " a pint of the driest there is in the club ; speak to the steward, send him to me, that's the best thing, there's a brut of eighty or something of that kind, I think——"

While Cordiner was thus trying to defend himself as much as possible from the penalty of his favorite sin, Sam had said, " Good-morning, old fellow," and a few minutes later was bowling away to his chambers in Sackville-street. And very pleasant chambers they were! Four rooms—three for himself, one for his man, Devereux, a calm, serious, quiet man of forty, looked sixty, and might have lived all his life with a bishop.

" Morning frock, white vest, grey trousers," said the master.

" Yes, sir," said Devereux.

" White silk tie, usual boots."

" Yes, sir," said Devereux.

" The brougham at four to the minute."

" Yes, sir," said Devereux.

" That's all."

" Thank you, sir," said Devereux.

They were, indeed, very pleasant chambers—not your usual kind of bachelor chambers, decorated with pictures of ballet-girls, or studies from Etty, or racehorses, or illustrations of prize-fights, or pictures of yachts, but good, common-sense, respectable rooms : a dining-room, furnished in light oak, with a dado to match, a few paintings by the best modern masters, a cabinet for wines and spirits, a couple of old arm-chairs, an oak over-mantel, with a few nice specimens of Nankin blue, and on the polished floor a thick Turkey carpet. The adjoining room was arranged for smoking and cards ; not that there was much play at any time in Selwyn's rooms, but his friends liked a hand at whist or poker, and he believed in making them comfortable.   He had keys for every-thing—his cigar cabinet, his cards, his counters, his spirits; he was business-like—not that he did not trust Devereux, who kept in a special cupboard a reserve of spirits, wines and cigars, but Sam liked his bunch of keys; they were, with their bright chain, a form of personal decoration : the chain represented a sort of male chatelain when he thrust his hands into his pockets on dress occa-sions, and he rattled it and his keys with something of a housekeeper's pride.

There were a few cards stuck in his over-mantel—private views of pictures, two or three At Homes, invita-tions to smoking concerts; and prominent among the society cards, as Sam called them, was Lady Forsyth's Every Wednesday Afternoon in May and June.

"Quite ready, sir," said Devereux, in his ecclesiastical manner.

"Thank you," said Sam, retiring to his bedroom, the very model of a sleeping apartment, with a spacious bath-room beyond.

What could a fellow like Sam Selwyn want with a wife while he possessed all these luxuries and privileges—such a servant as Devereux, who had never been known to be in drink or out of temper, and with an improving business, a growing balance at his banker's, and financial prospects generally of the rosiest.

These questions in a vague way presented themselves to Sam as he began to dress for Lady Forsyth's At Home; they occurred to him probably because the prospect of his having a wife now seemed further off than ever; as his means had increased—just, indeed, as he could afford with a clear conscience to have said to Dolly Norcott, "Be mine"—she had drifted further away, nay, right

away from him ; she had engaged herself to be married to
another, and the match was considered to be a good one
all round. 。

"And yet, somehow," he said to himself, "I don't say
die ; might as well, of course ; to hope is like locking up
stock that you know is as dead as last week's quotations
with a view to the future ; may look up some day ; do to
leave in one's will as a possible asset, or to schedule in
bankruptcy, as Cordiner would say, when he is chaffing
old Smudger—might swell out the figures—unrealized
assets : unrealizable would be the right description.
Lucky at cards, unlucky in love ; can't have luck all
ways ; if I'd busted perhaps I should, in my despair, have
proposed and been accepted. No accounting for what's
going to happen in this world ; don't know as one can
either bull or bear the next, for that matter. Suppose I
mustn't complain ; I never ax'd her, sir, she said ; and
Fortune has favored me up yonder on 'Change. Cheer
up, Sam, don't let your spirits go down, there's many a
gal as you knows well—no, confound it, that's vulgar ;
I'm losing my grip ; hate those horrid comic, bragging
masher songs ; wouldn't have Devereux hear me chant a
thing like that for a fiver ; and I was thinking of Miss
Norcott, too ; Sam, what are you about ? The fact is, I
am not the kind of fellow for a girl like that ! Forsyth
has style ; handsome chap, too ; knows how to put on
side ; then his mother has a title ; he hasn't, that's one
thing ; father only a knight after all ; no better than Tom
Wylie ; no better than Vinous Harry ; I could get to be
Sir Samuel in time, if I liked ; easy enough, only give
your mind, and your stomach, to it in the City, Sir
Samuel Selwyn. Well, my forbears were swells down
in Yorkshire ; I shouldn't disgrace them ; perhaps I
should. Cordiner says one is most distinguished not to
be Sir This or That. Old Smudger would call me Sir

Samivel; but for all that my wife in the West End would
be Lady Selwyn; and after all that's the only good of a
title; it's either for the missus or the boy; at least in the
case of real grit; as for the Snooters who get titles up in
the City—well, but it is all right; surely, I am not making
a grievance of it; and as for Sir Richard Smyth, Sir Harry
Dane and those other two fellows who sprang up the
other day out of fish and fruit into knighthoods, they are
very good fellows after all."

"Carriage at the door, sir," said Devereux.

"Thanks," Sam replied. "My coat all right, Devereux?"

"Yes, sir," said Devereux, hitching up the collar and
pulling it down again with a professional air. "Good fitting
coat, sir."

"That's all right," said the master. "Shall dine at the
club."

"Yes, sir."

"Ready to dress at seven."

"Yes, sir."

CHAPTER XXVI.

LADY FORSYTH AT HOME.

AND half an hour later Samuel Selwyn, Esquire, looking
his very best, shook hands with Lady Forsyth, in a darkened room, and surrounded by a delightful mixture of
Somebodies and Nobodies, guests from Mayfair, and
callers from Brixton. Sam felt quite an important person
when he encountered little Lomas, the author of "City
Notes" in the *Society Snapper*, and who every Friday
made a point of looking Sam up for "a few financial hints,
don't you know." Little Lomas was quite conspicuous
on this occasion. "Made five and twenty," thought Sam,

" out of the Automaton shares which old Smudger let him have, carrying a little premium before allotment."

Little Lomas, however, represented the smallest of the Nobodies at Lady Forsyth's ; and the next moment Mr. Selwyn was struck, not with the apparition of a certain famous statesman, whom his enemies call a mere politician, but with the real genuine Simon Pure himself, and evidently in one of those amiable moods, about which newspaper interviewers wax eloquent. The great man was talking to Miss Spofforth, the new tragedienne fresh from the United States, at whose first appearance he had most kindly assisted. He was telling her to the delight of several listeners how much he admired America, how deeply he regretted he had not been able to visit that country, what pleasure it gave him to know that he had many good friends there, and so on.

Sam felt that it was not quite *comme il faut* to stand by and listen, but he could not help it ; and he was very much interested when the hostess ventured to introduce his Excellency Signor Ferrari to the illustrious statesman. Why Ferrari was his Excellency did not transpire, but Lady Forsyth was lavish with courteous titles and complimentary distinctions. The name of Ferrari set the statesman's mind traveling from America to Italy ; but Ferrari promptly turned the conversation to the Russian news of the day, with its startling details of a military conspiracy just unearthed by the police, and developing extraordinary ramifications. Ferrari, considering that he referred to himself as an old-fashioned loyalist, did not seem to speak of the affair with very great regret ; he even said that it might be a good thing to bring the Young Russian agitation to a head, so that once for all Europe should be relieved of the everlasting threat of a great Russian upheaval. The famous statesman replied with both frankness and caution, expressing sympathy with the Czar, but at the

same time regretting that the Emperor did not see his way
to give his people a Constitution. Oddly enough the
next day all this and much more appeared as the result of
an informal chat at a dinner party with an illustrious
statesman, and was quoted in a London evening paper.
Little Lomas had thus easily capitalized his excursion from
Brixton to Gower-street; and what did he care about the
protest of a high-minded London journal against the pub-
lication of private conversation? Or for that matter what
did anybody else care?

Lady Forsyth might well be proud of her afternoons,
of the one under notice in particular. The Hon. Member
for Blodgetts-in-the-Marsh brought his wife, who is supposed to inspire the smartest of the personal articles in
his clever journal of *Chat and Opinion.* He seemed to
be in unusually good spirits, and attended the distinguished
statesman to his carriage, chatting all the while about a
certain Party resolution which was to shake the Government on the following day.

The famous statesman did not stay long with Lady
Forsyth. When he was gone there was time to look
around and make note of the other celebrities, which, by
the way, was being done with a critical eye by Mr. Lucien
Lightfoot of the *Social and Political Review,* which he
represents with a deep sense of its importance and circu-
lation. Mr. Lightfoot has the run of the highest society,
not alone as a journalist, but for his own sweet sake; he
gives At Homes himself on a large scale, and is in the
confidence of no end of Society people, who seek his
advice as to " the right thing to do, don't you know," on
certain occasions. Since the eminent Mr. Jenkins, of the
Post, joined the majority, and the journal of the upper
circles went down into the ranks of the Conservative
Democracy, no newspaper man has made so distinguished
a mark in Mayfair as Mr. Lightfoot, a past master in the

modern art of Society journalism. He is not only a
famous paragraphist, but in his social records knows exactly where to draw the line. "There are At Homes and
At Homes," he said to Selwyn. "One does not care to
meet Little Lomas nor to be hobnobbing with the Member for Ballyraggan, but Lady Forsyth leavens the stodgy
lump of mediocrity with blood and distinction;" and if
you had read Lightfoot's account of the Forsyth At Home
you would have come to the conclusion that the company
consisted of the most ultramarine of the aristocracy. He
knew how to give the affair sufficient tone for the *Review*.
In Lightfoot's narrative the great statesman came with his
intellectual and charming wife ; the Duchess of Malapert
brought her niece, the Hon. Miss Stannyward, whose contributions to the fiction of the year had lifted her at a
bound into the foremost ranks of lady novelists ; the Misses
Flaherty wore delicious Empire gowns. The calm eyes
of the Irish leader surveyed the scene with interest, except
when he was comparing notes with his friend the American
essayist, who had just arrived in London from cultured
Boston. The Russian came with his handsome mother ;
several members of the Chinese embassy were present ;
Miss Rollin, the Shakesperian reciter, gave Portia's speech
with much classic correctness, and Mr. Garrick Macready
electrified the company with "The Spanish Mother ;" Sir
Peter and Lady Freame, fresh from the Royal function at
Windsor, put in a brief but welcome appearance ; and on
the other hand the latest political thorn in the side of the
Government, Mr. Stewart Montrose Morency, and his
sister, the founder of the Home for Distressed Socialists,
was welcomed by the hostess with her well-known Cosmopolitan views of the world, of society, and politics.
And so on ; it is an education in the ways and peculiarities
of society, artistic, Bohemian and Royal, to read Mr.
Lightfoot's accounts of men and things in the *Review*.

Lady Forsyth, in a grey Irish poplin, was ubiquitous, and it must be confessed that she was a very agreeable hostess. Selwyn wandered about more at his ease with Philip Forsyth than with Dolly Norcott. He thought Dolly tried to avoid him; he was sure Philip did; but he was not in the humor to be avoided by anybody who, as he said, *was* anybody.

"Will you forgive me for saying you look charming?" he said to Dolly, with whom after several efforts he was enabled to have a word.

"I would forgive you for even saying something much more disagreeable," said Dolly, in her liveliest manner.

"Then forgive me for congratulating you—of course, I am delighted at anything that pleases you, or Walter, or Mrs. Milbanke; but of course every young fellow in London will be jealous."

"What are you trying to say, my dear Mr. Selwyn?" Dolly asked, knowing, of course, exactly what he was trying to say.

"I was trying to congratulate you on your engagement to Mr. Forsyth," he answered.

"Oh, thank you," she said, slightly discomfitted at Sam's prompt reply.

"Of course, he is the one to be congratulated," he went on, wondering all the time at his own temerity.

"I hope so," said Dolly, defiantly. "You seem to think it a good joke."

"It is no joke for your other admirers."

"Nor to Mr. Forsyth, nor to me, Mr. Selwyn," said Dolly, drawing herself up to her full height and passing on.

"There now, what a fool I am," said Sam to himself. "I have offended her; determined to be bold I have over-done it, I suppose. Here comes her sister, I'll apologize. Awfully sorry," he said to Jenny, "I think I have offended your sister. I was trying to congratulate her, you know ; and I think I was too frivolous, as your good husband, Walter, would say."

" I am sure you did not mean to offend her," said Jenny, " and therefore she must not be offended."

" Will you say to her if there is anyone in the world it would break my heart to offend it is Miss Norcott ; except, perhaps, her charming sister, Mrs. Milbanke."

" I am sure of it," said Jenny.

" Besides, my dear Mrs. Milbanke, I will confess to you, strictly between ourselves ; but perhaps I had better not."

" Oh yes, do by all means, you may confide in me ; let us retreat to Lady Forsyth's Rosamond's bower, as she calls it, where you may give me a cup of tea and your per-fect confidence, will you ? "

Yes, he would and did, and Jenny was very much in-terested.

" The truth is, my dear Mrs. Milbanke, if something had happened last week that happened yesterday I should have been daring enough, impertinent enough I ought to say, to have proposed myself to Dolly—I can't help call-ing her Dolly when I think of it."

" Yes ? " said Jenny encouragingly.

" But I could not, alas ! offer her a week ago what I could to-day ! "

' Yes? " said the sweet little insinuating voice of Mrs. Milbanke.

" Last week I was only worth a couple a thousand a year from my business—my vulgar business I fear you will say—but business is business, and England has made her name and fame by it, and her greatness after all is business."

" Yes ? " repeated the still small voice of Mrs. Milbanke.

" And to-day I have in addition to that two thousand a year a good solid thirty thousand pounds."

"Then Nitrates have turned up trumps, as you city men say," remarked Jenny.

"They have," said Sam, "and next week they may land me another thirty thousand for all I know, and I have not a single losing investment; but to-day, unfortunately, is this week, not last, eh, Mrs. Milbanke?"

"You are a very good fellow, Mr. Selwyn, and we shall always be glad to see you at Westbury Lodge."

"And you will apologize to Dolly for me, won't you?"

"I include Dolly, when I say we shall always be glad to see you at Westbury Lodge. I must go and speak to Lady Forsyth. Good-bye, if we don't meet again; we are going soon." She gave him her hand. "Walter always said you would get on. You are cautious and clever. I congratulate you on your good fortune. Come and see us soon; we must always be good friends."

"Thank you, Mrs. Milbanke," said Selwyn, pressing the plump, generous little hand.

And both drifted away in different directions. Selwyn found himself hushed into silence while a lady of the opera sang a mournful love song that made him feel lonely, and Mrs. Milbanke hurried to Dolly to tell her what Selwyn had said. Dolly remarked that she was very glad to hear of Mr. Selwyn's good fortune; she should always take an interest in him; she was not in the least offended at what he had said; she had turned away from him because she thought it was the right thing to do; but she really felt complimented, because it was clear that he envied Philip.

"And Philip?" said Jenny.

"Oh, he is very good, awfully penitent, says he never saw me look so lovely, is quite ready for Venice or anywhere else so long as I am there, his apparent neglect was really anxiety for his art because he wants to be worthy of me, and indeed he was ever so good, he has gone to be presented to one of his mother's foreign friends. Why, here is Walter!"

And sure enough Walter had hurried from his city office and driven straight to Gower-street.

"Thought I would like to come," he said, "was bothered about Forsyth; has he turned up?"

"Oh, yes," said Jenny, "came to bring us here, was full of apologies. I talked to him like a sister."

"And he replied like a brother," rejoined Walter, in his comedy-dialogue fashion.

"He did," said Jenny.

"And all is well, eh?"

"Yes."

"That's right. Where is he?"

"Talking to the Baron Von Something, who has just arrived from Berlin."

"The Berlin-gloved old gentleman with the collars and the glasses?"

"Yes."

"I see. He must come to dinner, and we will settle the Italian business: I would like you to be ready by Monday."

"We are ready now," said Mrs. Jenny, "have been ready this three weeks."

"Of course, of course," said Walter, "but Philip wasn't ready; he's ready now, eh?"

"Oh, yes, quite," said Dolly.

"Very well, then; we'll be off at once."

"Not this minute?"

"No, next week. Oh, yonder is Selwyn; must speak to him; he has made a fortune since we saw him last— yesterday, in fact. But here is Philip. Ah, Forsyth, my dear fellow, glad to see you; how well you look! Will you dine with us to-night *en famille*—a very real phrase to you now at Westbury Lodge—and go over our Italian route, eh? We propose to start on Monday; we shall be in time for the royal function we were talking of the other day; something too tremendously gorgeous even in the history of Venice; have got our rooms all right; quite a favor, but the hotel people knew us. Can you be ready?"

"Oh, yes," said Philip.

"We shall stay in Paris a few days; so if you have any little arrangements to make at the last moment, you can join us at the Grand, eh?"

Walter was full of the trip, and so delighted to find things all right again between Philip and his girls, as he called the sisters, that he went on talking out of sheer exuberance of spirits.

CHAPTER XXVII.

PHILIP'S LOVE FOR DOLLY.

"YOUR countess left London for Paris this morning, *en route* for St. Petersburg," said Lady Forsyth to Philip, when her last guest had departed and they were sitting down to a quiet cup of tea together. "Her secretary, Signor Ferrari, was here; did you see him?"

"No."

"I introduced him to the famous statesman."

"Indeed. He is the man Chetwynd talked so much about; always in attendance, I understood."

"I believe so; but all rules have their exceptions."

"Who and what is this countess, mother?" Philip asked.

"A very remarkable woman," Lady Forsyth replied; "has the *entrée* into the very best society, political and otherwise: curiously fascinating, is she not?"

"Has she a mission?" Philip asked, without noticing his mother's question.

" Probably."

" Why did Lady Marchmount say she was not in her box when she was ? "

" Don't ask me conundrums : at the same time, my dear boy, let me tell you that I would not believe Lady Marchmount on her oath ; they are a self-seeking lot, the Marchmounts ; they could make nothing of loyalty and Toryism and that kind of business, so they came over to us, and now they out-Herod Herod in their intrigues and pro-fessed ambitions."

" Then they might be taking hand in a Nihilist plot ? "

" They would not mind engaging their dirty hands in anything," said Lady Forsyth, with a tone of unsup-pressed contempt.

" But the countess is a staunch Russian of the old *régime*."

" Is she ? " asked Lady Forsyth.

" Is she not? " was Philip's rejoinder.

" What is it to you or me, Philip dear, what she is ? For the moment she is interesting, has had a romantic career, is beautiful, has sat to you ; for heaven's sake, let us be content. If you ask me what sort of a woman it is who has such a secretary as Ferrari, I should say she might be anything—a Nihilistic adventuress, or a duchess who loves curiosities."

" Whatever she is, mother, depend upon it she is a high-minded and noble· woman, and if she had devoted herself to some great act of national duty that might involve her life, I should not be surprised."

" I hope she has not inspired my dear boy with some romantic fancy," said Lady Forsyth. " In the first place, she is ten years your elder ; in the next place, she has been married twice ; how often she may have been divorced, who can say ? "

Philip felt the color come into his checks at the suggestion that the countess had made an undue impression upon him, which did not escape his mother's notice.

"She is not more than thirty," he said; "but whatever she may be, surely there is no harm in taking an interest in her."

"Not at all. One may take an interest in a baboon, or in the Irish secretary; but these Russian princesses, these Polish countesses, these Jewesses, who marry old lords and play at politics, regal or democratic, are women to be wary of; you are in their trap before you know where you are."

"Yes, mother, I quite understand. I was only seeking information, not warnings."

"Very well, my dear, you have got both, and I hope they will do you good. You know how I love you; there is no one in the world who can give such good advice and information as mine; and in the matter of information, my dear Philip, you will be glad to hear that you are to take me with you this evening to dine at Westbury Lodge."

"Delighted," said Philip.

"Mrs. Milbanke confided to me that there had been just the suspicion of a little misunderstanding; and when I tell you that I saw the shadow of the Countess Stravensky in the affair, you will not be surprised at my venturing to warn you."

"Has Mrs. Milbanke been talking me over, then?"

"Not at all: what she said sprang out of a remark of mine, and her reply was quite natural and spontaneous."

"But it was rather in censure of me, was it not?"

"No, it cannot be put in that manner. She hinted at lovers' quarrels."

"Nonsense," said Philip; "we have had no quarrel."

"The countess had detained you, and she was alone with you at the studio?"

"Of course she was."

" Did you do much work, Phil?" his mother asked, with a humorous twinkle in her eye.

" Not much," said Philip, smiling in spite of himself.

" You talked a good deal, I make no doubt."

" We had some conversation, of course.'

" She has wonderful eyes?"

" She has!"

" And hair that Titian might have painted—you said so last night?"

" It is true."

" And her voice, a sympathetic voice—eh? I know you, Philip; your father was just the same : he admired red hair and violet eyes, and had as sharp an instinct for a pretty woman as any man in the world, God rest him, and one of the kindest fellows that ever broke bread."

" Of course he had an eye for beauty, mother," said Philip, rising from his chair by her side, taking her face in both his hands, and kissing her heartily.

" Well, that's all I've got to say," went on his mother, after kissing him in return, " except that I think Miss Norcott the most desirable match you could possibly make—sweet, pretty, admires you, and a good income well invested and securely settled. If your father had settled the whole of his fortune on me before he lost half of it on that horrid exhibition, we would not have had to consider these vulgar questions of money. I only wish I could go to Italy with you, but I am glad you are going, it puts an end at all events to the possibility of any non-sense in that Russian quarter. I should hate a Russian alliance, just as much as the English Parliament would, even if you had not to change your religion for it ; if I am not much mistaken,the countess is a Jewess, and if the Forsyths cling to anything, it has always been—so your poor father told me—to their Protestant faith."

" Yes, of course," said Philip, but the fact of his mother

14

making so much of the countess also set the young man
thinking about her afresh, and with just a scintillation of
something like a chivalric sense of duty in regard to the
defence of persons accused in their absence.

But when he gave an arm to Dolly and an arm to Mrs.
Milbanke, and followed his mother and Walter in to
dinner soon afterwards at Westbury Lodge, he was quite
at his ease again, and the countess might have been in
Paris or St. Petersburg or anywhere else for all he cared;
you see it was rather a convenient disposition, Philip's;
and yet he had the quality of constancy too, no doubt,
once it was fairly invoked.

Dolly, in the daintiest of dinner gowns, considered with
due regard to the tone and style of her sister's dress, and
also taking into artistic account the surrounding decorations, looked divine.   Mrs. Milbanke was in her best
form.   Walter was genial as host could possibly be; and
Lady Forsyth, in black Irish poplin (she was mindful of
her country in everything she did, thought, or wore), with
her emeralds and her shamrock, a handsome example of
the British old lady; fair, well-nurtured, with long, white
hands, grey hair and plenty of it, a voice that was still
young, and a natural, easy gracefulness, that did not ape
youth, either in dress or manners!

The Italian trip was discussed at length over dinner,
and Philip began to find himself positively yearning to be
off.   Venice had always been to him like a fairy tale of
mediæval romance, with a floating city in it; with costumes of Oriental loveliness, and with warriors of Oriental
picturesqueness and Anglican valor; with women golden-
haired, violet-eyed, and with that Venetian form of mouth
that was made for love and pictures. • He had seen with
his dreaming eyes the brown and yellow sails on the
many-hued lagoons, and he had heard the tell-tale whis-
perings of the outgoing sea as it slipped by the gorgeous
palaces on moonlight nights.   There was only one break

in the perfect romance and beauty of his idealization of
the city of the sea, and that was to his mind the impossibility of telling its story on canvas. Turner had suggested it, Canaletti had tried to give it all its realistic
beauty, but even these masters did not rise to the prosaic muse of Rogers, whose lines you could treat as
texts to build palaces upon, and set to dreams of sea
and sky and old romance. Philip was a poet in sentiment
and feeling, and Chetwynd, his friend and art-adviser,
believed he would one day bring a noble creative power
into his work ; at present Philip was rather embarrassed
with something like a material interpretation of the poet
according to Festus—poets are all who love, who feel
great truths and tell them—and the truth of truths is love ;
and he made up his mind to love Dolly with all his heart,
and if Mrs. Milbanke had had any doubts previously
about Philip's devotion to Dolly they were all dispelled on
this evening.

Philip had even astonished and delighted his mother by
the earnest and even enthusiastic efforts he made to please
his betrothed and to shine in the eyes of her family. One
says family without considering it necessary to bring in
Dolly's father and mother, who lived at Norwood in a
quiet suburban way, two old people with their old servants,
and their old-fashioned ways, and with whom Dolly spent
some of her time, who occasionally visited at Westbury
Lodge ; but they considered their day was over ; they had
brought up a family of three, well and successfully ; their
eldest son was a Judge of the Supreme Court of India,
and their two daughters were the happy sisters of this
truthful narrative ; and this is all that it is necessary to
say of Mr. and Mrs. Norcott, very worthy and well-to-do,
kind, pleasant people, whom Lady Forsyth expressed a
desire to call upon, and to see whom Mrs. Milbanke promised to drive to Norwood any day Lady Forsyth pleased.

Her father and mother had no special day, but were always at home to their friends every day ; and her father's cook was good enough even for Walter ; so no more need be said as to the Norwood hospitality.

As the narrator has already remarked, Philip, on this pleasant occasion, did all he could to make himself agreeable. He even sung those little lullaby German songs in which his studio friends always found a special charm. He also told the several little Russian stories which belonged to a mythical age of tradition, of which the Tartars might hardly have been suspected ; and Dolly discovered that Philip had more accomplishments than she had suspected—a declaration which his mother capped by regretting they had not a guitar at Westbury Lodge, an omission which Mrs. Milbanke promised to remedy the very next day.

" My dear," said Lady Forsyth, " these little German ditties should be sung either to the guitar or zither, and Philip is quite a master on both."

" Nonsense, mother ! And besides, I have not seen either guitar or zither for months."

" My dear Philip," said Walter, " we will have both on the Grand Canal ; we will be our own galugenti ; we can already sing ' Finiculi, Finicula,' can we not, Dolly ? "

Dolly smiled, and Walter sat down to the piano.

" Come, Jenny," he said. " When first we heard this song and chorus, floating as we were by moonlight along the canal towards the quay, we all fell madly in love with it ; tried to get the song in Venice, tried in Milan, tried in Paris. Get everything in London ; only one place in the world where you can get everything. You must join us, Philip." And Walter, in a light but effective tenor voice, led off with the solo, and the chorus followed ; and Lady Forsyth said she would certainly keep this performance in view for her next charitable concert in aid of the Irish

distress in her own sweet native vale of Acushla. And
so the evening passed away with music, love, and pleasant
talk ; and the Venetian trip and studio, and the future of
Philip looked as rosy as his mother and their dearest
belongings could desire.

CHAPTER XXVIII.

THE COUNTESS, THE JEWS, AND THE GONDOLIER.

BUT Lady Stravensky had to be reckoned with in the Philip and Dolly business. The Jewish woman of Czarovna
held a brief from Fate in regard to Lady Forsyth's pleasant
calculations of matrimonial happiness and prosperity for
her son. None of them knew or suspected how nearly the
fortunes of the countess touched theirs. It was a bad day
for Philip when he saw that face at the Opera. How far
it was bad for Dolly and her sister Jenny, for Walter Milbanke and other persons in this drama of life, remains to
be seen. The narrator is perfectly well aware what is 'o
happen to Philip, and what must be the end of the countess.

These things are foreshadowed by those who read between the lines as well as on them. But Dolly Norcott
floats gaily along the stream, and who knows where she
shall find a port, or what it will be like ? She has charming qualities. One would like her to be happy. For that
matter, Philip Forsyth is not undeserving of good fortune,
but surely he is destined to have trouble. He dreams
dreams. He mixes his professional ambition with his love.
He is not stable. His impulses are fine. He is constant
while he is with Dolly ; but on his way home he sees
visions of the poetic face of the countess, her violet eyes,
her deep-red hair. She is the central figure of his unwrit-

ten romances, the heroine of his unpainted pictures. And just as a certain set of people go mad over Ibsen's unwholesome plays, so Philip was going mad over the aspirations of young Russia, checked for the moment by the shadow of the Countess Stravensky, whom he regarded as one of those accidental endowments of birth which belong to a bad cause as if in fatal mockery of heaven.

When Philip was with Dolly, the pretty English girl had it all her own way; when he thought of the foreign countess, ten years his senior, as his mother had reminded him, his pulse rose and his face flushed. He put these physical manifestations down to ambition, to art fervor, to a nameless something that suggested destiny. This did not argue well for the domestic happiness of Dolly Norcott when she should be Mrs. Philip Forsyth.

While it is placed on record that the Countess Stravensky had to be reckoned with, in the warp and woof of the lives of Dolly and Philip, in the plans of Lady Forsyth and the pretty sisterly intrigues of Mrs. Milbanke, let it not be understood that our unhappy queen of the ghetto had any desire or intention to interfere with the matrimonial or worldly prospects of Philip Forsyth, except in so far as she might help him on his way. He had deeply impressed her. For a moment he had reawakened feelings which had been dead since her love, her best instincts, her womanliness, her faith in heaven, her hope in the great Father, had been literally cut out of her heart and soul by the Russian knout. It was only for a moment; and in that moment she saw herself an innocent girl sitting at the feet of her lover in the peaceful home of her childhood. In that moment the perfume of a lovely past fell around her; and she gazed upon the young artist, who had Losinski's eyes and hair, and Losinski's voice and gait. As the mist cleared, it came to her to think that this was but a vision intended by Fate to whet her appetite of ven-

geance—a whisper from the red grave of the murdered
rabbi. Then she remembered who and what she was; the
outrage of the governor Petronovitch; and with that
memory came grateful recollections of the devotion of Stravensky, who in his heart had loved the beautiful maid of
the ghetto, and in his age, stricken with death, had
endowed her with his name, and combined with hers his
own passion of vengeance, and his aspirations for a free
Russia. Anna's interview with Philip Forsyth had for the
moment given a tone of sentiment to her otherwise rugged
ambition when she found herself all suddenly in love with
him, to discover as suddenly that it was love by proxy,
the revival of a passion that belonged to the dead. But
the passing weakness over the retrospect that had come into
her reflection now tended to strengthen the arm that was
rather made for loving embraces than to wield the vengeance of a conspiracy. Fate has its own inscrutable
purposes that make havoc with every human intention,
and provide perpetual surprises for those who come to the
conclusion that they can no longer be astonished.

Lady Forsyth understood that the Countess Stravensky
had gone to Paris *en route* for St. Petersburg, but this was
not the fact. Ferrari had traveled to the gay city alone.
It was seldom that he left the side of the countess, whom
he served with the devotion of a slave, but with the authority also of a member of the same band of Russian
regenerators. She had no wish to stray from the patriotic
path upon which they traveled together ; and if she had,
it would have been the duty of her secretary to hold her to
her bonds. Immediately after Lady Forsyth's " At Home,"
Ferrari had sudden business in Paris and Venice ; and the
countess withdrew to an almost equally foreign country in
London, namely, to Soho, an English land of exiles, conspirators, and Nihilistic wire-pullers, in the heart of a
peaceful metropolis.

While Ferrari had many disguises, the countess had only two, and they were hers by right; they infringed upon the personality of no other being ; she was the countess, and she was Anna Klosstock. As the countess, she was what we have seen, a lady of position, recognized by the Russian Court, and in the very highest European society. As Anna Klosstock, she was the friend and accomplice of that very Brotherhood of which Ferrari had spoken to the count on that never-to-be-forgotten day, when he had ridden into Czarovna to see if he could be of any assistance to the Klosstocks and their co-religionists. At the time when Philip was singing his lullaby ditties at Westbury Lodge, Anna Klosstock, in the guise of a poor Jewess, was sitting in council with three members of the Brotherhood, and they were congratulating themselves upon the vast extension of the military conspiracy which had that day been chronicled in the English papers ; the fact that the plot had been discovered was atoned for by the proof of its immense ramifications all over the Empire.

" You are a Russian born, Paul," said Anna, addressing one of the three, a tall, picturesque-looking man of fifty, muscular, with a flat face, sallow complexion, fiery eyes, gray hair, and a mouth that seemed to smile on one side of his face and sneer on the other; "you were born in Russia, in Moscow ? "

" Yes, sister ; my father was born there, and my mother too, and there were five of us in family."

" And you are the only one left ? "

" That is so."

" Siberia and the knout only spared you because you got away ? "

" If there is work to do it is not necessary to remind me of these things ; I never forget them, nor my oaths—nor my pleasure."

At this last remark both sides of his mouth seemed to smile.

"You know Venice?" asked Anna with the manner of one who repeats a fact and invites information upon it.

"I was there with our brother Ferrari for three years."

"You were a gondolier?"

"Yes."

"He was a merchant?"

"Yes."

"He employed you?"

"Yes."

"You respect and honor him apart from your oath?"

"Yes."

"As friend and chief?"

"Yes."

"You have friends in Venice?"

"One."

"He can be trusted?"

"Yes."

"A gondolier?"

"Yes."

"You will leave London by the next train, and boat for Venice?"

"Yes."

"The King of Italy is to be received in state by the municipality. The Countess Stravensky will be your mistress in the procession of boats. She will be attended by her secretary, Signor Ferrari ; you and your friend will be her gondoliers ; your uniform red, the decoration of your gondola red ; you will await the countess by the Pesaro Palace until she makes her appearance ; the old watchword ; your rendezvous with Ferrari will be at the little hotel of the Beau Rivage. In three days hence you will be there ; he will have arrived ; seek him and know the rest."

"I shall," said Paul, holding out his hand for the bank-notes which Anna drew from the pocket of her black dress.

"Withen ten days Ferrari may expect me. The Royal function which the Countess Stravensky is to attend, and at which General Petronovitch is to be present, will take place two days after my arrival, when it will be shown that the arm of the Brotherhood is strong and long-reaching."

The double smile came into Paul's sallow face, and the two other men remarked in different words, but with the same meaning, that the patriots needed encouragement.

"You have seen a detective from Scotland Yard?"

"Yes," said Paul.

"About the visit of the German princes?"

"Yes. We are safe in our asylum here so long as we respect it; that was the police message.'

"All must be free to come and go, eh?"

"That is so. Anything happening to any one of England's guests, and we shall be cleared out."

"So far as we can, let us obey the mandate; it is just. Any other reports?"

"None."

"Good-night."

During the next two or three hours, Anna Klosstock made her way through certain malodorous quarters of the East End, where the sweater demon held his grim court; among Polish and other Jews, refugees, paupers—miserables of all kinds.

Wherever her shadow fell upon them, it brought comfort. Anna Klosstock was an angel in these benighted regions. She spoke the language of the sufferers. They told her their woes; how they had been shipped from their native land like slaves; how they arrived in London penniless, friendless; how they labored night and day for bread and shelter; and their chief complaints were against their co-religionists. As a rule, the Jew is good to his people; but in London, the English Jew seems to take advantage of his foreign brother; the sweated and the sweater in the

East End are mostly Jews. Why England should allow these waifs and strays to be cast penniless upon her shores, was one of the questions that puzzled Anna in her studies of English freedom. But she did not stay to debate these or any other questions, she only remembered the sufferings of her race, and in whatever city she found herself she sought out poor and wretched Jews, and gave them her bounty with words of sympathy and hope, "for surely," she said, "our term of probation is drawing to a close, and the day of promise is at hand."

CHAPTER XXIX.

THE HEART OF A MAN IS DECEITFUL.

IT is not for the author of this history of Love and Adventure to attack or defend his hero. Philip Forsyth will fulfil his destiny, whatever his biographer or the reader may have to say to it. He is not the first who might have exclaimed in regard to two women, "How happy could I be with either, where t'other dear charmer away." Or, at all events, not the first who had thought in this wise of two desirable ladies.

The psychological novelist, or the student of physical and spiritual motives in man, would no doubt bend his intellectual energies upon an investigation of the difference between the influence of the countess and that of Dolly Norcott on the sentiments and emotions of the young and impressionable artist. Did he love the countess? And were his feelings toward Dolly the mere outcome of passion? Were the Westbury Lodge influences physical and worldly, and the Russian impressions spiritual and divine? Or *vice versa?* Philip, it is plain, stood, as between the countess and Dolly, somewhat in the position of Garrick between Tragedy and Comedy, though he would not have admitted it to himself. If he had never seen the Countess Stravensky, he might have had a calm, domestic career with Dolly Norcott ; but the Russian Jewess exercised a strange fascination upon him, and he upon her. To what extent they were each under the other's influence was made clear to them, as it will be to us, under somewhat prosaic circumstances. The Milbankes had started for Venice *via* Paris, and had left it for Philip to join them at the little hotel in the Rue Castiglione, where Walter Milbanke had taken a very pleasant suite of rooms. Philip had gone down to Charing Cross close upon train time, and had found every seat occupied, except one in a *coupé* nearly at the end of the train, upon which *coupé* the forbidding notice " Engaged " was very prominently displayed.

As Fate would have it, the *coupé* was occupied by the Countess Stravensky, and as if that same watchful fate had been more than usually active in the interests of Anna and Philip, the lady was thinking of the person who was seeking a seat in the Dover express. The countess had composed herself to a journey of silent thought. She was alone. Her maid was in a second-class carriage, having a flirtation with Ferrari's servant, for Ferrari deemed it necessary to be attended on occasion, for appearances and conveniences, by a valet of knowledge and experience. The countess, however ostentatious her establishments in Russia or Paris, only confided in one maid, who found her service both profitable and pleasant.

The queen of the ghetto was troubled with sensations that were entirely new to her since the tragic days of Czarovna. It was a relief from the dark and hypocritical ways of her woman's life to cherish the gleam of sunshine that had somehow crept into her heart with her visit to Philip Forsyth's studio. Though she might never see the

young artist again, she would cherish his memory ; and
while she was feeling this rather than expressing it, even
to herself, it came into her mind to think that Fate was
demanding another sacrifice from her in this consent to
part from him. She knew that nothing good could come
of her association with him ; that if there were love passages between them, they could only be for her a passing
relaxation of thought, the chief charm of which would be
to try and dream herself back again into the arms of
Losinski in that far-off time when she was betrothed to
him. But it was strange, she thought, that on the eve of
seeing, as it were, the other Losinski, she should be on her
way to that city of the sea they had talked of and arranged
to visit together, that city which Losinski loved, which
Ferrari knew so well, where Jew and Gentile were friends,
as they were in London, where the ghetto was a name
merely, and where " the badge of the tribe," if worn at all,
was only treated as an ornament.

It was a pleasant day. The sun was shining brightly
even into Charing Cross Station, and the countess, laying
aside the light wrap which her maid had handed to her,
was reclining in the furthest corner of her *coupé*, given
over to her reflections, and her reflections, as we have
seen, were more particularly occupied with Philip Forsyth,
with whom, had circumstances permitted, she could have
fallen desperately in love. This thought gave her pain
and pleasure ; but she suffered the pain for the sake of the
little sweetness of fancy that took off the sharp edge of the
bitter. She contemplated from the carriage window the
bustle of the station without seeing it. Her thoughts were
in that Primrose Hill studio, and her fancy had trans-
planted it to the head of the street in the Jewish quarters
of Czarovna. Right in the midst of her fanciful picture of
the past and the present, there was suddenly interposed
the living figure of the young artist. For a moment she

could not realize the truth of it, starting up as it did amidst the prosaic surroundings of the railway platform, of which she now became conscious.

With the persistence that belongs to railway travelers in search of seats two minutes before the train starts, Philip looked longingly and inquisitively into the engaged compartment, and his eyes met those of the occupier. He stood at the window as if transfixed. She smiled at him a dreamy recognition, and then suddenly came forward, and at a wave of her white hand the guard opened the carriage door. Philip stepped inside, and the next moment the Dover express was gliding on its way.

"Why, my dear countess," exclaimed Philip, "what a delightful surprise! I thought you were in St. Petersburg. How glad I am that I was late, and could not find a seat. How very kind of you to take pity on me."

"I shall be rewarded for my compassion in your pleasant companionship."

She looked at him, as she spoke, with what seemed to Philip to be an inviting sympathy of interest. He felt the blood rush into his cheeks.

"You are very good," he stammered; "and so is Fate. I don't know what I have done to be so highly favored."

"By Fate?" she said, interrogatively.

"By Fate," said Philip, "and by you."

"Fate and me," she said thoughtfully, and with her pretty accent, "what a partnership; but it is a strange world, and it might be Fate that brought us together here in this carriage, without our consent or our interposition."

"Fate is not always kind."

"Is it kindness to bring us together again when we had parted for ever?"

"Had we parted for ever?" Philip asked.

"I thought so," said the countess.

"Did you hope so?" he asked.

" I think so."

" Why ? "

" For many reasons."

" Tell me one."

" Because I thought you were more interested in your model than in your picture."

She looked at him steadily, but with a softness, he thought, of expression in her eyes. His heart beat violently, and she felt a strange desire to give herself over to the spirit of memory which Philip was once more stirring within her. In a navy-blue serge suit, with a white silk handkerchief tied loosely about his neck, his deep, black eyes ablaze with his unconcealed passion, his black hair hanging about his temples, Anna saw again her love of Czarovna, could have sworn she heard his voice ; and in Philip's trembling accents she felt the thrill of an old love. She had experienced so much suffering in the world that Fate seemed to be whispering in her ear, " Why suffer always, why cast aside this chance of happiness ? Remember of the past only that which is pleasant." And she leaned back on the soft cushions, and gazed at the flashing eyes of the young painter, who at that moment forgot everything, everybody, but the woman who sat before him, to his mind a living dream of beauty.

" My dear countess ! " he exclaimed.

She smiled and gazed at him. A blush seemed to steal into her pale cheeks. Her lips parted as if she were about to speak.

" My love ! " he said, encouraged by her tender looks, and stealing to her side he took her hand.

She neither moved nor spoke. He pressed her hand to his lips. She turned her face towards him. There were tears in her eyes.

" I love you, I love you ! " he exclaimed.

She withdrew her hand from his and shuddered.

"God help you," she said, "and forgive me; if He does help—if He does forgive," and she covered her eyes with her hands.

Philip only repeated " I love you," while the train went gliding along through green meadows, whitened here and there with the first blossoms of the spring.

"You must not love me," she said presently, " I can be to you nothing more than a memory, not even a friend."

"You can, you must," replied the passionate youth, utterly oblivious of his engagement to Dolly, with no thought or sense or feeling but what belonged to the moment.

" I wish it might be," she said, struggling against her fate.

"From the first moment I saw you," he exclaimed, stimulated by her expressed wish "that it might be," and with the belief that to love or passion everything is possible, "on that night at the opera, I adored you; from this happy day forth I am your slave!"

" Forbear!" she said. " It will not prove a happy day. I would love you if I could, if I dared. It is impossible. Our destinies are as far asunder as the poles."

" They shall be brought together," he replied passionately, "as close as our lips." And he had kissed her before she could make even a show of resistance.

Then there was a pause, but she let the hand he had seized lie passively in his; and the train went beating along its iron way, past farm and station, skirting woodlands and pastures. The clouds went racing along too, and Philip's hot blood coursed through his veins in sympathy.

He stole his arm about her waist, as no man had since the days of Losinski.. She permitted it, forgetting why she had at first shuddered at his touch, and allowing herself to drift along with the fond embrace and honeyed words of her lover, who was beside himself with the success of his attack upon this stately, beautiful, mysterious beauty.

Presently she drew herself away from him and assumed an air of entire self-possession.

"Philip, I hope you may learn to forgive me for this weakness, this temptation to forget a bitter past, in an unlooked-for visitation of sweetness. Nay, listen, do not speak. You are young and impulsive. You will have time to forget. The world is all before you, full of glorious possibilities, love, fame, happiness. For me, there is but a hard, thorny road, and I must tread the path alone. If you could know all, you would say it is so ; you would never seek to alter it ; you would indeed shudder at the depth of the precipice you have stood upon ; stand aghast at the escape my self-denial gives you, for I could love you ; yes, not alone for the sake of the past, but for your own ; but—and here I beg you to take note of my words—you might as well think of allying yourself with the worst woman your fancy can depict as with me."

"You are saying this to disenchant me ; you love another : or——"

"I am not saying it for any purpose but to save you and myself from a crime, a sin, and you from a future of humiliation. I do not love anyone ; I am a widow ; I was widowed from my love on the eve of my marriage ; I was only a girl, and there are sufferings in this world worse than death, humiliations worse than the gallows."

Her lips quivered as she spoke, and the expression of terror and anger, of something between madness and grief, between defiance and vengeance, which Philip had noticed in that face at the opera, seemed to convulse her. All this, instead of discouraging Philip, stirred in him the defiant desire for some opportunity to show to the woman either the madness or the sincerity of his passion.

"I care not what you are, what you have been, what

you may be—if we had to descend into the bottomless pit together, I love you, and will for ever and ever 1"

" You are mad," she exclaimed.

" I may be."

" You are mad," I say; "would you consort with a murderess 1"

"You are none," he replied, with a lofty smile.

" For you I am worse," she said ; "and I tell you now, my dear, misguided friend, that this love of yours, of mine if you will, is not only madness, it is folly, it is worse ;" and then noticing how firm was his madness, how impossible to shake it, she made a tremendous sacrifice of her feelings, her pride, everything that woman holds dear, and whispered in his ear, "What is worse than a murderess, what is worse than anything man considers bad in the woman he loves? I am that! yes, I am that !"

"My God !" the boy exclaimed, moving away from her in horror, "is it true ? "

"It is true," she said, and burst into tears.

"I pity you from my heart," he said, "I pity myself."

She sobbed or affected to sob. He sat silently, stunned by her confession. The train ran along just as smoothly, just as swiftly as before. Neither of them spoke again for some time. At last, secretly congratulating herself on the success of her stratagem, and at the same time stung to the quick that he should believe her, Anna said, "And now let us be a man and woman of the world.; what has passed between us is our secret ; let us respect it ; let us talk no more of love ; if we meet again, we can know each other as persons in the world, you can know me or not as you wish ; we can think of this as an incident of our lives in which there was a little sweet, and very much bitter, as there is in all incidents of this life ; and some day, when you are happy with your honest love and with your children about you, and you are a great painter, you will think of me as kindly as you can ; and one day in that future you shall, if it interest you, know my life all through ; and then you will forgive and pity me."

" As I do now," said Philip tenderly, " as I do now."

Her confession had done its work. She knew it would. She had reckoned up the passionate poetical nature of the young fellow quite truly. There is one sin which not the most romantic lover can overlook ; one crime which love cannot condone in the object of its worship. But Philip was in a miserable state of mind ; and in his misery he had the audacity to think of Dolly Norcott for the first time since he had encountered the countess at Charing Cross—so selfish, thoughtless, ungrateful is it possible for the heart of man to be. And as he thought of her, he wished the woman before him was as good, and virtuous, and truly lovable—a piece of ingratitude which only a master in the analysis of the psychological evolution of love and passion can understand or excuse.

" Shall we meet again in Paris ? " Philip asked, as the train slowed up for Dover.

" Not by appointment," she answered, " and it would be best that we should never meet again."

" I do not know what to think of you," he said.

" Do not think of me," she replied.

" I will not believe that you have told me the truth ; will you not give me a rendezvous ? "

" Not now ; at some other time I will."

" You will ? "

" Yes."

" When ? "

" I do not know. You may hear of me at 20, Rue de Bach ; but do not seek to find me ; wait until I write to you or send a message to you. I know where to address you."

" But I am leaving London for a month or two."

" You remain in Paris ? "

" No, in Venice."

" In Venice ! " she repeated ; but he did not notice the expression of surprise that passed over her face.

" My address there will be the Hotel Beau Rivage."

" The Hotel Beau Rivage," she repeated slowly, as her maid presented herself at the *coupé*. The countess, giving her hand to Philip, said " Good-bye," to which he promptly responded :   .

" We shall meet on the boat."

" Perhaps not."

" In Paris then ? "

" Not until you hear from me," she said firmly.

" But it is *au revoir ?* " he asked appealingly.

" Yes, *au revoir !* " she answered.

CHAPTER XXX.

PHILIP TRIES TO FORGET.

As Philip made his way to the night boat for Calais, he found himself staggering down the gangway. The intensity of his sensations had shaken his nerves. He felt as if he had just come out of a fever, as indeed he had. Reaching the deck, he sat down to recover his mental and physical equilibrium. He was dazed. He remembered once awaking from a terrible dream, with something like a similar feeling of a bitter happiness, a sense of wicked joy, pierced with the sting of remorse. Philip sat on the deck, staring at the sky. There was a young ethereal looking moon. He saw the passengers arriving, and watched them and their luggage being thrust aboard. They seemed to roll down the gangway in a confused mass.

It was a lovely night. There was not a ripple on the water by the quay, nor outside the bar. He wondered if she had come aboard, or if she would ; wondered with a strange feeling of curiosity ; and one moment he hoped she would not, and the next he hoped she would.

All at once, when he thought of Dolly Norcott, he felt wretched ; then as suddenly a sense of triumph crept into his troubled brain. To have held the woman of the opera in his arms ! To have stirred the heart of the woman with that sadly beautiful, inscrutable face ! To have her promise that they should meet again ! To have her confession that there had been a time when she could have loved him ! This was tantamount to an encouragement to believe that there might be a time in the future when she would return his love ! All this was delightful ; and yet it was a delight that he felt he had no right to embrace. It was the same kind of delight that belonged to the tragic bliss of Francesca and her lover in the story ; and it was wrong ; his was a worse crime then theirs. He was engaged to be married to a sweet and innocent girl. On his way to join her, he had entirely and sinfully forgotten her. He experienced a sudden contempt for himself. For a moment it occurred to him to reflect whether he might not be justified in disappearing altogether from the sight of both women, and betake himself to some distant corner of the globe, the world forgetting, by the world forgot.

The pleasant breeze that sprung up when the boat was under weigh, refreshed him, and he paced the deck, steadied with a modified sense of the enormity of his conduct. He began to philosophize about it, and to find excuses for himself. A man is not responsible for the outburst of these sudden attacks of passion, especially if he has been endowed by nature with an excess of feeling, with the temperament of the poet, and who has had no relf-restraining influences about him, no mentor to check his exuberance of fancy, none except Dick Chetwynd, who would, Philip felt assured, be rather inclined to regard a severe flirtation as something that might happen to any man, given the opportunity. Mrs. Chetwynd herself, Philip thought, as he drifted into this exculpatory vein, would only have smiled at the idea of his making love to the countess ; and his mother would not have minded it at all so long as it did not interfere with his engagement to Miss Norcott.

Whether he did these worthy people an injustice or not, this was the new way in which Philip's thoughts now began to sail along over the increasingly calm plain of his mind, just as the moon went sailing along behind the ship.

Presently he lighted a cigar, went below, ordered a pint of champagne and a biscuit, drank the former, threw the latter bit by bit into the sea as he stood by the gangway, pulling himself together, as the phrase is, and trying to dismiss from his memory the scene in the railway carriage ; and yet all the time he was wondering whether the countess was aboard. He had, in that vague, unwatchful condition previously described, observed the passengers come on deck, and he had not seen either maid, servant, or coun-tess. His curiosity was piqued. He would find out if her ladyship had come aboard. He did find out : she had not. Satisfied of this, he became more contented with his position, and began to find the railway adventure going further and further away as he neared the French shore. He would forget it. He could if he wished. And he could all the more so if he made up his mind to be true to Dolly ; and he would make up his mind. No good could come of his intrigue with the countess. There was some mystery behind her. A scandal perhaps. She had been quite emphatic in her intimation that what he desired could never be. And, as his mother said, she was ten years his senior. Moreover, he could not pursue the impulse that had made him rash and unscrupulous without creating a scandal, to say nothing of breaking Dolly's heart, perhaps, and making no end of trouble.

Yes, whatever happened, he would be guided by what was honorable and wise. He would forget the countess, except in so far as she belonged to his picture. His memory of her should belong only to that. She should be for him an artistic dream. Greater is he who conquereth himself than he who conquereth a city. He would devote himself to Dolly.

If Philip had been called upon to criticize the conduct of someone else who had made these vows, after such a lapse of memory in regard to his fiancée, he would probably have said it was all very well to go on protesting in this way in view of a pleasant time with Dolly, the other dear charmer away; but that if he were Dolly, he would not feel safe of the permanent fidelity of such a lover.

Poor Dolly! If she could only have suspected, much less known, what had happened between Philip and the countess on that memorable journey to Dover, she, with indignation and scorn, would have relieved Philip of his vows; for, despite the worldly streak in Dolly's nature, she had a true woman's good opinion of herself. If Philip had a better opinion of the countess or of any other woman, Philip might have gone over to that other woman, and Dolly would have professed herself glad to be rid of him, however much she might have secretly suffered.

And Jenny! Why, Mrs. Milbanke would have made London ring with his unworthiness, even though she would have felt it necessary to say that Dolly broke it off, that she had been over-persuaded to accept him by her family and friends, while really not caring as much for him as a woman should for the man she is willing to marry. Jenny would have kept Dolly's position clear,

but at the same time she would have " made it hot " foi
Philip, as Sam Selwyn would have put it.

What, by the way, would not Sam have given to have
had the encouragement to hope which a knowledge of
Philip's declaration to the countess would have war-
ranted ?   If he could only have had the assistance of Don
Cleofas of the two sticks, and have seen the shadow of
Philip's insincerity cast forward upon the path which now
looked so certain to lead to Sam being one day invited to
the wedding reception of Dolly and Philip Forsyth, at
Norwood or at Westbury Lodge !

By the time Philip reached Paris he had contrived to
forget a great deal of what had transpired during the day,
or, if not to forget, to so far ignore it as to meet Dolly the
next morning at breakfast in the cheeriest holiday frame
of mind.   And she looked " so awfully nice, don't you
know," as Swynford would have said ; so fresh and sweet,
so paintable, and so lovable too, as Philip said to himself.
Mrs. Milbanke was none the less charming in her matronly
fashion.   Both of them were dressed in light frocks, suggesting a pleasant fussiness of frill and collar, of ribbon
and tabs, of dainty flowers at the neck or waist, matching
the white apartment of the well-kept hotel.   Their rooms
looked out upon a courtyard which was gay with tubbed
laurel, and tented tables, and bright with April sunshine ;
April beginning to verge into May, and verging with all
due respect to morning dresses, white rooms, open windows, and breakfasts *al fresco.*

The Milbanke rooms filled one side of the courtyard
and were *en suite,* Philip Forsyth being allotted the furthest
chamber, which Walter had made especially pleasant with
an addition of a choice box of cigarettes, and Dolly with a
jug of roses.   They were a very representative party,
everybody in the hotel thought, thoroughly English, both
as to their complexions and their easy extravagance.   The

landlady, a plump, cheerful widow of thirty, did nothing but admire them as they came or went; and she made a point of going into their rooms herself to see that the breakfast was all that they could desire, and it was, from the long brown roll of Paris bread to the spring chicken, half buried in cresses and potato chips.

Philip had donned a new grey tweed suit, with a white silk neckerchief and brown walking shoes, and was all the handsomer in the eyes of the landlady, and possibly in Dolly's, that he was unusually pale, his eyes more than usually bright, and his black hair more than usually inclined to straggle over his forehead. If he had had hazel eyes, he might perhaps have been a more stable and reliable lover; but his eyes were blue, as has been previously remarked—a clear blue, which made his face remarkable without the observer at first quite knowing why. His complexion was naturally somewhat sallow; his eyebrows strong and dark, his hair raven; he was English in his manners and speech; but in person more like an Italian than an Englishman.

The two or three days of their stay in Paris was a delightful time. Walter Milbanke was the most thoughtful of travelling hosts. He managed everything.. No one else found it necessary to give a thought to anything except enjoyment. Walter anticipated the wants of his party with the consideration of an affectionate friend and the efficiency of the best of courtiers. And what a genial fellow he looked and was! Always in a good temper; never argumentative; that is, not in earnest; if he opposed anything it was in a spirit of pleasant badinage. He was mostly dressed in a suit of navy blue serge, his coat nattily faced with silk; and he pinned his dark red scarf with a diamond horseshoe. His thoroughly English complexion warmed up under the work of piloting and providing for his party, and gave him the appearance of robust health,

which in good sooth he possessed, thanks chiefly to an
equable temper and a generous heart. Walking or driving
in the Bois, he looked very proud of his wife and friends.
Mrs. Milbanke changed her dress twice or three times a
day, and was up to date in the matter of fashion, a trifle
ahead of it indeed; for she carried almost the first of the
husband quellers, as the club-like parasol handle has been
ironically called, and her hat was the tallest and prettiest,
too, in all Paris, not even excepting Dolly's, which soared
amidst ribbon and flowers, and gave an added piquancy by
contrast to the retroussé suggestion, the pretty tilt, as Sam
Selwyn would have said, of her incomparably piquant little
nose. But, oh her complexion! It was the envy of every
Frenchwoman who looked upon it; so pink and white, so
peach-like, and so real: and her large grey eyes and rich
yellow hair! Mrs. Milbanke was quite justified in admiring
her, though she was her sister.

Philip kept by Dolly's side everywhere, with a quiet
appearance of devotion that might have deceived even a
cynic; and it did entirely deceive Mrs. Milbanke and
Dolly; indeed, it deceived Philip himself. In the picture
galleries, in the shops of the Palais Royal, at the Comedie
Française, on a river trip at Versailles, he was a gallant
chevalier and devoted lover. He was at his best in every
way. He talked well, was a most entertaining companion
for all of them; knew the histories of the great pictures;
moralized eloquently at Versailles; talked of the war,
interspersing the incidents of the entry into Paris with
appropriate reminiscences of his young life in Russia.

And at night, after the light, elegant supper, which
Walter insisted upon as the proper finale to the play,—
Philip would take a hand at loo, or whist, or poker, for an
hour, and win and lose with a pleasant grace that had not
been suspected as one of his special charms.

"You never know a fellow until you have traveled with

him," Walter said to his wife on the third night of their stay in Paris (it was on the fourth that they continued their journey towards Venice), " and the more one sees of Forsyth, the more one must like him."

" It is quite wonderful," said Mrs. Milbanke, " quite ; I am deceived in him; I would have expected him to be a little exacting in regard to the programme of the day, and a young man of moods and whims ; but he is perfectly amiable."

" I am glad you agree with me, my dear," said Walter ; " I never came across a pleasanter fellow, nor one better informed, and, by Jove, if he does not know a thing, he has the knack of seeming to, and of extracting the neces·sary knowledge from some one else, or from a book, or in some way or other just at the right moment ; a thoroughly good-natured, agreeable fellow; Dolly may indeed be congratulated."

" I think so," said Jenny. " I hope so, and I believe so ; though Sam Selwyn with a big fortune would have been hardly less desirable. There is something I like about Sam ; he is so transparent, so good-natured, and so de-termined to be rich."

" Have you not liked him a trifle more since he made those two large sums of money ? Eh, now, my darling, confess ! "

" I have respected him more, Walter, that's all; and don't you think there was something very considerate and thoughtful in his not proposing to Dolly because he did not believe he had money enough, and saying he would have proposed if it had not for other reasons been too late the moment he was sure of his good fortune."

" Oh, I like Sam, and we must not lose him as a friend because we cannot have him as a brother-in law."

" Just so, dear," said Jenny ; and before Walter had finished his next sentence, Mrs. Milbanke was sleeping the refreshing sleep of a contented mind. Walter very quickly followed suit. There is an everlasting and non-injurious narcotic in the knowledge that your banker's balance is all right, and your investments secure.

CHAPTER XXXI.

DOLLY SEES THAT FACE IN HER DREAMS.

ALTHOUGH the weather was fine and sunny in Paris, with pleasant promise of May flowers, it was not until our friends had traveled all night from the gay city, to awake the next morning at Ambruel, that the world began to look green and floral. The trees in the Bois, it is true, had put forth indications of green buds; but the branches were still bare and brown. Here and there on the banks of the Seine there were villages about which fruit trees were beginning to blossom, and everywhere you felt the coming of the Spring, bright and perfumed. But after a night of travel, Philip woke up in the midst of a landscape backed by the mountains of the Savoy, that looked like fairyland, with tall green poplars, running brooks and clusters of picturesque cottages with overhanging roofs, and in the fields, men and women fixing up poles for the green vines that had begun to need them.

None of Philip's fellow travelers were up. They had a sleeping carriage all to themselves, with a small dining coupé attached. Philip stood upon the platform of the Pullman car in the early morning, and the incidents of the journey from London to Dover went further and further away in the distance. The continuous travel, and the entirely new surroundings, helped on "Old Time" and his hour-glass wonderfully. Philip took out his sketch book and began to make pictorial memoranda of the country through which the train was carrying its sleeping passengers with a calm, steady regularity of speed that seemed to be quite in keeping with the panorama. Here and there a river would swell out into lake-like pools, which reflected the adjacent country as in a glass, following which the stream would break out into turgid rushes of yellow turbulent water. Then you would come to the banks of shingle and dots of houses and blue smoke.

At one place Philip was very busy with his sketch book, the train having slowed up at a signal, and he brought into use a small case of water colors, that he might at least have a note of the bits of delicious color that appealed to the eye and to the imagination. A company of field laborers were at breakfast, men and women ; they had been busy with the vines ; the men wore jackboots, and had handkerchiefs round their heads ; it was in a green and flowery valley with fruit trees in rich blossom ; and for a background there was a double range of mountains, the front range a black battalion, the furthest away range white sentinels, guarding the valleys against the march of Summer, the spring vanguard of which, nevertheless, made its way to the plains with silent tread and gay with floral banners.

In the valleys there were houses like Swiss châlets ; these repeated themselves now and then ; but not like the mountains, which, as the trains went pounding along, seemed to come and go, and march on and off, like the supers in a theatrical army. Now and then the white peaks would go right up into the sky, as if to challenge the sunshine. Once in a way a streak of silver would appear on the mountain sides ; it was alive, and making its way down the great hills to run off into the meadows at their feet. By and by the country became more and more Italian, softer outlines of foothills, vaster mounts of distant snow. Near one station a company of soldiers were engaged at rifle practice ; and henceforth there were frequent church towers and steeples among the poplars.

Then came prettier villages and whiter roads, and the vine grew taller; the sun was more powerful; the train was running into summer weather.

At Turin the little party breakfasted, and Philip delighted them with his sketches. From Turin the country was green with tall grass and yellow with mustard in bloom. There were miles of pollard willows, and the meadows were white with daisies. There were acres of green wheat, and towns with red roofs, and in the distance still marched the everlasting hills, white at their summits, a blue haze in their valleys. There were wayside stations with red-capped officials, and fields yellow with dandelion. Then came signs of an approach to some large city; carts and waggons on the highway; a countryman with greyhounds in a leash, men and women in the fields, picturesque in form and color, the women suggesting Lancashire in their handkerchief head-dresses; but there were oxen yoked to the plough to take away the English reminiscences. Presently the train pulled up at Milan; and it was summer, for not only had the locomotive run out of Paris into the city of La Scala and the famous Cathedral, but it had run out of April into May; it was May day, and it looked May Day, and was perfumed as May Day should be.

Walter Milbanke had timed their arrival and made his arrangements accordingly. It was the dinner hour at the Grand Hotel Continental, a fine new house with a picturesque courtyard, courteous officials and the electric light. After dinner, Walter and Philip smoked, while the dear girls, as Walter called them, went through the artist's scrapbook, and traveled the pleasant day over again.

Looking out into the street beneath their open windows, attracted by a marching band of vocalists, they found that the wedding party of a popular workman was being escorted home by a company of friends, who were singing as they went, which led to a chat upon wedding customs, and set Jenny and her sister talking of the one wedding in particular, which was already beginning to interest Jenny very much.

"Of course," she said, when they were parting for the night, Jenny visiting her sister in her white bedroom, that looked out upon the courtyard, "of course it must take place at Norwood; it would never do for you to be married from your brother-in-law's house, it would look as if your father and mother were nobodies, as if they were not living in good style; and they are; and I think some of our friends will be astonished to see in what good style they do live, and what kind of a house."

"It is all one to me, as Sam Selwyn would say," remarked Dolly.

"Why quote Sam Selwyn, dear?" asked Jenny, somewhat reproachfully.

"Don't we always quote him when we want to use a good phrase that is more or less slangy?"

"Yes, we have that habit, but I don't think it is a good one; besides, it is just as well that we should try and relinquish the habit, now that we have finally made up our choice of Philip and let Sam slide."

"As Sam would put it," remarked Dolly, interrupting her sister with a laugh.

"Poor Sam," said Jenny, "he is a good fellow, and we must not lose him as a friend; even Walter is worldly enough to say so."

"But is there anything particularly worldly in keeping friends with Mr. Selwyn?" Dolly asked.

"I don't know; he will be very rich, everybody says so; is now, I believe, for that matter."

"And somehow, after all, much as you preach the other way, Jenny, you do not seem to have quite made up your mind that there is not a chance for Sam yet."

"Nonsense, Dolly; how can you say so?"

"I don't know how I can, but I say so because I think so."

"Then, my darling, pray think so no longer ; I am more than delighted with Philip, I am charmed and astonished."

"At what in particular?"

"At his pleasant manners, his amiability, his devotion to you."

"Are you? well, what did you expect then? What else can he be? Do we not make ourselves agreeable? Am I not always ready to listen to all he says ; to be charmed with his sketches ; and who could be anything else than amiable upon such a journey as this, and with such a companion as Walter, who thinks for everybody, gives nobody any trouble about anything, even looks after the baggage if necessary, and makes our tour a sort of royal progress? I cannot imagine the most awful curmudgeon, as Sam would say, being anything but gay under the circumstances."

"Oh, I do not know that Philip is gay," said Jenny, "but he is happy, contented, ready to do anything we suggest, pleasant, agreeable, and, what is more to the purpose, charmed with his pretty little *fiancée.*"

"Then say good-night to his pretty little *fiancée,*" said Dolly, smiling. "I am very tired, dearest."

And so they said good-night ; and in this kind of closing chat, which brought all the Milbanke nights to an end, Jenny told Walter that she could not quite make Dolly out ; she really did not quite know whether she loved Philip or not.

"Love him! why, of course, she does," Walter replied ; "he sat by her all day when he was not sketching ; and at dinner he never forgot to see that she had the best of everything ; and when we looked out and saw that wedding business going on, he was particularly attentive, and he whispered something to Dolly and she laughed. What more do you want, Jenny? You are so speculative about things."

"I love Dolly," she replied, "with all my heart and soul, and if she were not happy in her marriage it would break my heart."

"I know, I know," said Walter, "and it would compel me to drink more than would be good for me, I am sure; but she will be happy; there are various ideas of happiness—to be good is to be happy, the poet says; angels are happier than men, because they are better, don't you agree with that sentiment?"

No reply.

Walter looked up from his bed at the other end of the room. Jenny was in another world; prose and poetry were all one to her, as Dolly had been saying of something else—she was asleep.

"Good-night," said Walter in a whisper; "I think we are having a very pleasant time."

Philip Forsyth was trying to think so, too. But there was a shadow upon his reflections; he had got rid of it so long as Dolly and the rest were with him—so long as he could talk—so long as there was change of scene and sub-. ject; but now that he was alone he was once more back in London; once more with the Countess Stravensky; once more under the influence of her violet eyes; once more listening to her deep, sweet voice; once more at her feet morally, poetically, and to his own satisfaction. He tried to shake the pleasant shadow off; tried to think it was not pleasant; tried to eclipse it with the face of Dolly; tried to exercise it with the repetition of his vows of love to Dolly, and with his later vows made to himself to be true to Dolly, to love and esteem her, and to forget the woman of the opera-box except as a model, an idea, an artistic accessory, a something outside the affections, a mere acquaintance; but the god or demon who is sup-

posed to have power over the heart, who controls the loves
of mortal men and women whether they will or no, would
not have Anna Klosstock eclipsed by Dolly

Whether or no Dolly was governed by that fine instinct
which is the peculiar possession of women, or whether
she had a sneaking kindness for Selwyn, it is not for the
chronicler to say ; anyhow, she was not altogether satisfied
that Philip loved her as sincerely as he professed ; and
when she slept, she had uncomfortable dreams ; and when
she awoke, she did so with a shudder, as the imaginary
face of the woman in Philip Forsyth's picture faded into
the darkness.

CHAPTER XXXII.

AT VENICE BY MOONLIGHT.

"MAKE the acquaintance of the city of the sea as a matter
of choice by sea and in the sunshine," says Yriarte.   But
approach Venice how you may, or when, her aspect is
impressive beyond description.

If it is magnificent to sail into the lagoons from the
Adriatic, it is bewitching to glide into her waterways from
the mainland and by moonlight.   Furthermore, whichever
way you may approach your destination, you will find it
equally impossible to analyze the sensations that overcome
you ; in the end you will probably turn to Rogers, whom
you have hitherto regarded as a writer of mere prose,
tricked out in blank verse, and recalling your unjust estimate of the banker's muse, will in imagination place a
chaplet upon his brows as tribute to the poetic picture of
your waking dream.

> " There is a glorious city in the Sea.
> The Sea is in the broad, the narrow streets,

Ebbing and flowing ; and the salt seaweed
Clings to the marble of her palaces.
No track of men, no footsteps to and fro,
Lead to her gates. The path lies o'er the Sea
Invisible ; and from the land we went,
As to a floating city—steering in
And gliding up her streets as in a dream."

Across the long viaduct that joins Venice to the mainland, the train glided over a world of swamp and marshy
flats that reminded Dolly of the flats about the great river
in Norfolk, where it enters into the wide sea. It suggested
to Philip some faint memory of the Russian steppes, all
unlike though it was ; and while Walter Milbanke found it
more Dutch than English, he took especial interest in
noting the impressions of the approach to fairyland made
upon Philip and Dolly ; for he and Jenny knew Italy well,
and had already visited Venice on two occasions. Walter
was theatrical in his tastes, and he found the approach to
Venice like the preliminaries to the transformation scene
of a Drury Lane pantomime, beginning with dark mysterious gauzes, that suggest Cimmerian darkness, swamps,
strange waters, and slithery shores of ooze and weed.

The moon shone upon the vast mud-banks. Far away
there was a glimpse of sea ; and further still, a passing
hint of a distant sail close upon the horizon ; but no city,
no lofty campaniles, no silvery cupolas, no golden domes
and towers; only a morass lighted by the moon, a flat
watery waste, through which the panting locomotive seemed
to feel its way ; and at last when it glided into an ordinary
railway station—with gaslights and porters and all the other
belongings of locomotive travel—though they had arrived
at the glorious city in the sea, to both Dolly and Philip it
still seemed further away than ever.

" Mr. Milbanke," said a stalwart Italian, stepping up to
the party, hat in hand.

"Ah, Beppo !" was Walter's response.

"It is a joy to see you," said the Italian ; "I will attend to the luggage."

"Is your gondola here?"

"Close by," said Beppo, "and I have my comrade with me."

"That is good," said Walter, handing him the wraps, which were of the lightest, and at the same time giving him his tickets for the baggage.

Beppo was a gondolier, picturesquely attired. He spoke English with a soft purring kind of accent. Walter Milbanke had employed him during his previous visits to Venice ; and on this occasion had also hired Beppo and a comrade, with a special gondola, to be at the disposal of the party during their stay. He had also commissioned an especial uniform, with a bit of color in it, on account of the royal festivities.

When first Walter had suggested the Italian trip and the Venetian holiday, he had not counted upon arriving at Venice on the occasion of a royal function and a fine art exhibition ; but on discovering that Venice was to be en fête he secured the best suites of rooms at the Hotel Beau Rivage and a gondola and gondoliers. The larger of the two hotels on the quay was already full of guests, when he made his dispositions for their stay in Venice ; but the same proprietary controlled the smaller house, and here the Milbanke rooms were ample, and almost facing the grand statue of Victor Emanuel, which the King and Queen of Italy were to inaugurate, and in connection with which ceremony the city was to revive some of her ancient glories in the way of fête and pageantry.

Presently the Milbankes and the lovers stepped into the Venetian cab. It was lying by the station steps. It had no wheels, nor any horse. It was not "the gondola of the London streets ;" it was the gondola of Venice, solemn looking enough, but not so solemn as others with their hooded decks. Walter had been minute in his instructions, "for," said he, "I always remember my poor father's first and last visit to Venice ; it was winter, but daylight ; the gondola to him was a floating hearse ; to enter it when it is in its full panoply of service you have to back into it ; my father lost his hat in doing so ; the weather was wet and cold, it rained, the palace where he was lodged was chilled with a little charcoal stove ; the next day he left the city in the sea ; and there you have the prosiest possible idea of Venice."

"Walter, be still," said Mrs. Milbanke ; "the relation of the reminiscence is like throwing a stone at a lovely monument ; don't you see we are afloat?"

"I only wanted to cap Philip's disappointment at the start ; to put the finishing touch to the mudbanks and the stark prosy realism of the railway station."

Philip made no reply, for by this time they were in those quiet streets,

> "As in a dream
> So smoothly, silently—by many a dome
> Mosque-like, and many a stately portico,
> The statues ranged along an azure sky ;
> By many a pile in more than Eastern pride,
> Of old the residence of merchant kings ;
> The fronts of some, though Time had shattered them,
> Still glowing with the richest hues of art,
> As though the wealth within them had run o'er."

Philip said not a word. Dolly's hand had somehow found its way to his. She sat beside him. He was wrapped in the spell of his first sight of Venice. She, too, felt the strange witchery of it. Dolly's was not exactly a poetical nature ; but like the dullest of us she had her moments when the mind soars and feels a consciousness of its divinity.

The air was balmy. There was no breeze. The moon shone steadily down upon them. It was an azure sky as

the poet hath it though it was night. The blue was dark
but blue, and the more blue for the one or two silvery
stars that twinkled about the silent reflective moon. The
queen of night was surely contemplating the queen of cities.
" We are the two queens of the world," it might have been
saying, so high, so lofty, so dignified, so proud, she looked
up in the heavens ; and so majestic, so pathetically majestic looked the dreamy city of the sea, where moon and
palaces glassed themselves in the calm waters.

The one or two gondolas that accompanied our friends
when they started, disappeared mysteriously round bends
of the Grand Canal, where lamps glimmered now and then
in a half-hearted kind of competition with lighted windows
that sent streaks of gleaming darts or broad beams of yellow down into the deep, making the rippling wavelets that
accompanied the gondola rise and fall with splashes of
color that had the effect of molten gold. But this was
only momentary ; the gondola slipped and stole along, like
some shadowy boat in some imaginary city, where the
palaces rose like architectural spectres out of the bosom
of the dreaming waters.

Philip pressed Dolly's hand. She responded faintly.
Somehow she felt inclined to cry. Walter had lighted a
cigar ; he had one arm around his wife ; he was thinking of
the supper he had ordered, and wondering whether he
would ask Beppo to stay and take them out later.

There was music on the water far away. It fell upon their
ears like the moaning of an Æolian harp. From one of
the palace windows there came the ripple of laughter.
Beneath the balcony there shot forth from a little canal, a
gondola gaily lit with lamps ; it sped away with great swift-
ness, and Philip watched the fading lights until they disappeared as if the sea had swallowed them. How solemnly
beautiful it all was !

Palaces on either hand, carrying the mind back to the

most romantic days of the world's strange life, full of heroic
passages of human history, gay with love ditties, red with
tragic story, ramping with war and blatant with defiant
trumpets. And oh ! how poor the modern lay of the Venetian glories, how dim the words that burned, how inter-
mittent the thoughts that breathed when Venice has been
the theme. Byron, Otway, Musset, George Sand, how flat
in comparison with the reality, ran Philip's thoughts ; how
wise that American writer, Howells, who did not strive to
describe the indescribable, but wrote a book of thoughts
and facts and impressions ; for Venice is a fact ; it was a
dream to Philip, though he fully realized that it was a fact
—it and its palaces, its Doges, its great wars, its rebellions,
its Bridge of Sighs and its historic Rialto, its pageants and
its pictures, its San Marco of the grand old ancient days,
and its Florians of the frivolous present. " But who shall
paint it ? " he thought, " and why has the poetic Ruskin
tried to catalogue and set forth the details of its beauties
as if it were a pile of architectural bric-a-brac ? "

There was one thing Philip resolved and that was, not
to paint Venice. The queen of cities, she was to be suggested, not painted ; she was an Undine not to be limned
as an anatomical study but to be indicated, to be dreamed ;
the very thought of Canaletti's pictures of her serene
beauty made him shudder ; but he felt that Turner had
understood the city in the lagoons with her sinking sun,
her shimmery waters, her white and golden towers, her
lazy sailing boats, lumbering in from the sea. Philip was
hardly responsible for what he felt or thought. If he had
eaten the insane root that takes the reason prisoner, he
could not have felt more unlike himself, nor could he have
been happier in his dreamy helplessness. In the shadow
of a great steamer from the Eastern sea flying the flags of
England and the P. and O. they pulled up at the stairs of
the hotel ; and on their left, like a great white ghost, was

the robed statue of Victor Emanuel, waiting the coming of the King and Queen to have .:s fair proportions disclosed to the people.

"Supper!" said Philip, when Walter invited him to that necessary repast. "I feel as if it were a sacrilege to be hungry."

"Not at all," said Walter. "It would be if I had not taken care to order a repast; but just as nothing makes one so hungry as a good play or the opera, nothing is more exhausting than the first impressions of Venice. I remember when first I came to Venice, that trip down the canal made me as hungry as my first experience of Don Giovanni."

Jenny and Dolly appeared at supper with bright eyes and in bright costumes. Dolly was not so radiant as Jenny. The truth is, Dolly was not quite happy. Alone during those last touches of the toilette, which Dolly and Jenny often performed together, Dolly had said to her sister, "I really do not quite know whether Philip does not see a little too much in nature and art outside me, I mean, of course, to be quite happy with me; I don't want to have nature and art always in competition with fashion and me."

"My dear," said Jenny, kissing her, "you are in yourself the highest embodiment of nature and art."

"Not at all; if we were both put up to auction, I shouldn't have a chance in competition with one of those old palaces or with a moonlight night on the Grand Canal."

"You are a queer girl," Jenny replied, "he will get tired of Venice in a week. Venice is always the same; a beautiful woman is always different."

"Now, girls," said Walter, putting his head inside the door, "supper, and shall I keep Beppo for a floating siesta afterward?"

Yes," was Jenny's reply, " what is the time ? "

" Ten," said Walter.

So Beppo and his comrade ate their polenta and drank a measure of wine, and smoked their cigarettes by the quay, while the merry English party had their supper near the hotel balcony, where you could see Carlo, the head waiter, flitting to and fro in his dress coat, enjoying the chatter of the guests. Beppo and his comrade agreed that the ladies were very pretty girls. Jenny would have been much complimented if she had heard Beppo speaking of her as a girl.

" They are so free and pleasant," Beppo said, as he lay back in the boat looking up at the hotel windows. " Most English ladies are, they are like our Queen ; she is for a queen wonderfully free and pleasant-spoken. Just the queen for a free people, eh, Bettina ? "

Beppo called his comrade by his nickname Bettina, which had been given to him, because he was supposed to be womanish in his manners and had never been able to grow a beard, but who in his build and in his strong arms was quite unlike a woman : and he was still more unlike in the fact that he rarely talked, only as a rule said. " Yes " and " No " when he was not simply content to smile or frown his yeses and noes

" Yes," said Bettina.

" She will be here to-morrow, Bettina, and the King will unveil that noble statue of his royal father, Victor Emanuel, under whose banners we fought in the war, Bettina."

" Yes," said Bettina.

" And conquered, eh, Bettina ? "

" Yes," said Bettina.

" And at the base of it there is Italy in chains and Italy free ; and we helped to break her chains, eh, Bettina ? "

" Yes," said Bettina.

" And these English people are our best friends, Bettina,

and when next we have to fight they will fight with us on
shore and at sea."

"Yes," said Bettina.

While Beppo was romancing about what Italy would be
like after the next great war, the English party came out
with pretty cloaks and gauzy wraps upon their arms, the
men with cigars in their mouths. Beppo, hat in hand, was
ashore in one moment to be handing his passengers into
the gondola the next, and helping Walter to arrange the
cushions so that Dolly and Jenny should be at their most
perfect ease, with Walter and Philip at their feet, the moon
dancing away down in the sea beneath them, and sailing
majestically above them with two attendant stars.

CHAPTER XXXIII.

THE RED GONDOLA.

SOON after eleven they were once more afloat, the moon
higher and brighter, the water still and silent, the great
ocean steamer lying calm and solid at anchor, the opposite
island, with the Church of the Maggiore, sleeping in the
moonlight; a cluster of coasting craft lying in the shadow of
St. Maria della Salute ; and, as they steered by the steps
of St. Mark's, the Campanile, the Moorish towers, and the
flagstaff holding communion with the silvery stars.

Along the water line from the quay, past the Bridge of
Sighs, and by the Palace were a row of leafless trees,
mechanical contrivances of lamps, which were to be lighted
before the week was over. Even these curious additions,
artificialities that were singularly out of place, were inoffensive things in the moonlight, which softened their
harsh outlines and made them almost picturesque.

Perhaps it was the Capri that had loosened Philip's
tongue. For a time he was a very chatty companion.

He talked of the " Merchant of Venice," of the old days of the Rialto, of the Jews and the ghetto (which led to some mention of the treatment of the Jews in Russia), all in a quiet, unrhapsodical kind of way ; until they arrived at the apocryphal palace of Desdemona. Here there were lights and evidently junkettings, and under the window was a barge crowded with minstrels, who sang the " Finiculi Finicula," at which Jenny and Walter were delighted, and afterwards the Ave Maria of Gounod, which came like a sudden and unexpected benediction after the " Finiculi " chorus.

" The Moor has just killed his spotless bride," said Philip, " and this Ave Maria is her dirge."

And so they lingered here to listen to the music, and them moved slowly on towards the Rialto.

If Philip could have interpreted the echoes of the revelry going on in that palace under whose balcony they had passed ! It was a reception given by the Princess Radna, wife of the famous General Petronovitch, that made the Desdemona palace gay and festive on this third night of May, the first of Philip's first visit to Venice. The general and the princess were lodged here by the courtesy of an Italian noble, who had something more than his title upon which to maintain the dignity of his ancient house. Venice, and indeed Italy, was distinctly honored by the general's presence here with his lovely wife, during the festival prepared for the King and Queen. The general, it was understood, had a semi-official mission which also flattered the military and naval vanity of the nation.

A couple of Italian ironclads were slowly steaming through the lagoon to the quay, while the reception was going on to do honor to the sovereign, one of them to be at the disposal of the Russian guest, General Petronovitch, who had won a great reputation both as Governor of Vilnavitch, and as a commander in the field, having in this capacity rendered good service against some of the hostile tribes in Central Asia; and he had married one of the most popular women of the Russian Court, a princess and heiress to great estates. This trip to Venice was considered by the general as part of their honeymoon, and the Venetian ladies as well as the Venetian men were all agreed as to the bride's beauty; it was not Venetian; nor was it exactly Russian; it combined the French manners with the reposeful face of Gretchen.

It was known that the general had much for the lady's wealth as for her beauty and her position at court. He was a universal admirer of the sex, and hard things had been said about his infidelities even during his honeymoon; but it is a censorious world. There had come to Venice a certain distinguished stranger whose charms had already, it was said, given the Princess Radna cause for uneasiness; and whose appearance at the Opera the night previously to the princess' reception had divided the attention of the audience with the stage, so exquisitely was she dressed, so radiant were her jewels, so lovely was her red-gold hair, so pathetically beautiful the expression of her deep violet eyes.

While Philip and his friends were dreaming about Desdemona under her hypothetical balcony, this lovely stranger was just leaving her gondola at the palace steps to be received by the princess, who was already jealous of her—and had protested in vain against being compelled to receive her. In the old days of Venice, when every lover more or less carried his life in his hands among these splendid palaces, with their mysterious windows and alcoves looking out upon dim canals and gondolas that lay hid in shaded nooks, the princess would have had no difficulty in ridding herself of her rival—had the reward been a favor to some lover of whom the general might

have had equal cause for dislike, as the princess imagined
she had, to hate the lovely stranger. But who knows
whether under the inspiration of a great love or an equally
intense hate, the Venice of to-day may not have tragic
inspiration enough for a fatal intrigue?

"Could you have believed anything on this earth could
be so absolutely beautiful?" asked Jenny, as the gondoliers paused by the bridge of the Rialto to permit their
passengers to contemplate the Fondaco dei Turchi, upon
which the moonlight was falling in silvery splendor,
whitening the marble columns of its open logia, and casting a broad, steady reflection upon its antique façade.
What a history there was there to dwell upon! Walter
had looked it up, and was enabled, much to his own satisfaction, to mention its salient points.

"This is, of course, the old palace restored," he said.
"It repeats the original as nearly as possible. It was
built in the thirteenth century by the family of the Palmien
of Pesaro. In 1331 it was bought by the Republic and presented to the Marquises of Este, Lords of Briare, who
gave entertainments here, at which Ariosto and Tasso
were guests. The Fondaco dei Todeschi, and it is now
simply a museum, nothing more nor less, the Museum of
Venice."

"But many a noble palace along the Grand Canal has
come to a worse destiny?" suggested Philip.

"Oh, yes, and the fact that there are lodging-houses
and other show places, in which relics of their glories and
miscellaneous bric-a-brac are for sale in the marble halls,
make Venice to my mind all the more pathetic," Walter
replied, with an accent of sorrow in his voice that for a
minute or two quite troubled his wife.

"What's the matter, Walter?" she asked.

"Oh, nothing, my dear; I was only trying to get into
tune with Forsyth, who, of course, is looking at the poetic
side of things, and here the poetic is the pathetic."

"Ah," said Philip, "if one only had imagination enough to see the other side of this wonderful picture," as the boat floated once more out of the broad moonlight into the shadow; "if one only had the heart to think only of its glories, its pageants, its color, its victories, its laughter, its merry-makings."

"Yes," said Dolly, thinking she felt all this, but mistaking the depression that had fallen upon her fancy for something more than the woman's instinct of trouble that was beginning to cloud it. "Yes, indeed, it seems impossible to think of the happy side of life in those days when Venice was mistress of the seas."

"But you don't mean to say, Dolly, that you are languishing under the shadow of her degeneracy and downfall?" remarked Walter briskly.

"Yes, I am; at least I feel sad, and I don't know of any other cause for my sadness than lies in the contemplation of these beautiful remains of greatness."

"I wonder," thought Philip, "how she would feel had she the cause of tribulation that afflicts me?" for as in human faces that Jewish face we wot of was the most tenderly sweet and pathetic, so the sad glamour of it associated itself in his mind with the ruined palaces, the silent halls, the sleeping moonlight, the whispering waters, the wailing music of this midnight travel. He thought of Milan. The memory of the journey to Dover had grown old. He believed when the locomotive was panting on its way to its Venetian marshes that he was putting miles and miles between himself and temptation. He was resolved that if it were not so, in fact, it should be so in regard to his conduct. Walking with Dolly in the sunshine at Milan, and also when listening to the organ in the great Cathedral, there he had repeated these vows to himself, and had shown special marks of attention to the girl who was to be his wife, insomuch that Jenny had remarked to

Walter, "how Philip loves our dear Dolly ;" but Dolly, by that subtle instinct that woman is blessed with, or cursed with, as the case may be, felt the hollowness of all this, detected the want of a true ring in Philip's loving words. She noted the embarrassment that Philip felt now and then, when the face and memory of the other woman obtruded themselves in the course of his tender speeches ; and this night, on the Grand Canal, while his thoughts would wander to the Russian-Jewish woman, her heart beat plaintively to her doubts and fears, touched with suspicion and melancholy that she endeavored to debit to the past and its faded glories, to the stories of Desdemona and Juliet, to the mournful episodes of Venetian history, and the emblematical structure of the Bridge of Sighs that seemed to be the natural pictorial epilogue to the gloomiest of Italian tragedies.

"It is difficult to talk," said Philip presently, when Jenny had remarked upon their general silence.

"It is not necessary," said Jenny, "we can pretty well interpret each other's thoughts."

"If we could ! " said Philip with something like a sigh,

" And what then ? " said Jenny, laughingly. " I will give you a penny for yours."

" You don't bid high enough."

" I will give you all you dare ask," said Dolly, half jestingly, half archly, half in earnest, and with her heart at the moment full of a strange curiosity.

" Pardon ! " said Beppo, interposing with a drag on his oar, that brought the gondola to a sudden standstill, " this is the palace where the lady of the red gondola is. staying, very rich, very beautiful, a Russian, arrived here three days since, everybody talking about her. Yesterday she went to the ghetto and distributed a thousand marks among the poor ; and this is her gondola coming from the reception given by the Princess Radna, wife of General

Petronovitch, the famous Russian general who has come to attend the fêtes to the King and Queen."

As he spoke there bounded out from beneath Desdemona's balcony, a gondola, with two rowers, the one at the stern tall and broad of limb, the other lithe and neat. Beneath the awning of the boat reclined the figure of a woman, and apart, in an attitude of respectful attention, that, of a man in evening dress, the gondoliers were in crimson uniform, and red was the prevailing color of the decorations of the boat, which was lighted with one or two lamps, one near the stern falling upon a long drift of crimson brocade that swept through the water like a flag dipped to a conqueror, or the red signal of some tragic thought or deed. The boat swung past them without a cry or salute from the gondoliers of either vessel ; and the Milbankes and Dolly strained their eyes to see the face of the lovely occupant, but 'twas either veiled or in shadow.

Philip's heart beat with a quick anxiety as he asked in a tone of voice which he strove to make indifferent, " Who is the lady ? "

" She is called the Countess Stravensky," said Beppo.

CHAPTER XXXIV.

" THE Countess Stravensky ? " said Philip, repeating Beppo's information.

" Yes, sir, a Russian who looks like a Venetian."

" Your friend ? " remarked Jenny, with a curious note of interrogation in her tone and manner.

" I presume so," said Philip, as calmly as he could, with his heart beating at double quick time, and all his good virtuous resolves evaporating.

" An unexpected surprise," said Walter.

" You should surely say an unexpected pleasure," re-

marked Dolly, who was instinctively and otherwise jealous
of the Russian beauty.

"Did you know she was coming to Venice?" asked
Jenny.

"No," said Philip. "I understood she was going to St.
Petersburg."

"Did she know we were coming to Venice?" Dolly
asked.

"I don't quite remember; perhaps my mother may have
mentioned it," said Philip, suddenly finding his voice. "She
is no doubt here for the fêtes."

"No doubt," said Jenny.

They slackened speed by the Bridge of Sighs, where a
barge-load of musicians were entertaining a little cluster
of gondolas in which were many merry people, who joined
pianissimo in the chorus of "Finiculi, Finicula."

The moon shone full upon the canal, and the scene
had a soothing and fascinating effect. Philip found himself strangely under its influence. None of the little party
spoke for some time. Dolly's hand found its way to Philip's
in a timid inquiring fashion. Philip struggled hard to
hold it with the sincerity that had a few minutes before
actuated all he had said and felt in regard to Dolly and
the futute of their two lives; but the red gondola had left
behind it a trail of feverish sentiment, and he was once
more in imagination traveling with a certain passenger by
train from London to Dover. How mean and untrue he
felt all at once, how unworthy of the confidence of the
pure-spirited, high-minded, kind-hearted London girl!

"We will return now, Beppo," said Mrs. Milbanke.

"Yes, nadame," said Beppo.

The two gondoliers bent their backs to their work, and
the boat rushed through the moonlit waters. In a few
minutes they were at the hotel.

"It is a showy boat, that red gondola," remarked Jenny
to Beppo, as he gave her his hand for the shore.

17

"Oh, yes," said Beppo.

"But we shall look as smart as that to-morrow, eh, Beppo?" said Walter.

"Yes, yes," said Beppo, grinning; "your excellency has good taste."

And he had; for the next day when Beppo and his comrade took off their hats at the steps and offered their broad palms to assist the ladies into their pretty vessel, both Dolly and Jenny expressed their surprise and delight.

"Beautiful!" said Jenny.

"What a change! Is this the same gondola?" asked Dolly.

Beppo showed his white teeth, and his fine figure was complemented by his fine dress, a rich blue cloth with crimson sash. The gondola was elegantly furnished with blue silk cushions and Oriental rugs, and at the shining steel prow there fluttered a tiny silk Union Jack, the red and blue of which the bluish-green water reflected back again as if in token of amity and admiration.

It was a glorious day. The sun was far away in a blue sky. There was not a cloud. A pleasant breeze came in a warm genial ripple from the Adriatic. It seemed like an invitation to every sentiment of love and friendship. "All the world is happy," it might have been saying, "and this is the loveliest spot in all the world." Philip tried to think so. On the other side of the lagoon the Church of Santa Maria del Giglio was decorated for illumination at night. On the left, beating up towards them were a couple of the great boats of the River Po, with pointed stern and enormous rudder, the sun finding out rich tones in the ridges of their furled sails, the red-tasselled caps of the sternsmen presenting grateful points of color on the black and brown of the hull and deck.

As Beppo leaned upon his oar, the gondola shot away from the shadow of a great P. and O. steamer gay with

bunting and sparkling with tiny lamps. The statue of the
King was still enveloped in its white covering like a daylight ghost ; and along the riva the glassy trees ready to
be lighted at night had an odd out of place appearance.
But there was a gay stream of people walking, and quite
as much bustle on the water with flashing gondolas and
gay barges getting ready to join in the aquatic procession.
Ahead, the Campanile shot right up into the blue sky, the
banners of St. Mark's flew in front of that dazzling church.
On the right, by the Custom House, a little fleet of coast-
ers rested at anchor, but with their sails still more or less
set, brown and yellow, and here and there decorated with
strange devices. The Church of Santa Maria della Salute
slept on the water, in spite of its frame work of Vauxhall
lamps, which at night were to mark its beautiful architectural lines against the starry sky. Flags were flying everywhere. From the windows of the gorgeous palaces hung
rich brocades and Oriental draperies, tapestried stories of
ancient days. In the balconies were pretty women, and
below were picturesque men. Crowds were hurrying from
all sorts of by-streets, and boats working their way from
all kinds of mysterious canals.

It was a wonderful scene. It dazed Philip. He had
never beheld anything so impressive in its picturesqueness. All his memories of Russia, and his recollections
of English out-door displays, found nothing to compare
with this informal kind of public demonstration, unregu-
lated alike as regards the people as it was in regard to
the decorations of the palaces, the varied colors of the
flying boats, and without a single obtrusive hint of a master hand in the preparations for the illuminations at night.
Nothing seemed to have been designed, and yet everything was perfect in arrangement and color, and so overwhelming was the beauty of the architectural avenue
through which they were making their way, so superb the

sunshine, that even the theatrical tokens of the night to come were absorbed, and became unobjectionable.

There was on all hands a general air of delighted expectation.   Here and there between the palaces and at odd points, are steps leading to distant water streets, and these were coigns of vantage for the sovereign people, who filled up the open spaces.   Among these democratic assemblies were some of the most beautiful women in the world.   The poorer citizens of this city in the sea have inherited a physical loveliness, the tradition of which has come down to us from classic history, and which lives in the never dying art of Italy, in the pictures by famous masters, and better still in the women of this nineteenth century, who still go about the streets of Venice bareheaded and with slippered feet.

Presently the fleet of gondolas and gorgeous barges came as it seemed to a sudden anchor.   All the varying and flitting colors of the moment stood still in one spot, as if the finger of Fate had paused in turning life's kaleidoscope to permit of a restful observation of some specially lovely design that had been developed after many changes.   It was a happy jumble of artistic form and tone, of radiant color,   and subdued hues of brown and blue in the shadows.   So beautiful was the picture that it looked as if it might   fade away at any moment, and leave Leicester Square or the Strand mockingly behind.   This is how Philip felt, and how he phrased it in his mind in one of those moments when he was not on the look out for the red gondola.   At length the distant whistle of a railway train was heard.   Then everybody knew that the King and Queen of Italy, the idols of the people, and justly so, were steaming across the marshes.   Next there was a firing of big guns; then the music of military bands, the air El Rey ; anon there is a movement ashore, and in sympathy therewith a movement on the canal ; at last the picturesque

chaos begins to assume something like a pleasant irregu-
larity of order ; the day's pageant has begun.

Picture the scene. It is almost impossible to describe
it. You might be told the names of every great barge ; the
period of the costumes of the rowers ; it would be easy
to give you a running fire of historic titles and architectural characteristics of the palaces that are ranged on either
side of the procession, each one with a wonderful history ;
but by and bye you would begin to skip the record and
search for the red gondola. It is therefore best to supply
you with material for fancy. You can fill in the details
from Ruskin, George Sand, Ouida, Triarte, Howells, Rogers, and the established guide books. Get into your
mind something of the atmosphere of the most romantic
period of the world's history. Think of the haughty Doges
in their magnificent robes. Try and realize what Venice
was. Then remember what she is, a poetic and pathetic
wreck of her imperial greatness—the stage remaining with
its gorgeous properties, its superb sets, its noble architecture, its glorious sky, the actors dead and gone ; but to-
day moved and radiated with the new life of a better age,
with nobler aspirations, without, it is true, the inspiration
of barbaric and cultured art to make the day shine and
glitter with gold and precious stones, yet exhibiting
artistic links between then and now.

Think of these things, and then look around you and
note this modern pageant with its relics of the past, its
superb costumes, and animated with an ambition quite as
laudable as that which built St. Mark's and decorated it
with beaten gold. Imagine yourself with the Milbankes
and Philip and Dolly Norcott in the midst of this procession, the most impressive since the government of the
Council of Ten. It is a moving mass of energetic life and
brilliant color. There has been nothing so gorgeous on
these classic waters since the Carnival pageants of the four-

teenth century.   Among the guests and visitors are representatives of the most famous of the ancient Doges.   There
is a family of Greeks who claim descent from a famous
chief of Venice.   They are here in a gondola decorated
after the ancient manner, and with their gondoliers attired
as in the olden days.   Making its way to a prominent
position is a stately barge rowed by a dozen men, who
might be servants to the Capulets in Romeo and Juliet;
and close by, another that might belong to the Lady of
Belmont.   Here is the small red fez, the long hair, the
slashed sleeves that one has seen so often on the stage and
in pictures of the time; in companionship with the men
who are propelling the Greek barge are a party of rowers
befrocked as one sees them in the illustrations to Byron's
Corsair.

In competition for place is a superb gondola that looks
like an exaggerated toy of gold taken from the top of some
giant bride-cake, the rowers in blue sailor costume with
yellow sashes.   Rising gaily upon the busy waters with
swan-like motion in the wake of the rest, and making for
the King's barge, is a barge of white and gold; it is
followed by another of blue and white—the white being
Venetian lace which trails with the velvet at the stern of
the barge, joining many other draperies and brocades,
silks, and laces, that dabble the water with color, and add
to a reckless generosity of wealth flung hither and thither,
as one can imagine in Italian displays of the past.   Foremost among another group of gondolas, is one which is
manned with rowers who recall the glories of English
county life in the days of Fielding; a second, not unlike,
with servants in plush breeches and tall hats; a third is a
gondola of a barbaric style, with a hood of fantastic shape,
and with men fantastically dressed, the whole effect defiant.
Imagine these and a hundred other notable boats, gondolas, barges all making their way to surround the taller

vessel of the King with its magnificent golden eagles at the prow and a typical figure of regenerated Italy. You take your glass and you find that around the King's barge are other State vessels, the Bucentor, for instance, with its tradition of the bridal of the Adriatic ; and all at once the whole throng of aquatic vehicles begin to dance and make their way to the Royal Palace, amidst the discharge of distant artillery and the clash and bray of trumpets. The palaces of the Grand Canal rise up as if from the bosom of the waters. They are brave with color, and alive with excited people. The sun shines. The sky is a pale ultramarine ; the whole thing a fairy tale ; and so real that it makes more than one of the Milbanke party feel emotional.

Philip is lost for the time being in this feast of form and color. Dolly sits perfectly still by his side. Jenny is up and down twenty times to catch glimpses of the Queen. Walter hands his glass to every one by turns because it is a very powerful one, and he continually thinks he has spotted the best incidents of the show. Long before the cheers from the Rialto have been broken up with other demonstrative sounds they find themselves really part of the royal procession indeed, almost alongside the royal barge, and partaking of a share of the gracious recognitions of both King and Queen, who smile their acknowledgments of every loyal cheer, and bow to many a passing and accompanying boat. Jenny noticed that the King gazed approvingly upon their gondola, because it carried the flag which Italy most honors among the nations.

At the height of the enjoyment which Mrs. Milbanke felt in being so near the royal barge, the spirits of the party were somewhat dashed (though none of them except Philip could quite explain why they felt the shadow of the incident fall upon them more than upon any other boat) by the sudden appearance of the red gondola. It came shooting forth from one of the little canals right into the midst of the procession, and attracted universal attention. It stood out from the rest, not only on account of its positive color, but for the singular distinction of the lady who sat enthroned at the bow, in a simple silken costume of white silk and Venetian lace, her gondoliers in red and black, with velvet caps; and her secretary, Signor Ferrari, in the ordinary morning dress of the time.

The red gondola took up a position near the royal and state barges, and alongside the yellow and black gondola of the Russian general and his wife, the princess. The general bowed to the countess with much empressement, the princess contented herself with the slightest recognition that might pass for courtesy. The countess, Jenny declared, fairly ogled the general; but Jenny did not like the countess, and might have exaggerated the expression of the countess' face. Philip noticed that the countess was also honored by the gracious smiles of the King and Queen. He would not admit to himself that there was something in the glance of General Petronovitch that he did not like; but he had not seen how the countess had appealed to the vanity of her distinguished countryman (if a Jewess may be said to have a country or a countryman outside the pale of her co-religionists), in the drop of her violet eyes and the play of her ostrich fan.

When the procession arrived at the canal steps of the palace, the red gondola had vanished as rapidly as it had previously appeared, for no sooner had their Majesties landed, than Jenny and the rest, looking round for the red gondola, did not find it. Beppo, guessing their disappointment, remarked that Madame the Russian, who looked like a Venetian picture out of its frame for the occasion, had directed her men to make for the Fazio Palace the moment the King and Queen had left their barge, and he must own that they were a couple of clever gondoliers, though he had not seen either of them on the canal for years ; curious men ; Jews he thought, born in Venice, but of a roving disposition ; fought in the war, brave enough, but rolling stones, never know where to have them ; and so on, Beppo talking to himself as much as to Walter and the rest.

The reader of the first chapter of this section of our story has already met one of the men of whom Beppo was speaking — Paul Petroski (with the strange sinister face that was comedy on one side, tragedy on the other), commissioned for Venice by Anna Klosstock in the room of a back street in Soho. The other man was the friend he had mentioned at the London meeting of the Brotherhood, and both are here to obey the orders of Anna Klosstock 𝒴 and A'ndrea Ferrari, in a great cause.

CHAPTER XXXV.

PLOTTERS IN COUNCIL.

THE two gondoliers of whom Beppo had spoken in complimentary terms as to their skill and bravery passed the Milbanke party in the hall of the Beau Rivage after the procession had broken up. They were guests in the house, as the Milbankes and Philip were ; but they occupied apartments with the servants of the hotel, and took their meals humbly with them, supplementing, however, their polenta and fish with a bottle or two of Chianti, and entertaining their fellows with stories of the war, and incidents of their apocryphal travels. They all agreed that the King was worthy of his father, and that Italy enjoyed an exceptional liberty, won by the courage and with the blood of the sovereign people.

While Paul Petroski and his comrade were discussing politics and Chianti, the Milbankes were recalling the incidents of the morning over afternoon tea in the best room of the little hotel, the balcony of which overlooked the riva and was nearly opposite the linen-covered statue of Victor Emanuel, which his son and the Queen had arrived in Venice to inaugurate.

The countess and Ferrari at about the same time were in council at the Fazio Palace, in a back room that overlooked a canal more than usually gloomy, more than usually confined, but the waters of which were more than usually swift, probably the result of the narrowness of the channel, which hardly seemed to give room enough for two boats to pass.   Here also was a balcony, very different from that of the Hotel Beau Rivage, with its open view of the Lido in front and on the left the blue waters of the Adriatic.   This balcony was spacious.   It looked upon the dead wall of a dead palace, dead as the Doges who had visited its once illustrious owner ; dead as the valiant inscription beneath its Oriental portico ; dead as the decaying poles at its bricked-up doorway.

You could hardly see the sky between the two palaces, unless you looked down into the water that reflected the grey lichen decked walls.   As you turned your eyes to and fro and inspected the locality, you could realize the truth or probability of all the Venetian love stories you had ever read ; you felt that this spot above all you had seen was made for romance, for intrigue, for silken ladders, for mysterious gondolas and serious masqueraders.

The Fazio Palace had recently been restored in parts. The front, which gave upon one of the most important branches of the Grand Canal, was radiant with gold and bright with restored frescoes ; but the back, with its balconies upon the narrow way to which reference has been made, remained just as it was in the days before Falerio ; and the rooms of this out-of-the-way wing were also more or less in a state of dilapidated picturesqueness.   The

Countess Stravensky liked the privacy of the balconied room, away from the general staircases, with its picture-panels, and its tapestried vestibule. She had examined the place with Ferrari, and had found a doorway provided with great oaken shutters that completely isolated this portion of the palace ; and here the countess had set up a boudoir where she could be private at any time ; where she could read and write without the possibility of disturbance, and where, if she desired it, she could receive a guest in secret.

" You have done your work most excellently and com-pletely," said the countess, who had changed her proces-sional dress for an easy tea gown. " I thank you for your devotion, and applaud your taste."

Ferrari bowed his head and drew the curtain of the vestibule.

" It is all we could desire, you think so ? "

He showed her a little room inside the vestibule which might have been a dungeon, so thick and strong were its walls, so dim its light, and so generally gruesome its atmo-sphere.

" What tragedies have been done in this strange weird city of the sea," said Anna, as she looked into the room.

" Mere stage-plays compared with those of the Kremlin, the House of Preventive Detention, Schluusselberg, the Ravelin of Troubetzkoi, and the bagnios of Siberia."

" Yes," she replied. " Yes, and the mines ; but I was thinking just at that moment, Andrea, of romance. Last night I was reading Byron ; and this morning these Stories of the Bridge of Sighs."

She took up a new book as she spoke, but Ferrari only said :—

" I am glad you entirely approve of all this," and as he said so his ferret eyes glanced from the window to the vestibule, from the vestibule to the countess.

"It is well," she replied. "I will rest now."

Ferrari left the room for a minute, returning with a number of letters.

"These are the last replies to your invitations for Monday."

"Thank you," she said.

He placed them upon a table inlaid with various marbles.

"You are not well?" he said inquiringly. "Did you see the gondola with the two English ladies, and the British flag?"

"Yes."

"I thought otherwise."

"I saw it," she replied, "and *he* saw me. It makes me sad, dear friend."

The accent with which the countess spoke gave an added tone of pensiveness to the expression of her words. Ferrari, accustomed to her manner and her moods, did not notice this perhaps, but he felt that there was a softness in her tone of voice which was unusual. He had long enjoyed the privilege of an intimacy that gave him perfect freedom to say whatever he thought well for Anna and the cause in which they were both engaged. Never once had he made love to her ; never once had he dreamed of doing so. From the first moment of their renewed acquaintance after the tragedy of Czarovna she had made him understand that the relationship between them might be that of a man's friendship, the bond of two souls pledged to vengeance upon their mutual enemies, and more particularly in her case upon one who seemed until the last few months destined to elude their best laid plots and snares. By a tacit understanding they were to each other simply devoted friends and fellow conspirators ; they had in their memories the conflagration at Czarovna ; but above all the knout and the steppes and the prisons of Siberia.

Ferrari's devotion to the Brotherhood of which we have
already heard had nobler springs than Anna's, who had
but one dominant passion of revenge. They had both
found their companionship a comfort in its way, because
they could both make allowances for each other. Ferrari's
memory for Anna's once happy home and its desolation,
was as fresh as if he had seen her lover beaten to death
and the lashes of the knout falling on her own fair flesh
only yesterday. They were companions in adversity and
plots of vengeance ; in a desire, also, to help their people ;
but there the union of mind and hope and thought ended,
it had nothing to do with love, nor had Anna shown the
least sign of the revival of woman's tender feelings since
she left the Russian hospital until she met Philip Forsyth ;
her marriage to Count Stravensky being a political marriage, solemnized, as we know, on the death-bed of the
rebel count.

" He saw you ? " said Ferrari.

" Yes, I think so," she replied.

" Did he know you were coming to Venice ? "

" No."

" You knew he was coming ? "

" Yes."

" You have no secret from me in this, eh ? "

" None," said Anna.

" You traveled with him from London to Dover ? "

" Have I not said so ? "

" He loves you, eh ? "

" I think he does, in a mad boyish fashion that belongs
rather to your Italian country than to England."

" And you ? "

" Ah, Ferrari, I thought I was a heroine. I thought the
woman in me was dead and gone ; it is not. Do you not
think this English youth is like what our dear young rabbi
was ? "

" I am glad you speak of him as a youth," Ferrari replied.

" Why ? "

" Because you will regard his passion as that of a boy, and not let it move your woman's nature that you speak of."

" But, Andrea, it has, it has! I am miserable as a consequence, miserable. I have the feeling of a dream that blots out all but my father's house in the sweet time you know of."

" Before I came and pulled it all down about you."

" No, no, Andrea Ferrari."

" Yes, yes, I say, it was I. But for me you would have been happy; it was I who gave the excuse for butchery, and worse—and worse," he repeated significantly.

" No, no; some other excuse would have been found."

" But why this confession, Anna Klosstock, Countess Stravensky—why ? "

" Not to alter our plans, Andrea, but to relieve my mind."

" If I had not been old enough to be your father," said Ferrari, sitting by her side and taking her hand, " old enough, but not good enough ; if I had been young and had been made for what women call love, it would have been well, Anna, if we could have joined what is called hands and hearts.'

" And would you after what you say is worse than butchery ? And would you with the brand of the knout upon her ? "

" Ah, my child," Ferrari replied as if they were discussing a more or less ordinary matter, " that brand is an honor. But you love this English painter, eh ? Is it so after all your vows, after your pledges, and with the work you have to do that is so far away from such ideas, and the hottest

of it so near? Well, well, and yet we go on trusting women in the Brotherhood. Then the English youth must be
one of us, eh? Is that what you mean?"

" No, no ! Not for worlds ! "

" What then? "

" I know not ; but have no fear about the cause and the
work. I feel better for what I have said. And now to
sleep and dream."

" And get rest, the needful armor of battle and victory."

She took from a small cabinet a phial, poured a few drops
into a wineglass of water.

" Au revoir," she said. " Order the gondola one hour
before midnight. We shall take him on board at eleven."

' Him !" said Andrea, his thoughts on Philip.

" Him ! " said the countess.

" But whom? " asked Ferrari.

" General Petronovitch," she replied, laying her hand
upon Ferrari's arm.

" Yes," he said.

" Paul will find a person in the dress of a civilian standing near the ferry by the Rialto ; when the gondola appears
he will raise his right hand ; Paul will take him on board
and row towards the Lido until I tell him to return. The
general will alight here."

" Here ! "

" At the front entrance of the palace, and will then take
his leave ; he will desire to enter, but I shall give him the
rendezvous for Monday night an hour before the reception."

" Yes, yes ; that is understood. Countess, forgive me
if I doubted you for one moment, your courage, your word,
the fulfilment of your oath to me, and to the dead."

" Call me Anna, friend," she replied. " I forgive you,
Andrea Ferrari. Send Marie to me at ten, I shall sleep
until that hour."

"One word," said Ferrari. "Should he recognize you?"

"It is impossible, I tell you. I have told you so a hundred times. Who could recognize the Queen of the Ghetto, the simple modest know-nothing of Czarovna, in the Countess Stravensky?"

"I recognized you."

"But you knew the count."

"Petronovitch knew the count."

"But not as you knew him—not as one of us."

"You feel safe in this?"

"Perfectly," she replied. "Petronovitch thinks me dead. Who that had seen me borne to the hospital could think otherwise?"

"Who indeed, poor soul!" said Ferrari.

"Then be of good cheer," she replied. "All will be well."

"I kiss your hand," said Ferrari, his face brightening. "You are worthy to lead the Brotherhood."

"Even the sun has its dark clouds, Andrea. I shall not play you false. Look to yourself, and put your discreet soul into the minds of Paul and his comrade. And now I must sleep."

As she said this, she drew aside a portiere opposite the vestibule and disappeared.

CHAPTER XXXVI.

SHADOWS FALL ON THE MERRY SISTERS.

IF this were a history of the Venetian fêtes, the glories of the Art Exhibition, the inauguration of the Victor Emanuel Statue, the launching of Italian gunboats and the magnificent incidents of peace and war, of which these events were incidents in what might be called the grand *denouement* of Italian unity, the author would have to dwell upon details that belong rather to the journalist and the historian than to himself. The task would be pleasant enough, the general subject of sufficient importance for accuracy of date and circumstances ; but the occurrences in question belong to this present narrative only by way of accessory fact and color.

It will be sufficient in respect of the adventures we are chronicling to say, at this point, that after many days of busy preparation the night of illumination came, a night fraught with tragic significance to certain of the actors in the drama of the life of Anna Klosstock. The King and Queen had performed their important and interesting functions, and the municipality and citizens of Venice had prepared the last of the impressive demonstrations of the week—the after-dark decoration of the city.

Looking from the balcony of the hotel on the Riva degli Schiavoni a wonderful sight was spread out before our friends, the Milbankes and the lovers. The city in the sea with ships and boats all one lurid blaze of light above, the moon looking on with its calm attendant stars. The island and church of San Giorgio Maggiore loomed up from the lagoon, the shore lying in dark shadow, the quay alive with people walking between a long row of blazing Marguerite daisies in honor of the Queen Margherita, the church made strikingly distinct in its outline of pale green lamps which were in delicate contrast to the Bengal lights of some adjacent shipping. In the centre of the island the Lion of St. Mark's stood out against the sky, flanked with the letters U. and M. in colored fires.

On the left, looking down the lagoon, the Peninsular and Oriental steamer was gayer than the two Italian war ships lying off the Arsenal, the English captain having converted his slumbering vessel into something that might

18

have been fairy-like, but for the tremendous solidity of the steamer's ponderous hull, marked out with rippling fires and bearing aloft, in emblazonry of lamp and transparency, the flags and banners of Italy and Great Britain.

As far as the eye could reach on the right, away past the Bridge of Sighs, the steps of Saint Mark's, the Campanile, the Custom House and the famous adjacent church of Maria della Salute, the air was luminous with artificial light, and the water was alive with every class of boat and gondola, each vessel bearing variegated lamps of every shape and color. ' Songs and choruses came up to the Riva balcony in a curious complication of discordant sounds, with now and then flashes of melody; the National Anthem, and the cheering, defiant strains of that Neapolitan melody, the " Funiculi, Funicula," which had made so strange an appeal to the sentimental mind of Philip Forsyth.

It was not yet the hour at which they were invited to the Countess Stravensky's reception at the Palazzo Fazio. The idea of this brilliant function was to swell the moonlight parade of boats with a distinguished company between ten and eleven, at which time it was understood that the King and Queen would enjoy the scene and take part in it *incognito*.

Walter, Philip and Dolly were so much overcome with the scene before them, that, judging by their silence, they were at the moment indifferent to the social delights which Jenny anticipated at the Fazio Palace.

Philip, however, was far more engrossed in the possibilities of the future than in the contemplation of the present. His state of mind might be described as drifting. It was like a boat upon some calm, fascinating stream, making its way with the current, without compass or rudder, and content to glide on, fanned by perfumed breezes and lulled with sweet narcotics.

Dolly found herself a little out of tune with the situation. She realized that Philip was intensely absorbed, and that he answered her observations mostly in monosyllables.

Walter chatted and pointed out artistic effects, artificial and natural, and Jenny remarked more than once how kind it was of the Countess Stravensky to give them the opportunity of seeing a phase of Venetian life, which otherwise might have been outside their experience.

Continental aristocracy, Jenny went on to reflect, were less bound to the wheel of formality than the English. The countess had evidently the moment she heard of their presence in Venice despatched her messenger and cards to them without delay. It was a gracious piece of courtesy on her part, none the less pleasant that they had to thank Philip for it.

It may be said at once, for the reader's information, that the countess had a generous object in view when she invited Philip, the Milbankes and Miss Norcott to this reception.

She well knew that if ever there had been the slightest chance of a response on her part to the declaration of Philip, the tragic incident of the night had placed between them a still wider gulf. She was anxious to emphasize the finality of their separation by her marked reception of Miss Norcott as his *fiancée*, and by other indications of the purely Platonic sentiments she entertained towards him.

Philip, however, as the time approached for Beppo and his comrades to carry their English passengers to the Fazio Palace, found his thoughts drifting as far away from Dolly as they had drifted down the torrent of passion during that never to be forgotten journey from London to Dover.

" It will be very interesting," said Jenny, addressing Philip, " to see what society is really like in Venice,

When I was here before with Walter, we saw a little of it, but it was mostly professional ; tainted, I might say, if Walter will forgive me, with business connec'cd with a curious international law-suit."

" In which I succeeded for my clients," chimed in Walter

" Of course, of course," said Jenny, " that goes without saying, and your Venetian friend had indeed quite a touch of the grand manner of the ancient advocates who, I suppose, pleaded before the Doges."

" Why, my dear," interposed Walter, "and I mention it on the authority of Mr. Howells, in whose Venetian life you so delight, the best people in the best society in Venice are advocates; an order of consequence, as you suggest, even in the times of the Republic ; although shut out from participation in public affairs by a native Government, as it was, when Howells lived in Venice, by a foreign one."

" Austria was in authority then, I presume," remarked Philip, who endeavored to take at least a perfunctory interest in the conversation.

" Yes," said Jenny.

" Daniel Manin, the President of '48," continued Walter, " was of this professional class which, to quote your Republican friend again, ' by virtue of its learning, enlightenment, and attainments, occupies a place in the esteem and regard of the Venetian people far above that held by the effete aristocracy.' "

" Then I begin to fear we may have seen on our previous visit what may be called the best society in Venice," said Jenny.

" Not at all," Walter replied ; " the present is a very exceptional occasion. You will meet to-night not only the best people in Venice, but the best in Italy ; eminences, great generals, distinguished men and women of all classes, not to mention notable representatives of the foreign embassies. General Petronovitch and his beautiful Russian wife, a princess in her own right, I believe, are to be present. I think Philip can tell you something of these Italian guests."

" I have no acquaintance with them," said Philip. " I once heard Lady Marchmount speak of them. Petronovitch was the Russian governor who, I believe, put down the rising against the Jews some years ago in Southern Russia. He also rendered some great services to the Czar in Central Asia. Should there be another great European war, it is understood that he will hold a prominent command. He has been decorated by the Czar, and is probably entitled to the distinction of ' Prince,' but he is simply known as General Petronovitch ; very wealthy, very powerful, and fortunate in his marriage."

Philip went on talking in this strain, without taking any particular interest in what he was saying. Dolly sat looking out upon the lagoon.

" The Jews, by the way," said Walter, " hold quite an exceptional position in Venice. Next to the advocates in position come the physicians. Both are, as a rule, men of letters, and write for the newspapers, and many popular doctors are Hebrews. Howells mentions that even in the old jealous times, the Jews exercised the art of medicine, and took important rank. Oddly enough, the Venetian doctors pass most of their time sitting upon the benches in the pretty and well-furnished apothecary shops, where they discuss politics and art. Each physician has his own favorite apothecary, and has his name inscribed there on a brass plate against the wall, and, as a rule, if he is wanted, it is, as a rule, at the apothecary's that messengers seek him."

" You have read your ' Venetian Life ' as carefully as I have," remarked Jenny, laughing.

"Oh, yes," said Walter, "I always make a point of knowing as much as possible what has been said and written about the places I visit."

"When shall we see your proposed studio, Philip?" asked Jenny, suddenly changing the conversation into a fresh channel.

"Oh, in a day or two, Mrs. Milbanke," said Philip. "I have been too much absorbed in the beauties of Venice to think of it at present, but next week we will look the place up. My friend is away, but the keys are at my disposal."

"You will want models, of course?" said Jenny.

"Yes," said Philip, "and I hear they are plentiful. But Dolly is to be my first sitter. I think she will be quite as Venetian as the ladies in Mr. Fildes' pictures."

"Oh, do you think so?" said Jenny. "You do not like Mr. Fildes' Venetian studies?"

"Indeed I do," Philip replied. "They are pictures to live with ; might have perhaps a little more of the dreamy pathetic atmosphere of the Ocean City in them, but there is all its spirit of beauty and color, I fancy. It is very difficult to criticize pictures of Venice. It seems to me almost a desperate thing to attempt them ; and yet I should think the highest inspiration that can come to the painter should be found here."

Philip talked fairly well when he took up his cue, but it was painfully apparent both to Walter and his wife that Dolly took little or no interest in the conversation.

"What is the matter, Dolly?" asked Walter.

"The matter," she said, turning her gaze from the open window to the questioner. "Nothing is the matter. I suppose I feel as Philip felt last night on the Grand Canal, that there are scenes in the world so beautiful and surprising that they are apt to make one silent rather than talkative."

"It is indeed a marvelous sight," said Philip, "and I quite sympathize with Dolly."

"But it seems to me," said Jenny, "it is an entirely different thing from our first night's experiences. All is gaiety, brightness and light to-night; lanterns and music and festivity. I don't see why this should make anyone sad."

"Not sad exactly," said Dolly, but silent."

"Oh, nonsense, nonsense!" Jenny replied, getting up and putting her arm round Dolly's waist. "You are not well, or something is the matter. Perhaps Mr. Forsyth can tell us."

"Dolly is a little pensive, that is all, I think," said Philip. "Tired, perhaps; we have done a good deal to-day, you must remember."

"And have a good deal more to do," said Jenny. "Come with me, Dolly; you must lie down for ten minutes, and a little Eau-de-Cologne will refresh you. Walter and Philip will excuse us."

Jenny accompanied Dolly to her room, where Dolly, very much unlike her usual self, laid her head upon Jenny's shoulder and burst into tears.

"I knew something was the matter," said Jenny. "What is it, my dear?"

"I don't know," said Dolly. "I fell vexed and disappointed, and I hardly know why. Philip is very kind in his way, but very different from what I should have expected."

"In what way, my love?"

"I don't want to be engaged to a morbid, dull, dreamy person, who talks of nothing but serious things—destiny, the mysteries of the soul, the higher missions of life, and all sorts of subjects utterly out of place on a holiday such as this."

"But, my dear, why don't you tell him so. You should lead the conversation into the direction that pleases you."

"I can't," said Dolly, wiping her eyes and standing erect. "I feel as if he was talking for the sake of talking. There seems to be no sympathy between us, no thoughts in common. If I try to speak about music and art, and remember some of the great names and achievements of Italy, he caps me with some far wiser thought than mine, and does it, it seems to me, in a patronizing manner, as if I were a fool. But I will not bear it. If he is as disappointed as I am with the engagement about which so much fuss has been made, I would like him to break it off at once. Don't give me Eau-de-Cologne, I don't want it."

"My dear, my dear, you are beside yourself! At least put a little Eau-de-Cologne on your handkerchief and bathe your face. Your eyes are red, and you will be positively unpresentable at the Fazio Palace if you do not lie down and calm yourself."

"Very well, I will. Do forgive me, Jenny. I am very miserable. I meant to be very happy, and I will yet, in spite of Mr. Philip Forsyth. Cannot you see how strange he is? Of course you can—talking in that highly superior, poetic, dreamy, silly, idiotic way about Venetian models and rubbish !"

Dolly's fair face flushed with anger. She hardly knew what she was saying. But it is the privilege of the novelist to know something of what was passing in her mind. She could not help thinking how differently Sam Swinford would have behaved; what a merry party they would have been; how many pretty shops they would have visited; what ices at Floria's they would have enjoyed; what water-parties, what theatres, what gaiety ! Sam Swinford would not have left Walter to initiate everything on a trip of this kind; he would have been foremost with his pleasant suggestions, his passing jokes, his ever-open purse, his genial thoughtfulness, his anticipations of every possible want or desire that would have occurred either to her or to Jenny.

It is quite possible that even in this direction of pleasant companionship she might not have had to find fault with Philip Forsyth, had not that erratic genius had the misfortune to meet the Countess Stravenski.

———

CHAPTER XXXVII.

PETRONOVITCH AND THE COUNTESS.

COMEDY indeed walked hand in hand about Venice this night, the strange beauty of which the Milbankes were contemplating.

Already, as we have seen, the shadows of Philip's mad passion for the mysterious countess had begun to fall thick and heavy upon his betrothed, without anything more to justify the girl's forebodings of trouble than the instinct that governs the judgment of women.

The gloom of coming trouble also began to cloud Philip Forsyth's fancy, and to check once more the better sentiments of his nature.

Paul Petroski's double face, however, almost contrived to wear a smile all over it. He had been closeted with Ferrari during the day; had been shown over the Fazio Palace; had inspected the countess' boudoir, and expressed much admiration for the adjacent room that

looked like a strong stone prison; had poled a gondola
under the window where the countess had been sitting
thoughtful and still; not her gondola, not the red boat
which had charmed and delighted Venice, but the genuine
black-bodied boat with its funeral hood.

The red gondola was comedy; the black one tragedy.
The moonlit scenes on the canal were the bright comedy
pictures that were to lead up to the tragic *denouement.*

The meeting with Petronovitch on the previous night,
as forecasted in a former chapter, was the prologue to all
this; and a very delightful prologue it was to the Russian
general who had governed in Vilnavitch in the last days
of the ghetto at Czarovna. She, the divine, she of his
unholy Venetian dreams, was his companion. The rendezvous had in it all the piquant force of a romance that was
to be deliciously consummated.

Ferrari, it will be remembered, had had his fears in
regard to the memories that might be revived in the mind
of General Petronovitch; but Anna Klosstock had long
since faded out of the Russian's mental vision. His
remembrance of the unfortunate child of the ghetto had
been wiped out of his mind by other conquests, and he
had at no time ever been troubled with an unruly conscience. Petronovitch, indeed, had discovered almost in
his youth that conscience is just what you make it.

There is a good deal written that is true about the
prickings of conscience,.and ruffians of the deepest dye
have no doubt suffered from remorse; but Petronovitch
had no difficulties of this kind mixed up with his nature.
He had come into the world armed with a cast-iron conscience, or with one that he could mould at his will; it was
either adamant or it was whatever he desired to make it.
Anyhow it was not a factor in regard to his ambition or
his desires. He was a sensualist and a brute; not that
he lacked the polish of courts as a veneer of the *brusquerie*

of camps. He knew when to put out his gloved hand; when, his grip of mail. Among women of society he was greatly admired; he had the dash, and daring, and the knack of making the boldness of an unscrupulous lover appear to be merely the frankness of a soldier.

Petronovitch was what men call successful with women, and he regarded the impression he had made upon the Countess Stravensky as not the least gorgeous feather in his cap, and her love not the least renowned of the memories he hoped to enshrine in his unholy storehouse of past victories. He was on the march to that goal of illicit pleasure which now occupied all his wicked hopes. The outposts had been captured,·the citadel would capitulate at discretion. .

Know Anna again! Who could possibly recognize in the lovely and distinguished Countess Stravensky the victim of devilish conspiracy and lust whom Petronovitch had last seen broken and bleeding on the way to the hospital, through whose portals men and women went to their deaths or to everlasting exile in Siberia.

So far as Petronovitch was concerned the revolt of Czarovna was as old and forgotten a story as was the memory of his reception of the queen of the ghetto at his palace on the night of Losinski's arrest and judicial murder. General Petronovitch had risen to distinction and place since then; had marched roughshod through Turkish villages, and with fire and sword over rebellious multitudes away in Central Asia; had shaken his red right hand at the English flag; had offered to carry his victorious Cossacks right up to the Indian frontier and onwards; had been forgiven by his Imperial master for rash and impolitic speeches in very admiration of his daring and bravado.

In short, Petronovitch was a famous soldier and patriot of the mighty north, with whom, should the long forecasted great war take place for supremacy in the East, England would have to reckon in the first attacks upon the distant outposts of her empire. A great, successful, popular man, General Petronovitch; a libertine, unfaithful to his wife even in the honeymoon; a tyrant, but a soldier of resource; physically brave and a favorite of the Russian Army.

He went forth on that night prior to the illuminations of Venice, the night next to that of the countess' reception, with the feelings of a conqueror who could no more be resisted in the tents of Cupid than in the camp of Mars. And yet he sat at his inamorata's feet in professed humble worship of her beauty, grateful for her gentle condescension, and Anna plied him with sweet words and suggested promises that fooled him to the top of his bent.

She was dreamy, poetical, allowed her soft hand to be pressed. How Philip would have hated Petronovitch, and her too, perhaps, could he have had a glimpse of the wooing of the Russian general and the responsive murmurs of the violet-eyed countess.

It was well that the general did not see Anna's face, except in the subdued light of the moon; nor, indeed, note the satisfied smile of the principal gondolier, Paul Petroski, who was busy with thoughts that alternately influenced the sinister side of his mouth, and alternately the comedy side, though the sinister gave a touch of its cynicism to the other.

It was a glorious night, as Petronovitch had more than once remarked, and there was music on the water; and more particularly the song of pleasure, Funiculi Funcula, and the Ave Maria too. The gondoliers had joined in the last verses of the former, and Petronovitch himself had hummed the Italian words as he stole his arm round Anna's waist. She, too, had chanted some lines of the chorus with a merry *abandon;* for, with a gay ferocity, she looked forward to the morrow, when the companion of this moonlit hour should meet her in that quiet, secret boudoir of the Fazio Palace :—

> * Elle'è montata, il sai, lassù, montata
>   La testa è gia ;
>   E andata sino in cima e poi tornata
>   E sempre qua !
>   La testa gira, gira intorno, intorno,
>   Intorno a te
>   E il dore canta come il primo giorno
>   Ti spòsa a me !
>   Lesti ! Lesti ! via ! montiam su là !
>   Funiculi ! Funiculà !

CHAPTER XXXVIII.

FERRARI'S CUE.

It will be easy to conceive that after this excursion, the Countess Stravensky would find no difficulty in obtaining the general's consent to a private visit to the Fazio Palace an hour before the reception on the night of the illumina-tions.

As the clock struck nine, General Petronovitch, who had acted strictly upon the countess' instructions, left his palace secretly, dressed for the reception, but care-fully enveloped in his cloak, he walked along the shaded

---

* Ah me ! 'tis strange that some should take to sighing,
    And like it well ;
  For me, I have not thought it worth the trying,
    So cannot tell.
  With laugh, and dance, and song, the day soon passes,
    Full soon is gone ;
  For mirth was made for joyous lads and lasses
    To call their own.
    Listen ! Listen ! hark ! the soft guitar !
      Funiculi ! Funiculà !

trottoir of the little canal, and found the doorway of the
Fazio Palace open—the doorway leading to the passage
which opened upon the countess' private apartments.

These Venetian palaces, one would imagine, were built
as much for purposes of love and intrigue, as for artistic
luxury and architectural beauty. General Petronovitch
easily succeeded in making his way to the balcony room,
where the countess had given her instructions to Ferrari,
without exciting attention or remark. He found her ladyship reclining upon the yellow cushions of a rich silken
couch, her beautiful figure enveloped in an ample tea-
gown. He had closed the doors behind him as she had
requested; had met no one coming or going, heard no
signs of life ; felt that he had obtained a precious privilege,
and this thought was the essence of his opening salutation.

He did not know how closely and fatally those doors
had closed behind him. He was in a fool's paradise ; and
the fool was happy ! A sensualist, he was proud of his
conquest. His small eyes gloated upon Anna's pale face
as he kissed her hand, and took the seat it had indicated
by her side.

"You think me very weak, I am sure, general," she
said ; "but what is woman's strength but weakness ? "

" Her strength," said the general, pressing her hand,
" lies in her generosity."

" And man's ? " she said interrogatively.

" In his appreciation," he replied, promptly.

" Ah, you have made these affairs of the heart a study."

" What else in life," he said, " is worth serious attention ? "

" Oh, there are other matters of moment. You must
have felt them in the exercise of your noble profession
many a time."

" Never as keenly," he said, " as the natural interest a
man feels in a beautiful woman ; especially when she

grants him the delicious privilege you have granted me."

He stole his arm about her as he spoke. She made a gentle movement which was neither compliance nor resistance, and continued the conversation.

" But you are a great general, sir. You must in your career have taken part in many heroic scenes. Your victory over the Kurds was magnificent."

" You think so ? " he said, smiling. " I prefer my victory of to-night."

" Your triumphant march through Central Asia is historic."

" My meeting with the Countess Stravensky at Venice will be longer remembered."

" Tell me, general, what was your first great achievement in the service of our good father, the Czar ? "

" Great achievements, my dear countess, become small when the achiever talks of them."

" But remember, general, that a woman loves to hear her hero narrate his victories. Don't you remember that it was with the eloquent tongue of the soldier that Othello won Desdemona, and it was here, on one of these balconies that the Moorish commander came and held friendly and romantic converse with the maiden and her father ? "

" Yes," said Petronovitch, " and it was here, also, I presume, where she fell a victim to the black man's jealousy. If I had been Othello—for your sake I would even have been black—and you had been Desdemona, I should have understood you better ; should have loved ánd trusted you. I would never have been jealous ; I would never have killed you, except with kindness ; and then we would have crossed the dark river together ! "

" My dear general," the countess replied, turning her great eyes full upon him, and with to him what appeared to be a most fascinating smile. " if all this be true you are indeed in love."

"I am," he said; "most truly, most devotedly."

She laid her head upon his shoulder, and a little shiver of hate ran through her veins.

"He didn't like the parting with his daughter, that old Venetian," she said. "I had a father once—have now, somewhere in the world; and I would give my life to embrace him once again!"

"You are in a very reflective mood," said the general.

"Yes," she said, "the mood comes with thinking of your victories and the shadows that follow their sunshine. You triumphed once, did you not; most completely and with great honor in suppressing the rising against the Jews, in the Province of Vilnavitch? Ah, that was kind of you, to protect with your strong Russian hand those poor Hebrew people! You know, of course, that I am a Jewess?"

"No other race could give to the world so beautiful a creature," said the general, pressing his lips upon her forehead.

"It is the nature of love to flatter," she said; "and you do not care to talk of your generous deeds. Our Russian fellow-subjects had a fit of madness, had they not, in those days against my people? At a place called Czarovna, if I remember the name rightly, they had made for themselves, as far as possible in Russia, what may be called a paradise. It was as if their father Abraham had brought them at last to something like a land flowing with milk and honey."

"Yes, I believe so," said the general, absorbed in his admiration of the woman whom he pressed still closer to his side.

"You helped the poor people, and put down the insurrection, is it not so?"

"Well, not quite that, I fear," he said, "I was the Czar's officer; I tried to do my duty."

"Yes," she said, "you would, dear general, and in so doing show your appreciation of the fine character and domestic instincts of the Czarovna Jew—I am sure you did. It
was like you, like Russia, like our holy father the Czar!
Do you remember the name of Klosstock? My dear dead
Count Stravensky, I remember, mentioned him to me as a
very worthy man ; I think he had some business dealings
with him.'

"No, I don't remember," said the general, a little out
of patience with the direction in which the countess forced
the conversation. "It was so long ago, and so many
events have happened."

"You do not care to talk of these things," she said. "I
am very sorry."

He felt that she drew herself from him, and no longer
responded to his attempted embraces.

"My dear countess, I care to talk of anything that may
interest you. Believe me, I have no other desire than to
be your slave."

"There was a young woman in Czarovna—I think it
must be talking of Desdemona and her father that has
made me recall some strange circumstances which came
to the knowledge of my dear dead husband, Count Stravensky—they called her 'Queen of the Ghetto,' do you
remember?"

"Yes," he said, "I think I·do ; but as I said. before, it
is so long ago, and so many things have happened in the
time that has passed between then and now."

"Oh, no," she said, "it is not so long ago, my dear
general ; not to her, at least, nor to her father, nor to the
rabbi to whom she was betrothed!"

Petronovitch felt an increasing resistance of his blan-
dishments, as the countess recalled to his mind the
tragedy of Czarovna, which he now began himself to remember with unwelcome distinctness.

19

"To her," she said, rising and putting aside his arm, "it is as yesterday. To her the pain is as keen this moment as it was then."

She faced him calmly, but with flashing eyes, as he rose to his feet, and her hand was busy with a diamond buckle at her neck.

"Do you remember how you kept your promise to that woman? Do you remember the base proposals she resented? Do you remember how you undertook to release her lover? Do you remember how you outraged your promised protection? How you slew her lover and left the cruel marks of your savage nature upon her, body and soul? You do: I see you do!"

General Petronovitch had turned pale as she spoke, had stepped back from her as if to receive the spring of some wild animal.

Unclasping the diamond buckle, she flung aside her robe and disclosed the peasant costume of Czarovna, and there stood before him, his victim, Anna Klosstock.

This was the cue for which Ferrari had waited. Before Petronovitch could utter the exclamation of surprise that was on his lips, the lithe stealthy form of Ferrari had seized him from behind, and his grim assistant, Paul Petroski, stood by the doorway.

The general made no resistance. He had received a moral blow from Anna Klosstock that for the moment had struck him down as firmly as any physical assault. He was bound and gagged, and flung upon the couch where, a few minutes previously, he had congratulated himself upon his conquest over the beautiful woman who had so soon become the talk of Venice.

"I will not indulge myself," said Anna, "in the further recall of that crime of Czarovna. I have looked forward to this day for years, hourly—had it in my mind every minute—and have seen myself revelling in the denunciations

I should fling at you. But that is past! My mission is no longer one of revenge, but of justice. You pronounced the verdict upon the Rabbi Losinski—you pronounced the verdict upon Johannes Klosstock, the best man, the kindest father that ever drew breath—you, first ruining your victim beyond all repair, pronounced the verdict upon his daughter, Anna Klosstock—she now pronounces the verdict upon you ; not in her own name, but in the name of the patriotic Brotherhood of the Dawn, who have sworn as far as in them lies to rid their beloved Russia and all the world of such pests as you. The only torture you will undergo is that which must now afflict you. You sent my people of Czarovna before the High Throne of God with their sins thick upon their heads. Your Church declares it possible for the sinner to be forgiven at the last moment. You have ten minutes to make your peace with the God you profess to serve : and the joyous music of the Countess Stravensky's reception will be your requiem ! Remove the enemy of God and man. Report to me his death at ten '. "

CHAPTER XXXIX.

AFTER FERRARI'S REPORT.

As gondola after gondola came dashing along the Grand Canal, and pulling up with that sudden and remarkable precision so characteristic of this famous Venetian boat, the Countess Stravensky left her boudoir and prepared to receive her guests. Ferrari at the same moment passed out of the adjacent room, the steps of which led down to the palace's tiny quay beneath her ladyship's window.

" Czarovna is avenged," he said, taking the white hand she held out to him and kissing it.

" Dear old friend ! " she said, " I give you the kiss of gratitude."

She kissed him on both cheeks.

" Come to me at midnight—the same way," pointing to the ante-room, " we must confer."

The old clock by the doorway solemnly beat out the hour of ten.

" Punctual ever," she said, " and true, dear friend. To-night we will talk of Czarovna and the ghetto."

" And of to-morrow," said Ferrari, significantly.

" Yes," she replied, " of to-morrow ! "

The next moment she disappeared behind the portiere into the adjoining room, where her maid awaited her, and thence with stately tread to the head of the grand staircase of the palace. She was radiant.

Her dress was nothing short of an inspiration, so plain was it, yet so effective. The general impression it seemed to convey was that of a rich brocade which, despite its splendor, gave to the figure and fell in pliable and ever-changing folds. With the exception of a rich lace stomacher it was made high to the throat, as were all the countess' costumes, for reasons which the reader may probably guess. Lest he should be in doubt, let it be at once remarked, by the way, that the stripes of the Russian knout go down to the grave with the victim who bears them.

The hostess had referred to this in her tragic address to the cruel Governor of Czarovna, the famous Russian general, who, in his death agony, had heard that requiem music of which she had spoken.

While the festal strains were still rippling from the hidden orchestra, he lay dead and awaiting the silent disposition of his executioners.

The countess knew this, and her cheeks flushed ; she knew it, and her heart beat with rapture ; she knew it, and thought of her father away in the Siberian wilds ; she knew it, and more than once had to make an effort to keep back her tears.

The lights of hundreds of wax candles played upon her red-gold hair, and deepened the deep red shadows in her brocaded gown. A great solitaire diamond flashed in a thousand changing hues at her throat, and the star of some Russian order lay upon the faded lace of her stomacher.

The palace was a blaze of light, the atmosphere sweet with the perfume of flowers, the soft, winning harmonies of lute and zither came from an unseen orchestra.

Philip and his friends were among the first arrivals. In his wildest dreams the young artist had not yet realized the impressiveness of his gracious model's beauty. On this dreamy night in Venice, in his eyes she looked like the divine impersonation of the city itself. There was an added touch, it seemed to him, a deeper, richer tone in her wavy red-gold hair; there was an unaccustomed flush upon her usually pale cheeks ; her violet eyes reflected back the blazing lights around her. She seemed taller in his estimation, and moved about with the dignity of Juno and the inviting grace of Venus. He saw no one else, heard no other voice than hers. He left the side of Dolly abruptly to greet her, then in the same fashion returned ; felt himself under a spell he could not break.

The countess noticed his confusion, and thought of her betrothed of the ghetto. Philip, in her excited state of mind, seemed for the moment as a recompense sent to her by Fate. But she shook herself free of the thought as quickly as it came, and tried to place herself in the position of his fiancée. The next moment it occurred to her that Philip did not love the English girl, that she herself swayed his heart. The great object of her life accomplished with the death of Petronovitch, it crept into her mind to reflect again how bitter her lot had been, how little of love, how much of misery ; and as a fascinating temptation, the suggestion crept into her soul to accept the incense Philip was ready to burn at her altar; nay, to respond as her heart was inclined to his passion! But better thoughts came almost simultaneously with the bad ones—the antidote with the poison.

"I am so glad to see you," she said, taking Mrs. Milbanke by the hand with special cordiality, "it is so good of you to come."

"It was so sweet of you to ask us," Jenny responded.

"How beautiful your sister is! You English have such superb complexions!"

Then receiving Dolly, she said, "My dear, I congratulate Mr. Forsyth; forgive one so much your elder for venturing to offer a criticism; you are lovely, and what a becoming dress! Ah! here is your *fiancée*. Mr. Forsyth, I congratulate you; how happy you must be! And what do you think of Venice? Does it realize all you dreamt of? It is strangely beautiful and romantic, is it not?"

"Indeed it is," said Philip, his hand trembling in hers, his voice quivering.

"Full of subjects for the painter; and what tragedies in its history! Ah, well you must not think of them; light gay comedy is for you, is it not so? And this is Mr. Walter Milbanke. I am sure I do not require an introduction, I have heard so much of him."

"You are very good to say so—not too much, I hope," Walter replied. "But we must not keep you from your guests; there are so many waiting for the pleasure of your recognition."

"Thank you," said the countess, bestowing a general smile upon the entire group, "we shall meet, no doubt, on the canal later; the illuminations are something wonderful; you know my gondola; do not let us pass each other later without a salute. I shall be so delighted to see you all again."

Then she gave her attention to other guests, and Philip
followed her with his eyes as one in a dream. Jenny spoke
to him, Walter spoke to him, Dolly stood by his side. He
heard them not, saw them not. Several guests noticed his
wrapt attention and smiled. It was plain to see that the
hostess had made a conquest of the young Englishman, and
that he did not attempt to resist the spell she had cast
upon him.

"She is indeed a magnificent woman," remarked one
Venetian to another, "a Jewess, I believe ; might be a
Venetian instead of a Russian ; has the features of the old
masters, the hair too ; our own Titian might have painted
her."

"The young fellow. who is evidently annoying his lady
companions is perhaps an artist, and thinking as you think,"
said the other, disappearing among the throng.

Jenny overheard this, and for a moment tried to think as
the stranger suggested, that Philip's admiration was the admiration of the painter ; but she soon gave up that excuse
and felt herself insulted through her sister Dolly.

Presently Philip, with some foolish excuse or other, left
them only for a moment, he said, to speak to an artist
whom he would like them to know ; but a few minutes
later it seemed as if this was only an excuse to be once
more within the brilliant circle which continually surrounded the countess.

Jenny could no longer restrain herself. All her desire
to see and be seen in Venetian society, all her worldliness,
all her love of society, vanished in her sense of pride and
in her love for Dolly.

"My dear," she said to Walter, the moment there was
an opportunity to speak to him, "he is madly in love
with that woman. We·have made a mistake ; his engagement to Dolly is ours rather than his ; it must not go on ;
Dolly must not be sacrificed to her match-making sister."

"My dear Jenny," said Walter, "you are beside yourself. It is his artistic temperament that is at fault, not his heart. And what do you mean by 'match-making sister?' You have done nothing to force this engagement."

"Yes, I have; yes, I have," said Jenny quickly. "Sam Swinford says there is an underlying stratum of snobbishness in what we call our social life in London; he is right, and we have sacrificed Dolly to that wretched fetish."

"My dear, my dear," said Walter, "don't excite yourself. People are looking at us."

"Philip isn't," said Jenny, "he has eyes for no one but that woman. Look at our poor Dolly—she sees it; so does the countess."

"Well, well," said Walter, "my dear, be calm. For heaven's sake, don't let us have a scene. We will leave."

"But the gondola?" said Jenny.

"Oh, that's all right," said Walter.

"I mean the procession—I don't know what I mean. Were we not going out to join the company on the canal?"

"Oh, yes," said Walter, "and we will if you will be calm. There is no chance of saying or doing anything at present; we will talk it over. I will discuss it with Philip. Don't let us lead up to the usual criticism of the English abroad. Here comes Dolly."

"And there goes Philip," said Jenny. "He is crazy."

"He is looking for Dolly," said Walter.

"Not he," said Jenny.

"But he is, my dear," said Walter, "see, he is turning now." At which moment Philip came towards them, following Dolly, who answered the inquiring gaze of her sister with a defiant expression in her eyes, but not without tears.

"My dear, there is something wrong," said Jenny, drawing Dolly on one side, "your instinct was right; I have not mentioned anything you said to Walter ; but he and I both have been very sensible of Philip's behavior to night ; be calm, love ; don't fret ; we will put it all right ; take your cue from me. You shall not be sacrificed."

Dolly pressed Jenny's arm, and Mrs. Milbanke put on her best manner. She had some of the gifts of the natural actress. Now was the time, she thought, to give them play.

" Delightful, is it not, Philip ? " she said, " a lovely scene."

" Yes," he said, " it is."

" The countess is a lovely creature."

" Is she not ? " he replied.

" Everybody can see you think so," she went on, laughing coquettishly. " Oh, you men, you men ! "

Philip blushed and looked at Dolly, who tossed her head defiantly, and took Walter's arm.

" I want to show you the canal from the balcony," he said. " Philip will give his arm to Jenny."

Philip did so.

" We will follow Walter," said Jenny.

Philip had now an opportunity of seeing that the countess was not the only woman present who was attracting attention. Both women and men noticed the youthful English beauty. Dolly was not blind to this unspoken admiration. Her gait had all the healthful firmness of her tennis-playing countrywomen. She held herself with a natural gracefulness. Her complexion was fair as it was rich. Her lips red, her smile sweet, frank and unsophisticated. In her pale blue Duchesse dress, and with her white round shoulders, her shining yellow hair in a high coif, and her deep blue eyes, she was an exceptionally fine type of British beauty, and may be said to have divided the honors of the evening in the opinion of a brilliant assembly, so far as beauty and distinction were concerned, with the hostess herself.

" How well Dolly looks to-night," said Jenny to Philip.

" Yes," he replied, " but she always looks well."

" Lacks that pasty kind of complexion that painters admire, though ? "

" I think not," he said.

" Has not the charm that foreign women have then, is that it ? "

" I think she has every charm a woman can desire, or a man who seeks a good and beautiful wife."

" My dear Mr. Forsyth," continued Jenny, " you are either a fool or you think Dolly is.   Don't start, it will be noticed.   If I were Walter, do you know how I should view your conduct to-night ? "

" Mrs. Milbanke ! " exclaimed Philip.   " I do not understand you."

" I think I understand you, sir," said Jenny, losing all that wonderful calmness and control of herself which she had resolved five minutes previously to exercise.

" If you do, it is hardly polite to say so in such offensive terms."

" Do not let go my arm," said Jenny.   " I do not wish to attract attention ; you have done enough in that direction already."

" I ! " Philip exclaimed.

" You," said Jenny.   " You have had no eyes for anyone, no thoughts for anyone since our arrival except for this countess, this mysterious woman who gives you sittings and makes her appearance in Venice unexpectedly, when she has learnt from you that you are paying a visit to the place.   Your neglect of Dolly to-night, sir, your continual, your undivided attention to that red-haired woman, sir, has been in the nature of an insult to Dolly, to me, and to Walter.   Keep my arm, sir !   The honor may not be repeated, and, as I said before, I do not want to make a scene."

Jenny was simply beside herself with passion.

" Pray, my dear Mrs. Milbanke, moderate your words ; we will discuss my conduct at the hotel; I will explain, and you will explain ; I assure you, meanwhile, nothing is further from my thoughts than to desire to be unkind to you, or to Dolly or to Walter ; if I have seemed strange I am sorry, but pray do me the justice to believe that it would be impossible to insult you ; I may have seemed strange ; I have felt so, but——"

He was interrupted by Walter, who turned round on the moment to direct their attention to the assembling of the boats outside the palace, and the pause in the general gathering to witness and greet the new arrivals. " I think we ought to make our way to the exit now," said Walter, " I see Beppo and his comrade ; and (waving his hand) they see me. Yes, I will let them know that we are com- ing." Walter waved his hand again, and then proceeded to lead the way, following them amidst the general exodus of the company towards the grand staircase.

The scene was novel beyond description. The marble staircase gave upon the grand canal which was all alive with traffic, and all ablaze with color. The night was lighted up by one lamp above away in the shining heavens, and by millions down below, making the water one vast moving sea of emeralds, diamonds, and precious gems ; but Walter and Jenny and Dolly no longer enjoyed the glory of the scene. The gorgeous fête was out of tune with their feel- ings. The music was harsh, the bells rung backwards.

And when they had pushed off amidst the splendid crowd, and were already part of the show themselves, with the brilliant lanterns which Walter had ordered Beppo to provide, they found that Philip was no longer of their party.

" To the Telegraph Office, Beppo," said Jenny, a very prosaic order for so splendid an occasion.

" The Telegraph Office," exclaimed the gondolier.

" The Post," she repeated.

" But not to see the sights ? " he asked, for the first time hesitating to obey orders.

" Not yet," said Jenny, and with a firmness of manner which Walter did not care himself to resist.

" You wish to send a telegram somewhere ? " Walter asked.

" Yes," said Jenny.

" Take the next turn, Beppo ; we are close to the office."

" Yes, excellency," said Beppo ; and the gondola presently swept out of the light into the comparative darkness of a narrow waterway, the shadows of which were now more in harmony with the feelings of the little English party than were the lamps and music, the flashing boats, and the merry laughter of the Grand Canal.

CHAPTER XL.

SAM SWYNFORD IS SUMMONED TO VENICE.

THE London season had fairly commenced its course of comedy and tragedy, while the Milbankes and Philip Forsyth were in the midst of their adventures in Italy.

To Dick Chetwynd and his wife, however, it was but the first day of the season, which to them opened with the Spring exhibition at the famous art club and gallery of which Dick was the moving spirit. Bond Street was crowded with carriages taking up and setting down handsomely dressed visitors to Chetwynd's fashionable exhibition.

It was a delightful May day, almost as bright and sunny as Venice. The Bond Street tradesmen had put out their awnings, and filled their windows with fine displays of art and industry. . Dick Chetwynd, in faultless summer costume, with a button hole of lilies of the valley, assisted his aristocratic directors to receive the first distinguished crowd of the season.

Since the winter exhibition of the "Rosetti," the quadrangle, previously used as a carriage entrance, had been transformed into a delightful winter garden with an Oriental fountain, noble palm trees and Eastern exotics, amidst which the contributions of sculpture were deftly and daintily arranged with pleasant lounges, one picturesque corner leading into a pleasant tea-room.

Among the visitors was Sam Swynford, who had for the day laid his city business aside to indulge in the first of the great Art functions of the year.

With the defeat of Sam's matrimonial hopes, his financial prosperity had increased ; not simply day by day, but as it would seem almost hour by hour. He had heard nothing of the Milbankes since their departure for Italy, but he had read in that morning's paper an account of the fêtes at Venice, and had felt, in spite of himself, envious of the happiness and good fortune of Philip Forsyth. It was to him a matter of melancholy delight to meet Mrs. Chetwynd at the " Rosettis' " in this bright London May time, for she at once commenced to talk of Dolly and Philip and the Milbankes.

Mrs. Chetwynd appeared to take no active part in her husband's work.' While she heartily shared with him his artistic and occasionally his literary labors, she was rarely in evidence as more than an ordinary workaday wife busy with her domestic and family affairs. She had, therefore, on this occasion plenty of time to chat with friends and generally enjoy the occasion. She knew Swynford to be somewhat of a patron of the Arts to the extent at any rate of making occasional purchases ; she had heard all about his disappointment in regard to Dolly Norcott; she knew that he took a deep interest in the Milbankes ; that Dick liked him ; and she responded at once sympathetically to his questions.

"The Milbankes seem," he said, "to be having a delightful time in Venice."

"Then you have heard ? " replied Mrs. Chetwynd.

"Oh, no. I don't know that I expected to hear ; but I have been reading this morning's descriptions of the Venetian fêtes."

"Yes ; very picturesque and impressive, no doubt," said Mrs. Chetwynd. "Dick expected to have had a line or two from Philip ; but not a word."

"When people are very happy they are not given to very much letter writing, I expect."

"I should have thought you would have heard from Walter Milbanke ; he is a great friend of yours, is he not ? "

"Oh, yes," said Swynford, "I like Walter very much ; a good fellow ; comes into the city occasionally and does a little speculation ; just the same to him whether he wins or loses ; always cheerful."

"I suppose," replied Mrs. Chetwynd, "it is hardly what may be called etiquette to congratulate you upon all I hear about your successes in that mysterious part of London you call the city ? "

"Oh, I am not much of a man for etiquette, Mrs. Chetwynd, and whatever you might say to me would only be pleasant, I'm sure, under any circumstances. I have been very lucky lately, that is one of the reasons why I am here to-day. I must ask your advice about one or two pictures. It's a dispensation of Providence, no doubt ; if a man's lucky one way, he's unfortunate in another."

"But a man," replied Mrs. Chetwynd, "has so many resources, so many various means of consolation."

"You think so ? I suppose you are right. I may be the exception to the rule. But there is one kind of disappointment which a fellow never gets over."

" Ah," said Mrs. Chetwynd, "a fellow thinks so for a week or two or a month or two ; but he is easily consoled at last, and comes to regard what at one time he would call a disappointment as a very fortunate circumstance."

" No, Mrs. Chetwynd, not a bit of it. The only consolation he has is in trying to get all he can out of the proverb that 'While there's life there's hope.' Did you see the Milbankes before they left? "

" Well, to tell you the truth," said Mrs. Chetwynd, " I have seen very little of the Milbankes. I have heard a great deal about Miss Norcott and Mrs. Milbanke from Dick, and of course I have seen a great deal of Philip Forsyth."

" Yes," said Swynford, "very clever, interesting young fellow."

" You have met him, then? " said Mrs. Chetwynd.

" Oh, yes," said Swynford, "dined with him not very long ago at the Milbankes'. Will you forgive me, Mrs. Chetwynd, for pressing my confidence upon you? You see I am, as one might put it, more than usually a bachelor in every sense of the term ; no sisters, no mother, no woman-folk, as they say down in Yorkshire, to consult. You know all about what has happened to me, and what has happened to Miss Norcott. Has it occurred to you that the engagement was rather hurried and probably unduly supported by Dolly's relatives? "

" Well," said Mrs. Chetwynd, " I really can't say ; and you need not apologize for asking me the question. I know that Dick has always thought that marriage would be a good thing for Philip, and we did not know until the other day how much you are reported to have liked Mrs. Milbanke's sister."

" We are chatting between ourselves now, are we not ? " said Sam, anxious to have a *confidante.* " Liked her ! Mrs. Chetwynd, I would have given twenty years of my life to be in the position of Philip Forsyth ; and what troubles me a good deal is the feeling that it is quite possible that Dolly Norcott liked me just as much as the man she has become engaged to. I have an idea that Walter Milbanke and his wife considered Philip Forsyth a better match socially and in other respects than myself, rightly, no doubt ; he is a clever, handsome young fellow ; also an artist ; in society and likely to make a position at the West End. Dolly is passionately fond of her sister and her brother-in-law, rather easy-going, kind hearted to a fault ; and the more I think of it—and I never think of anything else—the more I come to the conclusion that if I had proposed two days before Forsyth I should have been accepted."

" Then, my dear Mr. Swynford, why didn't you ? " asked Mrs. Chetwynd quickly.

" I was too fond of her," said Swynford. " I told her sister the day after I understood she was engaged to Philip that if a certain thing had occurred two or three days earlier, I should have spoken to her and Walter upon the subject, and taken my chance with Dolly."

" May I ask what your reason was for delay ? "

" I was too fond of her," repeated Swynford. " The day after her engagement I was a rich man ; two days before I was only a moderately successful stockbroker. Two days afterwards events occurred on 'Change which I been hoping for and hardly daring to expect. I made fifty thousand pounds the day after I lost Dolly Norcott."

" Hello ! " said Chetwynd, passing at the moment. " How do you do, Swynford ? Agnes, my dear, the Marchioness of Thistledown is anxious to be introduced to you, and my chief director, Lord Singleton, asks me to make him acquainted with the city gentleman everybody is just now talking about."

" And who may that be ? " asked Swynford.

" Mr. Samuel Swynford," said Chetwynd, patting him familiarly upon the shoulder.

" Ah, we were just talking about that unhappy person," said Swynford, " I and your wife. I have been giving Mrs. Chetwynd a few points upon a subject in which we are all interested, I more especially."

" You must come and dine, Mr. Swynford," said Agnes, " and we will have a long chat."

" Yes," said Dick. " When will you come ? "

" To-morrow ? " asked Mrs. Chetwynd.

" With pleasure," said Swynford.

" Ah, here is Lord Singleton," said Dick. " Allow me to present Mr. Samuel Swynford."

" How do you do, Mr. Swynford ? " said Lord Singleton. " Very glad to make your acquaintance."

" Thank you very much," said Swynford.

" I want to show you a picture I have just bought, and, if I may, to have a word on business. Rather unfair to talk about money to you outside the city, but some people who are interested in a scheme you favor very much, I am told, have asked me to become a director."

" To-morrow, then, at seven," said Dick Chetwynd, nodding at Swynford.

" With pleasure," said Swynford. " I shall be there."

And the four gradually disappeared among the throng, Swynford congratulating himself in a melancholy kind of way upon the friendly intercourse he had struck up with the Chetwynds, more particularly pleased with Dick's amiable, sympathetic and handsome wife.

Lord Singleton presently carried him off to lunch at an adjacent club, where Sam entertained and instructed him in connection with certain investments which his lordship had made. Lord Singleton in his turn gave Swynford sundry valuable hints about certain pictures which Swynford intended to purchase ; not that he had much room for them

20

at his chambers, but he had recently resolved to buy a house on the Upper Thames where he could invite a few friends during the summer season, and have a snug retreat for high days and holidays when he could conveniently leave his business in the city.

It was rather late when he returned home to dress for a little dinner engagement which he had accepted at the Parthenon Club.   Nevertheless, he flung himself upon a couch full of cushions, asked Devereux for his slippers, and requested his servant not to disturb him for half an hour.

" You said you would dress at seven, sir."

" Yes, I know."

" It's now half past."

" Can't help it, Devereux.   Am tired ; must have forty winks."   .

" Yes, sir.   There are two telegrams for you."

" I won't open them," said Swynford, " at present."

" Right, sir."

" Come to me in twenty minutes."   . ~

" Yes, sir."

Swynford did not have forty winks.   He felt depressed and miserable.   He couldn't help all day long contrasting his position with that of Philip Forsyth.   He couldn't help thinking at the Rosetti Gallery how happy he could be if he had, as a companion, with future happy prospects, Dolly Norcott.   He couldn't help thinking how generously he could have ministered to her tastes and foibles, what pictures they would have bought together, what a delightful time they would have had in buying and furnishing that house, for which he had purchased those pictures ; and in contemplating himself he saw a special and individual example of the impossibility of perfect human happiness arising from the impossibility of a perfect cultivation of the virtue of contentment.

Sam Swynford possessed most of the things that could

make a young fellow happy. Good health, plenty of money, a genial and generous disposition, no social or political ambition; but he wanted Dolly Norcott. Once or twice during the day he had asked himself why he should not go to Italy? He could afford the time; there was nothing in his business at the moment that could not wait for him; he had no harassing speculations; the money he had recently made was the result of time-bargains which were over. Then he asked himself, supposing he went to Italy what satisfaction he could possibly get out of such a trip? He would meet the Milbankes and Dolly, of course; but between him and them stood Philip Forsyth, successful and in possession.

Devereux knocked at the door and came in while these varied thoughts and emotions were passing in weary repetition through his master's mind.

"Ten minutes to eight, sir."

"All right, Devereux, I am ready."

"Two telegrams, sir," said Devereux.

Swynford opened the first.

"Dinner will be quarter of an hour later than arranged, but happy to see you as soon as you like."

"That's lucky," said Swynford to his servant. "Needn't hurry."

"Yes, sir," said Devereux, handing his master the second message, which Swynford read twice over with an emotion he could not disguise from Devereux.

"When did this come?" he exclaimed, his voice full of its customary energy, his manner alert and excited.

"At one o'clock, sir."

"Good heavens, man," said Swynford, "why didn't you let me know?"

"I could not, sir," Devereux replied.

"No, of course not," said the master, striding rapidly across the room and back again, looking at himself in the mirror, then at Devereux, then at the telegram.

" Sorry to see you so much disturbed, sir. What can I do ? "

" Get me Bradshaw," said Swynford.

" Yes, sir."

" The Continental Bradshaw," said Swynford.

" Yes, sir," said the servant, laying the book upon the table before Swynford, who had now sat down with calm deliberation at his writing desk.

" Telegraph forms, Devereux."

" Yes, sir," said Devereux, handing the forms and pencil to him with military promptitude.

Swynford wrote :—

" *Thanks for your telegram; very sorry; am prevented at last moment from dining with you; will explain at future day; my sincere regards and regrets.*"

"Send that at once to the Parthenon Club."

" Yes, sir."

Devereux disappeared ; rang his own private bell for his own private servant, a boy in buttons as bright as his own eyes, who disappeared with the message.

When Devereux returned Swynford was deep in the study of Bradshaw.

" Pack my foreign trunk at once, Devereux. Order the brougham to be at the door at twenty minutes to nine to the minute. Pack what you think I shall require. I am going to Italy. Shall go straight through from Dover to Milan. Be ready to accompany me."

" Yes, sir."

" Leave the house keeper in charge here. Wire at once to Atkins that my address is Damiano's Hotel, Venice ; to send on his report and all letters from the city by first mail to-morrow. Now you have not a moment to lose, nor have I."

" All shall be ready as you wish, sir, to the minute."

" All right, Devereux. I will be back in a quarter of an hour."

Swynford, now all bustle and excitement, took up his hat and cane and walked to the nearest telegraph office, re-peating to himself the words of that second telegram from Venice to which he was now formulating his answer.

" *From Mrs. Milbanke, Hotel Beau Rivage, Venice :—Regard this as private ; but come to Venice immediately ; not direct to this hotel, but to Damiano's. I believe I can arrange everything to your satisfaction. Wire me at once, naming train you leave by.*

" JENNIE MILBANKE."

To which Swynford answered, writing the message with the calm deliberation which had succeeded his excitement, as follows :—

" *Samuel Swynford to Mrs. Milbanke, Hotel Beau Rivage, Venice :—A thousand thanks for your welcome telegram. Trying to understand it ; of course with sel-fish hopes. Am leaving by the Paris mail to-night. Shall go through to Milan and straight on to Venice. Wire me to Grand Hotel, Milan. Hope there is no mis-take about your message. Sincere regards.*

" SAM SWYNFORD."

The nearest telegraph office was at Burlington House. Sam had jostled several persons in Piccadilly on his way to it. An old gentleman called him a " bear." " Not always," said Sam to himself. " Sometimes a bull, but always the right animal, fortunately ; hope I'm going to reverse the old proverb about luck in love ; though my luck is not at cards, they say the Stock Exchange is as bad as cards. Am I really going to be lucky in love as well ? "

All kinds of romantic hopes went rattling through his

seem to have time to call a cab, and then the distance was so short. Besides, he did not want to speak to anyone but himself. He handed in his message, paid for the stamps, stuck them upon the form with the greatest care, and waited until he saw the despatch on the operator's desk.

At twenty minutes to nine to the second, the brougham was at the door. The luggage was inside and out.

"Too much luggage," said Sam in an interrogative fashion and somewhat fidgetty.

"Think not, sir."

"I can send for more clothes if I want them."

"Yes, sir."

'Will your assistant know what to send?"

"Yes, sir."

"Don't quite know what I'm going to do, or how long I shall be away."

"Have arranged accordingly, sir."

"You have."

"Yes, sir."

"That's all right. Don't want to be bothered."

"No, sir."

"Wire for cabin on board the boat."

"Yes, sir."

"And for special compartment from Calais."

"Yes, sir."

"Get one at Charing Cross to Dover if you can."

"Yes, sir."

Devereux accomplished everything as Sam desired. He always did. His silver and golden keys opened locks and hearts. And Devereux was just as generous in using Sam's money as the master was himself.

The boat was not crowded. Sam found a fairly comfortable cabin. But he paced the deck from start to landing. It was a starlight night. He built castles up in the clouds.

Not only built them but furnished them. His principal castle was a pretty detached house at Kensington. It had stables, a garden, and was decorated under the personal direction of Dolly Norcott, Jenny and himself. They spent most of the spring months in finding it and putting it in order. Before the season was over they were married at St. George's, Hanover Square. All this was pleasant dreaming. Of course the breakfast would take place at Westbury Lodge ; that is if they had a breakfast. Probably Mrs. Milbanke would prefer the new fashion of an afternoon wedding and an evening reception ; or rather was it evening or afternoon ; he forgot which ; but it was " the swell thing " he thought now not to have breakfast.

The night was very calm. Sam smoked. So did Devereux. The servant, however, kept clear of the master. He was one of those perfect retainers who know exactly when to be on hand and when not. Devereux had not read the telegram from Venice, but he had come to the conclusion that the expedition was one of a very personal character. He knew it was not a business trip. He knew it was not one of pleasure apart from the Milbankes. He knew that his master had no real pleasure outside that particular family. He knew his master was in love with Miss Norcott. He knew of the engagement of that young lady to his master's rival. He knew she had gone to Italy with her sister and brother-in-law. He knew that Mr. Philip Forsyth was traveling in their company. All London knew that the rising young student son of Lady Forsyth had gone to paint in Venice, and all the section of London which read the *Morning Post* knew that he was engaged to Miss Norcott, the daughter of the eminent and long since retired city merchant, and sister-in-law of the wealthy young city lawyer, Mr. Walter Milbanke. Therefore, Devereux was a trifled worried about his master's trip, although he had quietly said to himself that he should not wonder "if Samuel Swynford, Esquire, did not come out trumps in that affair yet."

It was not Sam's lot to engage in any adventure on his way to Milan. He met no fascinating beauty en route. Had he done so he would have compared her so much to her disadvantage with Dolly Norcott that she would not have stirred his imagination even into a desire for a flirtation. Moreover, he had no mysterious attachment, as Philip Forsyth had, when that gallant had renewed his acquaintance with the countess at Victoria Station. Sam was as true to his ideal Dolly as if she had never snubbed him, as if she had never warned him they could not be any nearer than friends, as if indeed she had not been engaged to his rival. He was a curious mixture, this prosperous young man of business. The secret of Sam's success on the Stock Exchange lay in his never losing his head, as his friends said. And yet, contemplating him in the midst of his city work, you might have doubted the truth of this judgment. Cordiner said of him :

" Sam Swynford is an enthusiast ; it isn't excitement, the apparent nervousness you think you detect in him when he is doing a big thing ; it is the enthusiasm of the moment, that's what it is ; the same kind of enthusiasm that gives a soldier the dash and pluck necessary in a charge ; the impulse, so to speak, of the moment. But that over, there is no firmer, no more solid operator than Sam Swynford ; a young fellow who never wobbles ; is never doubtful about what is the right thing to do ; doesn't ask advice ; is as firm as a rock and as hard for the time ; though, mind you, one of the most generous fellows living."

This description of Sam was no doubt correct, and will account for the quiet, steady, respectful way in which Sam approached his destiny at Venice.

"I can arrange everything to your satisfaction," he repeated calmly. "There is only one meaning in those words. She knows the only thing that can satisfy me. I told her I had made a heap of money ; I told her why I had not proposed to Dolly ; I told her that I would have done so if I had been in the position I then was at Lady Forsyth's party. What is it? Have they quarreled? Has Dolly rebelled? Has she discovered that she really does like me? We were always such good friends. She treated me as a sort of tame cat, I must allow ; a kind of poor relation ; a brother, say. But we were great friends, and she knew I worshipped her. Perhaps Forsyth thought she would worship him. A conceited chap, Forsyth ; like all those fellows who get their bread at the West End instead of in the city ; like all professional fellows as against trade and commerce and even banking. If Dolly likes it I'll be a banker, anything in fact. I have money enough to leave the city altogether if she wishes it. We shall see. Perhaps it is some trifling affair after all. Forsyth may be in difficulties? Or Mrs. Milbanke may have been speculating? Or Walter? No, that is too absurd. There has been a row. Mrs. Milbanke is a clever woman. She knows exactly what I feel about Dolly. She is going to play me off against the painter. Well, let her, I don't mind. I have thought sometimes that Dolly really likes me as well as she likes Forsyth. Besides, she is accustomed to my society. I know what pleases her. Women may pretend not to care for all sorts of little attentions : they may profess they don't like too much worship. I believe if I did not feel such a fool when I am with Dolly I should have got on better. Why am I such an ass when I am at the Milbankes'? It is only when Dolly is there that I don't feel like myself. Self-consciousness, I suppose. I don't suffer from that folly in the city, nor at the club."

At intervals along the journey this is how Sam's thoughts rambled on. It would have been very clear to Cordiner, if he could have had the smallest clue to Sam's feeling, that if he did not lose his head he had long since lost his heart. Let us hope that the worthy young man of stocks and shares and financial adventure may not have lost it in vain.

When he arrived at Milan he found the following tele-gram awaiting him :—

" Thanks, dear friend—no mistake—feel that you have guessed my object aright, your happiness and hers.

" JENNY MILBANKE."

Sam smiled as he read and re-read Jenny's message. All the world seemed new to him. The hotel could not hold him. He went out into the city. He walked for miles. He was in no hurry, as it seemed to Sam, to go on. What had come over him? Had things gone wrong? No, he was convinced that everything was going right.

" Pleasant city this, Devereux."

" Yes, sir.".

" Seen the Cathedral ? "

" No, sir."

" See it."

" Yes, sir."

" I shall not go on until the morning."

" Very well, sir."

" Want to arrive at Venice at night."

" Yes, sir."

" To-morrow night."

" Yes, sir."

" Shall go and sleep for an hour or two."

" You look tired, sir."

" I am. First train in the morning."

" Yes, sir."

Sam had not slept a wink since he left London. Jenny's telegram had given him a new spell of wakeful life. But now that he had built a number of fresh castles in the air, and with every prospect, as it seemed to him, of their realization, an exposition of sleep came over him ; and the man who never lost his head, according to Cordiner (who never took the heart into consideration), went to bed, and when he awoke after eight hours he thought he had not closed his eyes for more than a minute, though he felt wonderfully refreshed.

Meanwhile the last festal lamps were flickering out in Venice. Old Time, the scene-shifter, was preparing for further strange developments of this present drama of love and vengeance, of comedy incidents and tragic situations.

CHAPTER XLI.

EXIT PHILIP FORSYTH : ENTER SAM SWYNFORD.

"THE sooner we leave Venice the better," said Mrs. Milbanke to her devoted and genial partner. " Whether Mr. Forsyth remains or not is of no moment to us : we have done with Philip Forsyth forever, and I think we are well out of him."

" I suppose so," said Walter, lighting a cigar, and looking contemplatively across the lagoon. " I'm not sure, my dear."

" I think I am."

" It is all very sudden and very different from what we arranged."

" It is," said Jenny, taking a seat by his side and casting her eyes in the same direction, but speaking as if she were addressing an imaginary Walter somewhere in the neighborhood of the Lido."

They were sitting in the open balcony under a pleasant awning, the sun dancing upon the water beneath them.

and fro, and there was a great air of calm and repose in the atmosphere, which was in pleasant contrast with the recent bustle and excitement of the Royal fêtes. The King and Queen had left amidst salvoes of artillery and braying of trumpets, and whether the Countess Stravensky had followed in their wake or preceded them, was an open question upon which Walter could not satisfy his inquiring spouse. The mysterious disappearance of General Petronovitch was the talk of Venice, and it was half hinted on all hands that he had gone away to keep some mystérious rendezvous with the countess. His wife, the Princess Radna, still remained in Venice, but the courteous manager of the hotel had informed Mrs. Milbanke that her Highness had given instructions to her people for their return to Paris on the morrow.

Walter and Jenny had discussed these incidents of fact and gossip over breakfast, but without being moved by them very much either one way or the other, their immediate interest in life at the moment being concentrated upon Dolly and Sam Swynford. Walter was enjoying his after-breakfast cigar, and endeavoring to lay out his plans for the remainder of their Italian trip.

"You see," he continued, still looking across the lagoon and trying to blow a cloud of smoke after his thoughts, "I had made my arrangements for a stay of at least a month here in Venice; and indeed have taken these rooms for that time."

"I know," said Jenny, "but Dolly's plans were of a much more serious character than that. She had settled, not for a month, but for life."

"And her scheme still holds good," said Walter, smiling, "only she has changed her traveling companion."

"Well, and so have we," said Jenny, endeavoring to drop into Walter's semi-philosophic vein; "only that our trip is a summer holiday."

"You think she loves Swynford?"

"I'm sure she does," said Jenny, "and has loved him all the time, even when she accepted Mr. Philip Forsyth."

"Then why did she accept him?" asked Walter.

"Now, my dear," said Jenny, with the faintest suspicion of irritability, "don't let us go over that again. I am quite willing to assume my share of the blame of it, all the blame, if necessary; but I thought we had concluded our little controversy on that point last night. I'm sure I never slept a wink, what with your reiteration of the salient points, as you called them, and my thinking of them over and over again, afterwards. For heaven's sake let us say no more about responsibilities. Blame me, if you like, entirely."

"My dear," said Walter, taking her hand affectionately, still gazing out across the lagoon, "we are both to blame."

"Very well, then," replied Jenny, "there is an end of it. We have done the right thing at last."

"You really think so?" said Walter.

"I am sure so," she replied. "Mr. Philip Forsyth thought more of his art than of Dolly, and finally more of that intriguing countess than of either his art or Dolly."

"Has the countess really left Venice?" asked Walter.

"No doubt of it," Jenny replied; "and Philip has not been seen in this hotel for the last two days."

"You know that his luggage is still here," said Walter.

"Part of it—part of it," said Jenny, with some irritation. "It seems he took away his large portmanteau, and I am quite sure the porter has some secret understanding about forwarding the rest after him."

"It is all very strange," said Walter. "If he had said 'good-bye'—left a note—sent a telegram—done anything that we might have acted upon, our position would have been so much more satisfactory."

"His conduct," said Jenny, "is all the more scandalous. It is evident to me that there was a rivalry between this wretched General Petronovitch and Philip, a rivalry which we shall hear more of. The Princess Radna, I am told, intends to obtain a divorce ; she will lay her case before the Czar himself."

" Does it strike you at all," asked Walter, for the first time turning towards his wife and neglecting his cigarette, " that this General Petronovitch may have met with foul play?"

" No ; why should it? This is not ancient Venice. What foul play could possibly happen to him, except the foul play that is evidently part of his character ; the foul play of a reprobate?"

" And Philip?" continued Walter, interrogatively ; " you are quite satisfied in your own mind that he is under no restraint, that he left us voluntarily, and is away for his own wicked purposes?"

" I only know," Jenny replied, " that his conduct at the countess' reception was shameful ; that his manner towards the hostess was that of a weak fool under the fascinations of a designing woman ; that his withdrawal from our society the next day, and his appearance with the Countess Stravensky in her ostentatious gondola, are a sufficient justification of what we have thought desirable in the interest of Dolly."

" But you didn't see him, my dear, in the gondola."

" Beppo did," she replied, " and Beppo saw the boat turn into the little canal, which has a side entrance into the palace where she gave her very mixed and Bohemian reception."

" You thought differently of the reception, my dear, when she invited us, and were tremendously impressed with it until——"

" Philip made a fool of himself," exclaimed Jenny, interrupting her argumentative lord ; " and why you will go on repeating all this, and come back to it as if we were discussing it now for the first time, and had not sat up half the night similarly engaged, I cannot, for the life of me, understand. Philip deserted us, and practically threw over Dolly ; we shall not admit this outside our own little family circle, but that is the fact. Dolly was shamefully jilted. We only say that, I repeat, to ourselves. Sam Swynford comes upon the scene ; proposes for Dolly, as he had intended to do some weeks ago ; is accepted ; Dolly is happy ; Swynford is a good fellow, and he is happy ; and what in heaven is the matter with you, Walter ? "

" How came Swynford here at all ? It is that which puzzles me," said Walter. " If you had been perfectly frank with me, I don't suppose we should have had these discussions. You are keeping something back."

Again he turned his face interrogatively upon Jenny. She pressed his hand and rose to her feet.

" You are always in such a hurry, Walter. I should have told you all in good time ; and I am sure you will forgive me now if you compel me to confess before I meant to. The telegram I sent to my dressmaker was not to my dressmaker at all ; it was a private message to Sam Swynford, inspired thereto by our conversation at Lady Forsyth's, and suggested to him that he should come to Venice."

" I thought so," said Walter.

" If you thought so, why didn't you say so ; it would have spared us so much irritation."

" I am not irritated," said Walter, " and you know I would spare your feelings in every possible way ; your subterfuge about the dressmaker was unworthy ; and it was unkind also to keep me in the dark."

" I feel it was, dear ; I know it was. I confess it. I apologize ; my only excuse is that Dolly was with us when I told the little fib about the message ; I could not, of course, take her into my confidence ; as for you, dear, I humbly ask your forgiveness."

She flung her arms round her lawful critic, deposited her head upon his shoulder, and Walter gave her what he considered to be a triumphant kiss.

"Now then," he said cheerfully, "that's all right. I forgive you; we understand each other. I have no doubt you did the right thing; I have no doubt Dolly has done the right thing; I am sure Sam Swynford has; and I am quite sure that Philip Forsyth has behaved shamefully."

"Walter, you are a darling!" exclaimed his wife, returning his kiss. "And now, what are your plans?"

"To get out of Venice at once as you proposed," said Walter; and, as he said so, they both, by mutual impulse, left the balcony as if to pack; but they were both attracted by the entrance of the manager of the hotel.

"A letter," he said, "very urgent, for Mr. Milbanke."

Walter opened it. It was from Philip Forsyth—only a few lines :—

"Forgive me. Accept my abject regrets and apologies. Dolly will easily forgive me. I am utterly unworthy of her and of your friendship. Tell her so. We shall probably never meet again. I have left Venice on a long journey. My conduct on the night of the Countess Stravensky's reception may explain my change of plans and life. I feel it due to you to say this. No one need be alarmed as to my safety. I have written to my mother. If ever you and yours think of me again, remember me when most I seemed entitled to your respect and esteem.

"PHILIP FORSYTH."

"Thank you," said Walter, turning to the manager. "There is no answer."

"The messenger did not wait," said the manager.

"You have instructions to forward on the remainder of Mr. Forsyth's baggage?"

"Yes, sir, it goes to Paris."

"I am sorry," said Walter, "to tell you that this has broken up our little party. We shall leave to-morrow for the lakes and Switzerland; but we are very much indebted to you for your kindness and attention. We shall pay for your rooms until the end of the term for which I engaged them, and we shall hope to return next spring for a long stay in Venice. Any loss that you may have sustained by our monopoly of the hotel during the fêtes I shall discharge with pleasure."

"Monsieur is most generous," said the manager. "I hold myself at your command." With which the cour-teous host withdrew, and Walter and his wife returned to the subject in hand.

"That letter, my dear," said Jenny, "is our justifi-cation."

"Yes," said Walter, "it relieves my mind very con-siderably. I should have felt troubled about leaving Venice without having something definite from Forsyth. Now all we have to do is to try and forget the disagree-able part of our journey, to look upon what has happened as all for the best, and continue our holiday in a cheerful spirit."

"We never, my dear Walter, were more unanimous upon any subject. Where do you propose to go?"

"I think we might spend a few days at Verona, a week or two at Belaggio, and then travel quietly through Switzerland and home by Paris."

"Delightful," said Jenny, as Dolly and Sam Swynford entered the room. "Don't you think so?" she said, addressing Dolly and her new fiancé.

"The morning," said Dolly, "or what? Venice is certainly lovely. Sam has given me an ice at Florian's, and I have been feeding the pigeons."

"For sixty seconds," said Sam, cheerily, "I was afraid the pigeons were going to feed on Dolly. She was literally in a cloud of feathers. I had positively to rescue her."

"Not the first rescue," said Dolly, with a frank, affectionate expression in her dancing eyes that comprehended the whole group.

"Your sister," said Sam, "is a trifle mysterious or mischievous—don't know which; both, perhaps. She has been saying that all the way here, and yet I'm sure the ice was harmless enough. If it had been punch *a la Romaine*—well, there, I'll say no more about it, except between our four selves that this is the happiest moment of my life."

"There!" said Dolly, "and you've said that before."

"And on many occasions," said Jenny, merrily. "Walter always says it when he makes a speech."

"Come to think of it," said Sam, "you are possibly right. Don't remember that I ever made more than two or three speeches in my life, and I believe I have always rung in that convenient expression. But I hope that doesn't take away from its point to-day. If I had wings like those pigeons, I think I should just soar right up into that blue sky and come tumbling down again in very fun, just as one of the fluffiest of them did after he made the acquaintance of Dolly."

"I daresay," said Walter. "Have a cigar?"

"I'll have anything you like, my dear boy."

"Dolly," said Walter, as she stood there beaming upon him, "sit down, and don't look so miserable. If you have any little purchases to make, take a little rest and go out and make them; we leave Venice to-morrow."

"Leave Venice!" exclaimed Swynford, looking at Dolly.

"Leave Venice!" said Dolly, looking at Jenny.

"We are tired of Venice," said Jenny. "But we are not going home; don't be afraid. What do you say to the Lake of Como, Sam?"

"The Lake of Como," replied Swynford, "where the marble palace lifts its something to eternal summer and blushes forth in the midst of roses, or what is it? I'm not good at poetical quotation."

"Quite good enough," said Walter. "That's the place."

"And a little cottage in a shabby village when we get there?" said Swynford.

"By no means," said Walter.

'It was so in the play, you know," said Swynford, turning to Dolly.

"This is not a play," rejoined Walter, "and we don't want any of your comedy dialogue, Sam ; only a little of your common sense."

"All right," said Sam. "Proceed ; all my common sense is at your disposal. Not got much of it, but such as it is and all I have pray command me."

"Do you propose to give us the pleasure of your company?" asked Walter.

"I propose to give myself the pleasure of your company."

"For how long?" asked Walter.

"Until you're tired of me ; and as regards Dolly, even a little longer."

"You talked this morning of sending to London for some luggage."

"I have sent for my Sunday clothes," said Sam, laughing.

"To this address?"

"To the Hotel Milano."

"Do you think they are on their way by this?"

"I hope so."

"Very well, then ; you can give instructions at the Hotel Milano to have them sent on to the Hotel Belaggio."

"Consider it done, my dear Walter," said Sam.

"I am going up to the station now," said Walter "to arrange for a saloon carriage to Verona."

"Will Dolly come," said Swynford. "and Mrs. Mil-banke?"

"They had better rest a little," said Walter. "We will come back, and I propose that later we spend an hour in St. Mark's. There are some little things Jenny would like to buy, and then we will go over to the Lido and dine."

"You had better place yourself entirely in Walter's hands," said Jenny to Sam.

"Most happy," said Sam. "Walter, give the word; I am with you."

CHAPTER XLII.

MODERN LOVERS IN ANCIENT VERONA.

THERE is probably no more interesting city in all Italy than Verona, where Shakespeare's "Two Gentlemen" took their walks abroad, and Romeo and Juliet lived, loved and died. Whether the tomb they show you is Juliet's or not, the town is that of the Capulets and the Montagues, and the air pulsates with romantic possibili-ties.

To begin with, the place is delightfully situated on a rapid river; it is within the mighty shadows of the Alps; it has a Roman amphitheatre, more complete and beautiful than the Colosseum at Rome; it is a city of palaces and balconies, of frescoed houses, and narrow, picturesque streets.

Standing in the Piazza del Signori, you feel that not only is that story of Romeo and Juliet possible, but true. At night, meeting there two or three groups of noisy young citizens coming home from some local festival, you may feel assured they will bite their thumbs at each other.

English travelers bound to Milan, on the one hand, or to Venice on the other, rarely make Verona more than a resting-place for the night; but it is well worth the sojourn of a week. Your hotel is one of the fine old Scaligeri palaces.

It was the Saturday market on one of the days of the Milbankes' stay there, and they found the courtyard of the Palace of the Capulets full of market carts and tethered horses; the adjacent and surrounding buildings evidently humble lodging-houses, but even these had balconies, and were artistic in decay.

"Murray" says there are more balconies in Verona than in any other city of Italy. Walter was very happy in his pleasant allusions to modern Romeos and Juliets, and to those who flirted in the balconies of old. Sam was delighted at any reference to his engagement with Dolly, who had some little difficulty now and then in restraining what Jenny had informed her was a too jubilant view of her position.

"The fact is, my dear," said Dolly to Jenny, "I feel as if I had had an awful escape. If I had been rescued from a fire or shipwreck, and had got well over it; or, to be more prosaic, had been very ill in crossing from Calais to Dover, had quite recovered, and had a good dinner, I couldn't have felt more contented than I do now."

"But you mustn't let Sam see it."

"Why not?" said Dolly. "He is under the impression that I gave up Philip, not Philip me, and I really don't care whether he knows the entire truth or not. I have told him I am very happy, that even when I seemed to hold him at a distance I always loved him. You know, dear, you gave me a lot of advice about Philip. Don't you think it would be just as well to let me alone now to go my own way?"

"Well, perhaps—perhaps," said Jenny. "I own I was not very wise about the Forsyth business. But what is this? Why, this is the market-place. Walter, is not this the market-place?"

"Yes, dear," said Walter. "Don't you remember we saw a picture of it in the Walker Gallery at Manchester?"

"No," said Jenny, "I never saw a picture half so beautiful anywhere." And the present chronicler is almost inclined to agree with this admiring exclamation.

Imagine the market-place at Nottingham or Yarmouth, the houses tall, some frescoed, one a palace, all with balconies; at the north end a pillar bearing aloft the marble effigy of the lion of St. Mark; on the south a temple; in the centre an ancient fountain with a statue of the Virgin. Above this imagine a blue, far-away sky; and on the floor of the market numberless stalls, protected by great white umbrellas; at the base of St. Mark's pillar a group of Italian men and women from the country, looking exactly like a peasant chorus out of a grand opera, so much so that you expect them every now and then to burst forth into song. Then imagine the market itself full of vegetables and flowers, and cattle and poultry, mostly presided over by Italian women, with handkerchiefs about their heads (and occasionally a mantilla) not unlike the head-dress of Manchester factory girls; and all round the market busy shops; whenever you get a peep out of the square down some side street you catch glimpses of the façades, ancient palaces or narrow-gabled thoroughfares. Add to all this Italian soldiers, policemen (in tall hats, with silver-tipped walking-sticks), priests in solemn costume, wrinkled old men with equally wrinkled umbrellas, blue-eyed Italian girls, and stately housewives marketing. If you can put all this together in any kind of shape you may form some idea of the Verona market.

Among the cries of the miscellaneous vendors of goods and hawkers of minor articles of trade, "quatro chinka,

chinka, chinka," "stivola," "pollastro," seemed continually in oral evidence, the "chinka, chinka," of an old
lady (like the grandmother of one of Ouida's peasant hero-
ines, of a strange and an antique mould) rising calmly
above the rest. She sold four and five pieces of fish for a
penny. Her competitors dealt in boots and shoes, chickens,
cheese, crockery, flowers—what indeed, did they not
sell?

And this fine old market of white umbrellas, with the
sun playing all kinds of fantastic tricks with its various
wares, was the Forum in olden days. The building we
spoke of as a Temple we find was the Tribune, "to which
the newly-elected-Capitano del Popolo of the Free City,
after having heard Mass at the Cathedral, was conducted,
and in which, after he had addressed the people, he was
invested with the insignia of office." In after times the
sentences of condemned criminals were pronounced from
this Tribune. Proclamations were made from it, and debt-
ors were here compelled to submit to a humiliating punishment. In all bright scenes, however sunny, the shadow
always comes.

As they left the market, they met the prison van on its
way to the local Newgate; but even this conveyance had
a gay appearance. The officers in charge, in new cocked
hats and bright swords, were chatting with the driver, a
peasant, who was calmly smoking a cigarette. Beggary
does not excite your sympathy as it does in London. The
Italian mendicant is dirty, perhaps; unaffectedly lazy, but
he looks warm in his rags. There is a terrible reality
about most of the London beggars; and the professionals,
whom Mr. Ribton-Turner, in his book on Vagrancy, has
immortalized, can "assume a wretchedness" so keenly
that they compel your pity. Nevertheless no Verona beg-
gar made an unavailing appeal to Sam Swynford during this
happy time at Verona; and, full of his romantic success

with Dolly and the realization of his dearest hopes, the
poetic city now and then seemed to stimulate Sam into
unexpected flashes of intellectuality.

On the last night of their visit to Verona, the Milbanke
party were favored with special permission to visit, by
moonlight, the arena where the Christian martyrs were
driven from their prisons out among the wild beasts, to
audiences of captains, senators, ladies, priests, and the populace.   He would have been indeed insensible to poetry
or human sympathy who could have seen the moonbeams
falling upon the marble seats and the broken arches without
a pitying sigh for the past, and a grateful reflection upon
the privileges of liberty and toleration in the present. Sam
Swynford felt as they wandered through the great solemn
place, a strong inspiration of protection towards Dolly,
which she reciprocated in a more or less comfortable nestle
under the wing, or to put it without metaphor, under the
strong arm of her prosperous young London lover.

When they were most inclined to linger over sentimental reflections about the scenes in the arena, Walter Milbanke was busy with thoughts of his final show, which was
the Tomb of Juliet in the moonlight.   " Not," he said, as
he led the way with the guide to the carriage which awaited
them at the entrance of the Colosseum, " Juliet's Tomb
as ordinary visitors see it, but all to ourselves with this
glorious moon."

Driving through the pleasant streets, and saluted here
and there by the music of evidently social evenings which
gave occasional light and merriment to sundry houses *en
route*, they presently came to a quieter part of Verona,
lighted only by the great white moon.   They approached
the pleasant corner selected for Juliet's apocryphal tomb
through an old-fashioned garden, with patches of green
turf and blooming gilliflowers, rows of peas in blossom
that rivalled the white Marguerite daisies in the moonlight

and a rich perfume from beans in flower and the scent of many herbs. It was a mixed garden of the English kind; that seemed unconsciously to lend itself to the Juliet illu-sion of the English poet. Even Walter was subdued by its unostentatious beauty, and the little party followed the old lady who opened the garden gate upon the narrow way that led to the great stone coffin which, as a matter of sen-timent and imagination, the world is willing to accept as a relic of the Shakespearean story.

It was somewhat out of keeping with the romance of the scene to find the great stone sarcophagus half-full of visit-ing cards, the prosaic character of which was not quite redeemed by the one or two faded wreaths that hung about the tomb. But it was all, nevertheless, very lovely and im-pressive in the moonlight and without the presence of other sightseers; and the Milbankes, with their newly-engaged companions, drove to their hotel, being generally more or less under the impression that they possessed a far higher and poetic appreciation of the beautiful than any of them had imagined.

That same silvery moon, however—which seemed to look down with special approval upon Verona—cast only fitful and furtive beams upon a weird ghost-like figure that appeared to a party of Venetian fishermen sailing their picturesque vessel through the water-gateway of the Adri-atic into the shimmering lagoons of the City-in-the-Sea.

CHAPTER XLIII.

THE GHOST OF THE LAGOONS.

THEY were a fishing trio of the lagoons, Chiozotti, in fact, well known for their industry and their piety. They had been beating about most of the night without hauling in anything worth mentioning, until it was nearly morning, and then naving called down a blessing from the saint whom their brown illuminated sail glorified, their net had filled to overflowing. They emptied it with much rejoicing upon their reeking deck, and then spread their canvas to catch the morning breeze for Venice.

It wanted yet an hour or so to dawn, the first opaline advances of which began to move the curtains of the Eastern sky. Only a handful of pale stars remained in the heavens. The sea had been rough on the previous night, and a strong under swell was left in memory of the passing storm. The picturesque smack rose and fell with a regular cadenza of motion.

While one of the men steered and attended to the navigation, the other two were busy getting their fish into the hold, singing all the while a kind of answering chorus to the chant of the steersman.

Presently the soloist paused in his song to gaze intently to windward where he fancied he saw something in the water. It was not a boat, nor was it a fish. It might be a piece of floating wreckage. But it looked strangely like some awful vision of the deep. The helmsman said nothing, but crossed himself devoutly and looked in another direction.

The opaline glow that had at first been very faint now gave place to streaks of pink and grey and red; it looked like a stormy breaking of the morning.

There was an unusual shadow, too, upon the sea, the steersman thought. He feared to look to windward, though he tried to smother a superstitious dread that came over him in a repetition of his fisherman's chant, and again his mates took up the refrain. He no longer saw the strange weird something in the sea; it was still there, nevertheless, rising and falling with the swelling waves. Once in a way the first beams of the morning fell upon it as if with inquisitive glances. Then the shadowy forms of the Euganean hills began to assert their presence far away beyond the mainland. Further North the cold white Alps were getting ready to make their appearance on the distant background of the hazy picture. By and bye the islands of the lagoons would put in their claims to recognition, but for the moment there was only one object to be seen.

And now they all saw it. The fish with their shining scales and bright dying eyes had been stowed away, and suddenly the man at the helm pointed a long bony finger in the direction of the ghost-like object to windward. The thing was recognized in silence. It assumed an almost upright attitude with the rising of the waves ; and as they receded it floated backwards as a graceful swimmer might. It did not, in taking this new position, however, buffet the water as a live swimmer would, but rose and fell with a ghostly rhythm of motion. When its head topped the waves horizontally it showed a human face distorted, white and swollen, with dark hair.

All three toilers of the deep now saw the apparition. It was more than a ghost and less than a man. Was it some pernicious creature of the sea ? How should they avoid it ?

They tacked. They turned their eyes to leeward. They made as if they would sail for the open sea.

The morning hesitated at the portals of day. Once or twice it threatened to go back into the night. Unusual clouds began to gather about the East. A heavy fall of rain pattered down upon the sea.

The swimming figure followed the ship. They had both struck the same current. The sailors now saw it in a new quarter. They were afraid. Again they tacked. This time the prow turned towards the Lido. The men had resumed their course.

Presently a long streak of light illuminated the waters. The rain ceased. It was nearly morning. The sun forced silver lances up into the clouds.

And now there could be no mistake. The figure was human in form, but its face was a weird deformity. It was a goblin, a monster, a something horrible. It had great white hands that were steering it towards the ship. Its head rose and fell with the waves. They could all see the nameless thing. They fell upon their knees and commended themselves to their saints, and more particularly to her who had vouchsafed them their goodly haul of fish.

Then they took counsel and came to a decision. The monster was a ghost. They were convinced of it, these three Chiozotti. They crowded all sail to get away from it; when suddenly, as if under the influence of the god of day, the wind fell and there was a dead calm. The sea, however, still rose and fell. There were no waves. But the keel of the boat made a gurgle and a washing. The sea seemed as if trying to break into a wave, but it only slopped up against the ship's sides. One of the men thought there was something like a sob accompanying the bulging motion of the water.

They tempted the dead breeze from every point, but the ship lay still, and the morning in silvery splendor began to salute and glorify distant objects, flashing now and then through the clouds into a white path across the lagoon right up to the ship. In one of these passing illuminations they saw the ghost clearly.

" It is no ghost," said the bravest of the three ; " it is a dead man."

" Did you ever see a dead man swimming with its arms and legs as a live man swims ? " said the other, fortifying himself with a long drink from a bottle which he handed to his mates.

" It does indeed swim," said the helmsman ; " that's true."

" What harm can come to us," said the first, " having

commended ourselves to the Virgin and to our own much beloved and beholden-to saint ? "

" She did not help Pierre when we were wrecked and lost our mate," said the helmsman.

" Forgive him, Santa Maria ! " exclaimed the second fisherman ; " he knows not what he says !

" It is no ghost, comrades," repeated the bravest of the three, " only a drowned man ; let us take him in tow."

" What if he take us in tow ? " said the first of the Chiozotti.

" Truly, what then ? " exclaimed the helmsman. " Look at him ! Dead, do you say ? Yes, a dead-alive ; he swims, don't you see it, first on his breast, then on his side, and thirdly on his back. Do drowned men swim like that ? "

" It's the action of the waves," said the second fisherman, taking another drink.

" Strange action ! " said the first.

" Yes, I grant you," said the second ; " but are we cowards ? Have we been out in all weathers, and seen strange sights by night and day, and are we going to be afraid now that the sun is rising and Venezia begins to look across the water to the Lido ? "

" No," said the first spokesman.

" What shall we do, good comrade ? "

" Lower the boat and take the drowned man in tow ! " said the other, handing the bottle to the steersman, who emptied it and found himself more courageous by two wine-glasses full.

" But see," he said, " nevertheless it is coming along of its own accord. It needs no assistance ! "

" There will be a reward," said the second sailor. " I see gold lace ; it is the body of an officer in uniform."

" Don't romance," replied the first fisherman ; " it is the glint of the sun on the water."

By this time the sun was really getting up in the heavens. The sky was beginning to turn blue. Distant mountains came nearer.

" Lower the boat, boys," said the bravest of the three men. " I will fasten a line to the ghost!"

The helmsman crossed himself as he lent a hand to his mates, and presently the boat was slipping to the stern where the second man dropped into her and began to pull towards the strange figure which seemed to be literally playing with the waves.

" Yes," said the Chioggia fisherman as he approached it, "gold lace sure enough, but what a face ! and, mercy on us, how dead-alive it looks with its hands waving up and down. Ahoy, mate, heave to !" with which exclamation of personal encouragement he flung a thin rope across the body and so manœuvred it that in a minute or two he had fastened a stronger one to it, and the ghost of the lagoon answered to the tug of the boat which the fisherman began to pull for the smack.

The vessel hove to, and the adventurer having fastened his boat to the line flung out by the helmsman, scrambled aboard. The ghost floated in companionship with the vessel's boat, which dropped quietly astern. The Chioggia smack now hoisted her painted sails and steered for the channel by the Lido.

It was an ebb tide, and the water, as Mr. Symonds tells us in his " Italian Sketches " at such time, runs past the mulberry gardens of this pleasant hamlet like a river. The fishing boat, with its ghastly figure at the stern, swung into this rapid stream aided by a freshening breeze, and from the other side of the Riva no doubt looked a pretty object, as indeed it was if you took no note of its half-submerged cargo—the dead passenger with its great white hands and its equally white face, like soft, half-tanned leather.

On went the boat and its silent witness past the grove of acacia trees which rise out of its tall green grasses, where the first butterflies of summer were disporting themselves for their brief hour or two of gay and radiant life.

Presently the vessel's course was changed for the Custom House, and now she went gliding along with no swelling motion, except such as the wooing wind gave her.

The sun was up. Venice was alive. A little crowd of early workmen had gathered round the Victor Emmanuel statue. The last remnants of the decorations were being removed. The pigeons in the Grand Square of St. Mark's were fluttering over their first meal of the day. The two royal standards opposite the famous church were flying in the morning breeze.

A cluster of gondolas were lying by the steps in the shadow of the Lion of St. Mark's. Picturesque groups of men and women were standing near. The gorgeous palaces were glassing themselves in the Grand Canal with blurred effects of form and color made by the rippling water. Round the corner of the Pizarro Palace where the Countess Stravensky had looked down from the window of her boudoir, however, the water was still and showed every line of architecture, every lichen on the ancient walls, every bit of ooze and green slime that clung to the lower stones on the water's edge, but there was no trace of the tragedy of the recent festival any more than there was of those others which had preceded it in bygone days. Nor had the wavelets in front of the palace anything to show or to say of the magnificent reception, the gay and festal music of which had been the dirge which Vengeance had prepared for the Russian general who had presided over the outrages of Czarovna.

All the world looked so happy on this morning as if the bright sun, the soft breeze, the clear sky, the perfume of flowers (brought from the mainland by a passing boat) had been given as compensation for the closing of the royal festival; or as if the spirit of Venice had risen up to let her worshippers feel that the city in the sea needed nothing of festival or music or royal guests, or flags and banners, and painted boats to make her desirable, but that she was loveliest with aught else but her own beauty.

And yet trailing along her dreamy city was that bleached and ghastly thing that a little way off looked like a strong swimmer at his ease, his extending arms and legs rising and falling with the motion of the vessel in company with which he was enjoying the bright gay morning. But what a ghastly mockery it turned out to be when the Chioggia smack cast anchor and dropped her sails. And what a reception it had from the chattering crowd that collected on the quay—all talking at once, some crossing themselves, others professing to recognize the corpse, all presently making way for the Custom House authorities and the police.

"General Petronovitch," said one of the chiefs of police, "he who disappeared on the night of the illuminations; and this (taking from the body a dagger that was entangled rather with the clothing than with the flesh) the cause of death, perhaps."

On the blade of the rusted knife could still be seen deeply engraven a word of Arabic, which a learned priest translated into Italian, French, and English. They were the same Arabic letters as those that were embossed upon the amulet that the Countess Stravensky wore at Mrs. Chetwynd's reception, and the word was "Vengeance!"

Thus the judicial murderer of the Rabbi Losinski, the assassin of the household peace and joy of the Klosstocks, and the scourge of Czarovna, flung after execution into the sea, had come back again to Venice a witness of the far-reaching hand of Nihilistic vengeance,

CHAPTER XLIV.

POETRY, PROSE, AND THE DEAD SWIMMER.

FROM Verona to Como is a day's journey. Under any circumstances, there is no monotony in it, but traveling in pleasant companionship it is perhaps one of the most delightful of continental railway journeys. The scenery is never uninteresting, and there are always in the distance fine ranges of snow-capped mountains.

The happy English party from Venice, it need hardly be said, found the trip full of a new and special interest. Dolly was radiant. It needed no psychological student to discover that Sam Swynford was the selection of her heart. If he had been wise in his estimation of female character, he ought to have discovered in his earliest acquaintanceship with Jenny's lively sister that her "stand off-ishness" and sallies of wit at his expense were only feminine indications of interest, if not love. It was perhaps a little feline, while she purred, to make her lover conscious of an occasional scratch. Had the amiable young stockbroker responded with the manful intimation that he was not to be wounded with impunity nor without resentment, it is quite possible that the shadow of Philip Forsyth might never have fallen upon Dolly's fateful youth. She had in her secret heart loved Swynford none the less that she had occasionally made him suffer. It was only the trifling of a somewhat coquettish nature. Swynford had, in slave-like worship, flung himself at her feet, and she had placed her foot upon his neck, not viciously, but with something of the pride of conquest. She would have appreciated from

22

Sam the spirited response that such treatment would have received from Philip Forsyth, because she knew that Sam was devotedly attached to her. She had doubts of Philip, was flattered by his attention, urged to accept him by her sister, who had no other object but Dolly's social and happy advancement in life.

The truth is, the two pretty young women were as much above the average of their sex in genuine amiability as they were in appearance and manners. They had, in the course of their education and training, annexed unconsciously some of the snobbishness of the upper middle class in small social victories; delighted in being received in a higher grade of society than their neighbors; found in social success of this kind greater pleasure than should belong to the honest performance of their home duties; liked of course to be admired rather for their beauty than their intellectual qualities; were ambitious more or less selfishly for distinction in their husbands that they, the wives, might assume the role of superior persons; were, in fact, good women with women's weaknesses.

No hostess was more gracious than Mrs. Milbanke, nor more successful in her popular little parties, and Dolly might well be envied for her high spirits, her healthful constitution, her bright eyes, and her unquestionable beauty. Philip Forsyth had been proud to be seen escorting her in the tents of Vanity Fair, proud of the attention her happy, pretty face invoked, proud of the envy it excited among women, and the envy he excited as her prospective husband. But Sam Swynford, in his more common-place nature, had paid far higher tribute to Dolly's natural fascinations than was possible to Philip Forsyth. Sam had no ambition apart from her. In every speculation he was inspired with the hope of a future with Dolly. He administered to her little vanities in every way that was possible to his position as her admirer and an inti-

mate friend of the family. He remembered all the days
in which she was specially interested—Christmas, the New
Year, St. Valentine's, Easter, her birthday, Jenny's birthday, Walter's birthday. She always said he had excellent
taste in the choice of flowers, the binding of books, and
the selection of dainty bits of bric-a brac. But Jenny
could not forget that Sam had in his speech a suggestion
of North Country dialect, and was a little inclined to over-
dress, took no pains to cultivate aristocratic society, and
was, after all, only a stockbroker; so that when Philip
Forsyth, with his distinguished style and manner, his
artistic prospects, his promising position in society, and
his notable circle of friends, came along as a rival to
Swynford, Mrs. Milbanke took Dolly's future into her
hands and brought about the engagement which had
ended so disastrously. She now congratulated herself
and her three companions on continuing their Italian
holiday with the new love, and being entirely off with the
old, and confessed to Walter that there was something
nobler in life than some of the aims which had engrossed
her ambition, upon the sunken rocks of which she had
nearly wrecked Dolly's future ; but Walter would not
hear of the smallest thought of self-abasement on the part
of his pretty and affectionate wife, and he vowed that he
had always felt somehow or other that everything would
come right for Dolly, although he was anxious to make
believe that if anyone was to blame for hastening that unfortunate engagement it was he himself.

Altogether the party was under the influence of affectionate self-denial and mutual congratulation upon the
course events had taken. At present they did not, from
a sympathetic point of view, feel the shadow of Philip
Forsyth's strange disaffection, and they had no knowledge
of that sensation which the Ghost of the Lagoons had
created in Venice.

They arrived at Como, a picturesque city at the head
of the famous lake, where Walter had secured rooms at
the best hotel in the square by the quay where you take
the lake steamers or hire rowing boats. After an excellent dinner Walter and Swynford sat in the balcony,
smoked their cigars, and watched the sunset. Dolly and
Jenny unpacked their valises and talked over the day's
adventures.

The next morning they were to go on to Bellaggio.
Sam and Walter were up with the lark, interested in study-
ing the picturesque and busy secularization of Sunday in
Italy, which is strikingly illustrated in this little city of
Como. Jugglers, hawkers, vendors of iced drinks, and
holiday people were in the Square from the earliest hour
on Sunday morning. Later, there were steamers arriving
with bands of music and democratic societies out for the
day. Members of rival and friendly associations met
these political combinations on the quay, where they
palavered and exchanged emphatic civilities. Their bands
Swynford considered to be nearly as bad as those of the
Salvation Army in England; he hoped they had not
traveled all that distance to make the acquaintance of
such ribald music. Walter, discoursing with a bystander,
discovered that the musicians were hired for such occasions as these by political administrators and the Odd
Fellows and Foresters of Italy. The banners of these
Orders were, however, more easily carried than those of
our English confraternities. They did not indulge in
those tremendous pictures which in England stretch right
across the streets and are borne aloft in high winds with
much sweat and struggle by even the strongest and
doughtiest of Oddfellows and the most stalwart of Robin
Hoods.

The square of Como was very busy all Sunday, and so
were the streets; busy with people who were shopkeeping,

going to church, marketing, singing, working. At night the vocalists were in the ascendancy, but, as Walter remarked, they *did* sing and they were not drunk. They awoke the echoes of the surrounding hills with madrigals and chorus. If the square of Como had been a thoroughfare in an English city those bands of workmen and holiday-makers would, it is to be feared, have been roaring out some music-hall song or hiccoughing a vulgar chorus of the slums.

" One goes from home," said Walter, " not only to see how great England is in many things, but how small, not to say brutal, she may be in others."

In the afternoon our English travelers said their prayers with the rest of the church-going community, and towards evening made their first little excursion on the lake, which they navigated in dreamy sunshine on the morrow.

Sweet and gentle searchers after truth have discovered that Bulwer Lytton adapted his poetic description of the Lake of Como from a foreign source ; other philanthropic critics have at the same time ridiculed the poem as utterly overdone being applied to the famous Italian lake. Permit a humble worshipper of nature, and one who loves art none the less, to say that Bulwer's half page of suggestive description is only a faint indication of the spirit and beauty of the Lake of Como. Why, there is even an hotel at Bellaggio, half way down the lake, which goes near to be worthy of the well-known lines :—

> " A palace lifting to eternal summer
> Its marble walls from out a glossy bower
> Of coolest foliage, musical with birds."

The lake is a sheet of water thirty-five miles in length, and every yard of it a picture of romantic beauty—high sloping hills that hem you in now and then, making not one lake, but many ; hills that are clothed with foliage and backed at many points by distant Alps that are clothed in everlasting snow. As the steamer skirts the shore you see that the gardens of the innumerable villas are filled with flowers, that the houses are of all descriptions, palaces, cottages, chalets, lodges, hotels ; as they go high up into the mountains they dwindle off into the cots of vineyard-tenders or herdsmen. It is wonderful now and then to see up in the mountains villages which look like flights of buildings that have settled down in clusters as pigeons might, all in a heap, with a few trees above them, and always the sheltering elbows of convenient Alps. The season is late they tell me on the boats and at the hotel, yet the air is soft and balmy, great bunches of westeria decorate garden walls, lilac, rhododendron, Guelder roses, chestnuts are in full bloom, and at every village where the steamer touches, men and women are sitting out of doors, the men swinging their legs over quay walls, the women sewing or tending children, all in "summery" dresses, and we have long since discarded wraps and overcoats, and find the weather hot enough despite the breeze of the steamer in rapid motion. Bellaggio is probably the most delightful point of the lake. It is fifteen miles from its northern extremity, and divides the lake into two branches.

Here the travelers commenced their delightful experiences of Bellaggio. The weather was like July in England, though the time was early May. The sky was characteristically Italian. The windows of the hotel were open. From the great drawing-room came the voice of a prima donna of the lyric stage, whom some traveling companions had persuaded to sing a few snatches from "Othello" and "Lohengrin." The terraces of the hotel were reflected in the lake in deep colors of green and pink and red and yellow, repetitions of grass and flowers.

On the opposite shore the lake was bordered by a sweep of architecture that melted away into hill and dale; and far off on the right the snow mountains pretended they were white clouds capping the rich blue of the sky. In the little town there was a piazza out of which every now and then ran narrow street ways up to the hills; little streets literally of climbing steps. When you looked up these narrow ways and saw women coming down with children in their arms, or men lolling against curious doorways, you could only wish you were an artist with nothing else in the world to do but to put these pictures into black and white for magazines, or better still, into all their glory of color for popular picture galleries. When the lusciousness of full summer comes to Lake Como, and rests upon the clustering hills of Bellaggio, and dreams in a sunny glow down in the valleys, it is no stretch of fancy to imagine the perfumed light of some marble palace stealing through the mist of alabaster lamps, and every air

> " Heavy with the sighs
> Of orange groves and music from sweet lutes,
> And murmurs of low fountains that gush forth
> I' the mist of roses."

" Of course I like the picture," said Dolly, " but not for always, Sam." ·

" How do you mean ? " he asked, pressing her arm as they lounged upon the terrace watching the light and shade upon the distant hills.

" Beautiful for a visit," said Dolly; " perfectly lovely, but too good for the likes of I, as Walter's gardener says down in the Midlands."

" You really feel like that ? " said Sam. " I'm so awfully glad, because I was thinking somewhat in that direction."

" Really ? " she asked.

"Indeed most truly," he said. "I once knew an odd, simple kind of rich man who owned a palace in Worcestershire, but lived in the lodge which stood by the road at his gates. Of course, Dolly, I could live with you, my dear, anywhere, palace or cottage, a garret in Bloomsbury or a bijou villa standing in its own grounds at Kensington."

"Sam, you're so odd !"

"When I said garret," said Sam, "of course I only meant it as a figure of speech—a *façon de parler*, as Walter would say ; but without you I can imagine myself in this Bellaggio palace longing for a cottage on the hills opposite, or trying to negotiate an exchange of rooms with one of those loafing peasants who live at the top of the narrow avenues that give upon the Piazza, where those wrinkled old women we saw this afternoon sell toy distaffs and bric-a-bric."

"Our thoughts are certainly sympathetic, Sam," said Dolly. "I shall often dream of this lovely place. If we were to live here we ought to dress in costume, as they do upon the stage. I could never endure to go about in such scenery in ordinary clothes."

"That's because," said Sam, "you never see this kind of thing in pictures without Italian men and women in all sorts of fancy dress. The best studies of lakes and mountains and water-falls, with palaces and foreign costumes, seem to me to be like chromos ; but wouldn't those wrinkled old women on the Piazza make fine subjects for Professor Herkomer. Forsyth would have——"

"Don't mention that name, Sam ; not yet, at all events. It makes me feel as if I would like you to slap me in the face."

"Dolly !" exclaimed Sam, entirely forgetting what he was going to say about Forsyth.

"It does," said Dolly. "I don't wonder at those strong men in the East End of London beating their wives."

" Dolly, Dolly," said Sam, with his arm round her waist and " awfully happy," as he told her afterwards, " you'll make me feel miserable if you talk in that way. Besides, fancy drifting from ' glassy bowers, musical with birds, palaces lifting to eternal summer, and orange groves heavy with the sighs of music from sweet lutes,' into the barbarism of Whitechapel and women-beaters ! For goodness' sake, don't tell Jenny what we talked of, and don't mention it to Walter. We shall be chaffed unmercifully. Let us go back to poetry and sentiment."

" That's the bell for dinner," said Walter Milbanke, coming upon them unobserved, and calling their attention to the sounding gong beyond the terrace, " and here are the English newspapers. Such a discovery, by Jove ! How Comedy and Tragedy do go hand in hand ! They have found General Petronovitch floating with the tide from the Adriatic into the lagoons, stabbed to the heart with a dagger on which is engraved, in Arabic, the word ' Vengeance.' "

" How dreadful ! " exclaimed Dolly.

" It is believed," continued Walter, " that he was killed on the night of the illuminations and taken out to sea in one of the many boats we saw on that exciting night. By Jove, it's worthy of the ancient days of Venice."

" I'm glad we didn't stay," remarked Dolly.

" So am I," said Swynford, " and you'll excuse me, Walter, if I don't tear my hair over Petronovitch. I feel so awfully happy."

" You look it, my boy, you look it. Come along, then, we will dismiss the Venetian ghost and try the Bellaggio cuisine. I think it's all right. I have interviewed the *chef*, and discovered a brand of champagne that I think will even astonish you, you City sybarite ! "

CHAPTER XLV.

THE COUNTESS TELLS HER STORY TO THE BROTHER· HOOD AND PHILIP.

THE foreign quarter of London with which the public is supposed to be most familiar is in truth the least known of the many mysterious districts of the great metropolis.

Soho, in its own peculiar way, possesses as many strange ramifications as the black circle of Whitechapel, which environs the tragic footsteps of the most terrible of modern assassins. The police have the key to many of the retreats in which political exiles and foreign conspirators meet to hold friendly intercourse, and to hatch plots of social regeneration and personal vengeance. But Scotland Yard has no special reason for interfering with the meetings of these continental outcasts, so long as they do not offend the English laws.

The liberty of the subject in these islands covers the stranger as well as the native. To plot against the life of potentate, statesman or private citizen, however, of this or any other country would, of course, bring conspirators under legal restraint ; but it is not the business of the London police to act the part of spies upon political exiles ; and who is to interpret the secret thoughts of the solemn mysterious men and women who live quiet lives in the regions of Soho, or report to the police the spoken words of their private gatherings ?

England, America and Switzerland have for many years been the plotting grounds of Nihilists and Social ·Democrats.

If it were possible to separate the patriot whose faith
and hopes are satisfied by a wholesome agitation, from the
patriot whose bitter political programme is one of dagger,
dynamite, and violent social upheaval, the Government
would no doubt be ready to draw a hard and fast line on
the side of pacific operations as against the violence of
revolution.   But liberty is compelled to allow a large
margin for license, and it is better that an occasional cul-
prit, who might deserve death or life-long imprisonment,
should receive the protection of our shores rather than an
unchecked despotism should work its will upon the high-
minded agitator, whose only crime is a national enthusiasm for the regeneration of his country.

And so it comes about that London is the sanctuary of
the political exile, not being actually a proved murderer
liable to extradition ; though it must be confessed that
Soho has sheltered many a conspirator who has been
associated with attacks on authority entitled to condemnation as outside the pale of mere political conspiracy.

Of such was more than one of the persons met together,
some two weeks after the Venetian *fêtes*, at the Parisian
Cabaret, in a certain *cul-de-sac* known as Thomas' Alley,
within a stone's throw of Dean Street.

The Parisian Cabaret was a small unpretentious café,
at the extreme end of Thomas' Alley ; smuggled away in
one corner of it, as if it had been built into an uninten-
tional architectural vacancy—an after-thought in the
higgledy-piggledy plan of the original builders.   The lower
part of the house was occupied with a large bow-window
and a quaint doorway, with an over-decoration in the
centre of which was a date indicating that the architecture
belonged to the picturesque period before the age of
stucco and iron.   The upper stories were curiously
gabled ; and the quaint windows, glazed in much smaller
squares than is usual in these days, were prettily deco-

rated with French blinds, neatly tied back with colored ribbons. The place had a singularly clean look; and the principal, and, indeed, only saloon for eating, drinking and dominoes, had a white sanded floor and white painted pannelling that were pleasantly characteristic. The Parisian Cabaret was, indeed, much cleaner and far more agreeable to look upon than most of its customers, one or two of whom lived on the premises; notably Ivan Kos-tanzhoglo, who was a moving spirit of that brotherhood in which Ann Klosstock had been enrolled as one of the two women who had been considered worthy of its confidence.

Ivan Kostanzhoglo had been for some time stationed in London as a controlling agent of certain movements that had been made more or less in combination with other sections of the Young Russian party; but, under orders, he was about to run the risk of reappearing in St. Petersburg, where a rendezvous had been settled for himself, Paul Petroski, Anna Klosstock, Andrea Ferrari, and other earnest confederates.

The startling incident of the far-reaching power of Nihilistic vengeance at Venice, while it had stiffened the surveillance of the Russian police at all the ports of entry into Russia, and led to numerous arrests in the interior, had exercised a tremendous revivifying influence upon the widespread conspiracy which aimed at the overthrow of the Imperial power. The guides and chiefs of the party of action believed in following up the assassination of Petronovitch with a striking dramatic demonstration at headquarters.

It was in connection with this so-called patriotic action of the young Russian party that the private doors of the small underground apartment, which was rented by Ivan Kostanzhoglo, were open to receive company some two weeks after the Ghost of the Lagoons had startled Venice from its customary repose.

Sitting at a round table, lighted with a lamp, were our friends Ferrari, in his shirt sleeves, a loose light coat hanging over his chair (it was a very hot night) ; Anna Klosstock, in a simple sober black gown, without collar or cuffs, her hair gathered up beneath a black bonnet ; Paul Petroski, of Moscow, who had kept his faith at the little hotel on the quay at Venice, and also at the Fazio Palace ; Ivan Kostanzhoglo, a swarthy, thick-set Muscovite, attired in semi-fashionable French garments ; and three others whom it is unnecessary to name.

" I claim," said Anna Klosstock, " the right to acquaint him with my history in your presence before the final oath is administered to him."

" Madame knows best," said Ivan, who sat opposite to her, quietly rolling cigarettes and smoking them, as if to do so was the one chief duty in life.

" We know madame's history," said Paul. " Why repeat it in our presence ? "

" Have our friends," asked Anna, turning to Ferrari and then glancing at the three persons unnamed, " been made acquainted with our victory at Venice ? "

" We only know," said one of them, " that Petronovitch, our bitterest foe, has fallen before the triumphant onslaught of the Brotherhood."

" It will give encouragement to your hopes and strength to your arm to hear that recital.   I count it a part of my duty to record unto you an account of my stewardship, and that of our brethren, Ferrari and Petroski."

" We shall thank you for the revelation," said one.

" It is no doubt our due to know it," said the other.

" And there is nothing so inspiring as a general's own story of his victory," said the third.

" In a few minutes," said Anna Klosstock, " there will arrive, for admission to the Brotherhood, a young English gentleman, who is devoted to me and my poor fortunes. He has accepted at the hands of Andrea Ferrari the oath of secrecy; but not the oath of comradeship, which would entitle him to our pass-words and to share the glories and dangers of our cause. Brothers," she said, rising, "this young man has none of the motives that we have for the labors and dangers we have undertaken. He was born in Moscow, it is true, and in his early youth saw our brother and sister exiles of the past go forth upon their fatal journeying to Siberia. He has a sensitive and generous nature; the memory of those things has sunk deep into his heart; but he is young. His mother is a widow; a patriot, a devoted friend of all exiles. It is his misfortune to have fallen in love with your humble companion."

The smile that for a moment illuminated the face of Ivan Kostanzhoglo vanished at a glance from Ferrari; and Anna Klosstock continued to speak as if she were alone, unconscious of the men who sat around her.

"It is not necessary for me to say to what extent I have returned his strange devotion."

"Not very strange," whispered one of the unnamed to his neighbor, "if a lovely face and figure have anything to do with inspiring love."

"But," she continued, "I am unwilling that for my sake this young English gentleman shall further jeopardize his position and his liberty. He professes to be under the spell of our great cause, to desire no other life than one that shall be devoted to it, in memory of his young life in Moscow, and that he may be at least my comrade. He only knows me as the Countess Stravensky. To him Anna Klosstock is nothing. Her life, her love, her miseries, her motives for revenge, her part in our great victory of Venice are to him an entire blank. While reporting, as one of our secret brotherhood, to this meeting, I desire to convey to him the particulars of my career, that they may disenchant him and show him the abyss upon which he stands. Should he then persist in throwing in his lot with ours, I ask you to accept him."

As she sat down there was a murmur of dissent, question, and admiration ; and the entire brotherhood for a few moments seemed all to be talking at once, but not much above a whisper.

Presently Ferrari was heard alone.

" To me, madam's wish," he said, " is law. Throughout all our operations, in every instance of peril, madame has never made a mistake. I have to this young man administered the first oath of secrecy. I believe him worthy, and capable of being one of us. My vote is for madame."

" And mine," said Ivan Kostanzhoglo ; " though it is a dangerous element, the admission of a sentiment beyond patriotism."

" But love," said Paul Petroski, " is a power that has helped us often, and in many straits."

" And we agree," said one of the three unnamed, " that it is to the frank, open statement of madame, that we should not oppose her judgment in this, when it has always been true."

" Go, then," said Anna, to Ivan Kostanzhoglo. " In the saloon you will find our visitor. He will be sitting at the table in the right hand corner, by the pillar near the fireplace. He is young, dark, handsome. You cannot mistake him. His dress, a shabby disguise ; yet you cannot fail to see through it the features, the figure of a gentleman."

Ivan rolled another cigarette, and left the room through its double doorways, which was guarded until his return by Ferrari.

It was not altogether an uncomfortable apartment, though it lacked ventilation, which was obtained chiefly through an orifice in the chimney, where a strong gaslight

was burning, and around which there was a continual halo
of smoke from the cigârettes which all, including Anna
herself, were more or less smoking.   There were a few odd
engravings upon the dark wall-paper, one or two easy chairs,
a small book-case, and a map of Europe.

Anna leaned back thoughtfully in her chair, and breathed
a few whifs of smoke from an Egyptian cigarette, a bundle
of which lay before her.   She pushed these aside and ceased
smoking as Ivan Kostanzhoglo entered with Philip Forsyth,
who was indeed disguised in shabby habiliments ; and in
face and feature for that matter, his cheeks pale and sunken,
his eyes surrounded with a black rim, his hair long and
straggly.   He wore a pair of bluish French trousers and a
thin alpaca frock-coat, buttoned to the throat ; and in spite
of the hot weather and the closeness of the underground
atmosphere, he looked cold and chilly ; but when later on
he spoke, his voice was strong and his manner expressed
the physical strength, which, to look at him, you would not
have expected him to possess.

"Brethren," said Anna Klosstock, rising, leaving her
seat, and taking Philip by the hand, "this is our English
friend, whose heart has bled for the miseries of our country,
who is anxious to join our brotherhood, and who has sworn
the first oath of secrecy."

Philip looked round with a quiet inquiring gaze, and
then fixed his eyes upon Anna with an expression of aston-
ishment.

She was still beautiful ; but it was the beauty of the
street and the alley, the beauty of despair, the beauty that
shines sadly through the surroundings of rags and poverty.

Her figure seemed to have shrunk into her thin, shabby
black gown ; and the shadow that fell upon her, as she
stood by the radiance of the somewhat dim lamp upon the
table, gave a sombre look to her face which was unusual
in Philip's experience of its varied characteristics.

It was borne in upon his mind that it lacked even the
tragic beauty that belonged to the despairing, defiant face
he had seen at the opera and conveyed to his canvas.

"Welcome, brother," said the confederates, one after
the other, as they shook him by the hand.

"Be seated," said Ivan, "and we will pledge you to our
better acquaintance;" whereupon, turning to the little
bookcase and opening a cupboard beneath, Ivan brought
forward a couple of bottles of red wine, opened them, and
placed glasses upon the table.

Philip drank in a mechanical half-decided way, conscious,
as if by instinct, that something was about to take place,
hardly in keeping with those heroic aspirations with which
he had credited the countess and her confederates. Not
that he had expected anything like a rose-leaf council, or
a carpet conspiracy; but there was something in the change
from the bright, clean, cheerful saloon of the little Parisian
Cabaret, to the half-lighted, dull, prosaic, double-locked
apartment, and its heavy-browed, ill-dressed occupants that
chilled his spirits, and, for a moment, recalled to him his
unnatural exile from his mother and friends, who were at
that moment, so close to him and yet so far away. But
presently, when, unintentionally, Ferrari had moved the
lamp from before the face of Anna Klosstock, in such a
way that when she rose it illuminated her entire figure, the
old strange infatuation took possession of him, and he
listened as one in a dream.

"Brethren," said Anna, rising and laying down the cigarette which she had still held between her fingers, "I have
to report to you the result of the brotherhood's mission at
Venice; and for the information of our visitor, who seeks
for weal or woe to be our comrade in the great cause to
which we are pledged, I beg you to permit that I shall
mention one of the motives which brought us originally
together. When I was a young girl I lived happy and con-

tented with my father, who was the principal Jew merchant of Czarovna. There came to our village one Losinski, a young learned scholar, who was appointed Rabbi. I fell in love with him, he with me. We were betrothed. It was the eve of the solemnization of our marriage. But at the height of Czarovna's happiness there came a new governor, General Petronovitch, and with him the wicked risings against the Jews with sword and fire, which you all remember, less than ten years ago. This governor from St. Petersburg was a sensualist, a tyrant and an assassin. He found villainous excuse to attack our house, to confiscate my father's estate, to send him to that living death, Siberia; to seize upon the young and learned rabbi, my lover, to condemn him to the knout. Maddened with my despair, I sought the governor at his palace, a suppliant for mercy. By fair promises he induced me for a moment to trust him. The crime he committed against me was one worse than death."

Philip Forsyth felt his heart stand still. He clutched his chair and pressed his feet upon the floor to prevent himself from falling. One of the unnamed, noticing his trouble, clutched him by the arm and pressed wine upon him as Anna continued her narrative.

"The next day I witnessed the execution of Losinski, and raising my voice in revolt and defiance, excited my people of the ghetto into revolt. In the midst of their attack upon the fiendish despot, I was dragged to the scaffold myself, and there beaten out of all sensibility, to wake up finally in the hospital, a miserable wreck, with sufficient life still left to swear eternal vengeance upon General Petronovitch, the only effort of existence left to me, the one red spark of hope in my earthly dungeon. Surely it was that one hope that gave me life. My wounds dressed with salt—I spare you even a single word about the physical agony I suffered—I began to recover, and it was thought in time I should be well enough to undergo a continuation of my sentence which belonged to the gaol and the mine ; but by some unaccountable intervention I was released and carried away to a foreign city. There was one great, good friend of the Jew, who lived on the outskirts of Czar- ovna, a Russian noble, who had, under pressure of ingrati- tude and persecution from his master, joined a branch of this Brotherhood of the Dawn."

For a moment the speaker paused in response to sup- pressed but vigorous tokens of approval.

" The cause and the Brotherhood ! " almost shouted one of the unnamed, raising his glass and clinking it with those of his neighbors.

Philip watched the woman with an intent gaze of wonder.

" His name was Stravensky—the Count Stravensky. He knew my father, he knew me ; saw me on that fatal day, hurrying to the traitor's palace, endeavored to interpose for me on the scaffold, was rebuffed, and ordered to his home. His wealth and his early services to the Czar, the greatness of his family name, and his burning desire for vengeance, sent him to St. Petersburg, where he resolved to fight his way diplomatically to place and position, his left hand the Emperor's, his right hand for Russia. It was through his intervention that I was removed, through his intervention that I was reported dead. That was the only report the Government would accept ; and so Anna Kloss- tock died. In a few years there arose from that moral death a new woman. Educated in Italy by scholars, tended by devoted women ; with what object, with what ambition, they knew not, nor did I for a time half suspect how Fate was working for me. Day nor night did I ever cease to pray for vengeance upon Petronovitch, whose march of advancement I watched with a smile of hate, noted his achievements in Central Asia, his proud conquests in the field, his social and diplomatic victories. One day there came for me a messenger from my kind patron. I accompanied madame to Paris. There, after a few days of formality and instructions, I stood by the bed of Count Stravensky, was made his wife, and received from him the legacy of his patriotic aspirations, and his last benediction on my vow of vengeance. They only knew in St. Petersburg that the count had married a cultured, but humble lady of Italy. The count had laid his plans carefully and well. I was received by His Majesty the Czar, on my way to deal with my estates in Vilnavitch, in the neighborhood of Czarnova. I have held my own, I hope, as the Countess Stravensky, never forgetting the wrongs of Anna Klosstock, the persecution of the Jews, and my vows to this brotherhood."

Again she paused, for the suppressed demonstrations of her audience, who, much as they had seen of tragic trouble and romance, were carried away not alone with Anna's story, but with the majesty of the woman as she narrated it.

Philip still sat a dumb witness ; moved by deep emotions, but standing apart, as it were, altogether from his companions ; listening to Anna's story from a different standpoint, influenced altogether from motives they could neither follow nor understand.

"To the patient and the true, the day they hope for comes. It was at Venice, two weeks ago. You remember some of you, our parting here, the naming of our rendezvous for Paul Petroski, for Ferrari, for myself. We met again, I and the General Petronovitch ; once more, as the Countess Stravensky, Anna Klosstock again had the honor to find favor in his cruel eyes. Not as in the old days did she struggle to be free from that cruel evil glance. She invited it, sought it, courted it in the very presence of his wife ; won him to her side, as Gretchen might have won the Fiend, methinks, had she desired. I beckoned ; he came. I tolerated the pressure of his false lips upon this hand—upon this hand!"—she continued, raising her right arm aloft and clutching her fingers as if she held a dagger there—" that beckoned him to his death ! "

Amidst the general gasp of satisfaction which welcomed Anna's tragic declaration, Philip covered his face with his hand.

Anna looked at him for the first time during her confession.

" Does anyone doubt my right to the vengeance which has thrust the dagger of the Brotherhood into this supreme wretch ?   Let him look upon me ! "

Philip, feeling that these words were addressed to him, raised his head and again fixed his eyes upon the speaker.

" Let him know why I am a Nihilist of the Nihilists ! Let him behold my title to vengeance ! "

As she spoke she tore open her dress, exhibiting a lovely white arm and part of a beautiful bust, turning at the same time with swift rapidity to exhibit her right shoulder and her neck, no further than is considered correct by ladies of fashion at balls and in the opera stalls, but sufficient to thrill iron men who had themselves been witnesses of the worst of Russian tortures.   Red and blue, deep ridges and welts crossed and recrossed each other, with intervals of angry patches of red, and weird daubs of grey that blurred and blotted out all remains and tokens of the beautiful form with which nature had endowed one of its loveliest creatures.

Philip looked, and fell forward upon the table with a cry of horror, his head in his hands.   The others remained dead still for a few seconds, until Ivan Kostanzhoglo rose quietly from his seat, replaced the torn garment over the woman's shoulders, and kissed her reverentially upôn the forehead.

As Anna, herself much overcome, resumed her seat, Andrea Ferrari advanced to Philip and laid his hand upon his shoulder, at which the young fellow looked round.

" Philip Forsyth," said Ferrari, it will be against the wish of Anna Klosstock if you take the oath that will make you, body and soul, one of us. What have you to say?"

" Nothing," he replied. " Petronovitch is dead."

CHAPTER XLVI.

ONLY A WOMAN.

PHILIP FORSYTH's mad infatuation would have confirmed him, as Ferrari put it, body and soul a member of the Brotherhood, but for the persistent opposition of the Countess Stravensky. If Philip did not take the final oath he was, nevertheless, accepted as an auxiliary of the association. It was only for conscience sake that the countess resisted this last act of the young artist's wild devotion. As she put it to her comrades, he was sufficiently their ally without completing the treaty of secrecy and service.

Ferrari saw in this act of friendship, not to say love, the first sign of weakness in Anna's character. It did not occur to him that she had achieved the work of vengeance which had stimulated and held together her alliance with the Brotherhood.

Since the Ghost of the Lagoon had cast its lurid shadow upon Russian despotism, the Countess Stravensky had found little room in her heart for thoughts and feelings which hitherto had been engrossed in the one idea of her resurrection from death and torment in the Czarovna hospital.

On the eve of that supreme act of vengeance in the Venetian palace, Anna had been strangely moved, as we have already seen, by the infatuation of Philip Forsyth; not so much on his account, as for the memories which it revived of her happy girlhood. She had in lonely mo-

ments seen in this boyish love of the English artist something like a spiritual resuscitation of the youthful Rabbi
Losinski. Her thoughts, which for years had only gone
back to the village of Czarovna with shuddering remem-
brances of its tragic overthrow, now found opportunities
for contemplating the light and sweetness which preceded
the advent of the Governor Petronovitch. She had permitted her fancy to wander back to the great house at the
entrance of the ghetto, the Jewish celebrations of leaves
and flowers and harvest, of births and deaths, of religious
institutions and customs. She saw herself a child, sitting
at her mother's knee, and weeping at her mother's grave ;
noted how quickly in her infant mind this later memory
had mellowed with time into an engrossing affection for
her father, giving her almost womanly duties in her girlhood, and offering her sympathies towards every soul in
the ghetto. Even on the first day of her arrival to fulfil
what to her was a sacred mission at Venice, she had sat
for hours silently in her red gondola dreaming of this happy
past in the one model Jewish village of that great Empire,
where the fires of revolt and persecution are for ever
smouldering with threatening and awful possibilities.

Ferrari, with the instinct of his race and the subtle understanding of the born conspirator, felt that Anna's
sympathy for Philip Forsyth boded no good to the cause.
He ventured to say so, both to Philip and to Anna herself.

Anna answered him with reference to the successful
incident of the movement with which she had been associated ; dwelt upon the tremendous sensation that had been
created in the courts of Europe by the vengeance of Venice ;
and confessed that she could not find it in her heart to
make the one great sacrifice he now demanded of her, to
cast off Philip Forsyth.

" If I could cut him off from us," she said, " with the
assurance that he would return to his home and duty, you

might count upon me. But it his misfortune to have fallen under some strange spell which we possess."

" Which you possess," said Ferrari.

" It is all the same," she said. " My mission, he claims, is his mission. I do not disguise from myself that he is mad ; but I find in his companionship a strange pleasure."

" To confess which," said Ferrari, " is to confess that you are no longer true to the Brotherhood."

" True ! ! " she exclaimed. " Do you then impeach me ? In what respect am I untrue ? "

" You know," said Ferrari, " that you are the first woman I have trusted. You know that I have always been opposed to confiding our section of the Brotherhood to the constancy of a woman."

" In which you are," said the countess, " illogical. Was it not Sophie Provskaya who gave the signal for Rysakovis attack which carried off the emperor you most hated ? "

" But which," rejoined Ferrari, " you most condemn."

" I ? " she exclaimed.

" Have you not," he said, " changed our latest programme ? Have you not more than once declared ' we are conspirators, but not assassins ? ' Have you not repudiated the term Nihilist, as it is applied to the party of revolution and reform in Europe ? "

" For a foolish word," she said, " which does not interpret us or our ambition. Do I repudiate the rising we hope for ? Do I not rejoice in the coming revolt of the army ? Do I not glory in the agrarian fires of the peasant ? Do I pause at an act of vengeance—a life for a life ? Ask me to rival Sophie Provskaya, the risk of my own life for the annihilation of a thousand Petronovitches, one by one or in companies, and I am equal to the occasion ; but cast me for a dynamite plot, involving the lives of innocent people, and leading to no political result, but assuredly to be followed by the execution of some of our own comrades, and I resist ! "

" But," said Ferrari, " given the great result, given the signal for a general upheaval, for the rallying of the great forces of revolution, the overthrow of a vile and bloody tyranny, the establishment of a constitution, in short, for the fulfilment of the great and glorious programme of constitutional liberty and national freedom—what then ? "

" Assure me of this, Ferrari, and I am with you. Assure me that we may hope, in one great sacrifice, to break the Russian chains, and at the same time to bring our brothers and sisters to the promised land, flowing with milk and honey, and I am with you. But you must convince me, Ferrari ; otherwise, dear friend, I pause with the victory of Venice : and could I forecast the end of all for me, I would ask no other blessing than to die in my father's arms away in his Siberian captivity.· Nay, do not start, Ferrari ; I could say this to no other. You remember the good, generous, kindly merchant ; the devoted father, the staunch friend, the martyr ? "

" Then you have heard," said Ferrari, calmly, " from your father ? "

" Not from him but of him," she said, a melancholy smile stealing over her pale features.

" The despatch you received in Paris ? " said Ferrari.

" The same. It came through the Russian Ambassador."

" The one secret you have withheld from me," said Ferrari.

" Not withheld," said the countess " only postponed. The influence of the Count Stravensky, my dear friend and successor, was beneficial. It gave my father means ; it secured communication with Moscow and St. Petersburg. Not at once ? Oh no ! It took three years before relief of any kind came to him : four years, five years, six

—and to-day, Ferrari, he is in his own peaceful rooms in an agricultural village away beyond the mountains, tended by a Siberian servant, and resigned, waiting for the end. As you so long regarded him as dead to me, as I have so long accepted that position, so he has regarded us,—dead Ferrari, dead! If I should see him again it would be a foretaste of Paradise for him, for me perhaps."

" It is this romantic attachment of yours to Forsyth that has unnerved you."

" Then I thank him for it, on my knees, Ferrari. If he has relighted that human lamp within my breast which shows me the past in the present, what humanly I was, then thank God, Ferrari, for his interposition."

" So it do not cast its betraying light upon the forthcoming enterprise of the Brotherhood, I am willing to say ' Amen ' to that. I can find in my own heart, Anna Klosstock, one drop of patience, when I remember that it was I who brought down upon your father's house the hand of persecution and murder ; that it was I who made the trail of death, of the sword and fire which the Christian friends followed to the peaceful streets of the Czarovna settlement."

" You have had your revenge, Ferrari, and I mine."

" No, no, my sister. I have no love-tokens of the past, no young English woman to revive it if I had. My vengeance is never complete. No woman can come between me and my oath, between me and my righteous ambition, between me and my sacred duty, as Philip Forsyth comes between me and yours."

" I will not have it so, Ferrari ; and I claim your firm and faithful allegiance to me, an allegiance not of oaths or vows, but of mutual suffering and mutual wrong. If it has pleased our Father Abraham that in this alliance of ours the woman at last shall be weaker than the man, do not blame me. Judge of me in the future as you have known me in the past, but do not ask for the impossible ; do not ask for a destroying angel in a mere woman of the people ; do not ask for the spiritual in the mortal ; do not ask for a miracle—I am only a woman ! "

CHAPTER XLVII.

DICK CHETWYND SAYS "I WILL."

FERRARI'S instinct was true. His judgment of Anna Klosstock was confirmed by results.

It needed no traitor in the camp to frustrate the opera-tions which took him and Anna and the rest by the various routes to St. Petersburg. The mainspring of the move-ment was altered. It was a question of nerve. Ferrari had detected it. There had been no secrets between him and Anna until her previous visit to London, when Philip Forsyth crossed her path ; but he had been reassured, touching any fears he might have experienced in Anna's confession of deep interest in Philip, by her magnificent campaign of strategy and vengeance on the Grand Canal. Her outbreak of emotional memories, however, on the eve of the Brotherhood's united action in St. Petersburg, had, as we have seen in the previous chapter, shaken his faith in the mental and physical strength of his amazonian asso-ciate. But there was no course of check open to him in regard to the Nihilistic advance. All he could do in the way of strengthening the outposts, guards and sentinels of the conspiracy, he carried out with firm exactitude. He hoped to have kept the action clear from any association with what Anna called her auxiliary aid, Philip Forsyth, who traveled in her company to St. Petersburg, the Coun-tess Stravensky's private secretary, *vice* for the time being Ferrari resigned.

Her Italian comrade passed into Russia through a different port, and in one of his most complete disguises. The countess and her maid, accompanied by Philip and a courier, went openly to St. Petersburg, where the young artist was duly introduced into the highest society by his illustrious patroness. Her visit was understood to be simply one of rest and social duty, *en route* for the scene of her husband's estates, whither some business of charity called her. Within a few days of her arrival she set out for the interior, or was understood to have done so ; but what happened was an enterprise of an entirely different character

The countess made her *adieux*, and disappeared from society and the world of St. Petersburg, prior to taking her place in the ranks of the Brotherhood, accompanied by Philip in a disguise which she had prepared for him ; but not before conjuring him to leave her and her associates to return home, while he could return safe to his family and friends. But Philip had only one negative reply to all her warning, and in some strange, unaccountable way, the woman who had been for years the companion of strong men bound together by patriotic oaths and emotions of revenge, found the infatuation which she exercised upon the voluntary young exile from London reflected back upon herself. She tried to think that fate had given to her the comfort of his companionship as some sort of recompense for past sufferings ; that fortune, perhaps, had placed him by her side as a new human impulse, an added arm in the great work which, Ferrari assured her, would be the signal for the coming millenium of their race and the overthrow of the Colossus of Despotism which threatened to bestride the civilized world.

Ferrari had of late over and over again expounded to Anna Klosstock (in whom, after all, his hopes of success in the latest enterprise of his career were centred) the tremendous growth of the revolutionary strength in Russia which had taken place under the new Czar Alexander III.

While admitting the numerically small numbers of the organizing and executive forces, Ferrari had shown Anna, by documentary and other evidence, the vast extension of the movement towards which they occupied the van : and while receiving in secret conclave the reports of the advance which was being made right through the military services, they both chiefly rejoiced in the prospects of the propaganda among the peasants, who had in many districts and under more or less authoritative encouragement, worked their will upon the Jews, but had of late entered into secret agrarian alliances with their Semitic fellow-citizens against the nobles and landed proprietors.

Jews throughout the provinces most in sympathy with the holy cause had been welcomed into secret societies ; and it was set forth in a recent important work by Tikhomirov that one of the great significant facts of the moment was a definite transition of anti-Semitic into agrarian troubles.

The people, finding it difficult to form peasant parties, had organized secret societies, one of which, having wide and powerful ramifications, had contributed a new brother to the Ferrari organization.

Everything looked well and promising for the first signal of revolt, which, being made in St. Petersburg, was to act as a beacon-fire over a wide and extensive district of outposts, military, civil, and agrarian, in which many classes, official and otherwise, were engaged.

The train was laid. It was the patriotic duty of Ferrari and his confederates to light the match which should bring about that great popular rising which is the hope and purpose of the great popular movement throughout the Empire.

On the day which was to bring about such great results St. Petersburg was unusually gay, and to a stranger it might even have seemed as if, for the time being, both military and police had made some special relaxation in their discipline and duties of surveillance.

But everything in St. Petersburg is more or less mysterious. No man can account for the under-current, which ebbs and flows and rushes hither and thither beneath the surface of its ordinary life. It is a calm sea, that flows insidiously above jutting rocks, moving sands, and dangerous eddies.

The police of Russia are as secret as the Revolutionists. Both are as active ; and on this momentous occasion, the authorities, instead of having relaxed their watchful guardianship over the Imperial power, were especially lynx-eyed, well informed, and alert, as was only too completely manifested to the little band of conspirators under the leadership of Andrea Ferrari.

It is a rare occurrence in open daylight for the police to disturb the citizens by an important arrest. These operations are generally reserved for the stillness and repose of the night ; but on this busy sunny day a little troop of police and military were taking very devious routes outside the leading thoroughfares, quietly surrounded a house near the Tavreda Gardens, which had been for four and twenty hours under the eye of an astute detective force. The result was one of much greater importance to St. Petersburg and the Czar than his officers understood. It prevented the ignition of that train of fire which had been laid with so much skill and patience ; and it added to Russia's political prisoners, among others in whom the readers of this history are interested, Anna Klosstock, Andrea Ferrari, Philip Forsyth, Ivan Kostanzhoglo, and Paul Petroski. Fortunately, so far as their immediate existence was concerned, the plot, as it presented itself to

the police, was of a minor character; presenting under
their investigation none of those grave and serious features
which really belonged to it, and like many another revolutionary enterprise in, Russia, it was nipped in the bud
without exciting any particular attention. It formed, however, during several weeks an interesting political subject
in the hands of an English correspondent attached to a
great London journal, and it was through this medium
that Lady Forsyth and Dick Chetwynd became acquainted
with the unhappy position of the Countess Stravensky's
companion.

The newspaper correspondent informed the English
public that among the prisoners recently tried and condemned to a period of exile in Siberia, was a young
Englishman who, having first given an assumed name to
his captors, had confessed that he was Philip Forsyth,
an artist, of London, a student at the Royal Academy, the
son of an eminent engineer, who had lived and died in
Russia, leaving behind a son, Philip, and his mother, Lady
Forsyth, a widow, of London. The young fellow, said the
correspondent, had no doubt given these particulars in the
hope of some intervention on the part of his family. The
plot with which he was associated was not regarded as
of any very great importance by the authorities, except
that it compelled them to make an example of the persons
concerned, one of whom, an Italian Jew, named Ferrari,
having strangled his sister, had succeeded in committing
suicide in prison; another, Ivan Kostanzhoglo, was sentenced to lifelong imprisonment; a third, Paul Petroski, to
a short period of detention; and a fourth, a remarkably handsome woman, who having, as in the case of the
English artist, given at the outset a false name, had confessed under pressure that she was Anna Klosstock, and
that the object of her association with Ferrari and the rest
of the confederacy lay chiefly in the hope that she might

be sent to Siberia to join her father. It appeared that during the risings against the Jews some ten years previously, this woman's father had been sentenced to exile, which had been considerably modified under official influence, that she had lived a wandering life, thinking he was dead; but having been in the service of the Countess Stravensky two years previously in Paris, she had discovered that her mistress had already interested herself on behalf of her father, and had procured him some concessions in regard to punishment.

The story was, the correspondent stated, a curious romance in its way, seeing that the countess had exercised her influence in favor of the girl's father before Anna Klosstock herself came into her service. Amongst the few papers discovered on the occasion of their arrest, was a letter from the Countess Stravensky which had been found in the prisoner's possession, bearing out in various details the story of the woman's life. The police had made a special effort to receive endorsement of this from the countess herself, but had been unable to find her. She had passed through St. Petersburg only a few days previously, to the neighborhood of Czarovna, in the province of Vilnavitch, where her husband, the count, had formerly resided, and no doubt in due course the police would hear from her laydship.

In the meantime, however, the judge took a lenient view of Anna Klosstock's case, and he more or less benevolently sentenced to Siberia ; and it is understood that by the order of the Czar, who has taken some personal interest in these arrests, she will be permitted to join her exiled father.

The news of Philip's arrest and conviction created a profound sensation in London. Not a moment was lost in bringing to bear such influence as Lady Forsyth and her friends possessed upon the Foreign Office to put the

English Minister in communication with the Government in St. Petersburg, but the most practical and important action was discussed and decided upon in family council at Dorset-square.

" Yes, certainly, Dick," said Mrs. Chetwynd, "you are right ; it is the only thing to be done."

" I know the country," said Dick, "but it is a serious undertaking."

" All great enterprises are serious," said his wife.

" Every possible influence that is to be got, of course, I can procure," said Dick, thrusting his hands deep into his pockets and pacing the little breakfast-room, where the principal morning papers had been flung down after perusal ; the leading journal, however, still in Mrs. Chetwynd's hands.

" It will be a great sacrifice to make for both of us, Dick. If you had not traveled on far more dangerous missions I believe I would not let you think of it."

" It will be a costly service, too," said Dick, " not only as regards time but money. I think I know the Foreign Secretary in St. Petersburg, and my decoration at the hands of the late Emperor should serve me. It is a good thing for Philip that I happen to be commissioned to the Russian instead of the Turkish head-quarters."

Dick walked about and soliloquized, half responding to his wife's remarks, partly to his own reflections.

" Besides, you are lucky, Dick. I do not think in all your career you have ever made a serious mistake—not even when you married me."

" My dear," said Dick, taking her genial face between his hands and kissing her heartily, " the only danger of my life was the possibility of ever missing the good chance that brought us together; and I have never made a mistake except when I have not acted upon your advice."

" Dick, my dear," said Mrs. Chetwynd, firmly, " you

24

must go to Russia, and bring that foolish boy home to his mother."

" I will," said Dick.

_____

CHAPTER XLVIII.

ON THE ROAD TO SIBERIA.

FORTUNATELY for Dick Chetwynd's mission he was no stranger to St. Petersburg, and he had had some experience of official life in Russia, during both peace and war. He knew the value of English introductions, and how most effectively to use Russian gold.

Notwithstanding the supposed continual strain of the diplomatic relationships of the two countries, and the traditional hostility of international interests, Dick Chetwynd had full confidence in the courteous and friendly reception which he would receive at headquarters.

From the Czar down to the humblest Russian official, an Englishman properly accredited and backed by traveled experience and worldly knowledge, may rely upon courteous treatment.

No official is more polite thah the Russian under the influence of a stranger's authoritative indorsement.

It is true that Chetwynd met with minor obstructions and delays which easily gave way to major tips and considerations; but in presence of the great masters of authority, with his letters from the English Prime Minister, the Russian Embassy in London, and other documentary powers, he found his path both smooth and pleasant. Indeed it was with some difficulty that he succeeded in proceeding on his journey with anything like a gracious refusal of the many social invitations he received as tributes to his own personal charm of manner as well as to his remarkable official introductions. Moreover, the fact that as a war correspondent he had chronicled in one of the leading English newspapers the triumphs of the Russian arms on a great campaign, and had been honored with the personal recognition of His late Majesty after a certain famous battle, made him a *persona grata* in the brilliant Russian capital.

Having discovered that Philip Forsyth was one of the prisoners *en route* for Siberia, under the command of Captain Karakazov, and in all probability only despatched some few weeks previously from Moscow, he made rapid dispositions for prosecuting his journey. In the meantime he wrote encouraging letters full of good assurance of his own safety to his wife and of hopeful prospects to Philip's mother.

What surprised Chetwynd more than anything during his investigations at St. Petersburg, was the utter and complete disappearance of the Countess Stravensky.

The Assistant Minister of Foreign Affairs, a singularly well-informed and courteous gentleman, who from being reticent at the beginning of their interview became almost loquacious at its close, assured him that there was no doubt about the complicity of the Countess Stravensky in the recent plot. The police were engaged in unraveling her career. It was believed that ever since her remarkable marriage with the Count Stravensky, one of the Government's most devoted servants, she had been mixed up in the Russian propaganda. If this were so, the countess had conducted her affairs with great skill and daring. She had received complimentary recognition from the Russian Court, and indeed had been almost, in certain social directions, an accredited agent, and was certainly regarded as a friend to the reigning family. She had been received at the Russian Court, and was a distinguished personage in the highest Russian circles; but within the last few months the police had discovered what they considered to be a clue to her association with some of the worst enemies of Russia, and indeed, they believed she was an accomplice in the murder of General Petronovitch at Venice.

At present these charges were indefinite, and might possibly be difficult of proof; but they were considered to be strongly exemplified by the strange disappearance of the countess from Russia. She had arrived in St. Petersburg some few days before the failure of the latest dynamite plot, had observed the usual polite ceremonies of the Court, had been seen at the opera, and was a guest at a semi-official reception on the night before the nefarious scheme of the Propagandists was to have been consummated. From that moment there was no trace of her. She had disappeared as completely as if she had never existed. And the complete system of espionage that belonged to the police had failed to come upon the slightest clue; the telegraph had flashed inquiries and descriptions in every direction throughout Europe, but without result. They had hoped that the young Englishman, the prisoner Forsyth, would have been able to throw some light upon her proceedings and habits. Had he been a Russian subject it was possible that more than the ordinary pressure would have been exercised to obtain confessions from him; but he probably spoke the truth when he said that he did not know what had become of her, and he did not disguise for a moment that he had traveled with her from Venice to Paris, from Paris to New York, from New York to Havre, thence to St. Petersburg. Indeed, there would have been no object in his denying this, because one of the so-called Brotherhood of the Dawn had confessed it.

"Under pressure?" asked Chetwynd, accepting the cigarette which the Assistant Minister had politely offered him.

"Probably," said the official.

"You have severe measures in this direction, I know," said Chetwynd, "and I am deeply grateful for the consideration which has been shown to my friend."

"You have reason to be so, I think, from all I understand," said the official. "We are talking in confidence, but it may help you to a better understanding of my Imperial Master when I tell you that it was by order of the Czar that Forsyth's sentence was commuted to imprisonment; by order of the Czar, not in response to any diplomatic intervention, but out of consideration for his youth and his evident simplicity, and the fact that he was a young English gentleman."

Chetwynd was duly impressed with the consideration shown to him and his country, and on taking leave of the Assistant Minister expressed in a general way regret that England and Russia did not better understand each other than appeared to be the case in the opinion of leading Russians and some prominent Englishmen, and hoped the time might come when the boundary line of their mutual ambitions in Central Asia might be drawn with a severe and firm regard for the world's peace and happiness. Arrived at Moscow, he succeeded in finding his way to the penal establishment at Sparrow Hills, where the young English artist had rested with his fellow-prisoners *en route* for Siberia.

It was at this very spot where Philip, as a boy, had seen the band of exiles mustered and marched out, as mentioned by him to Chetwynd during his artistic inspirations at Primrose Hill in the English metropolis. The place was probably very much in the same condition when Chetwynd became acquainted with it, as it was in the days of Philip's father, and as it had been when Mr. Bremner, quoted by the author of "Stories from Russia," visited it thirty years previously.

Chetwynd found no difficulty in visiting the prison and witnessing an exodus.

On the next day the governor, a courteous official whose heart had not been hardened under his melancholy experiences, accompanied him in the early autumn morning, not to the great fortress, but to a series of strong barrack-like buildings, surrounded by a high wall, not of a very powerful defensive character, but carefully guarded by numerous sentinels.

The governor conversed pleasantly in French, and rolled perpetual cigarettes ; advising Dick also to smoke during their round of the penal institution.

The broad courtyard was already occupied by a large company of prisoners, each fettered by the ankles, not with heavy chains, but sufficiently galling, alas, for a general march of little short of six months to the dreary wilds of Eastern or Western Siberia. They included men and women, the former in the usual convict's dress, a long loose coat of coarse grey cloth, the latter in thick woollen dresses with a kind of cape or shawl fastened about their shoulders and another over their heads, worn very much in the manner of a Lancashire operative. A portion of their route, the governor informed Dick, would be made by river, in enormous barges upon which were constructed prison cages, where the men and women were separated, but by road they travel in bands together. It was true, he said, that some died by the way, and that political prisoners who could afford it were permitted to ride and also to take with them baggage and their families, many of whom lived after some years of severe discipline in a comparatively free and comfortable manner. He admitted that there were exceptions, but hoped that the exile in whom Chetwynd was taking so deep an interest might be one of those favored persons. It was not often, he said, that an Englishman was included among the exiles to Siberia, but during the last few years many foreigners had interested themselves unduly in Russian politics. Fanatics from Italy, France and Germany, calling themselves, he believed, Socialists and Regenerators of the World, and once in a way the police had, he understood, to pay their polite attentions to some English ally of the revolutionists. He could not understand why England, having so many political and social difficulties of her own to attend to, should take so much interest at it appeared she did in the internal affairs of Russia. Possibly, as Mr. Chetwynd confessed, this young English gentleman, Mr. Philip Forsyth, had been led away by the fascinations of the Countess Stravensky, whose disaffection to the Government had been as great a surprise as was her sudden and extraordinary disappearance.

Many of the band starting upon their awful journey had favors and privileges to ask, which in some cases were granted and in others refused, but on the whole the men and women seemed to be treated, at least at this stage of their trials, with a certain amount of sympathy, particularly on the part of the governor whenever he was addressed or his intervention was invited by subordinate officers.

At the same time when the gates were thrown open, the strong military guard on foot made a formidable show, each man loading his weapon in presence of the prisoners.

Part of the escort was mounted, carrying long spears ; they were probably Cossacks, and in the experience of Mr. Bremner, previously quoted, the commanders of this light cavalry were in the habit of using the poor creatures with unchecked cruelty, riding furiously about among them, striking them right and left with their strong whips, without any reason for their activity, just as brutal drovers might among their cattle.

On this occasion the men were banded together apart from the women, but Chetwynd noticed a far better disposition than Mr. Bremner had noted in the treatment of the exiles who marched out under his observation ; but he restrained his tears with some difficulty, when the gates were closed and he heard the melancholy tramp and clank of irons in which his imagination easily depicted his unhappy young friend.

In the interior of the prison he found most of the men and women unfettered, but the governor informed him that on the next day he might witness, if he remained, the riveting of their chains. At the same time it occurred to the officer to suggest that these poor creatures were more to blame than the Government. Some of them were criminals of a bad type; others were political criminals, little better, except that in most cases they had been well nurtured, and were educated men and women who had been too wise to accept and obey the laws under which they lived. He refused to accept for a moment Chetwynd's suggestion that many political prisoners in Russia were probably misunderstood, some unduly and unfairly punished on unfounded and occasionally manufactured evidence. Justice might make mistakes, the governor said, and did no doubt in all countries, but he begged Mr. Chetwynd not to forget that the late Emperor had been murdered in the streets, and that plots of the most diabolical character had been successful, while others which threatened the lives of innocent people had been prevented by the activity of the Government.

Chetwynd had to confess to his distinguished escort that these questions seemed to be more openly discussed in Russia than he had believed possible; but at the same time he was fain to regard the frankness of the officials whom he had met as a compliment to his special credentials and a desire to stand well with the English authorities.

Asked about the prisoner Forsyth, the governor had no particulars to give except to indicate the band of which he was a member and the name of the commander. He did not remember having seen or noticed Forsyth. There had of late been a great many prisoners passing through

Moscow on their way to Siberia, for there had recently been very serious risings and plots against the Government; but he thought it possible that if Chetwynd traveled with reasonable speed he might overtake Captain Karakazov and his command on this side of the Siberian frontier; certainly within a few days of its crossing the line. As a rule the journey was commenced earlier in the year, the prisoners passing through pleasant summer and autumn weather. It might be that the difficulties of the latest bands of travelers would be somewhat enhanced by winter snows; there were signs of severe weather coming upon them earlier than usual, but every precaution was taken for protecting the exiles, and if they had hardships to endure, the military escort, men and officers, were not exempt from atmospheric influences. This hint sufficed for Dick Chetwynd to decline the governor's invitation of hospitality on the next day.

From Moscow Chetwynd traveled night and day to Nijni Novgorod, where he halted in the midst of the latter days of the great autumn fair, which under other circumstances would have had for him a tremendous attraction. There is nothing like Nijni Novgorod in the world. In a small way one might be reminded of it by some of the seaside resorts on the other side of the Atlantic, where enormous hotels, giant caravanserais, are occupied during the season by thousands of guests, the seashore crowded with summer attractions and thronged with people ; where, during the winter, not a soul is to be seen, except perhaps one or two guardians of the vast house of entertainment, and a few wooden huts about it, all silent as the dead.

This is Nijni Novgorod during half the year. It is a vast city of shops, stores, houses, hotels, churches, wide broad streets, fine showy buildings, boulevards, theatres, market places, bazaars ; but in the early summer months entirely deserted ; shops barred and bolted, markets

closed, churches locked up, the whole a city of the dead,
to be awakened as it was when Chetwynd passed through
its busy thoroughfares, during the month of August, by
five hundred thousand traders from all parts of Russia,
brought thither by rail from St. Petersburg and the Bal-
kans, by canal from the White Sea, by the Oker and on the
broad bosom of the mighty Volga.

Chetwynd was compelled to remain here a day and
night, part of which time he occupied in writing letters
home, in completing his outfit, and arranging his method
of travel.

In the evening, with thoughts far away, he smoked a
cigarette, and listened to the military bands playing oper-
atic airs opposite the governor's house, and watching the
busy crowd passing to and fro over the pontoon bridge
which connects the lower and upper towns.

The music, which appeared to give great pleasure to
the crowd and to the officers lounging about the governor's house, smoking cigarettes and receiving with much
condescension the evident admiration of the crowd, was
not a little painful to Dick. It was a selection from " Carmen," the opera at which Philip Forsyth had first seen
the face which had brought him and his friends so much
misery and distress.

During the next few days our English traveler in search
of his friend was steaming down the Volga and up the
Kama in one of the vessels that run between the Great
Fair city and Persia, where Mr. George Kennan, the
American author, had his first skirmish with the Russian
police, and whose descriptions of Russian peasant life will
no doubt prove to be one of the most interesting and
important revelations in the modern literature of Russian
travel and political debate.

Dick Chetwynd found his credentials and authoritative
orders from St. Petersburg and Moscow a talisman that

opened all gates and ways before him, and the morning after his arrival in the city on the Kama he was once more *en route*, this time by the Ural Mountains railroad, for Ekaterinburg.

Two days of travel brought him to the station near the summit of the mountains. The weather was cold ; there had been heavy frosts in the hills, the faded foliage was beginning to shrivel and fall. The scenery was wild and impressive, suggesting Switzerland and the Alleghany Mountains, the country dotted here and there with mining camps and villages that might have belonged to the early settlements of Canada and the United States. The railway was a remarkable work of engineering, and, while Dick was loath to leave it at Ekaterinburg for the wilder and more difficult country beyond, he was nevertheless satisfied to have reached the point where his journey must be continued by road.

At this last railway station on the Ural slope he had information of a band of exiles who had passed through the city of Ekaterinburg at about the time mentioned by the prison governor at Moscow.

Dick was now some hundred and fifty miles from the Siberian frontier, and on a certain calculation with a local official he was informed that it might be quite possible to overtake Captain Karakazov before he reached the boundary.

While the distance from Ekaterinburg had to be covered by a public vehicle, well horsed, but traveling over difficult roads, its progress was very rapid compared with the slow march of the fettered prisoners. The journey was relieved at various posts on the way, where horses were changed, the rate of traveling being at about eight miles an hour ; the inn accommodation at night rough as it could be, but not inhospitable, and Dick found companions who were civil, but with whom he could hold little

conversation in the only language they knew. They relieved the way with much drinking of tea and smoking of
strong tobacco, and Dick continually bent his eyes forward and used his field-glasses frequently in the hope of
catching a glimpse of the miserable travelers ahead. On
the second day, and towards evening, after leaving Ekaterinburg, the driver, with a cry of " Vot granista ! " pulled
up his horses.

The weather had turned bitterly cold, and the snow was
falling.

Dick, muffled up in his fur cloak, had fallen asleep for
the first time during many hours, in the furthermost corner of the great boat-shaped, four-wheeled carriage, which
for some time had been carefully hooded and covered by
way of protection from the weather.

Starting up, he found his fellow-passengers alighting
and repeating the two words of the driver, " Vot granista."
(Here's the boundary.)

They were in a forest clearing.

Before them, by the roadside, stood a tall pillar, and
round about it a strange weird group of men and women,
soldiers on foot and mounted Cossacks, their spears bright
amidst light feathery flakes of falling snow, which was
transforming the surrounding country into a white world.

They had arrived at the boundary post of Siberia, a
square pillar, ten or twelve feet in height, of stuccoed or
plastered brick, bearing on one side the coat of arms of
the European province of Perm, and on the other the
Asiatic province of Tobolsk. " No other spot between St.
Petersburg and the Pacific," says Mr. George Kennan,
whose current work I have already mentioned, " is more
full of painful suggestions, and none has for the traveler a
more melancholy interest than the little opening in the
forest where stands this grief-consecrated pillar. Here
hundreds of thousands of exiled human beings—men,

women and children; princes, nobles, and peasants—have
bidden good-bye for ever to friends, country and home.
No other boundary post in the world has witnessed so
much human suffering or been passed by such a multitude
of heart-broken people. More than one hundred and
seventy thousand exiles have traveled this road since
1878, and more than half a million since the beginning
of the present century. As the boundary post is situated
about half-way between the last European and the first
Siberian étape, it has always been customary to allow exile
parties to stop here for rest and for a last good-bye to home
and country. The Russian peasant, even when a criminal, is
deeply attached to his native land; and heart-rending scenes
have been witnessed around the boundary pillar when such
a party, overtaken perhaps by frost and snow in the early
autumn, stopped here for a last farewell. Some gave way
to unrestrained grief; some comforted the weeping; some
knelt and pressed their faces to the loved soil of their
native country, and collected a little earth to take with
them into exile; and a few pressed their lips to the
European side of the cold brick pillar, as if kissing good-
bye for ever to all that it sympolized. At last the stern
order ' Stroisa !' (form ranks) from the under officer of
the convoy put an end to the rest and the leave-taking,
and at the word " March !" the grey-coated troop of exiles
and convicts crossed themselves hastily all together, and,
with a confused jingling of chains and leg-fetters, moved
slowly away, past the boundary post, into Siberia."

As Dick Chetwynd tumbled out of the tarantas, and
pressed forward towards the exiles, the stern order " Form
ranks ! " and the following word " March ! " were given,
and the prisoners prepared to resume their weary and heart-
breaking journey.

" Captain Karakazov ? " exclaimed Dick Chetwynd at a
venture, hardly daring to think that he had overtaken the

band he was following, but with a desperate hope that it might be so.

Whether he had not spoken loud enough to command attention amidst the clanking of chains and the miscellaneous orders and exclamations, his excited interrogatory passed unheeded.

"Is this Captain Karakazov's command?" he shouted in French.

No reply; but there was a movement in the ranks which attracted his attention.

"Captain Karakazov!" he shouted again at the top of his voice, his fellow-passengers now regarding him with both surprise and alarm. An officer who had been busy receiving the reports of some subordinate turned somewhat angrily towards him.

"I am Captain Karakazov," he said. "What is your business, sir, with me?"

"Thank God!" exclaimed Dick. "You have a prisoner, Philip Forsyth," at which moment one of the exiles fell forward from a group and was caught with difficulty, but with great solicitude, in the arms of a woman, who, turning towards Chetwynd and the officer, disclosed to the English traveler the weird face of the woman in the Gold Medal picture, the scene of which flashed upon Dick with a strange terrible realization; the winter background of lurid light, the snow, the bearded prisoners, the hooded woman, the mounted guard, the thoughtful student, the woman at bay. Before the officer in command had time to say another word, Dick Chetwynd was on his knees by the side of Philip Forsyth.

"Great God!" he exclaimed, whispering into the ear of the woman, "the Countess Stravensky."

She looked at him with a tearful light in her great violet eyes, and placed a finger upon her lips, with a gentle sibillant "Hush!"

Philip Forsyth, weary with travel and attacked with fever, had fainted, and his strange dreamy forecast of the two figures in that sketch which still lay upon the easel near Primrose Hill was realized, with this exception, that strong hands were near to protect and rescue him.

Dick Chetwynd had hardly put his arm round his friend than he was roughly dragged into the roadway and literally flung at the feet of Captain Karakazov, who saluted him with some coarse words in Russian. The next moment, Dick, on his feet, glaring at the officer, hurled at him a few equally strong expletives in English. Both having thus somewhat soothed their angry agitation, Dick, in French, said :—

" Sir, I have orders for you from the Minister of War at St. Petersburg, and a cipher also from His Imperial Majesty of still more importance."

" Permit me to see them," said the officer.

While they spoke the evening was rapidly changing into night. A lantern was brought, in the gleam of which Dick Chetwynd showed his authoritative writings to Captain Karakazov.

" They are sufficient," said the officer, "and I beg you will accept my apologies."

" If these orders are promptly carried out I assuredly will ; otherwise——"

" The orders will of course be promptly obeyed," reading the St. Petersburg instructions, and laying emphasis on the words. " The unconditional release of the prisoner, Philip Forsyth."

" By order of the Czar," said Chetwynd somewhat theatrically, quite contrary to his usual habit and manner, but inspired by the surroundings, angered by his rough usage, and anxious to emphasize to the fierce young Russian, by whose orders he had been assaulted, the tremendous Imperial authority against which he leaned his stiff English back.

Two subordinate officials were detailed to the service of the English traveler.

They carried Philip Forsyth, with his chains and long grey cloak, insensible as he was, and placed him inside the Russian carriage.

Dick gave the driver a handful of roubles, begging him to hurry on to the nearest post, which fortunately was within a short distance.

Anna Klosstock parted with her companion without disclosing any more emotion than was concentrated into her grip of Dick Chetwynd's hand. It was from the eyes of the stolid Englishman that the tears streamed, not from those of the suffering martyr, Anna Klosstock.

CHAPTER XLIX.

AN OLD MAN AND HIS DAUGHTER.

TRAVELERS who know Siberia and readers who have studied the literature of the subject need not be told that it is not always winter in that vast region of the Russian Empire, which is larger than Europe, and has nearly as much variety of climate. If this last claim, however, be somewhat exaggerative, it must at least be confessed that there are tracts of Siberia which can boast of flowers and gardens, song-birds, butterflies, clear streams, pleasant lakes, and fertile valleys. A great portion of the country in the provinces of Tobolsk and Tomsk, and including the steppes of Baraba and Ishim, are of rare fertility; they are, indeed, the granaries of Russia. The valley of the Yenesei, in Western Siberia, north of the Sayansk Mountains, is not unworthy in its summer months to be compared with the valley of the Severn in England.

Consult your Encyclopedia and you will find that the majority of the inhabitants of the central provinces of Siberia are Russians and Poles, who have been sent thither either as political or criminal exiles ; leavened somewhat by a respectable minority of colonists. The worst type of criminals and the prisoners who have given most offence to the reigning powers in the fierce political conspiracies, are condemned to hard labor in the mines ; others are detailed for work of a less fatal character ; and there is a third degree of punishment which gives to the political exile a large amount of freedom, in which many live more or less contentedly, with wives and families, and occasionally even preferring such limited freedom to a return to their former homes. They are relegated to specific districts under the surveillance of the police, but are permitted to employ themselves how they please. Some of these have entered upon their new life with their household goods, accompanied from Moscow by their wives. Many pathetic stories that are honorable to our humanity are told of lovely women thus sacrificing themselves on the altar of their loves, even marrying for the sake of such feminine martyrdom.

The general impression of the reader who has dwelt upon the gentle romance of Madame Cottin's " Elizabeth," is that around the heroine's humble home in the province of Ishim, the world was dark and dreary, and had but one sad tale of snow and chilly landscape, forgetting the author's description of the four months of summer that reigned even there with the perfumed blossoms of the birch-tree, which the exiles cultivated in their little garden ; the playful flocks of wild-fowl on the lake ; the genial character of the air ; the pleasant sunshine. It is true these delights were only enjoyed to the full by the natives of the country, the exiles still sighing for their liberty and the sight of old friends. Elizabeth, in the well-known story, at last found a merciful Czar, and this present history is not all one long record of Imperial tyranny, though the mercy found for the exile of Tobolsk, and the interposition of the direct Imperial power which marked the closing days of Anna Klosstock and her father, not to mention the release of Philip Forsyth, are romantic exceptions to the general outcome of those official "orders of the Czar," which fill the bleakest spots of the Siberian world with weeping and wailing and gnashing of teeth.

There are instances of exiles, as I have said, preferring to remain in the favored category of relaxed Siberian discipline, wretched men and women who have outlived their friends, and who no longer feel that they possess the capacity to begin the new life that is offered to them. Possibly these cases are few and far between, but thousands of exiles, after their term of detection has ceased, continue in the country, becoming farmers, traders, trappers, and following the occupations from which they had been carried off by the strong and too often secret arm of the law.

Johannes Klosstock had for some years been permitted the highest privileges allowed to the exile ; and he had accepted the relief with the same religious resignation that had entered his soul from the first.   He had long since ceased to suffer.   The past had become to him a dream. Happy Czarovna was still his world.   He walked out in summer days and saw Anna his wife.   He sat by the stove in winter and talked with Losinski and the famous Italian traveler Ferrari.   Once in a way there would come to him disturbing glimmerings of the bitter change that had left him all alone with only his dream.   But he was a religious man ; he bowed his head and prayed, and looked forward to the coming of the Messiah, and to the reality of a reunion of wife and child.

One summer afternoon, sitting at the door of his simple hut, where he was permitted to have the attendance of an old Polish housekeeper, who was devoted to the old man, he saw the apparition of his daughter Anna. She came out of the distant woodland, crossed the rough bridge which spanned the stream, a tributary of the great lake; then pausing, she turned towards the cottage. The old man smiled. The summer sunshine fell upon the much-loved figure in what he conceived to be his happy dream. " My dear, dear Anna," he said ; and the woman came on, flowers in her path, peace in her heart. She was no imaginary Anna walking in the silent land of the father's tender fancy ; she paused at the primitive gate that finished the rough fencing of the tiny garden, and saw her father. There was no demonstration on the part of either of them. Anna was dressed very much in the fashion of her early day. Her face was pale ; but the old light had come into her eyes. Her red-gold hair showed streaks of grey ; but her step was light, and her voice sweet and musical. When she entered the garden the old man rose to his feet. He passed his hands over his eyes, then stretched out his arms. " Father," said the well-known voice. " Anna," was the only response, and the old Polish woman found them locked in each other's arms.

In the closing days of this history Anna Klosstock and her father are removing to the pleasanter country between the post stations of Ceremishkaya and Sugatskaya, which Mr. Kennon has described as a rich open farming region, resembling that portion of New York which lies between Rochester and Buffalo ; and which may therefore on our side of the Atlantic be fairly likened to the wolds of Lincolnshire or the wealds of Kent, without, however, the beautiful hedgerow characteristics of the old country. The means of the Countess Stravensky, despite the disappearance of their owner, had in a great measure found their way into the hands of Anna Klosstock, and her father had received valuable assistance from his banking friends of Moscow

and St. Petersburg; so that here in the heart of the most
fertile of the Siberian country, father and daughter will end
their days together, with ample money for all their wants,
and sufficient for acts of charity and benevolence. This
very winter Philip Forsyth has learned, through private
sources of information organized by Dick Chetwynd, that
the Klosstocks had purchased a homestead near Sugatskaya, which many a wealthy Russian might envy; that the
old man, still dreamy in his manner and often wrapped in
reflection, nevertheless realized the happiness that had
come to him in his latter days; and knew how great it was
in contrast with what he had suffered in the first days of
his exile; while Anna only lived to give him pleasure, and
make her peace with heaven.

CHAPTER L.

THE GOLD MEDAL.

THE picture is finished : the gold medal has been awarded;
and "Tragedy" is the artistic sensation of the latest Royal
Academy exhibition. The barrier and the policeman have
once more appeared in the central gallery of Burlington
House.

Not alone for its exceptional merit is Philip Forsyth's
"Road to Siberia" the talk of the art world. Something
of the romance associated with it has leaked out. The
busy gossips of the society papers have told its story in
many and various ways. The facile pen of The Jenkins
of the *Review*, whom we have met at Lady Forsyth's
receptions, had, however, penetrated some of the darkest
shadows of the mystery. By no means correct in its
details, the *Review* had graphically suggested the courageous and friendly journey of rescue which had been performed by Dick Chetwynd; the telegram of the British

Consul at St. Petersburg; Dick's surprise on its receipt, his hurried councils with Philip's mother and friends, and his prompt expedition to Siberia were told with journalistic effect. Dick's kindly reception at the hands of the Russian officials, the usefulness of his early experiences as a war correspondent in expediting his march, his adventures by land and river, and the scene by the tragic frontier pillar were quoted in all the journals, and eagerly devoured by the public. But Jenkins secundus was altogether at fault when he endeavored to indicate the part which the Countess Stravensky had played in this extraordinary drama.

The mystery of the story indeed was untouched. The Countess Stravensky had disappeared as completely as if she had never existed. Neither the police nor Dick Chetwynd had solved the Stravensky problem, and Philip Forsyth kept his own counsel in regard to that notable person—kept it with a dogged silence that no one could weaken. The young artist had come home again entirely changed in manners and habit, and strangely altered in appearance. Pale, thoughtful, and with the strongest tendency to look upon the ground, Philip now appeared to live in a world of his own; and, happily for himself and for Art, he devoted himself with a calm intensity to his· work. Back again at the studio beyond Primrose Hill, he lived there for days together without making his appearance at his mother's, or visiting the Chetwynd household. On quiet evenings he might be seen strolling over the Hill, or smoking a cigar upon one of its highest seats. As a rule, he began work with daylight, and only laid down his brushes at the approach of night. His models were queer people, mostly selected from foreign emigrants and Eastern sailors at the London Docks. For months his only recreation appeared to be in continual visits to the Port of London. He made sketches of·the Jewish refugees from Russian Poland and other districts, and occasionally brought his models straight to his studio, lodging them close by ; finding vent for his feelings and direction for his art in subjects of modern Russian history, not painted with ostentatious political point, as might have been expected from his somewhat fanatical impulse, but with a pathetic fervor that permitted a margin even for the tremendous difficulties that belong to the Russian political situation. These studies, however, represent pictures yet to come ; and it is not within the space of this present chronicle to do more than forecast the future of Philip Forsyth from the standpoint of his remarkable work, "The Road to Siberia," which has sufficiently impressed the fathers of the Royal Academy to secure for its painter the first step to honors which he neither desires nor resents.

Once in a way he will stroll into the Arts Club, or the Hogarth, of an evening, and take a quiet, sober part in the social life of these pleasant establishments. Occasionally throwing off the shadow which has fallen upon his young life, there is no assumption of undue thoughtfulness or gloomy manner; it is quite natural to him, and is accompanied with a certain unconsciousness of singularity which disarms the personal affront of unsympathetic criticism. He has rivals in his art, and critics in the press entirely ignorant of his antecedents, who credit him with intentional airs of eccentricity, and characterize both his manner and his work as commercial and shoppy. But Philip has suffered, and is strong, and once a week when he goes to his mother's to spend Sunday and accompany her to the little Catholic chapel round the corner, Lady Forsyth finds a new pleasure and satisfaction in his companionship, which is restful, quiet, non-argumentative, and affectionate. He has a wholesome sympathy for the suffering, and even in his criticisms of the Russian rule, there is an appreciative sentiment of the obstacles which block the way of even the most charitable of Muscovite monarchs.

The diplomatic skillfulness and pleasant geniality of Walter Milbanke brought to bear upon the amiable and happy nature of Sam Swynford through the medium of Dick Chetwynd, have brought about a complete reconciliation between the Forsyths and the merry sisters. It is satisfactory to be able still to give them that familiar title, the merry sisters.

Sam and Dolly, at the suggestion of clever Mrs. Milbanke, have made their home in the best part of the fashionable regions of Kensington. The fortunate young stockbroker, lucky in his marriage as in his financial speculations, had been able to give to Dolly all her heart could desire, and at the same time to provide Mrs. Milbanke with a house of call not less luxurious and comfortable than her own. It is quite possible that under the influence rather of Mrs. Milbanke's ambition than the desire of her sister Dolly, Mr. Swinford may yet be heard of in the great legislative council of the nation; not that he cares for public honors, but he has made sufficient money to command the attention of one of the great parties in the City, is popular wherever he goes, has already refused a seat in the County Council, has been elected a member of one of the great party clubs. He and his wife are on the reception list of the Prime Minister's discreet and accomplished wife; and his coach at the last Hyde Park Corner meeting was the best appointed of the day, and certainly carried two of the most attractive women of the season, Mrs. Swinford and Mrs. Milbanke, the wife of the well-known conveyancing solicitor.

They met Philip Forsyth for the first time since their marriage at a quiet little dinner given by Lady Forsyth at Richmond. Philip was inclined to be somewhat bashful at the outset, but was speedily placed at his ease by the

wise discretion of Mrs. Milbanke, the pleasant lively conversation of Walter,.and the rare capacity of Dolly Swinford for talking about everything that was far away from
Philip's thoughts, and her charming facility for translating
pleasant ideas into music. She played and sang divinely
snatches of this opera and the other, never for one moment dropping into any suggestion of " Carmen," and
always keeping clear of anything calculated to stir the
emotions. It was altogether on one side a most agreeable
plot to make Philip ignore anything in the past that could
unpleasantly influence the present, and he and his mother
were sympathetically receptive of these pleasant efforts of
social friendship.

With all his influence Dick Chetwynd has not been
able to learn anything of the fate of Ferrari, Petroski, and
the President of the meeting at the French Cabaret in
Soho. The Italian and his comrades must therefore pass
out of this history as many other men in Russia have
passed out of all knowledge of their friends and associates,
some to die lingering deaths in stifling prisons, others to
grow grey in Siberian wilds. It may, however, be said
for Ferrari and his comrades of the Brotherhood that they
were always prepared for the martyrdom which they knew
they might at any moment be called upon to endure.
Moreover, Ferrari, if he had not lived to realize his best
hopes, had at least enjoyed the sweets of revenge on most
of his personal enemies. Whether his passion was a
righteous one or not, it was the chief motor of his life,
sanctified in his mind by the name of patriotism. So let
the memory of him be kept green at least for his courage
and devotion to the unhappy Queen of the Ghetto.

THE END.